Garfield ®
Snack Pack
BY JIM DAVIS

Volume Three

Ross Richie CEO & Founder • Joy Huffman CFO • Matt Gagnon Editor-in-Chief • Filip Sablik President, Publishing & Marketing • Stephen Christy President, Development • Lance Kreiter Vice President, Licensing & Merchandising • Arune Singh Vice President, Marketing • Bryce Carlson Vice President, Editorial & Creative Strategy
Scott Newman Manager, Production Design • Kate Henning Manager, Operations • Spencer Simpson Manager, Sales • Elyse Strandberg Manager, Finance • Sierra Hahn Executive Editor • Jeanine Schaefer Executive Editor • Dafna Pleban Senior Editor • Shannon Watters Senior Editor • Eric Harburn Senior Editor • Chris Rosa Editor
Matthew Levine Editor • Sophie Philips-Roberts Associate Editor • Gavin Gronenthal Assistant Editor • Michael Moccio Assistant Editor • Gwen Waller Assistant Editor • Allyson Gronowitz Assistant Editor • Amanda LaFranco Executive Assistant • Jillian Crab Design Coordinator • Michelle Ankley Design Coordinator
Kara Leopard Production Designer • Marie Krupina Production Designer • Grace Park Production Designer • Chelsea Roberts Production Design Assistant • Samantha Knapp Production Design Assistant • Paola Capalla Senior Accountant • José Meza Live Events Lead • Stephanie Hocutt Digital Marketing Lead • Esther Kim Marketing Coordinator
Cat O'Grady Digital Marketing Coordinator • Amanda Lawson Marketing Assistant • Holly Aitchison Digital Sales Coordinator • Morgan Perry Retail Sales Coordinator • Megan Christopher Operations Coordinator • Rodrigo Hernandez Mailroom Assistant • Zipporah Smith Operations Assistant • Breanna Sarpy Executive Assistant

kaboom!

BOOM! Studios, 5670 Wilshire Boulevard, Suite 400, Los Angeles, CA 90036-5679. Printed in China. First Printing.

ISBN: 978-1-68415-436-4 , eISBN: 978-1-64144-553-5

"GARFIELD IN WONDERLAND"
WRITTEN BY SCOTT NICKEL
ILLUSTRATED BY ANTONIO ALFARO
LETTERED BY JIM CAMPBELL

"JON ARBUCKLE'S VERY IMPORTANT SUMMER VACATION"
WRITTEN BY MARK EVANIER
ILLUSTRATED BY ANTONIO ALFARO
LETTERED BY WARREN MONTGOMERY

"SPRING BREAKUP"
WRITTEN BY MARK EVANIER
ILLUSTRATED BY ANTONIO ALFARO
LETTERED BY MIKE FIORENTINO

COLORED BY LISA MOORE

COVER BY ANDY HIRSCH

SERIES DESIGNER
GRACE PARK

COLLECTION DESIGNER
CHELSEA ROBERTS

EDITOR
CHRIS ROSA

SPECIAL THANKS TO JIM DAVIS AND THE ENTIRE PAWS, INC. TEAM.

Garfield in Wonderland

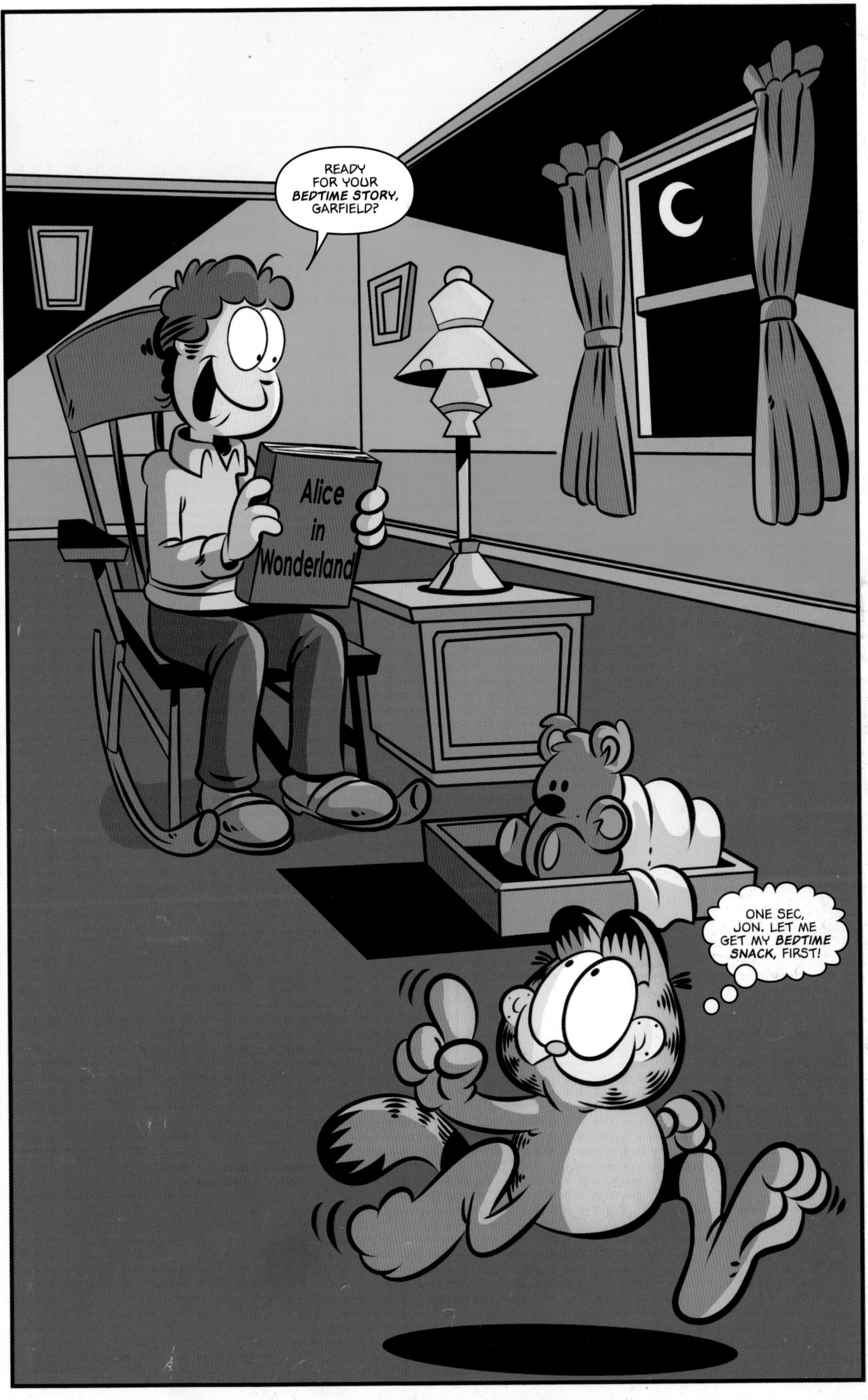
READY FOR YOUR BEDTIME STORY, GARFIELD?
Alice in Wonderland
ONE SEC, JON. LET ME GET MY BEDTIME SNACK, FIRST!

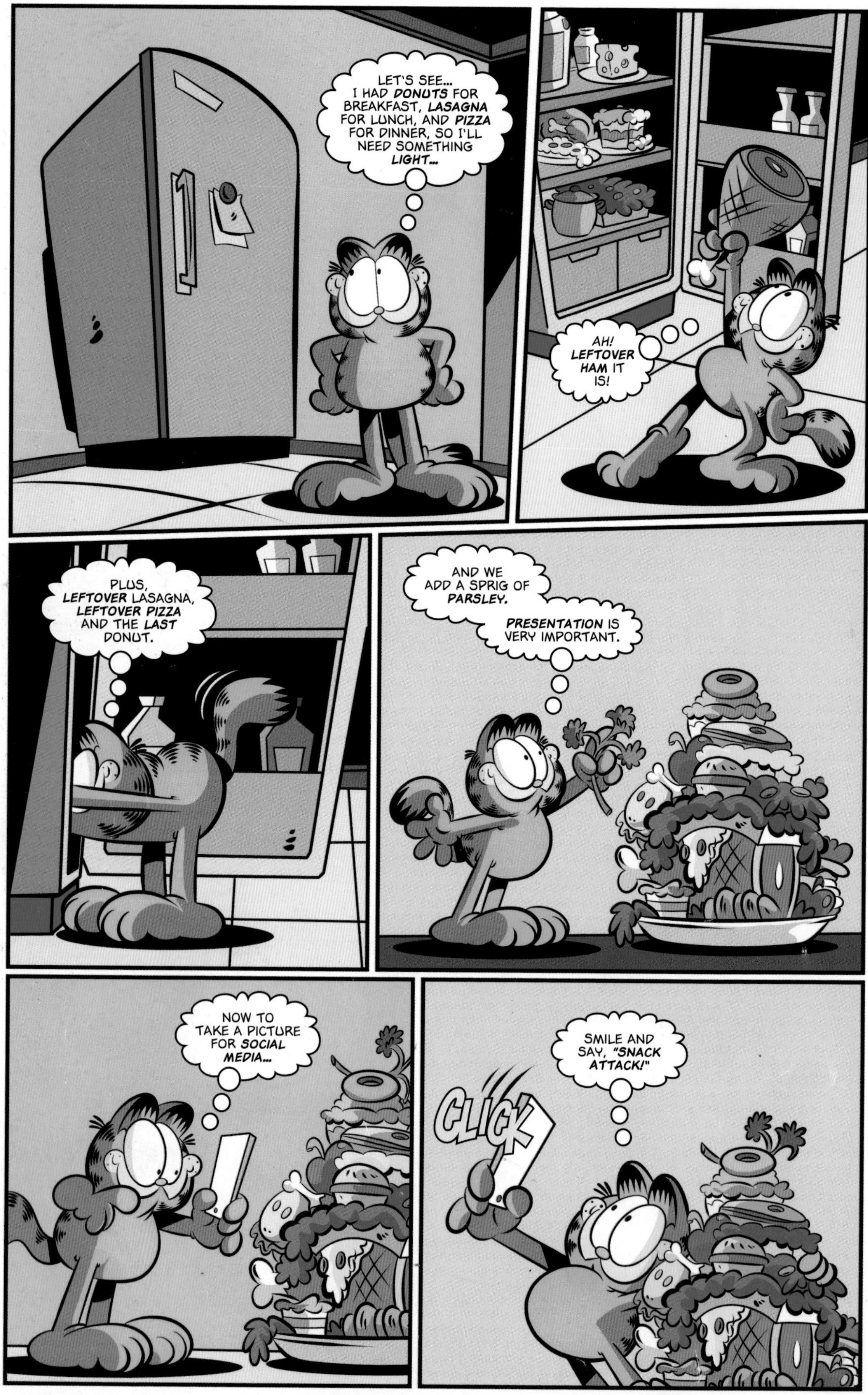
LET'S SEE... I HAD DONUTS FOR BREAKFAST, LASAGNA FOR LUNCH, AND PIZZA FOR DINNER, SO I'LL NEED SOMETHING LIGHT...
AH! LEFTOVER HAM IT IS!
PLUS, LEFTOVER LASAGNA, LEFTOVER PIZZA AND THE LAST DONUT.
AND WE ADD A SPRIG OF PARSLEY.
PRESENTATION IS VERY IMPORTANT.
NOW TO TAKE A PICTURE FOR SOCIAL MEDIA...
CLICK
SMILE AND SAY, "SNACK ATTACK!"

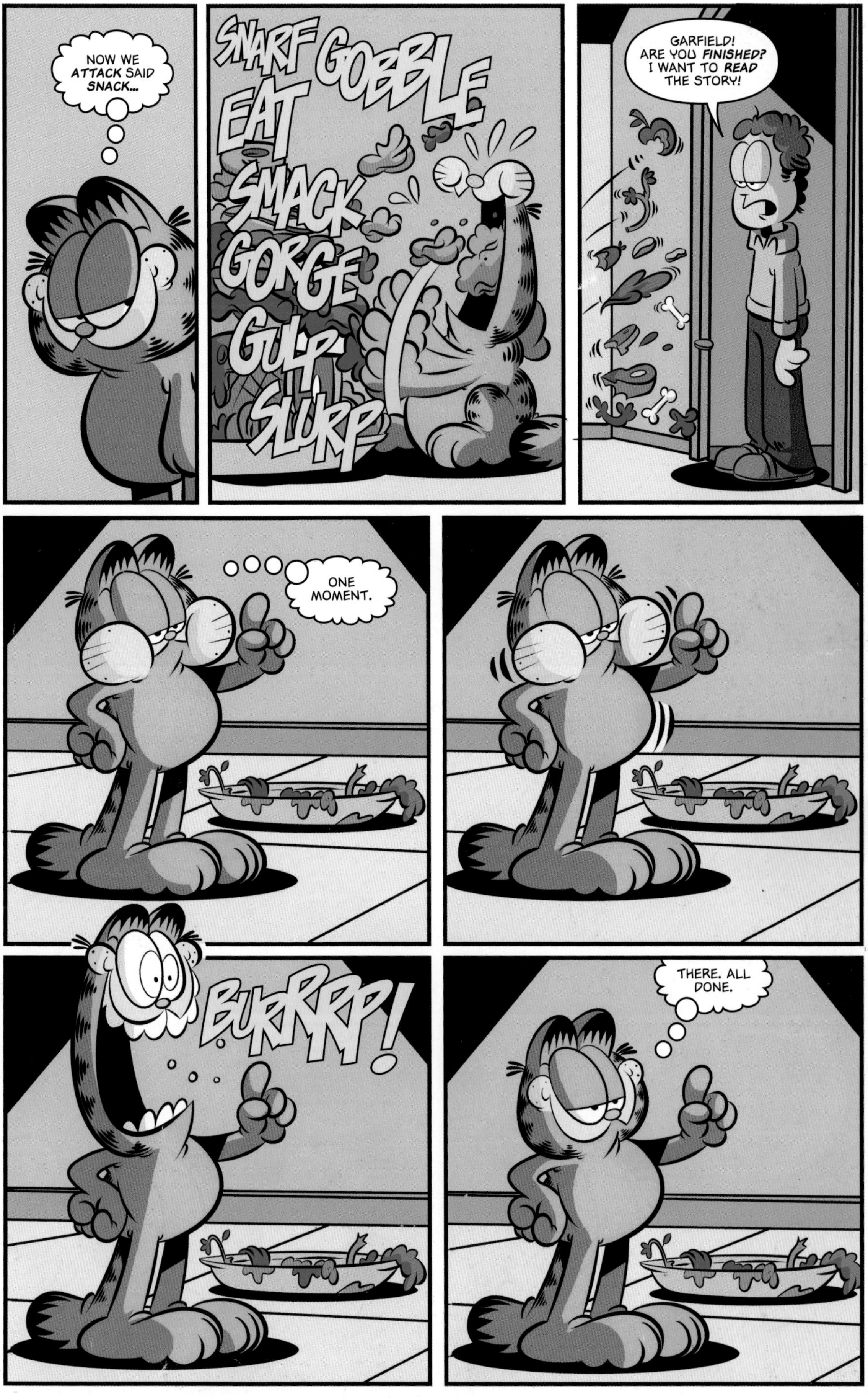
NOW WE ATTACK SAID SNACK...
SNARF GOBBLE
EAT
SMACK
GORGE
GULP
SLURP
GARFIELD! ARE YOU FINISHED? I WANT TO READ THE STORY!
ONE MOMENT.
BURRRP!
THERE. ALL DONE.

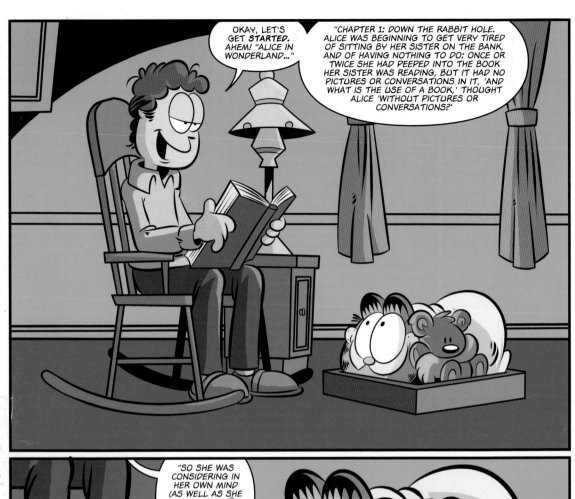

OKAY, LET'S GET **STARTED**. AHEM! "ALICE IN WONDERLAND..."

"CHAPTER 1: DOWN THE RABBIT HOLE. ALICE WAS BEGINNING TO GET VERY TIRED OF SITTING BY HER SISTER ON THE BANK, AND OF HAVING NOTHING TO DO: ONCE OR TWICE SHE HAD PEEPED INTO THE BOOK HER SISTER WAS READING, BUT IT HAD NO PICTURES OR CONVERSATIONS IN IT, 'AND WHAT IS THE USE OF A BOOK,' THOUGHT ALICE 'WITHOUT PICTURES OR CONVERSATIONS?'

"SO SHE WAS CONSIDERING IN HER OWN MIND (AS WELL AS SHE COULD, FOR THE HOT DAY MADE HER FEEL VERY SLEEPY AND STUPID)...

"...WHETHER THE PLEASURE OF MAKING A DAISY-CHAIN WOULD BE WORTH THE TROUBLE OF GETTING UP AND PICKING THE DAISIES, WHEN SUDDENLY A WHITE RABBIT WITH PINK EYES RAN CLOSE BY HER...

"THERE WAS NOTHING SO **VERY** REMARKABLE IN THAT; NOR DID ALICE THINK IT SO **VERY** MUCH OUT OF THE WAY TO HEAR THE RABBIT SAY TO ITSELF, 'OH DEAR! OH DEAR! I SHALL BE LATE!'...

LATE...

LATE...

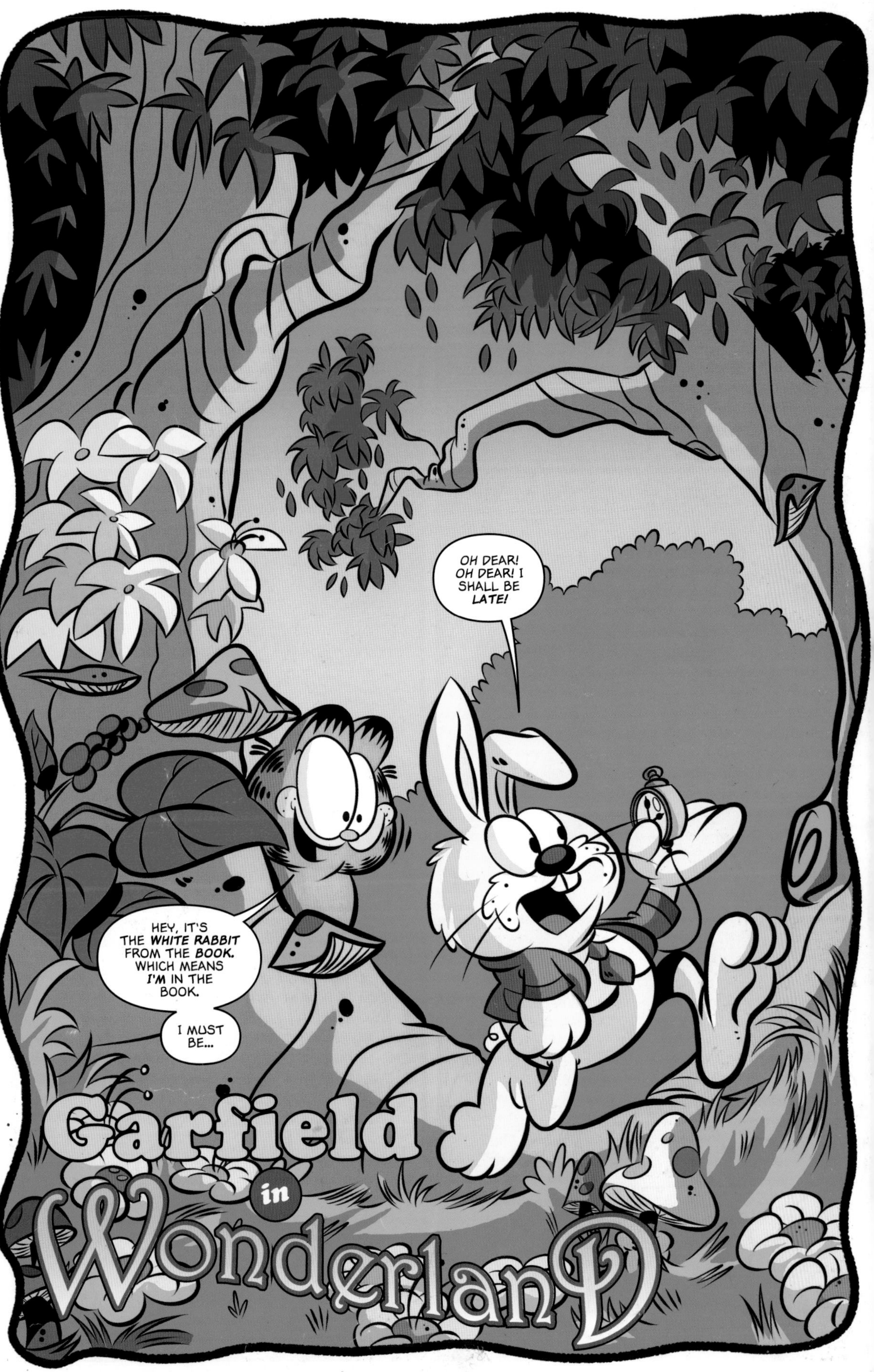
OH DEAR! OH DEAR! I SHALL BE LATE!
HEY, IT'S THE WHITE RABBIT FROM THE BOOK. WHICH MEANS I'M IN THE BOOK.
I MUST BE...
Garfield in Wonderland

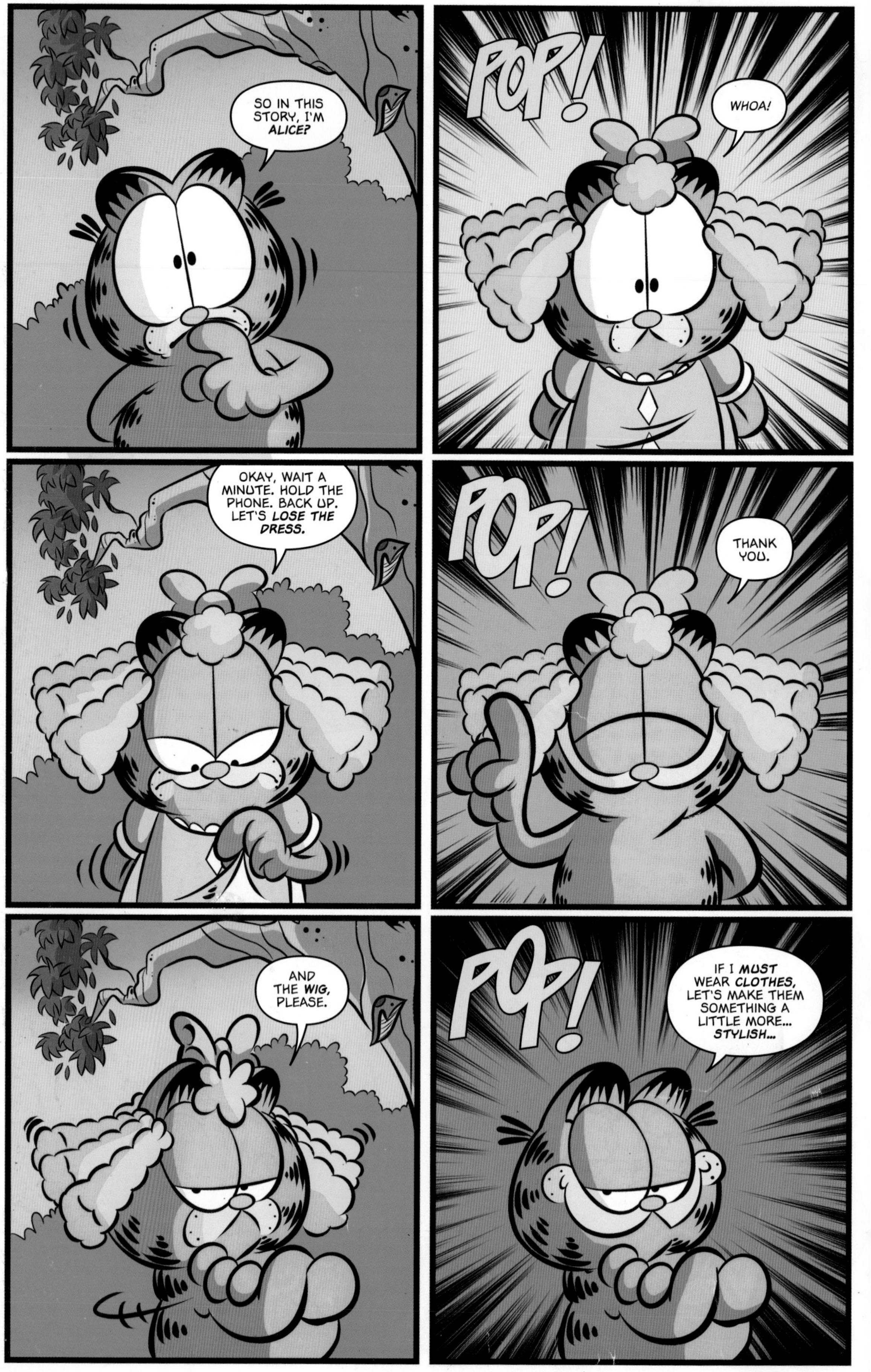
SO IN THIS STORY, I'M ALICE?
POP!
WHOA!
OKAY, WAIT A MINUTE. HOLD THE PHONE. BACK UP. LET'S LOSE THE DRESS.
POP!
THANK YOU.
AND THE WIG, PLEASE.
POP!
IF I MUST WEAR CLOTHES, LET'S MAKE THEM SOMETHING A LITTLE MORE... STYLISH...

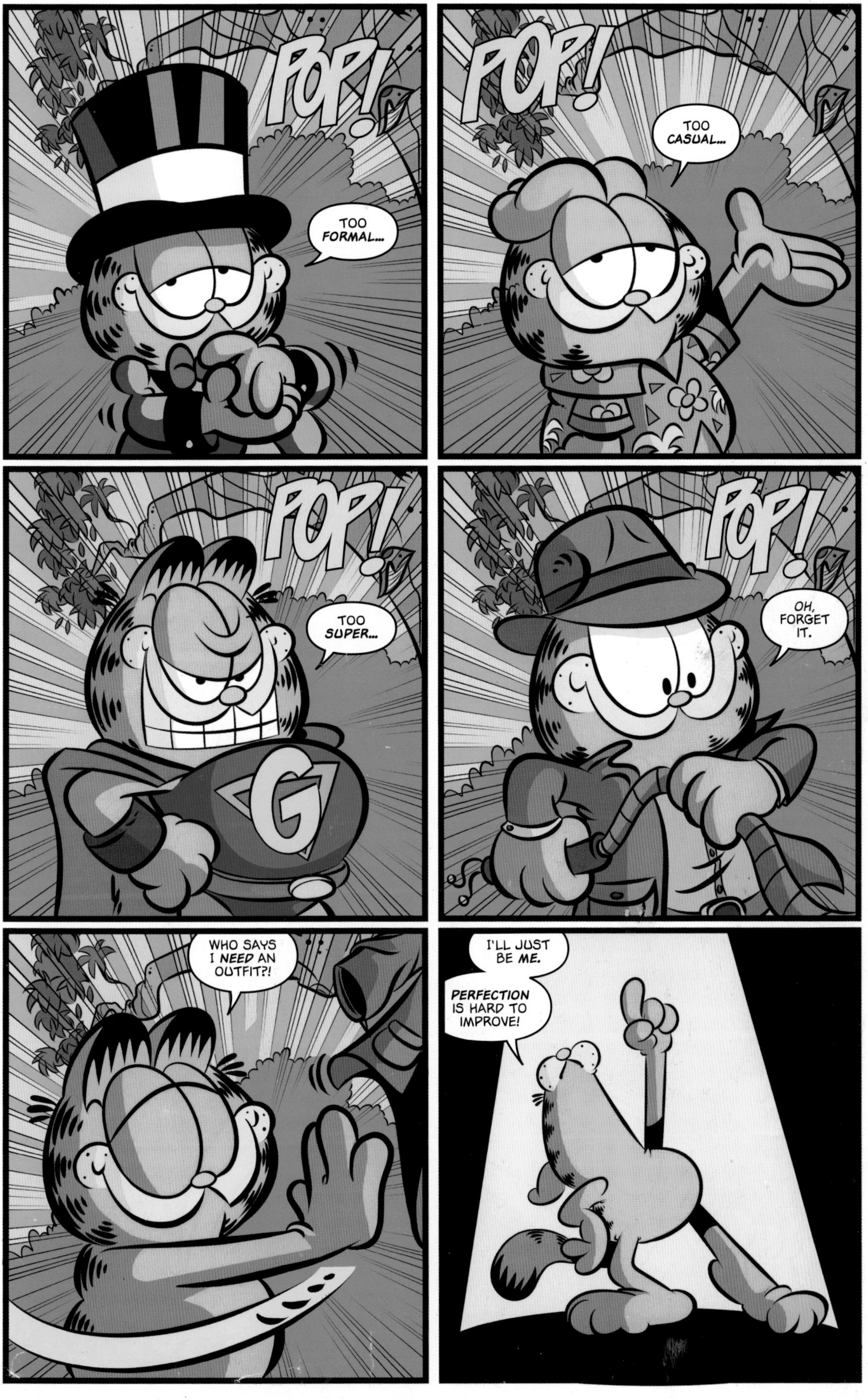
POP!
TOO FORMAL...
POP!
TOO CASUAL...
POP!
TOO SUPER...
POP!
OH, FORGET IT.
WHO SAYS I NEED AN OUTFIT?!
I'LL JUST BE ME.
PERFECTION IS HARD TO IMPROVE!

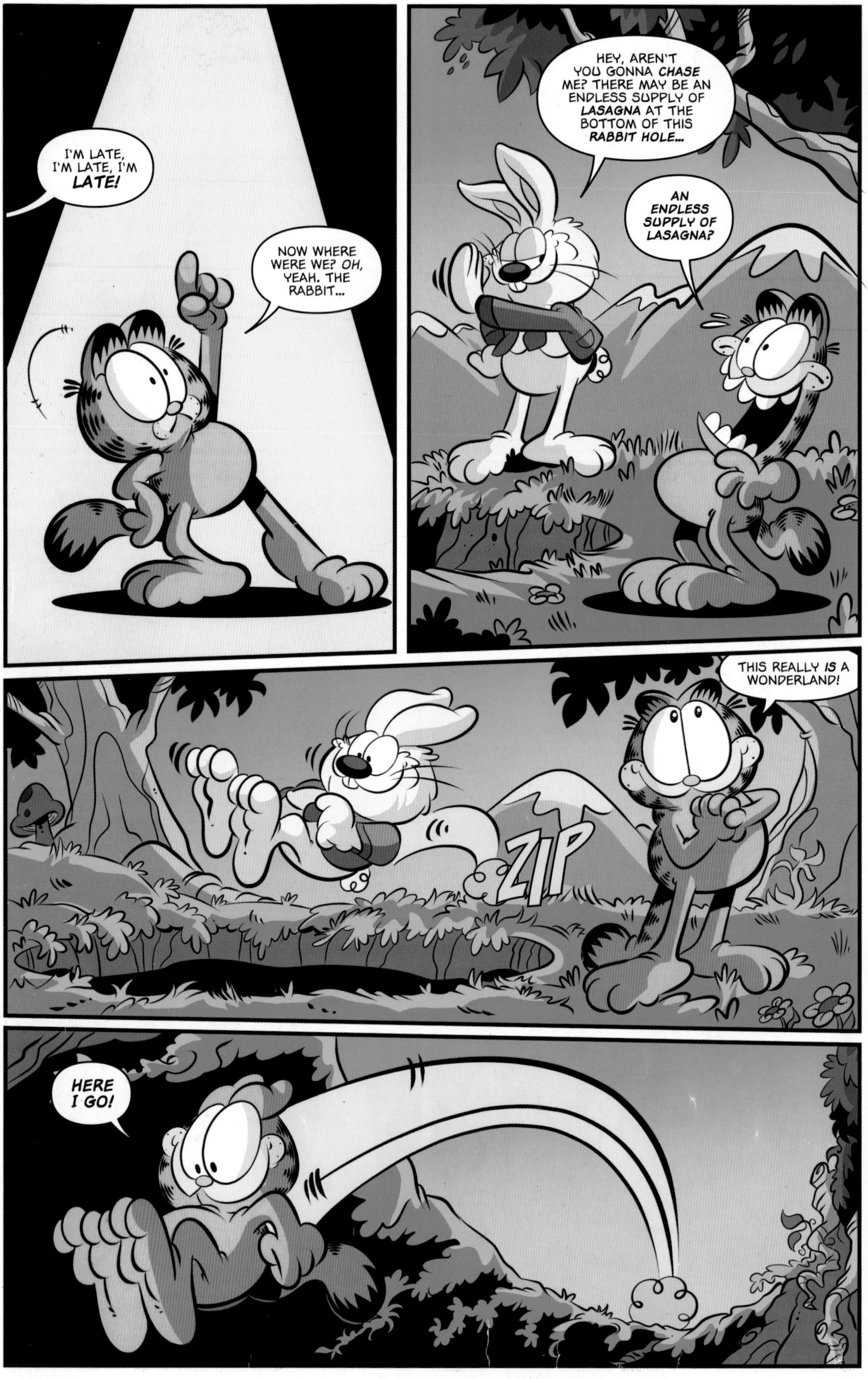
I'M LATE, I'M LATE, I'M LATE!
NOW WHERE WERE WE? OH, YEAH. THE RABBIT...
HEY, AREN'T YOU GONNA CHASE ME? THERE MAY BE AN ENDLESS SUPPLY OF LASAGNA AT THE BOTTOM OF THIS RABBIT HOLE...
AN ENDLESS SUPPLY OF LASAGNA?
ZIP
THIS REALLY IS A WONDERLAND!
HERE I GO!

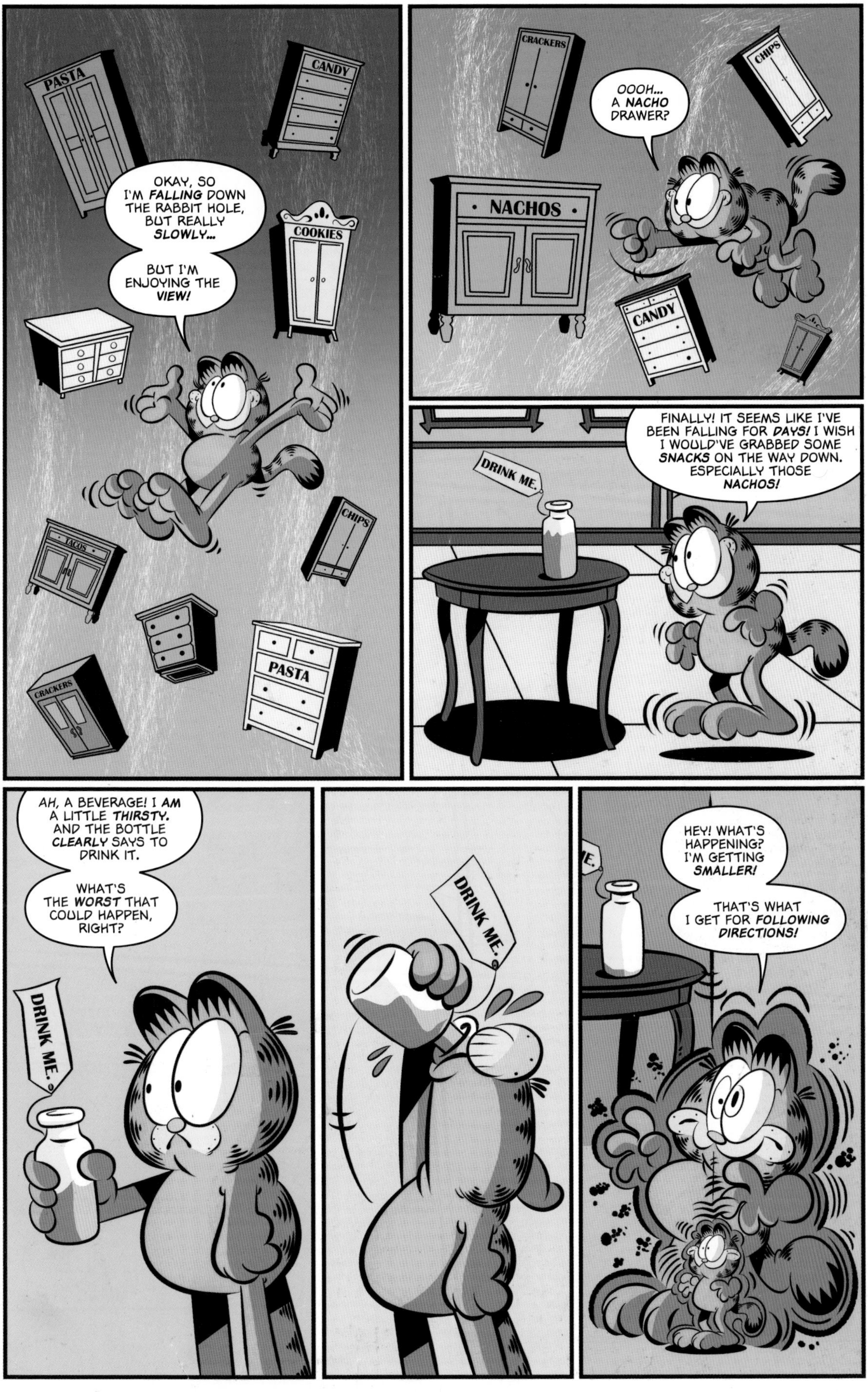

PASTA
CANDY
OKAY, SO I'M FALLING DOWN THE RABBIT HOLE, BUT REALLY SLOWLY...
BUT I'M ENJOYING THE VIEW!
COOKIES
CHIPS
TACOS
PASTA
CRACKERS
CRACKERS
CHIPS
OOOH... A NACHO DRAWER?
NACHOS
CANDY
FINALLY! IT SEEMS LIKE I'VE BEEN FALLING FOR DAYS! I WISH I WOULD'VE GRABBED SOME SNACKS ON THE WAY DOWN. ESPECIALLY THOSE NACHOS!
DRINK ME.
AH, A BEVERAGE! I AM A LITTLE THIRSTY. AND THE BOTTLE CLEARLY SAYS TO DRINK IT.
WHAT'S THE WORST THAT COULD HAPPEN, RIGHT?
DRINK ME.
DRINK ME.
HEY! WHAT'S HAPPENING? I'M GETTING SMALLER!
THAT'S WHAT I GET FOR FOLLOWING DIRECTIONS!

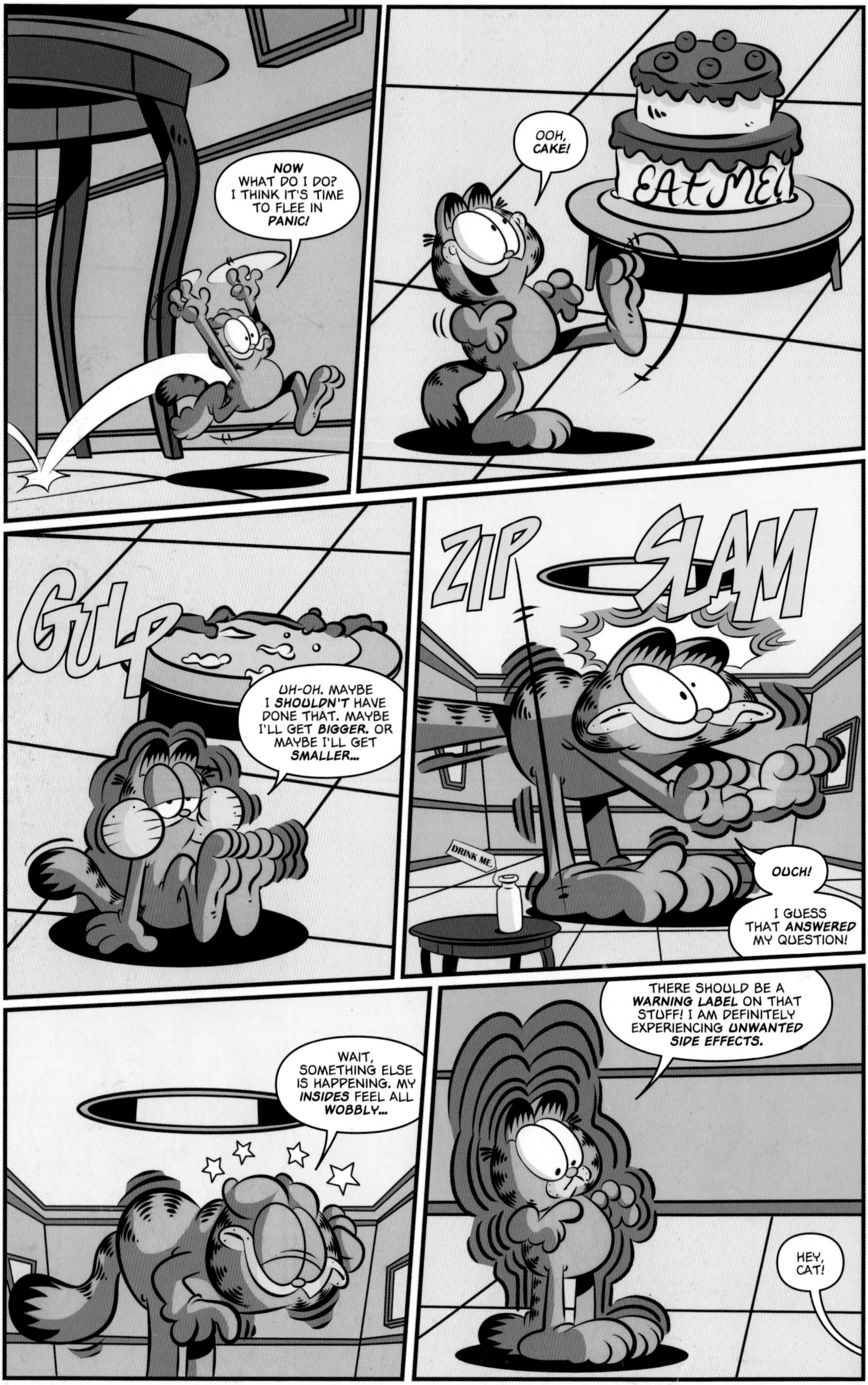
NOW WHAT DO I DO? I THINK IT'S TIME TO FLEE IN PANIC!
OOH, CAKE!
EAT ME!
GULP
UH-OH. MAYBE I SHOULDN'T HAVE DONE THAT. MAYBE I'LL GET BIGGER. OR MAYBE I'LL GET SMALLER...
ZIP
SLAM
DRINK ME.
OUCH!
I GUESS THAT ANSWERED MY QUESTION!
WAIT, SOMETHING ELSE IS HAPPENING. MY INSIDES FEEL ALL WOBBLY...
THERE SHOULD BE A WARNING LABEL ON THAT STUFF! I AM DEFINITELY EXPERIENCING UNWANTED SIDE EFFECTS.
HEY, CAT!

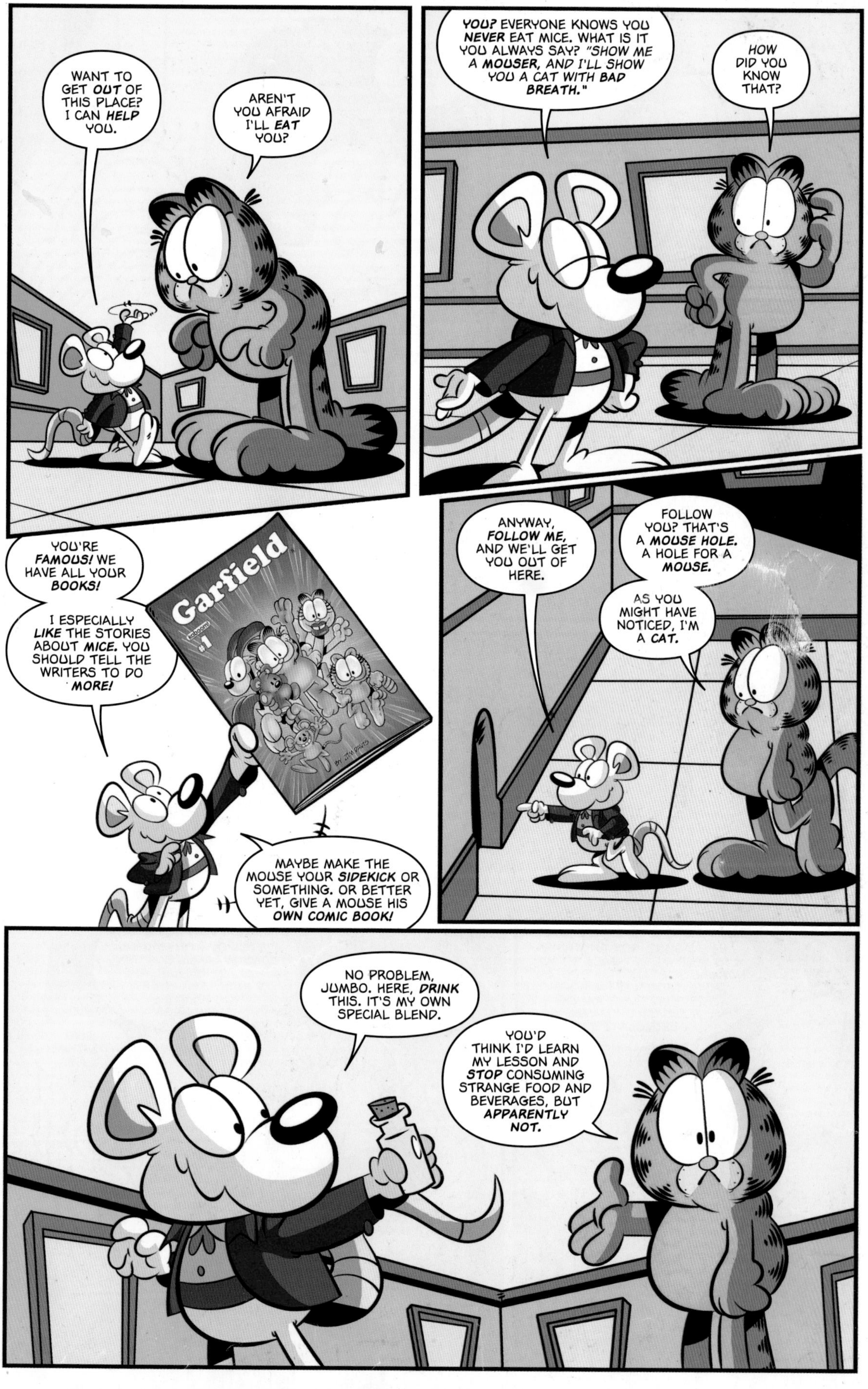
WANT TO GET OUT OF THIS PLACE? I CAN HELP YOU.
AREN'T YOU AFRAID I'LL EAT YOU?
YOU? EVERYONE KNOWS YOU NEVER EAT MICE. WHAT IS IT YOU ALWAYS SAY? "SHOW ME A MOUSER, AND I'LL SHOW YOU A CAT WITH BAD BREATH."
HOW DID YOU KNOW THAT?
YOU'RE FAMOUS! WE HAVE ALL YOUR BOOKS!
I ESPECIALLY LIKE THE STORIES ABOUT MICE. YOU SHOULD TELL THE WRITERS TO DO MORE!
Garfield
#1
MAYBE MAKE THE MOUSE YOUR SIDEKICK OR SOMETHING. OR BETTER YET, GIVE A MOUSE HIS OWN COMIC BOOK!
ANYWAY, FOLLOW ME, AND WE'LL GET YOU OUT OF HERE.
FOLLOW YOU? THAT'S A MOUSE HOLE. A HOLE FOR A MOUSE.
AS YOU MIGHT HAVE NOTICED, I'M A CAT.
NO PROBLEM, JUMBO. HERE, DRINK THIS. IT'S MY OWN SPECIAL BLEND.
YOU'D THINK I'D LEARN MY LESSON AND STOP CONSUMING STRANGE FOOD AND BEVERAGES, BUT APPARENTLY NOT.

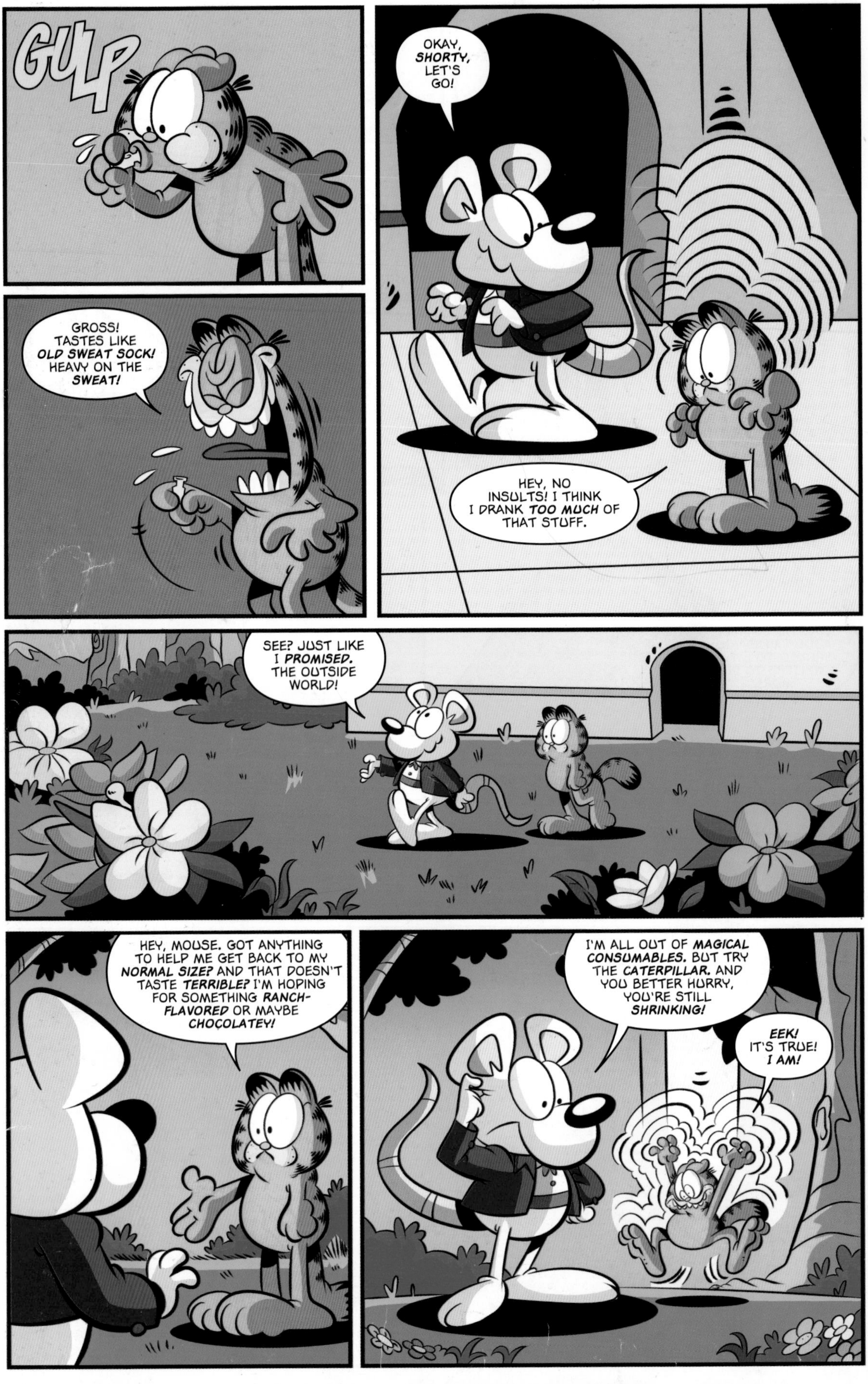
GULP
GROSS! TASTES LIKE OLD SWEAT SOCK! HEAVY ON THE SWEAT!
OKAY, SHORTY, LET'S GO!
HEY, NO INSULTS! I THINK I DRANK TOO MUCH OF THAT STUFF.
SEE? JUST LIKE I PROMISED. THE OUTSIDE WORLD!
HEY, MOUSE. GOT ANYTHING TO HELP ME GET BACK TO MY NORMAL SIZE? AND THAT DOESN'T TASTE TERRIBLE? I'M HOPING FOR SOMETHING RANCH-FLAVORED OR MAYBE CHOCOLATEY!
I'M ALL OUT OF MAGICAL CONSUMABLES. BUT TRY THE CATERPILLAR. AND YOU BETTER HURRY, YOU'RE STILL SHRINKING!
EEK! IT'S TRUE! I AM!

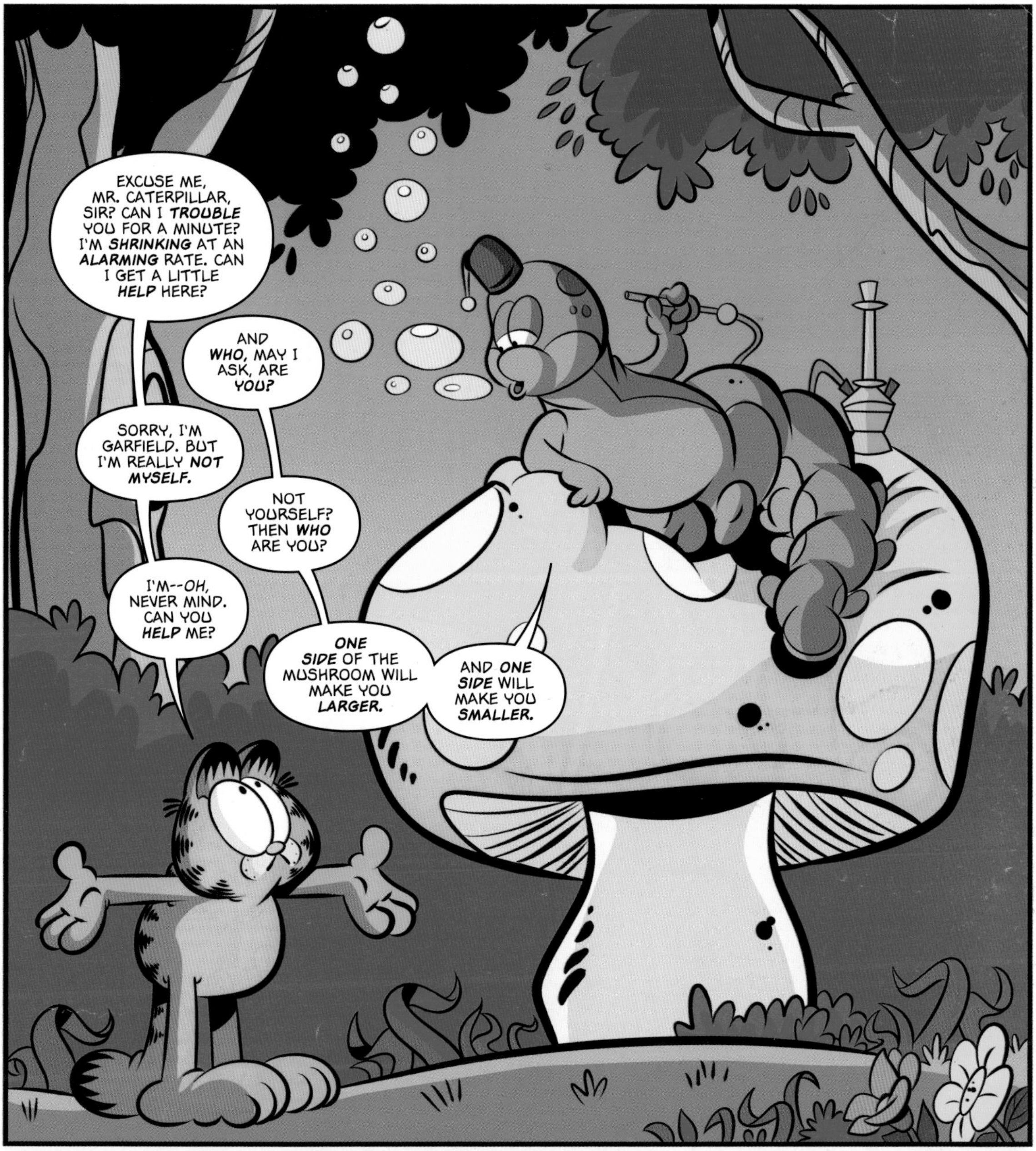
EXCUSE ME, MR. CATERPILLAR, SIR? CAN I TROUBLE YOU FOR A MINUTE? I'M SHRINKING AT AN ALARMING RATE. CAN I GET A LITTLE HELP HERE?
AND WHO, MAY I ASK, ARE YOU?
SORRY, I'M GARFIELD. BUT I'M REALLY NOT MYSELF.
NOT YOURSELF? THEN WHO ARE YOU?
I'M--OH, NEVER MIND. CAN YOU HELP ME?
ONE SIDE OF THE MUSHROOM WILL MAKE YOU LARGER.
AND ONE SIDE WILL MAKE YOU SMALLER.

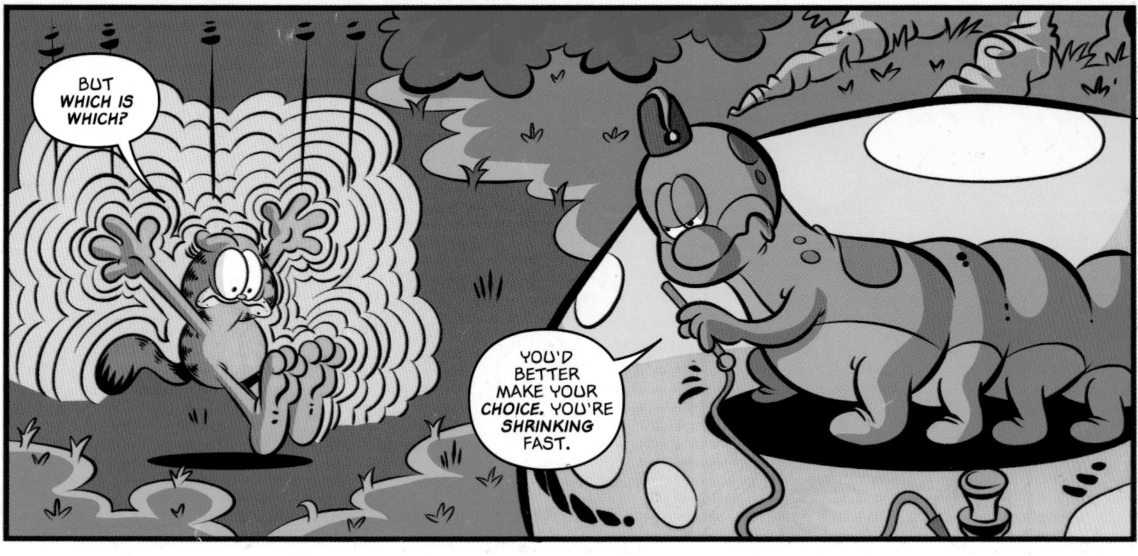
BUT WHICH IS WHICH?
YOU'D BETTER MAKE YOUR CHOICE. YOU'RE SHRINKING FAST.

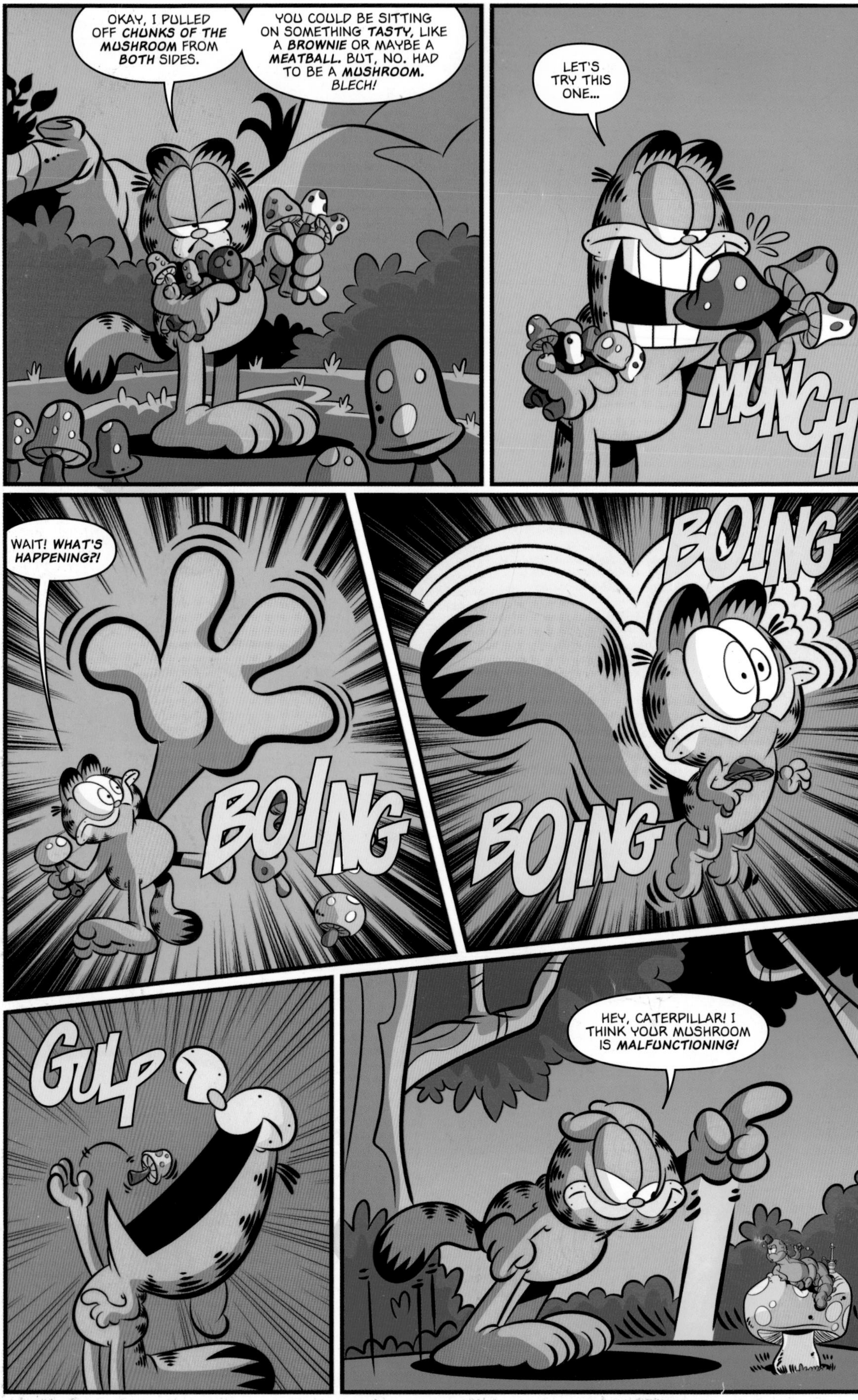
OKAY, I PULLED OFF CHUNKS OF THE MUSHROOM FROM BOTH SIDES.
YOU COULD BE SITTING ON SOMETHING TASTY, LIKE A BROWNIE OR MAYBE A MEATBALL. BUT, NO. HAD TO BE A MUSHROOM. BLECH!
LET'S TRY THIS ONE...
MUNCH
WAIT! WHAT'S HAPPENING?!
BOING
BOING
BOING
GULP
HEY, CATERPILLAR! I THINK YOUR MUSHROOM IS MALFUNCTIONING!

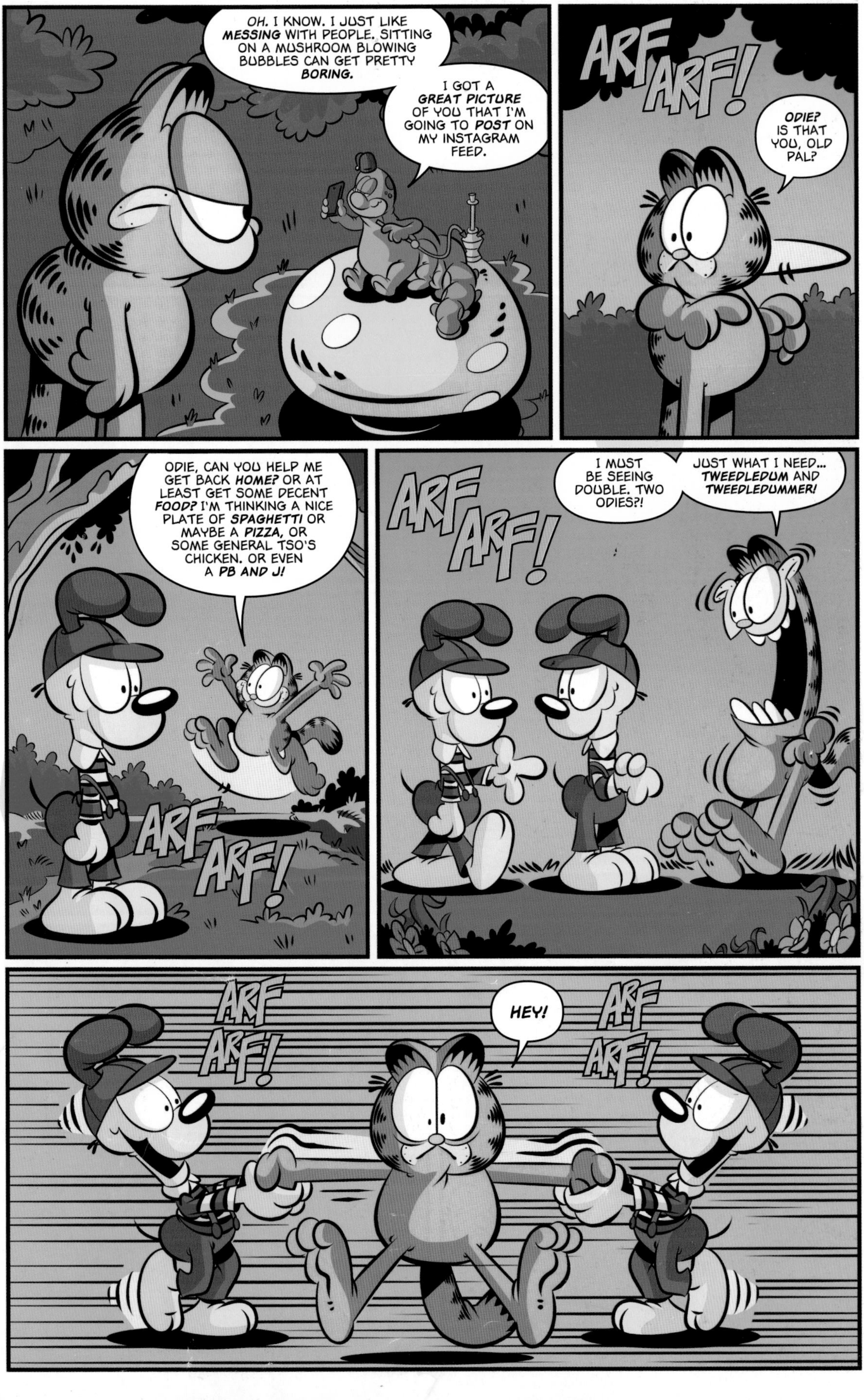
OH. I KNOW. I JUST LIKE MESSING WITH PEOPLE. SITTING ON A MUSHROOM BLOWING BUBBLES CAN GET PRETTY BORING.
I GOT A GREAT PICTURE OF YOU THAT I'M GOING TO POST ON MY INSTAGRAM FEED.
ARF ARF!
ODIE? IS THAT YOU, OLD PAL?
ODIE, CAN YOU HELP ME GET BACK HOME? OR AT LEAST GET SOME DECENT FOOD? I'M THINKING A NICE PLATE OF SPAGHETTI OR MAYBE A PIZZA, OR SOME GENERAL TSO'S CHICKEN. OR EVEN A PB AND J!
ARF ARF!
ARF ARF!
I MUST BE SEEING DOUBLE. TWO ODIES?!
JUST WHAT I NEED... TWEEDLEDUM AND TWEEDLEDUMMER!
ARF ARF!
HEY!
ARF ARF!

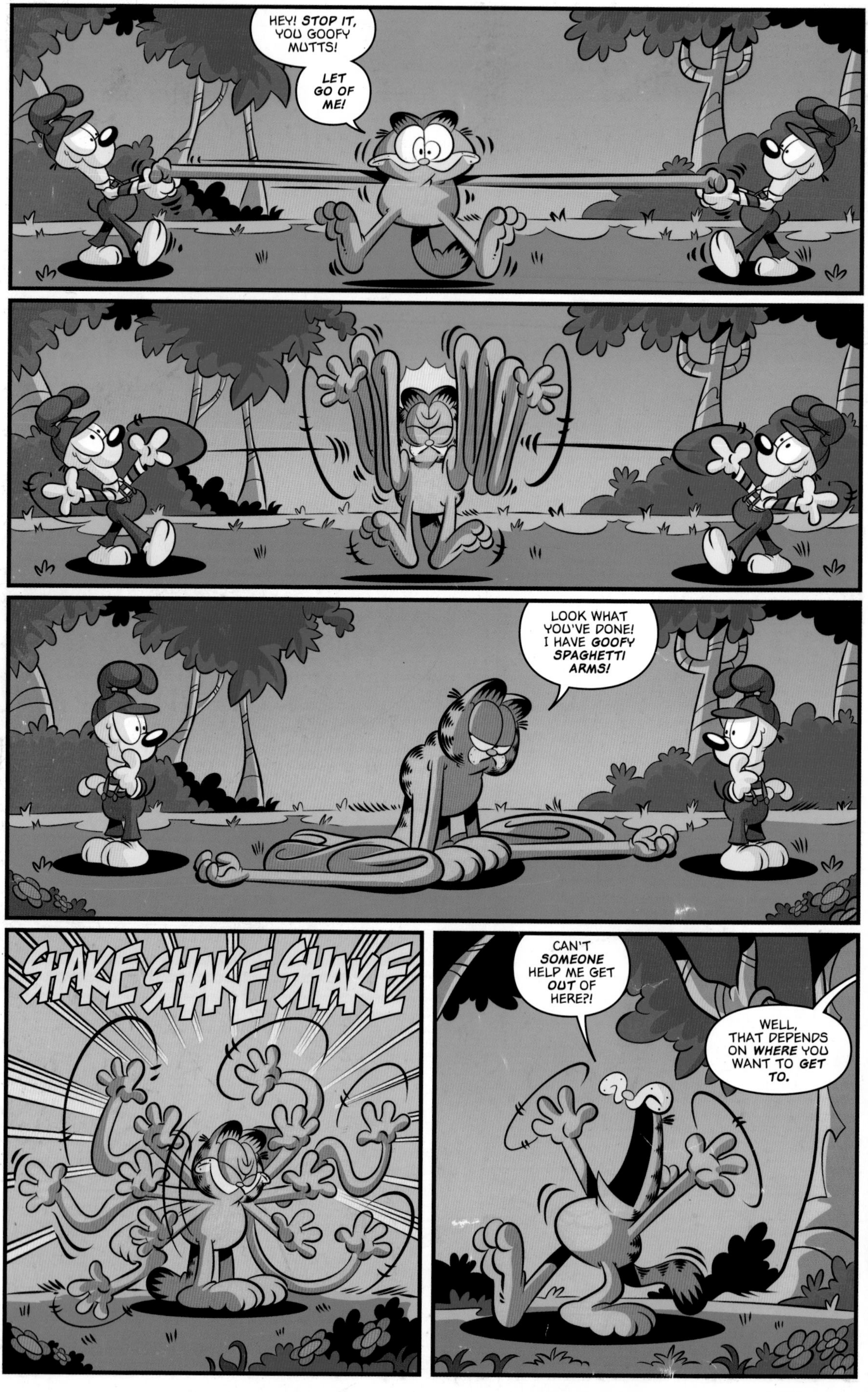
HEY! STOP IT, YOU GOOFY MUTTS!
LET GO OF ME!
LOOK WHAT YOU'VE DONE! I HAVE GOOFY SPAGHETTI ARMS!
SHAKE SHAKE SHAKE
CAN'T SOMEONE HELP ME GET OUT OF HERE?!
WELL, THAT DEPENDS ON WHERE YOU WANT TO GET TO.

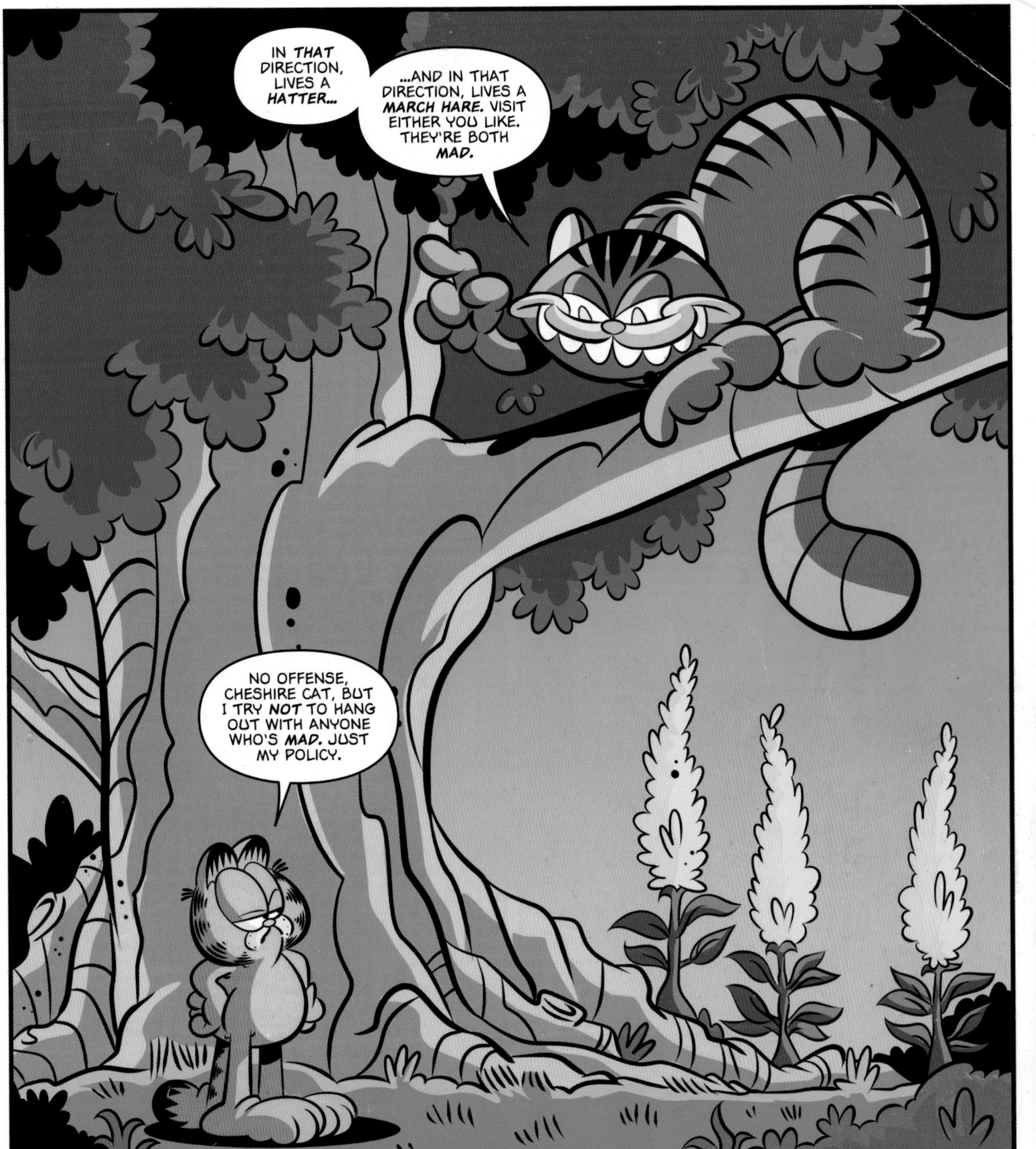
IN THAT DIRECTION, LIVES A HATTER...
...AND IN THAT DIRECTION, LIVES A MARCH HARE. VISIT EITHER YOU LIKE. THEY'RE BOTH MAD.
NO OFFENSE, CHESHIRE CAT, BUT I TRY NOT TO HANG OUT WITH ANYONE WHO'S MAD. JUST MY POLICY.

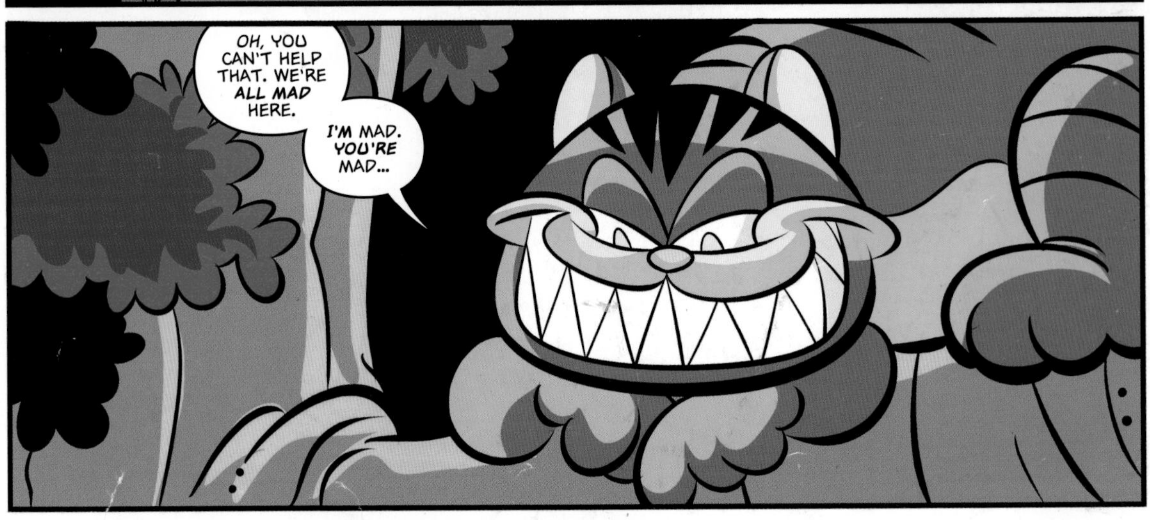
OH, YOU CAN'T HELP THAT. WE'RE ALL MAD HERE.
I'M MAD. YOU'RE MAD...

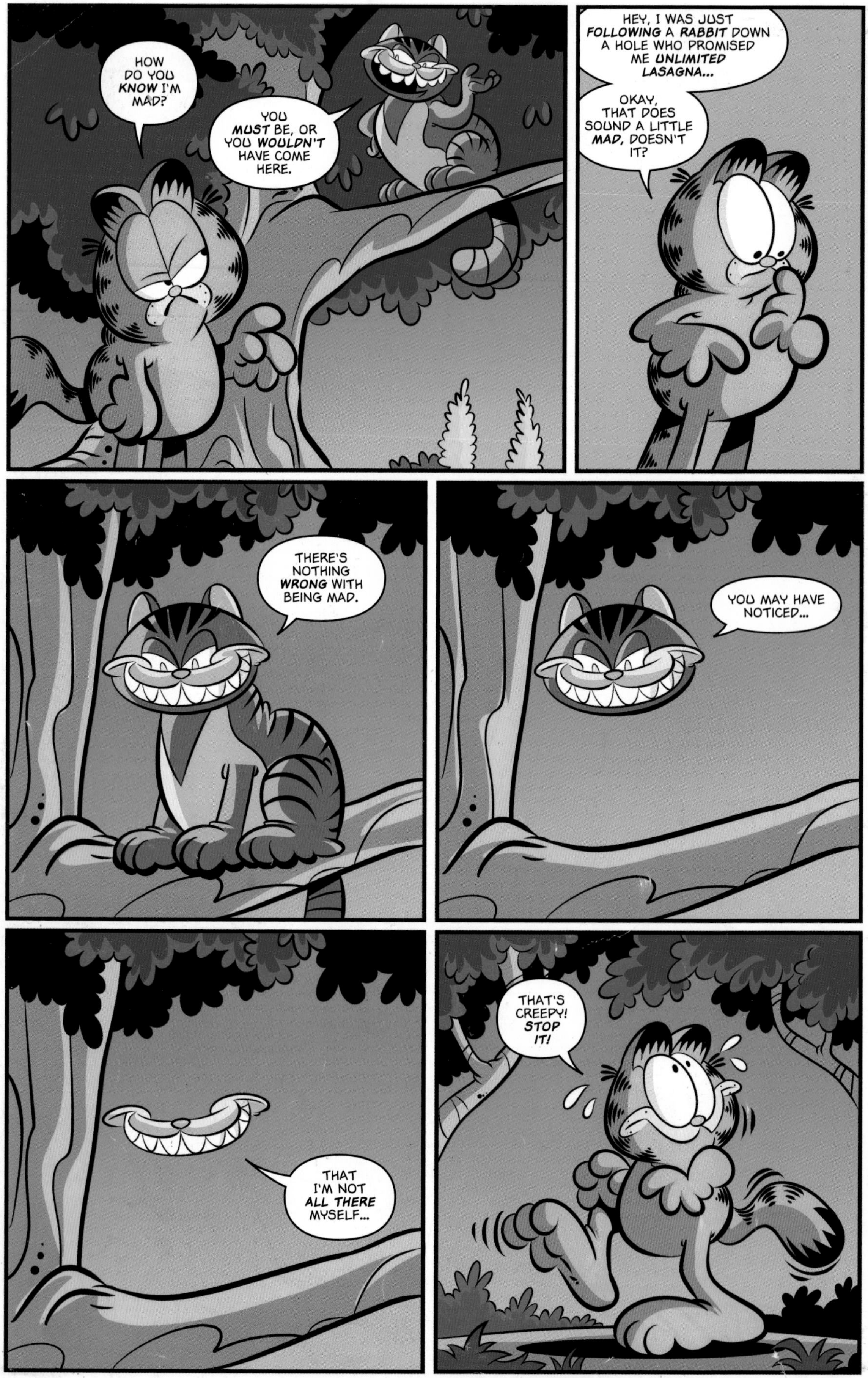
HOW DO YOU KNOW I'M MAD?
YOU MUST BE, OR YOU WOULDN'T HAVE COME HERE.
HEY, I WAS JUST FOLLOWING A RABBIT DOWN A HOLE WHO PROMISED ME UNLIMITED LASAGNA...
OKAY, THAT DOES SOUND A LITTLE MAD, DOESN'T IT?
THERE'S NOTHING WRONG WITH BEING MAD.
YOU MAY HAVE NOTICED...
THAT I'M NOT ALL THERE MYSELF...
THAT'S CREEPY! STOP IT!

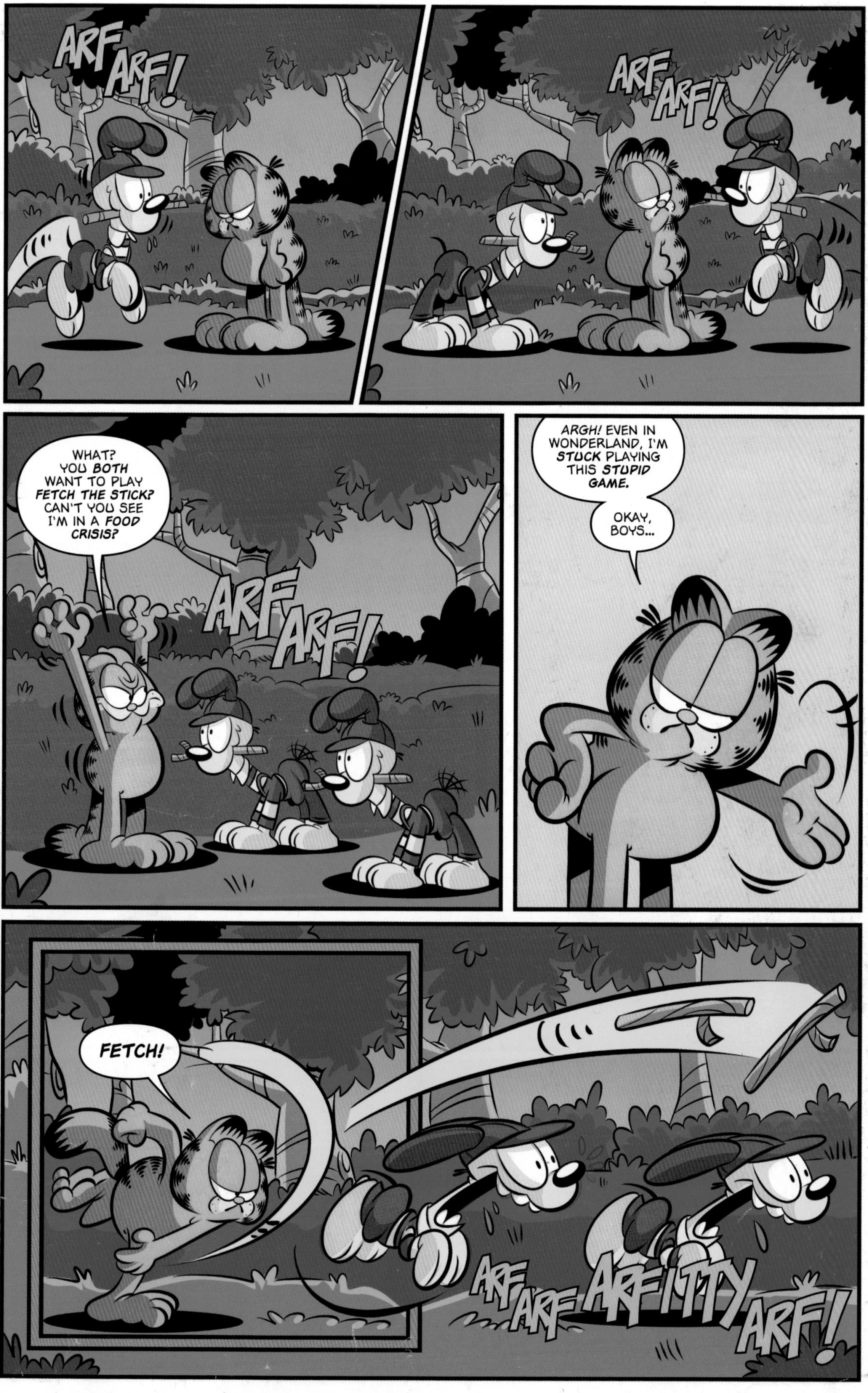
ARF ARF!
ARF ARF!
WHAT? YOU BOTH WANT TO PLAY FETCH THE STICK? CAN'T YOU SEE I'M IN A FOOD CRISIS?
ARF ARF!
ARGH! EVEN IN WONDERLAND, I'M STUCK PLAYING THIS STUPID GAME.
OKAY, BOYS...
FETCH!
ARF ARF ARFITTY ARF!

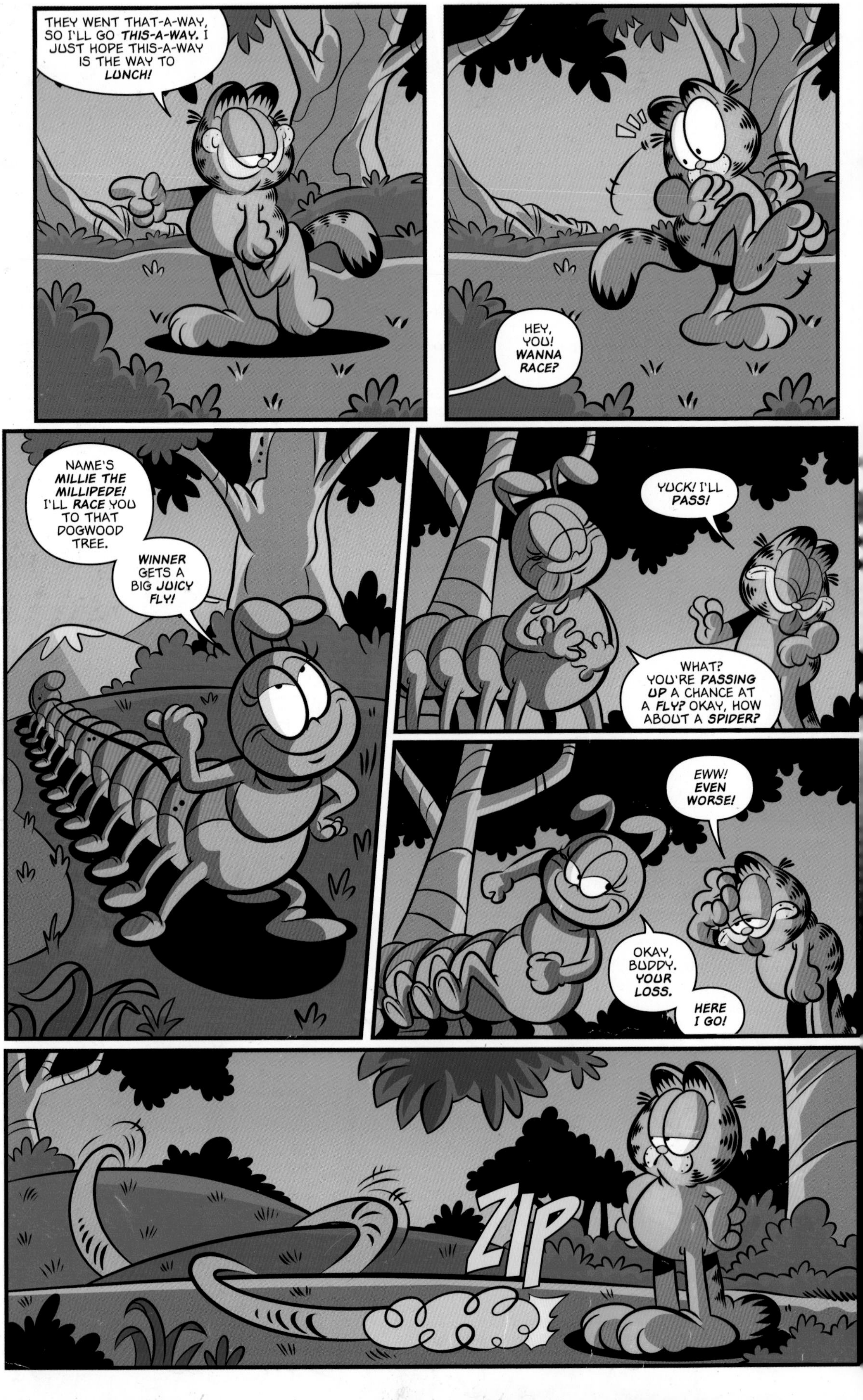
THEY WENT THAT-A-WAY, SO I'LL GO THIS-A-WAY. I JUST HOPE THIS-A-WAY IS THE WAY TO LUNCH!
HEY, YOU! WANNA RACE?
NAME'S MILLIE THE MILLIPEDE! I'LL RACE YOU TO THAT DOGWOOD TREE.
WINNER GETS A BIG JUICY FLY!
YUCK! I'LL PASS!
WHAT? YOU'RE PASSING UP A CHANCE AT A FLY? OKAY, HOW ABOUT A SPIDER?
EWW! EVEN WORSE!
OKAY, BUDDY. YOUR LOSS.
HERE I GO!
ZIP

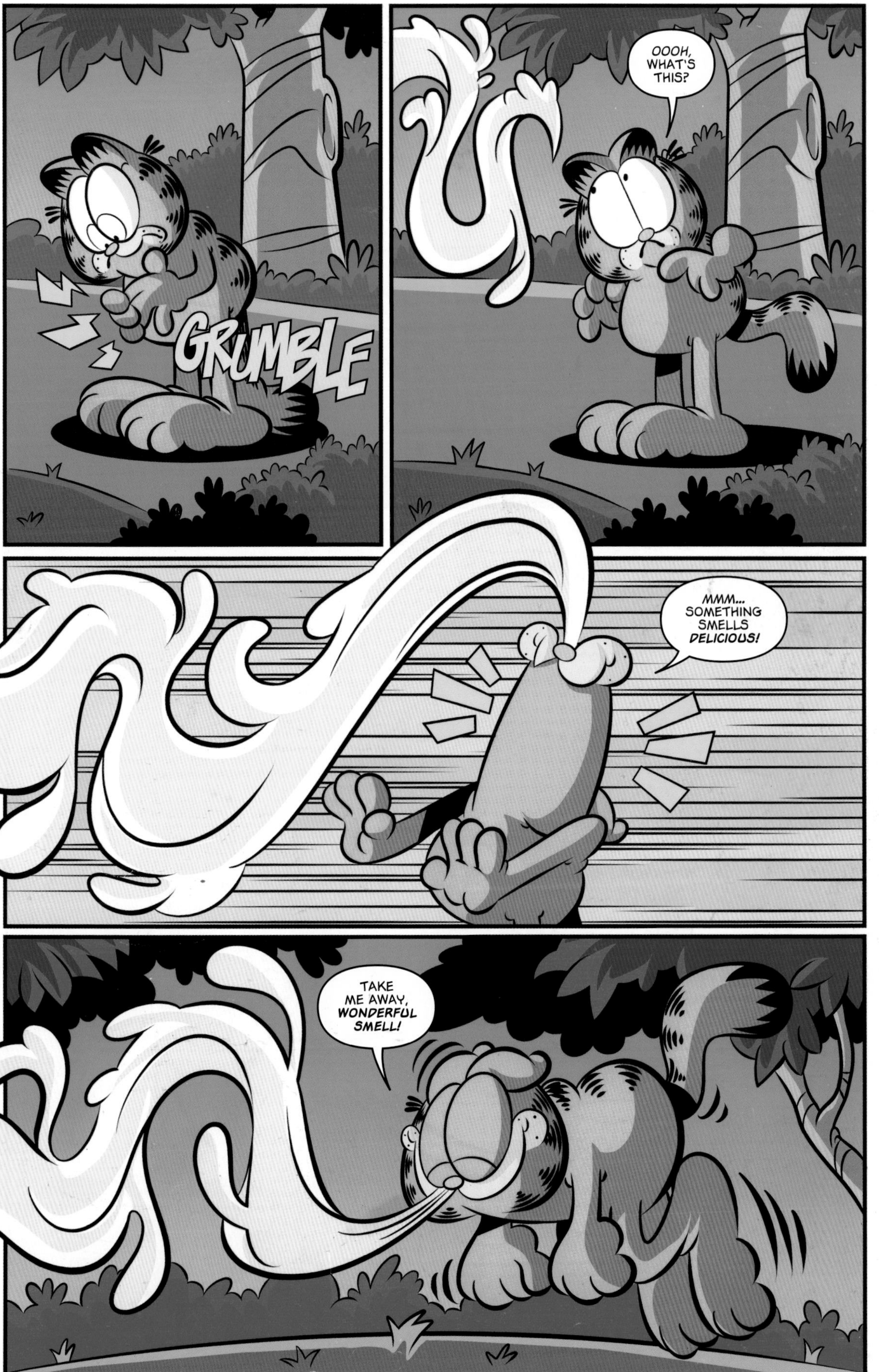
GRUMBLE
OOOH, WHAT'S THIS?
MMM... SOMETHING SMELLS DELICIOUS!
TAKE ME AWAY, WONDERFUL SMELL!

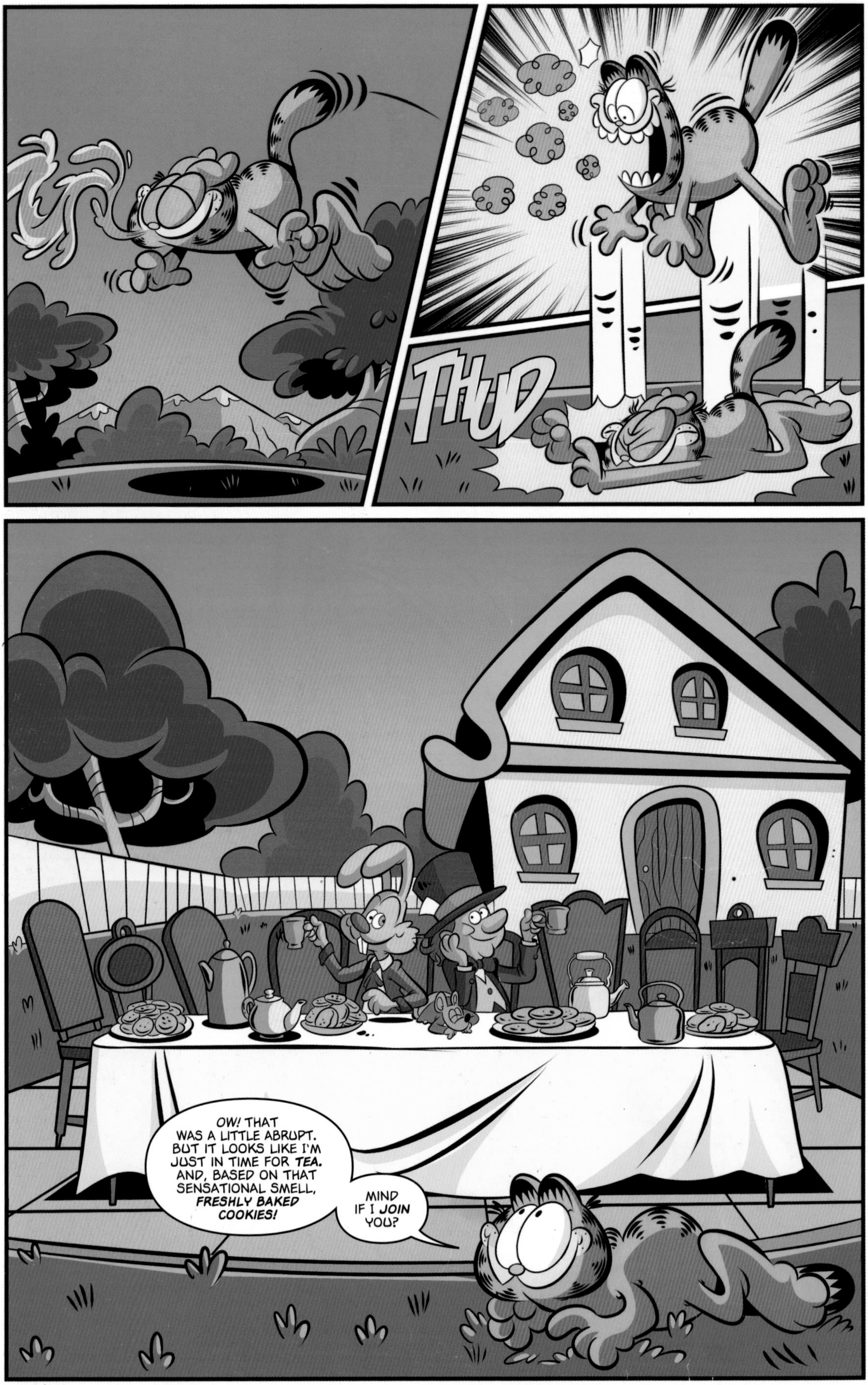
THUD
OW! THAT WAS A LITTLE ABRUPT. BUT IT LOOKS LIKE I'M JUST IN TIME FOR TEA. AND, BASED ON THAT SENSATIONAL SMELL, FRESHLY BAKED COOKIES!
MIND IF I JOIN YOU?

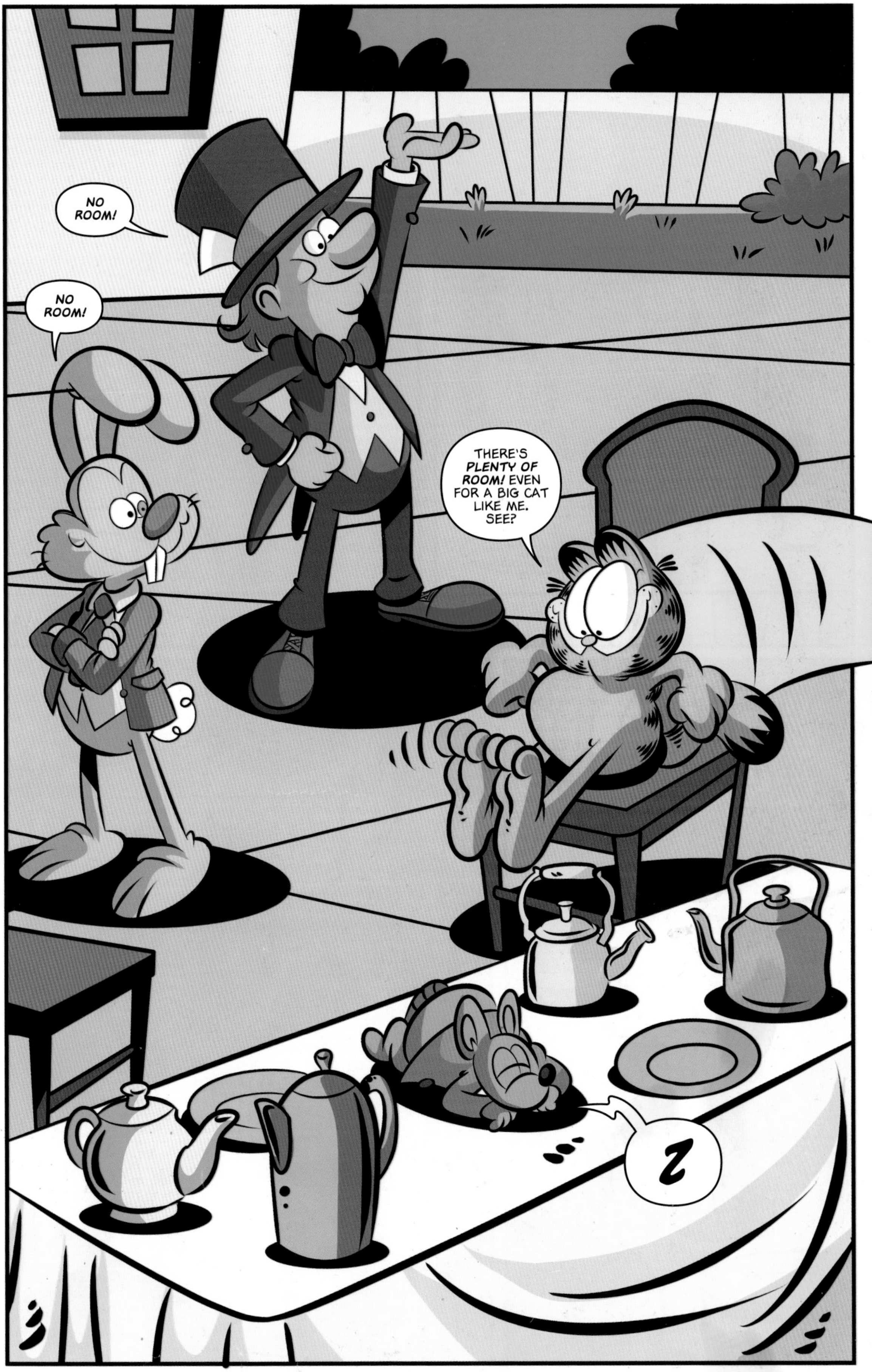
NO ROOM!
NO ROOM!
THERE'S PLENTY OF ROOM! EVEN FOR A BIG CAT LIKE ME. SEE?
Z

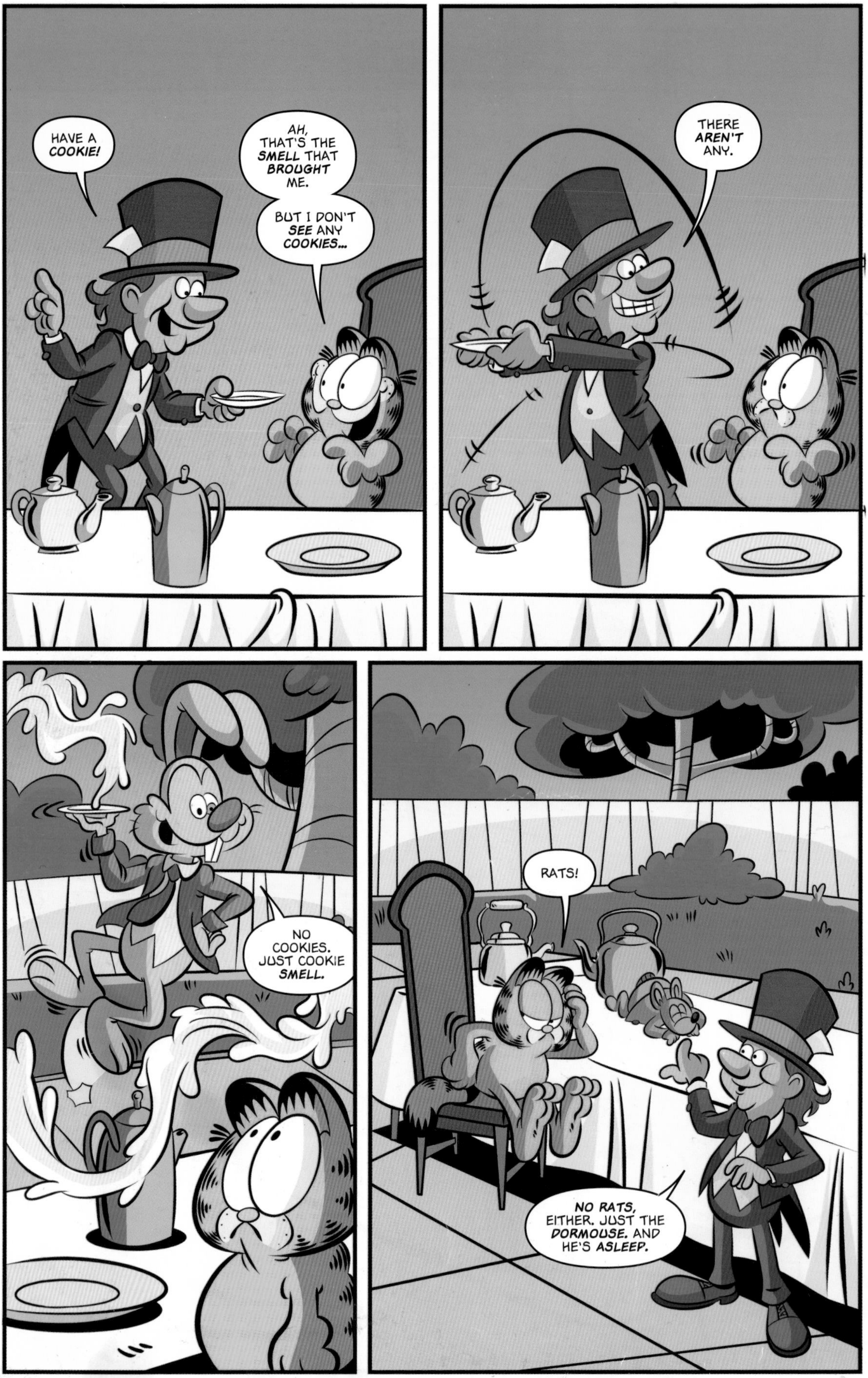
HAVE A COOKIE!
AH, THAT'S THE SMELL THAT BROUGHT ME.
BUT I DON'T SEE ANY COOKIES...
THERE AREN'T ANY.
NO COOKIES. JUST COOKIE SMELL.
RATS!
NO RATS, EITHER. JUST THE DORMOUSE. AND HE'S ASLEEP.

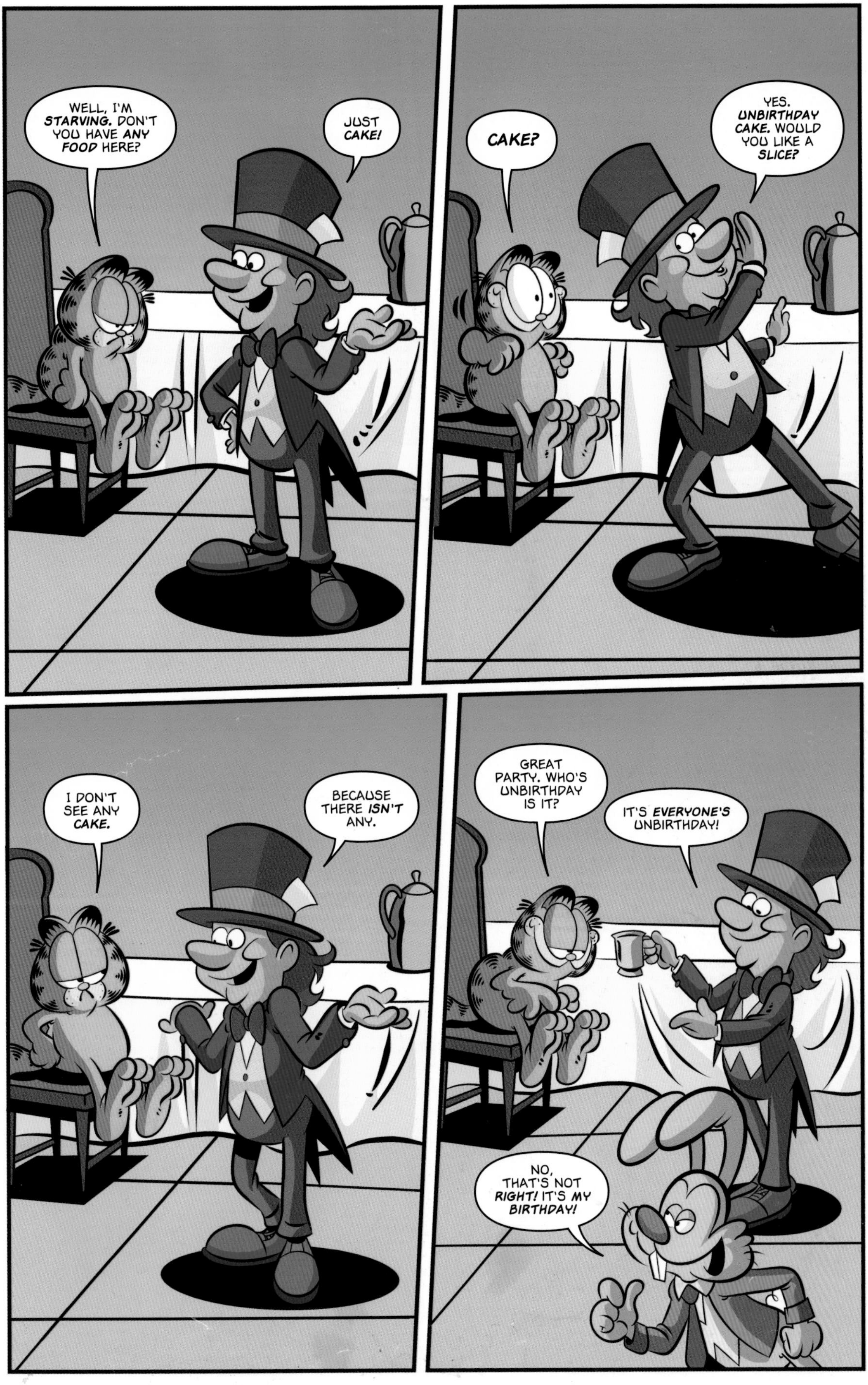
WELL, I'M STARVING. DON'T YOU HAVE ANY FOOD HERE?
JUST CAKE!
CAKE?
YES. UNBIRTHDAY CAKE. WOULD YOU LIKE A SLICE?
I DON'T SEE ANY CAKE.
BECAUSE THERE ISN'T ANY.
GREAT PARTY. WHO'S UNBIRTHDAY IS IT?
IT'S EVERYONE'S UNBIRTHDAY!
NO, THAT'S NOT RIGHT! IT'S MY BIRTHDAY!

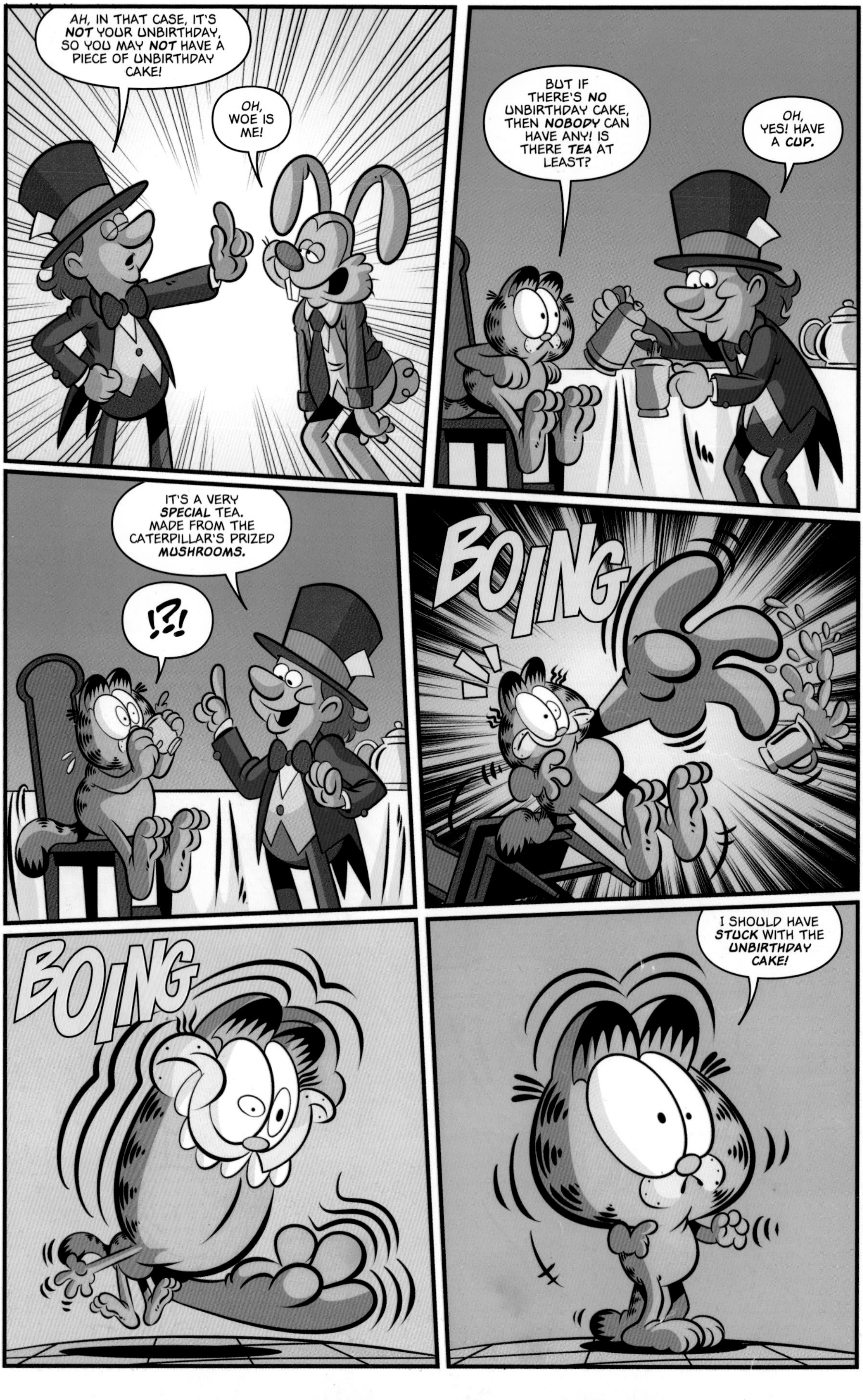
AH, IN THAT CASE, IT'S NOT YOUR UNBIRTHDAY, SO YOU MAY NOT HAVE A PIECE OF UNBIRTHDAY CAKE!
OH, WOE IS ME!
BUT IF THERE'S NO UNBIRTHDAY CAKE, THEN NOBODY CAN HAVE ANY! IS THERE TEA AT LEAST?
OH, YES! HAVE A CUP.
IT'S A VERY SPECIAL TEA. MADE FROM THE CATERPILLAR'S PRIZED MUSHROOMS.
!?!
BOING
BOING
I SHOULD HAVE STUCK WITH THE UNBIRTHDAY CAKE!

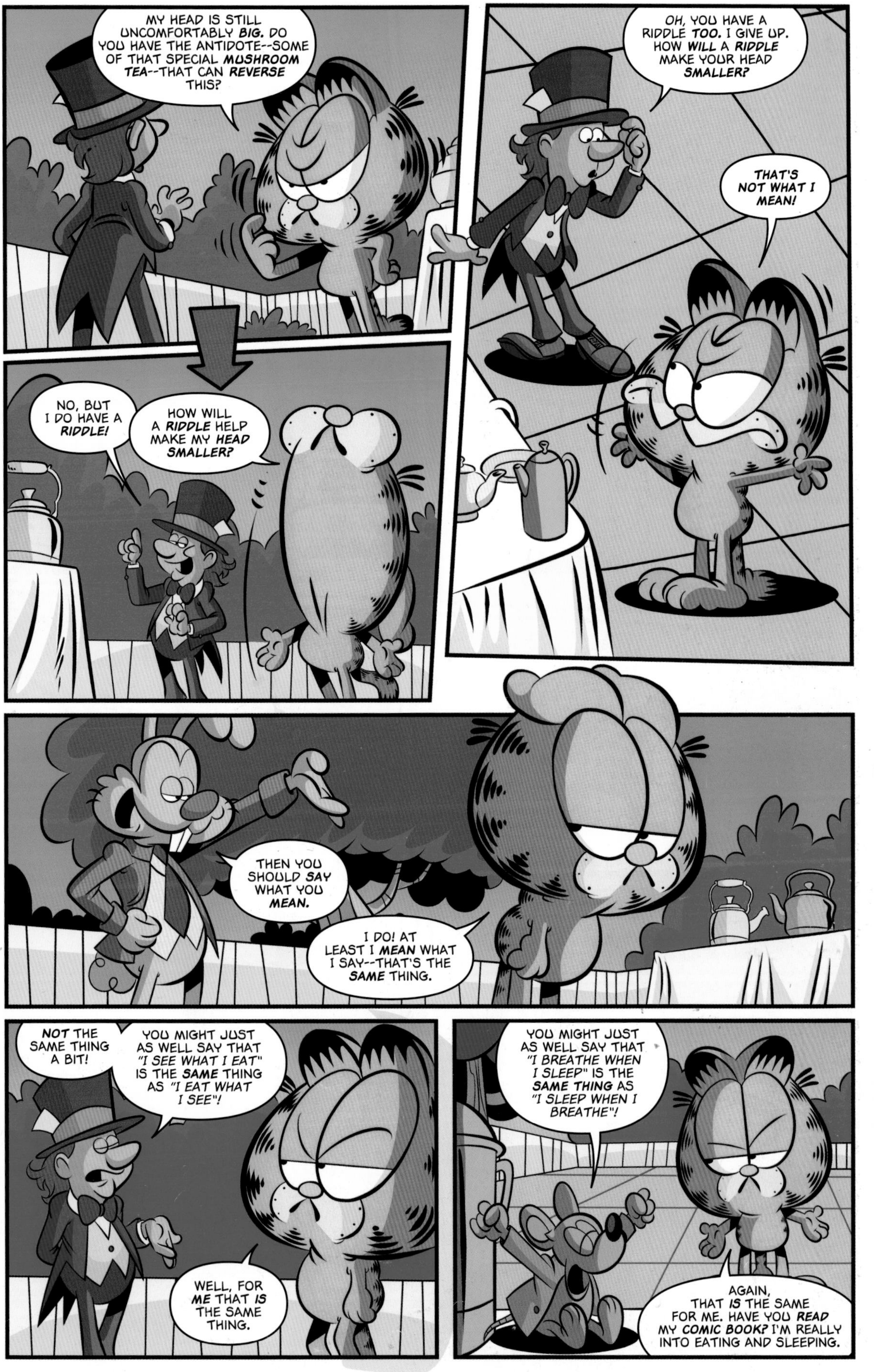
MY HEAD IS STILL UNCOMFORTABLY BIG. DO YOU HAVE THE ANTIDOTE--SOME OF THAT SPECIAL MUSHROOM TEA--THAT CAN REVERSE THIS?
NO, BUT I DO HAVE A RIDDLE!
HOW WILL A RIDDLE HELP MAKE MY HEAD SMALLER?
OH, YOU HAVE A RIDDLE TOO. I GIVE UP. HOW WILL A RIDDLE MAKE YOUR HEAD SMALLER?
THAT'S NOT WHAT I MEAN!
THEN YOU SHOULD SAY WHAT YOU MEAN.
I DO! AT LEAST I MEAN WHAT I SAY--THAT'S THE SAME THING.
NOT THE SAME THING A BIT!
YOU MIGHT JUST AS WELL SAY THAT "I SEE WHAT I EAT" IS THE SAME THING AS "I EAT WHAT I SEE"!
WELL, FOR ME THAT IS THE SAME THING.
YOU MIGHT JUST AS WELL SAY THAT "I BREATHE WHEN I SLEEP" IS THE SAME THING AS "I SLEEP WHEN I BREATHE"!
AGAIN, THAT IS THE SAME FOR ME. HAVE YOU READ MY COMIC BOOK? I'M REALLY INTO EATING AND SLEEPING.

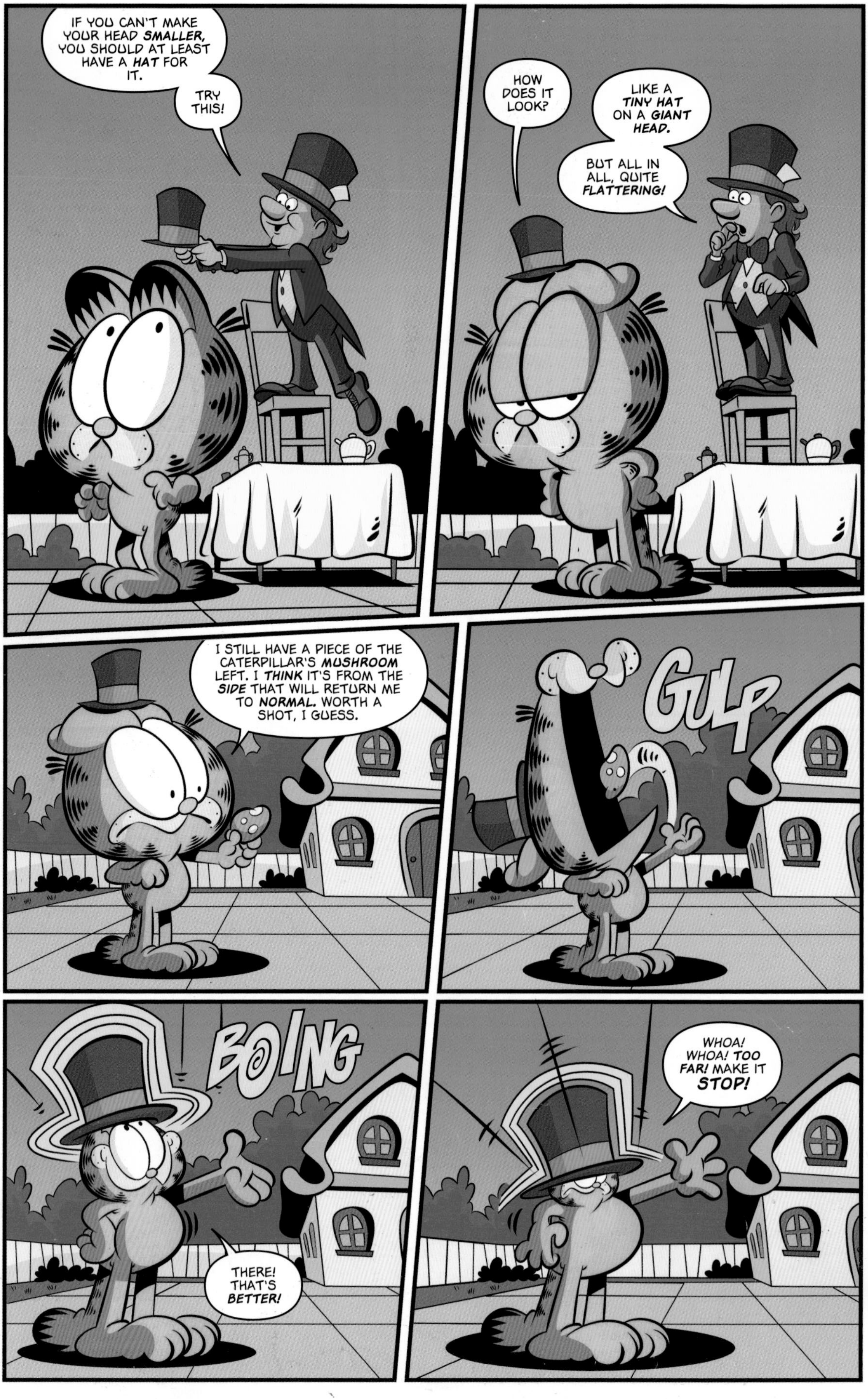
IF YOU CAN'T MAKE YOUR HEAD **SMALLER,** YOU SHOULD AT LEAST HAVE A **HAT** FOR IT.
TRY THIS!
HOW DOES IT LOOK?
LIKE A **TINY HAT** ON A **GIANT HEAD.**
BUT ALL IN ALL, QUITE **FLATTERING!**
I STILL HAVE A PIECE OF THE CATERPILLAR'S **MUSHROOM** LEFT. I **THINK** IT'S FROM THE **SIDE** THAT WILL RETURN ME TO **NORMAL.** WORTH A SHOT, I GUESS.
GULP
BOING
THERE! THAT'S **BETTER!**
WHOA! WHOA! **TOO FAR!** MAKE IT **STOP!**

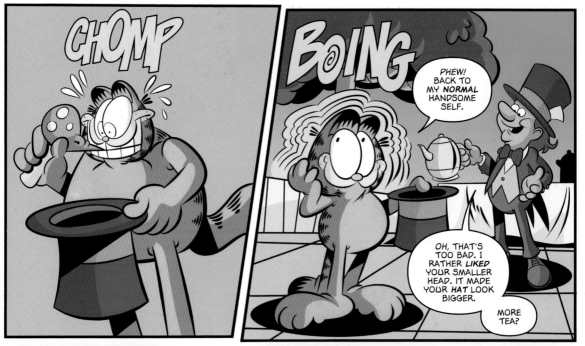

CHOMP

BOING

PHEW! BACK TO MY *NORMAL* HANDSOME SELF.

OH, THAT'S TOO BAD. I RATHER *LIKED* YOUR SMALLER HEAD. IT MADE YOUR *HAT* LOOK BIGGER.

MORE TEA?

NO, NO, NO. NO MORE *WEIRD MUSHROOM* TEA FOR ME.

IN FACT, I GOTTA *RUN.* STRANGE PLACES TO GO, NUTTY PEOPLE TO MEET. YOU KNOW HOW IT GOES.

MERRY UNBIRTHDAY!

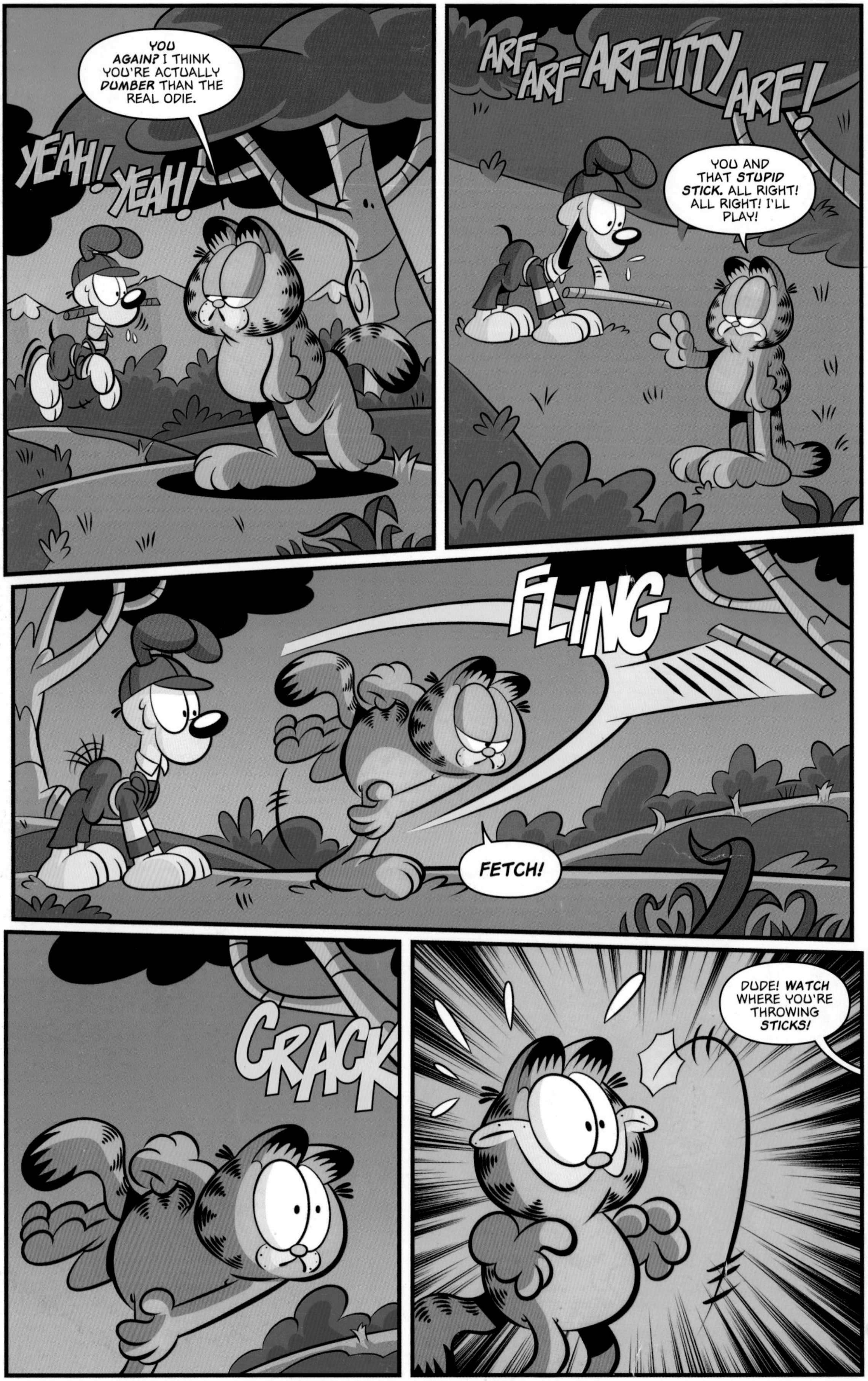
YOU AGAIN? I THINK YOU'RE ACTUALLY DUMBER THAN THE REAL ODIE.
YEAH! YEAH!
ARF ARF ARFITTY ARF!
YOU AND THAT STUPID STICK. ALL RIGHT! ALL RIGHT! I'LL PLAY!
FLING
FETCH!
CRACK
DUDE! WATCH WHERE YOU'RE THROWING STICKS!

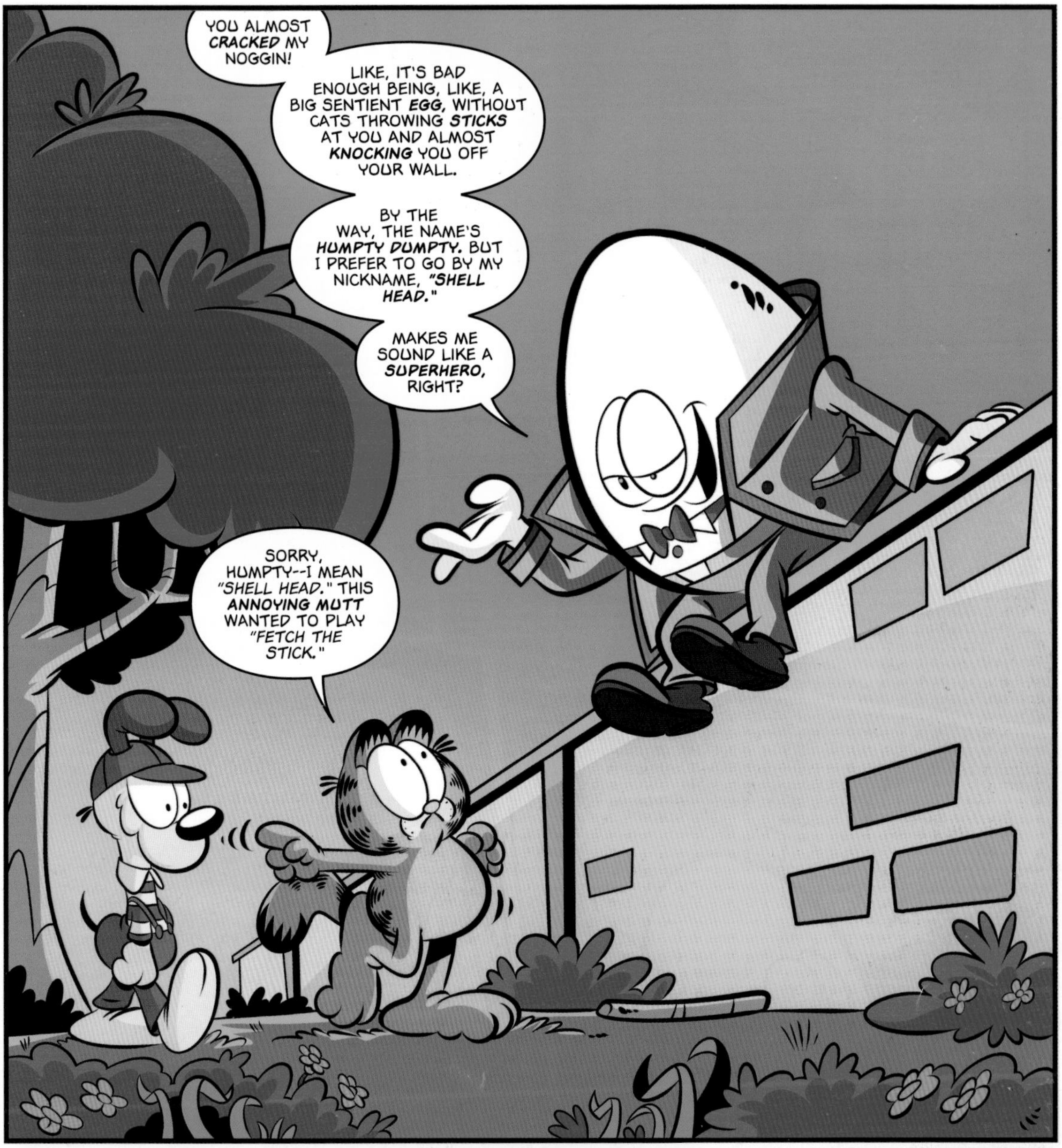
YOU ALMOST CRACKED MY NOGGIN!
LIKE, IT'S BAD ENOUGH BEING, LIKE, A BIG SENTIENT EGG, WITHOUT CATS THROWING STICKS AT YOU AND ALMOST KNOCKING YOU OFF YOUR WALL.
BY THE WAY, THE NAME'S HUMPTY DUMPTY. BUT I PREFER TO GO BY MY NICKNAME, "SHELL HEAD."
MAKES ME SOUND LIKE A SUPERHERO, RIGHT?
SORRY, HUMPTY--I MEAN "SHELL HEAD." THIS ANNOYING MUTT WANTED TO PLAY "FETCH THE STICK."
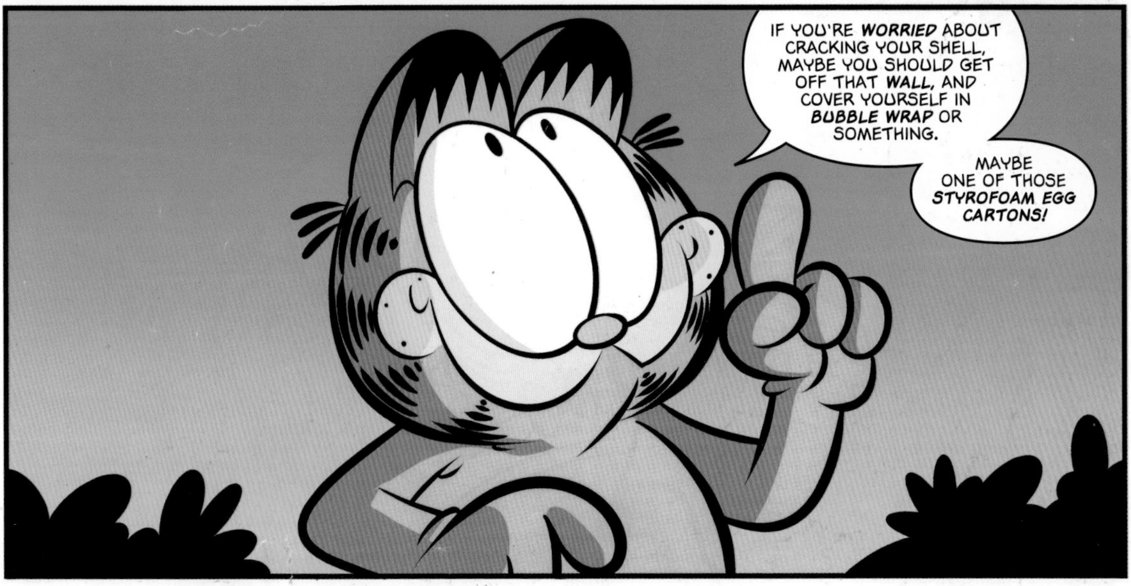
IF YOU'RE WORRIED ABOUT CRACKING YOUR SHELL, MAYBE YOU SHOULD GET OFF THAT WALL, AND COVER YOURSELF IN BUBBLE WRAP OR SOMETHING.
MAYBE ONE OF THOSE STYROFOAM EGG CARTONS!

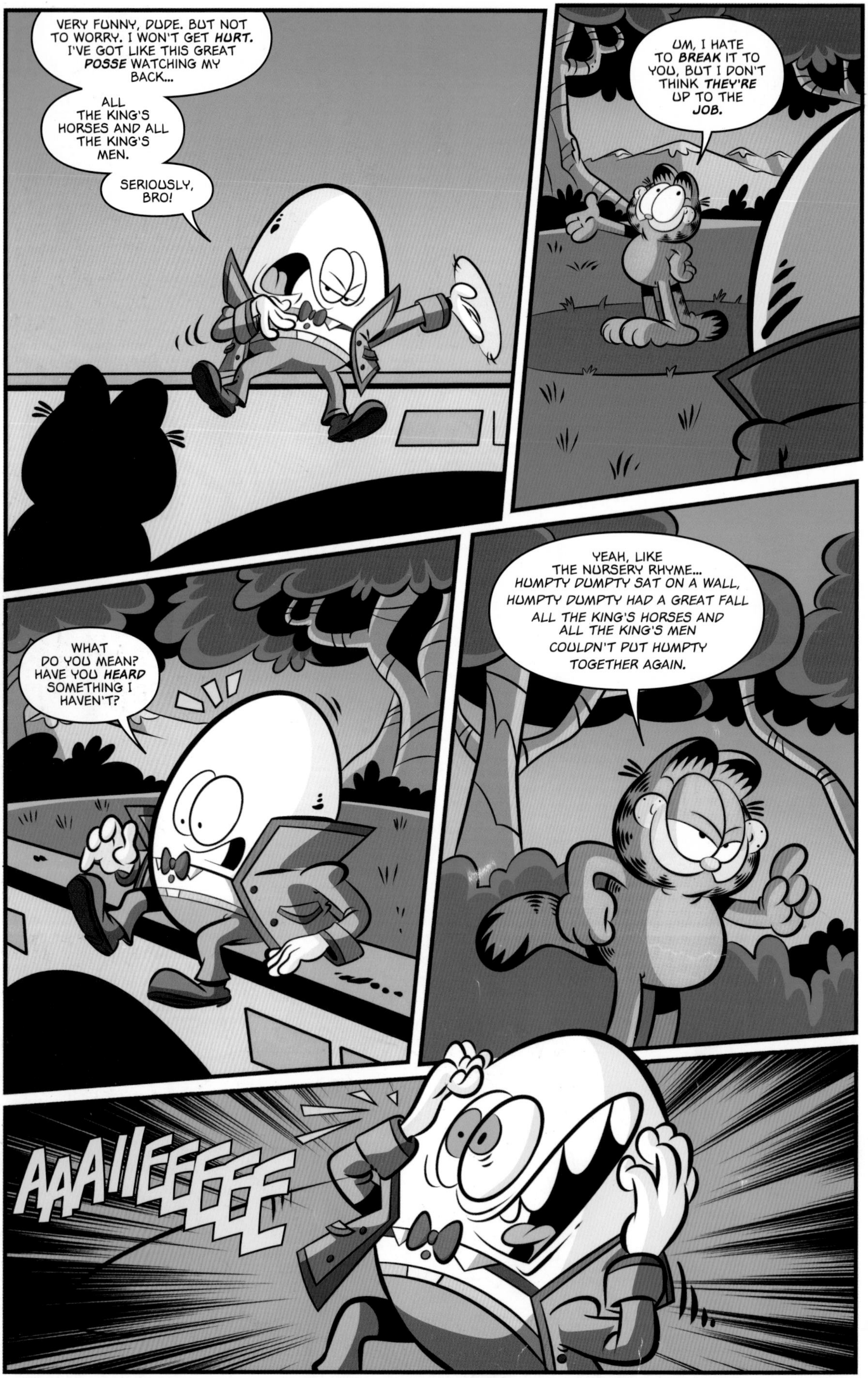
VERY FUNNY, DUDE. BUT NOT TO WORRY. I WON'T GET HURT. I'VE GOT LIKE THIS GREAT POSSE WATCHING MY BACK...
ALL THE KING'S HORSES AND ALL THE KING'S MEN.
SERIOUSLY, BRO!
UM, I HATE TO BREAK IT TO YOU, BUT I DON'T THINK THEY'RE UP TO THE JOB.
WHAT DO YOU MEAN? HAVE YOU HEARD SOMETHING I HAVEN'T?
YEAH, LIKE THE NURSERY RHYME... HUMPTY DUMPTY SAT ON A WALL, HUMPTY DUMPTY HAD A GREAT FALL ALL THE KING'S HORSES AND ALL THE KING'S MEN COULDN'T PUT HUMPTY TOGETHER AGAIN.
AAAIIEEEEEE

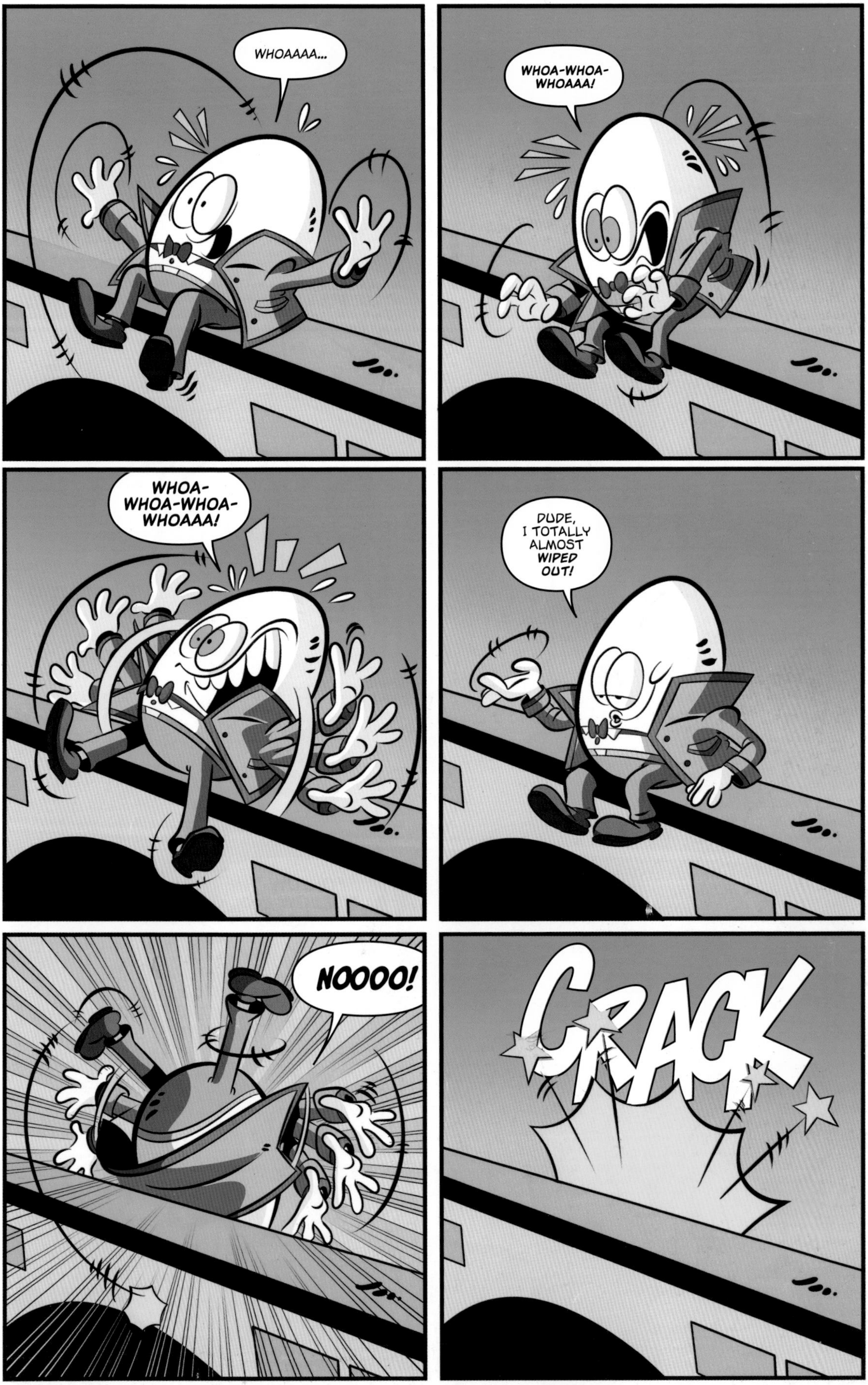
WHOAAAA...
WHOA-WHOA-WHOAAA!
WHOA-WHOA-WHOA-WHOAAA!
DUDE, I TOTALLY ALMOST WIPED OUT!
NOOOO!
CRACK

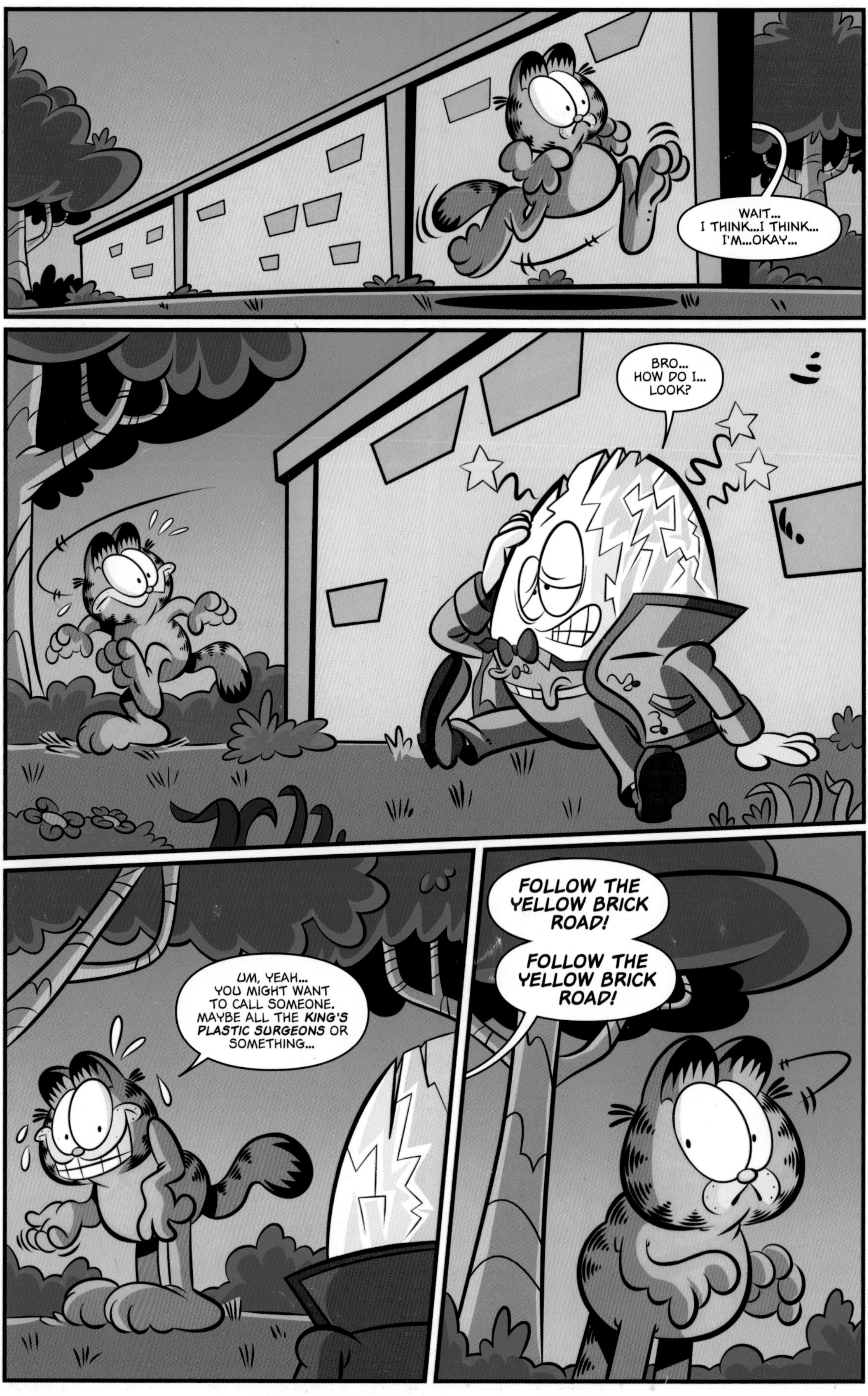
WAIT... I THINK...I THINK... I'M...OKAY...
BRO... HOW DO I... LOOK?
UM, YEAH... YOU MIGHT WANT TO CALL SOMEONE. MAYBE ALL THE KING'S PLASTIC SURGEONS OR SOMETHING...
FOLLOW THE YELLOW BRICK ROAD!
FOLLOW THE YELLOW BRICK ROAD!

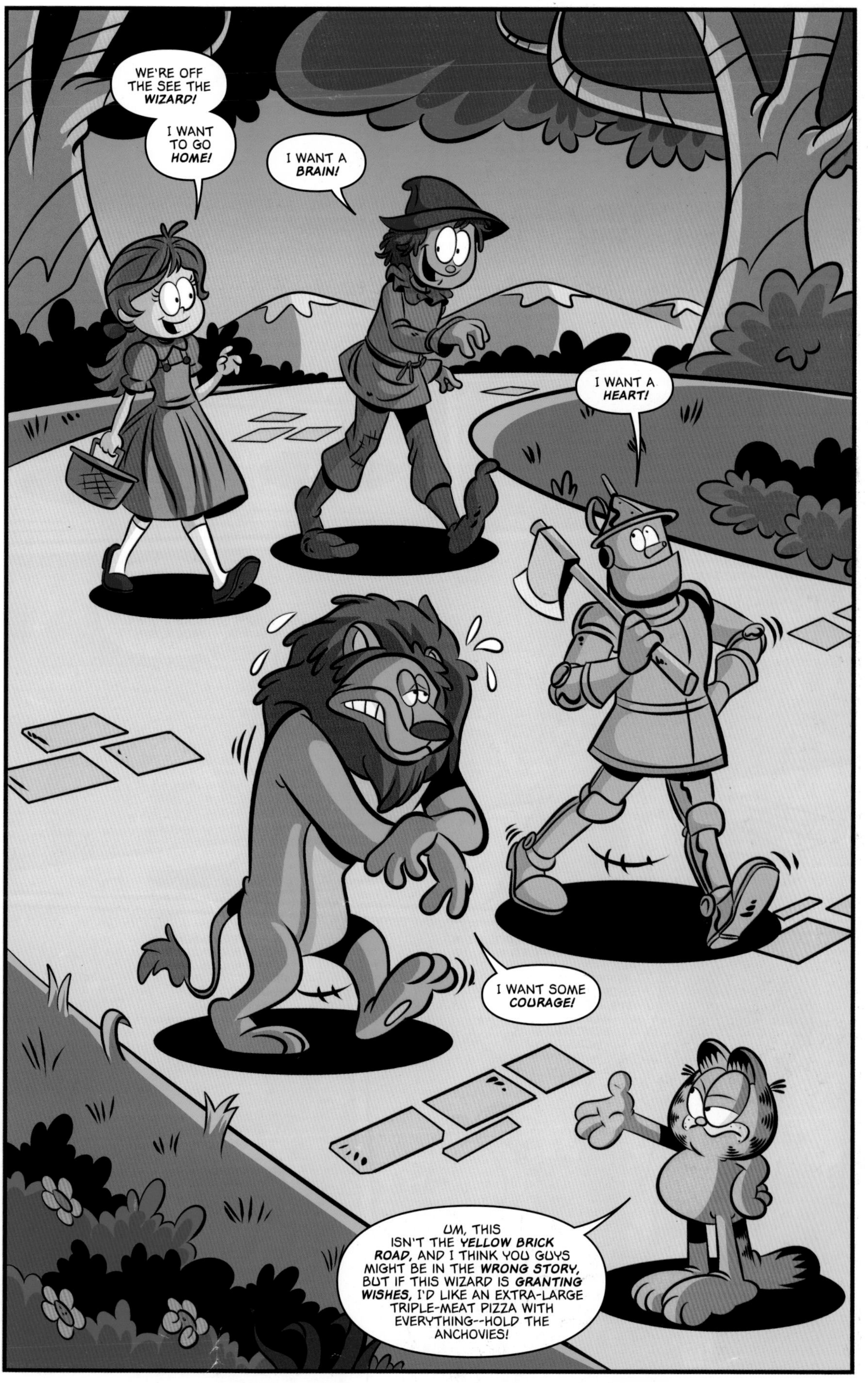
WE'RE OFF THE SEE THE WIZARD!
I WANT TO GO HOME!
I WANT A BRAIN!
I WANT A HEART!
I WANT SOME COURAGE!
UM, THIS ISN'T THE YELLOW BRICK ROAD, AND I THINK YOU GUYS MIGHT BE IN THE WRONG STORY, BUT IF THIS WIZARD IS GRANTING WISHES, I'D LIKE AN EXTRA-LARGE TRIPLE-MEAT PIZZA WITH EVERYTHING--HOLD THE ANCHOVIES!

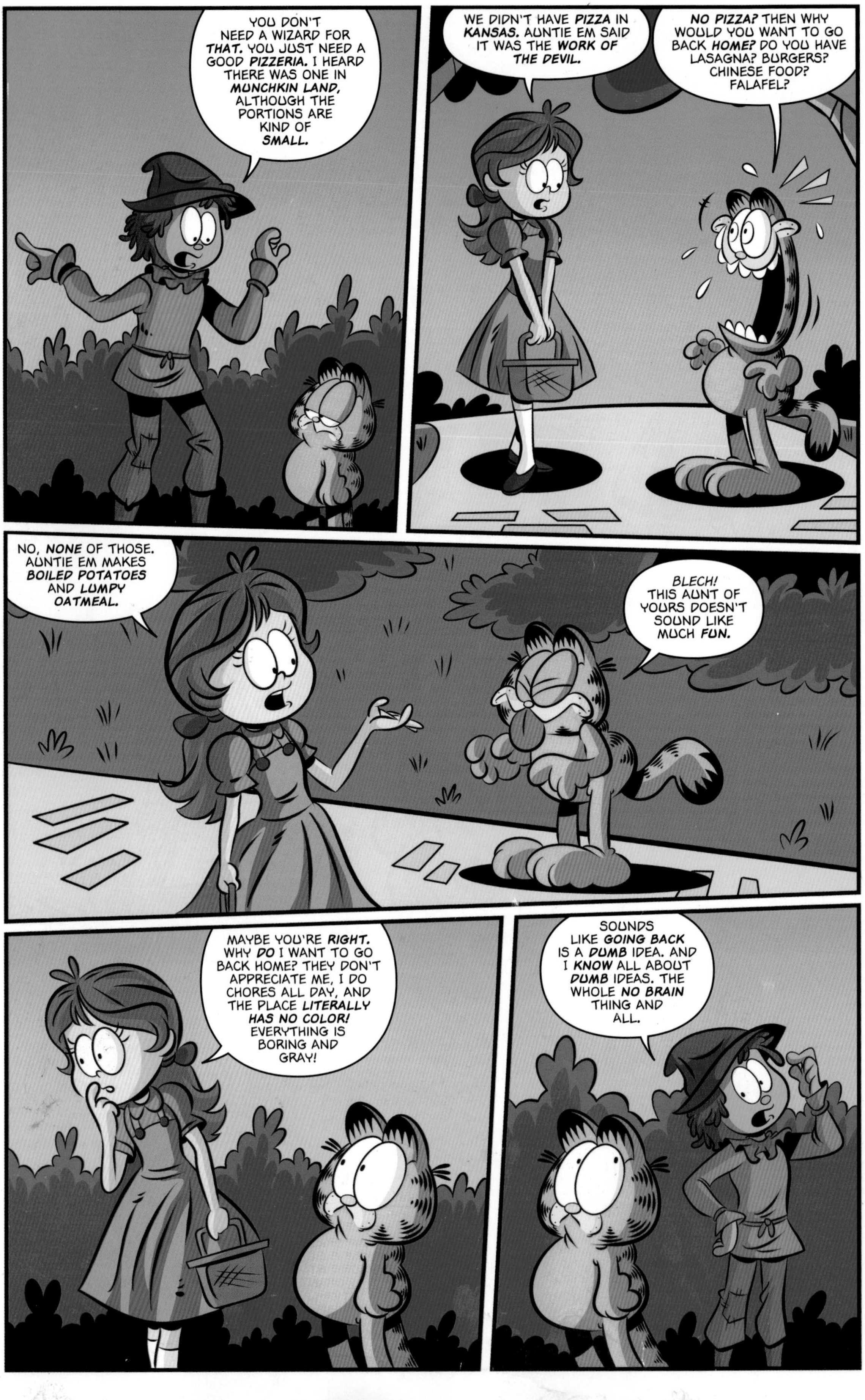
YOU DON'T NEED A WIZARD FOR THAT. YOU JUST NEED A GOOD PIZZERIA. I HEARD THERE WAS ONE IN MUNCHKIN LAND, ALTHOUGH THE PORTIONS ARE KIND OF SMALL.
WE DIDN'T HAVE PIZZA IN KANSAS. AUNTIE EM SAID IT WAS THE WORK OF THE DEVIL.
NO PIZZA? THEN WHY WOULD YOU WANT TO GO BACK HOME? DO YOU HAVE LASAGNA? BURGERS? CHINESE FOOD? FALAFEL?
NO, NONE OF THOSE. AUNTIE EM MAKES BOILED POTATOES AND LUMPY OATMEAL.
BLECH! THIS AUNT OF YOURS DOESN'T SOUND LIKE MUCH FUN.
MAYBE YOU'RE RIGHT. WHY DO I WANT TO GO BACK HOME? THEY DON'T APPRECIATE ME, I DO CHORES ALL DAY, AND THE PLACE LITERALLY HAS NO COLOR! EVERYTHING IS BORING AND GRAY!
SOUNDS LIKE GOING BACK IS A DUMB IDEA. AND I KNOW ALL ABOUT DUMB IDEAS. THE WHOLE NO BRAIN THING AND ALL.

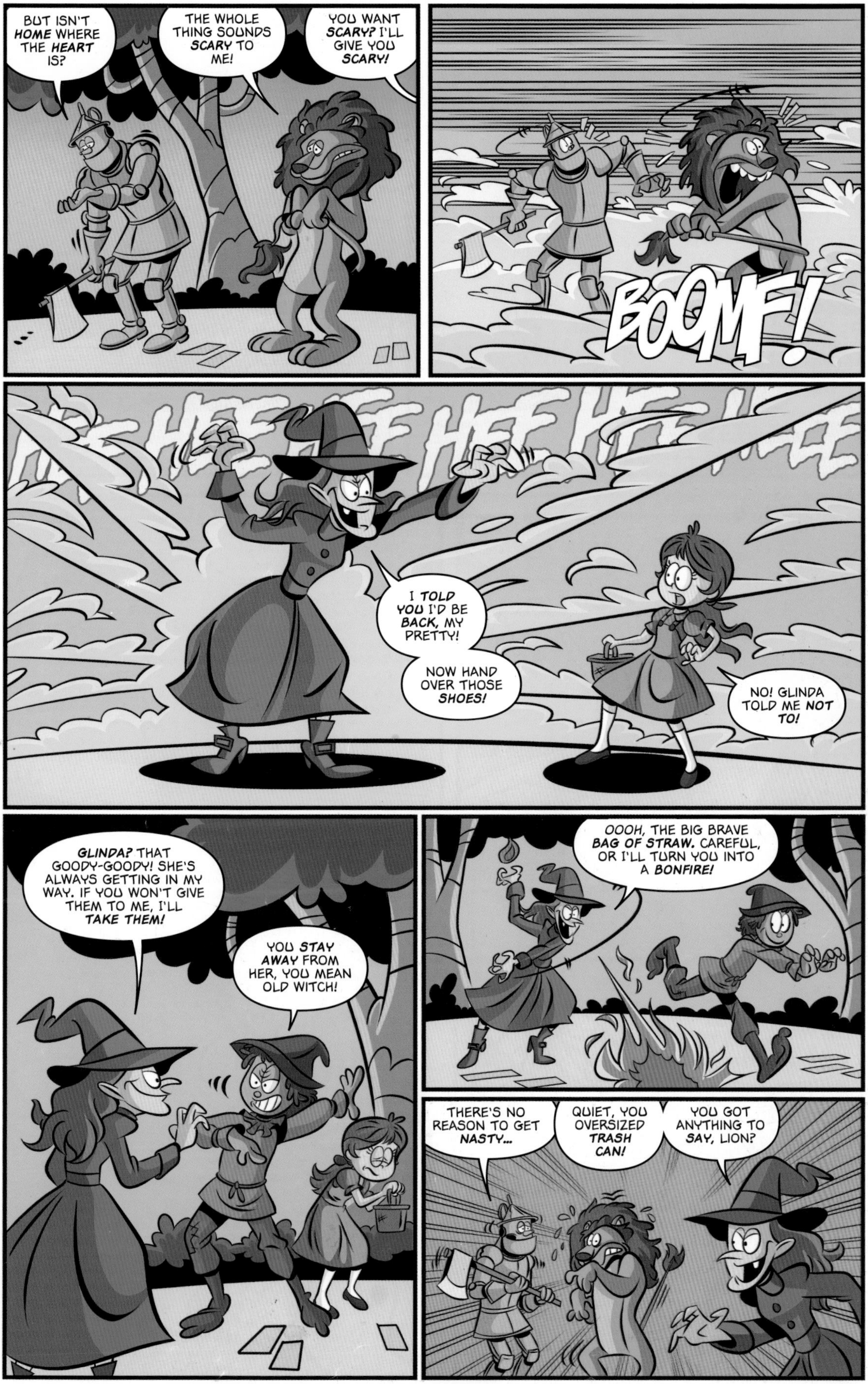
BUT ISN'T HOME WHERE THE HEART IS?
THE WHOLE THING SOUNDS SCARY TO ME!
YOU WANT SCARY? I'LL GIVE YOU SCARY!
BOOMF!
HEE HEE HEE HEE HEE
I TOLD YOU I'D BE BACK, MY PRETTY!
NOW HAND OVER THOSE SHOES!
NO! GLINDA TOLD ME NOT TO!
GLINDA? THAT GOODY-GOODY! SHE'S ALWAYS GETTING IN MY WAY. IF YOU WON'T GIVE THEM TO ME, I'LL TAKE THEM!
YOU STAY AWAY FROM HER, YOU MEAN OLD WITCH!
OOOH, THE BIG BRAVE BAG OF STRAW. CAREFUL, OR I'LL TURN YOU INTO A BONFIRE!
THERE'S NO REASON TO GET NASTY...
QUIET, YOU OVERSIZED TRASH CAN!
YOU GOT ANYTHING TO SAY, LION?

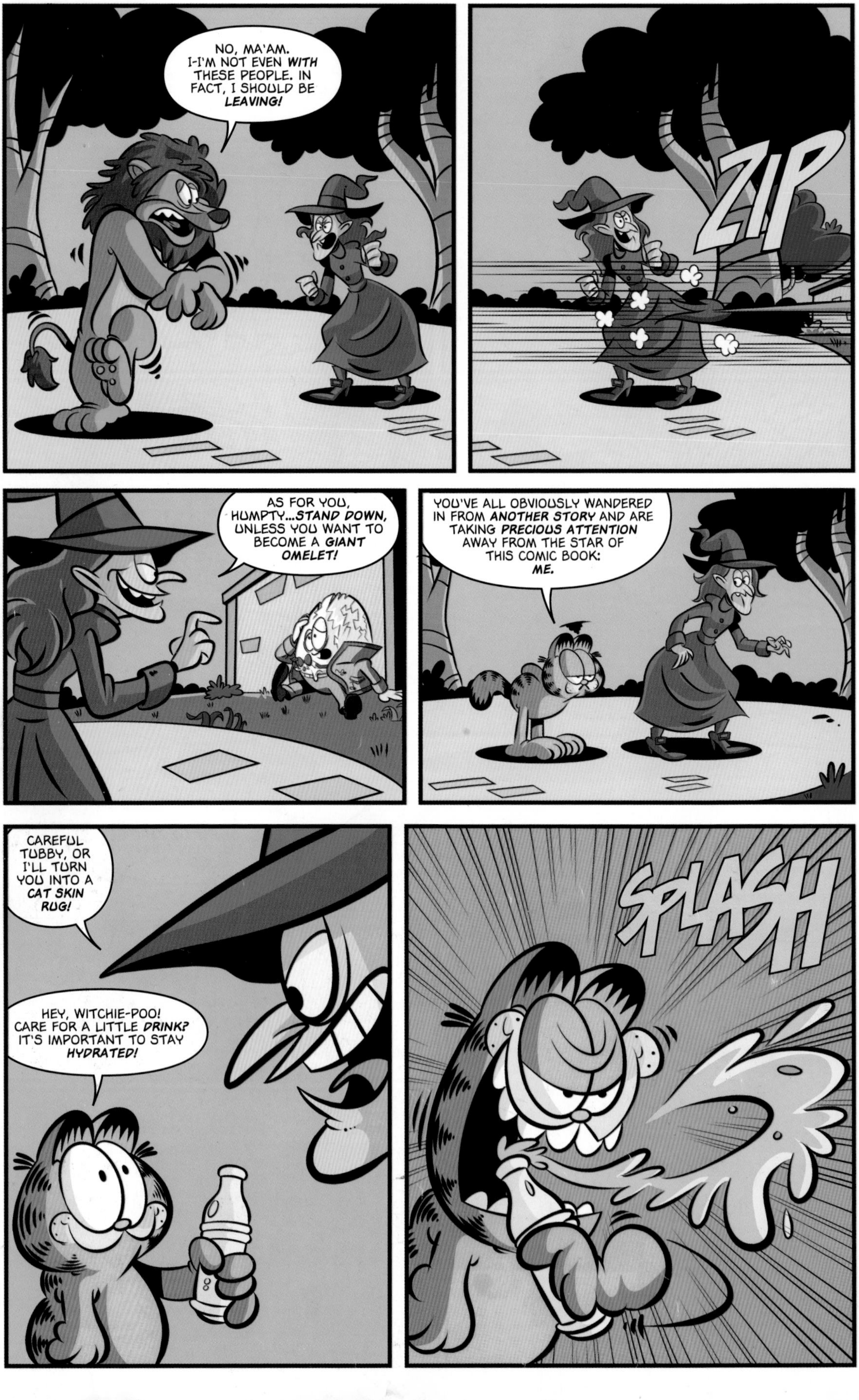
NO, MA'AM. I-I'M NOT EVEN WITH THESE PEOPLE. IN FACT, I SHOULD BE LEAVING!
ZIP
AS FOR YOU, HUMPTY...STAND DOWN, UNLESS YOU WANT TO BECOME A GIANT OMELET!
YOU'VE ALL OBVIOUSLY WANDERED IN FROM ANOTHER STORY AND ARE TAKING PRECIOUS ATTENTION AWAY FROM THE STAR OF THIS COMIC BOOK: ME.
CAREFUL TUBBY, OR I'LL TURN YOU INTO A CAT SKIN RUG!
HEY, WITCHIE-POO! CARE FOR A LITTLE DRINK? IT'S IMPORTANT TO STAY HYDRATED!
SPLASH

LUCKILY, I AM FAMILIAR WITH THE PUBLIC DOMAIN STORY OF *OZ*, AND, THROUGH THE *MAGIC OF COMICS*, CAN PULL OUT A *BOTTLE OF WATER* WHEN THE SITUATION DEMANDS.

NO... NO...

The Wizard of Oz

I'M MELTING! MELTING!

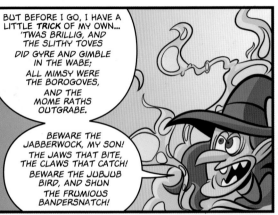

BUT BEFORE I GO, I HAVE A LITTLE *TRICK* OF MY OWN... 'TWAS BRILLIG, AND THE SLITHY TOVES DID GYRE AND GIMBLE IN THE WABE; ALL MIMSY WERE THE BOROGOVES, AND THE MOME RATHS OUTGRABE.

BEWARE THE JABBERWOCK, MY SON! THE JAWS THAT BITE, THE CLAWS THAT CATCH! BEWARE THE JUBJUB BIRD, AND SHUN THE FRUMIOUS BANDERSNATCH!

JABBERWOCK? WHAT'S THAT?

UH-OH...

SOMETHING'S HAPPENING. *SOMETHING BAD...*

FWOOOOOSSSHHH

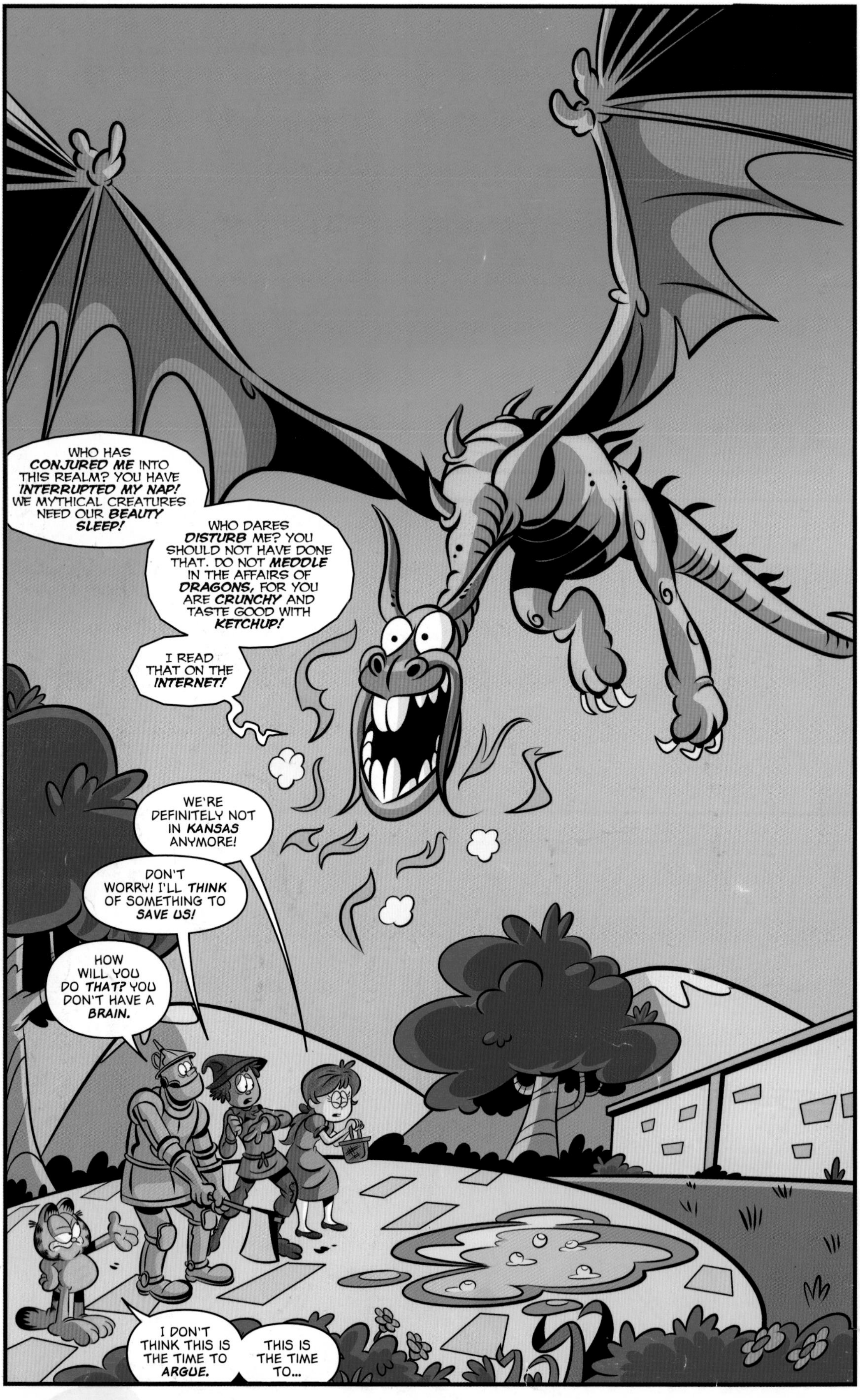
WHO HAS CONJURED ME INTO THIS REALM? YOU HAVE INTERRUPTED MY NAP! WE MYTHICAL CREATURES NEED OUR BEAUTY SLEEP!
WHO DARES DISTURB ME? YOU SHOULD NOT HAVE DONE THAT. DO NOT MEDDLE IN THE AFFAIRS OF DRAGONS, FOR YOU ARE CRUNCHY AND TASTE GOOD WITH KETCHUP!
I READ THAT ON THE INTERNET!
WE'RE DEFINITELY NOT IN KANSAS ANYMORE!
DON'T WORRY! I'LL THINK OF SOMETHING TO SAVE US!
HOW WILL YOU DO THAT? YOU DON'T HAVE A BRAIN.
I DON'T THINK THIS IS THE TIME TO ARGUE.
THIS IS THE TIME TO...

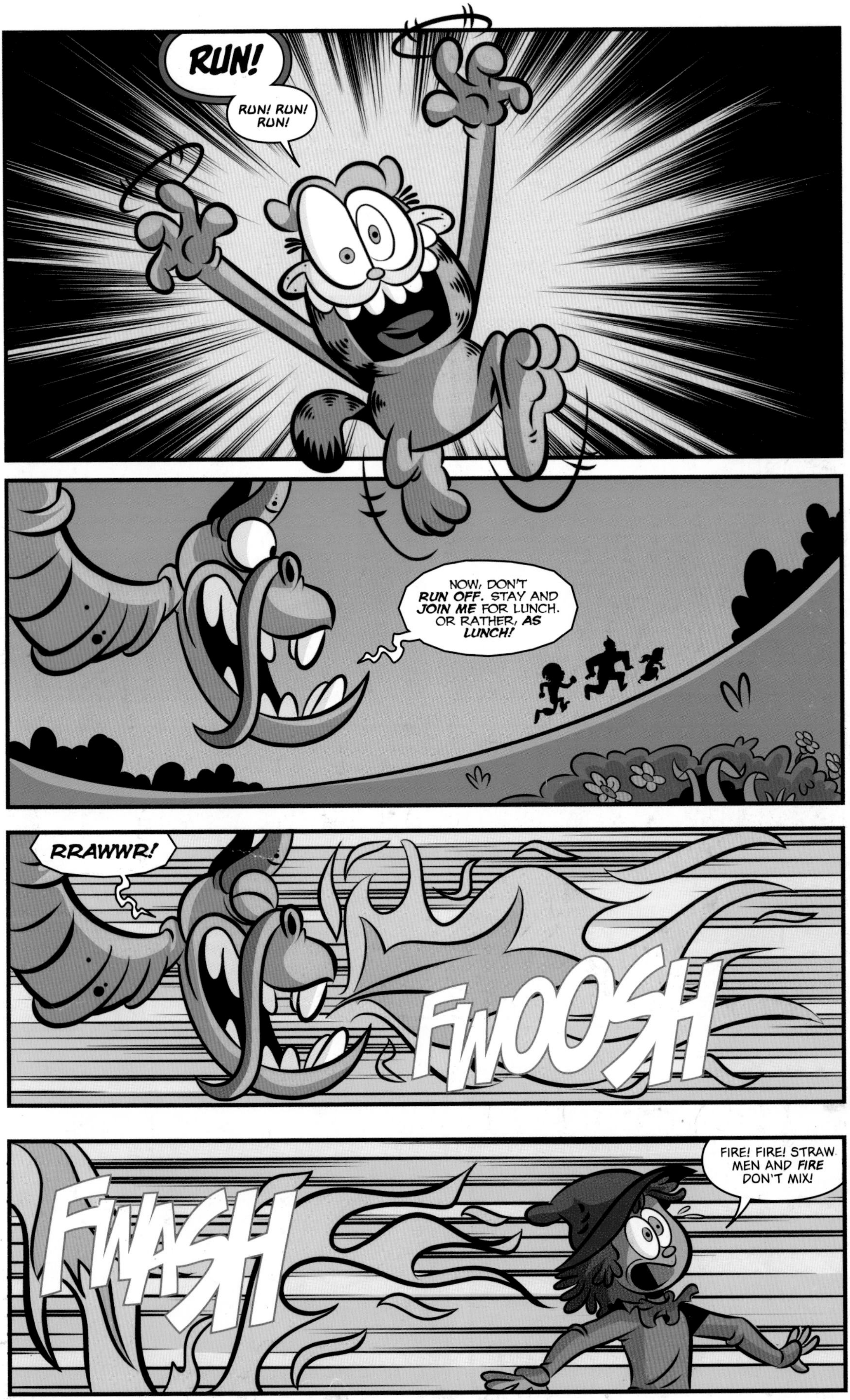
RUN!
RUN! RUN! RUN!
NOW, DON'T RUN OFF. STAY AND JOIN ME FOR LUNCH. OR RATHER, AS LUNCH!
RRAWWR!
FWOOSH
FWASH
FIRE! FIRE! STRAW MEN AND FIRE DON'T MIX!

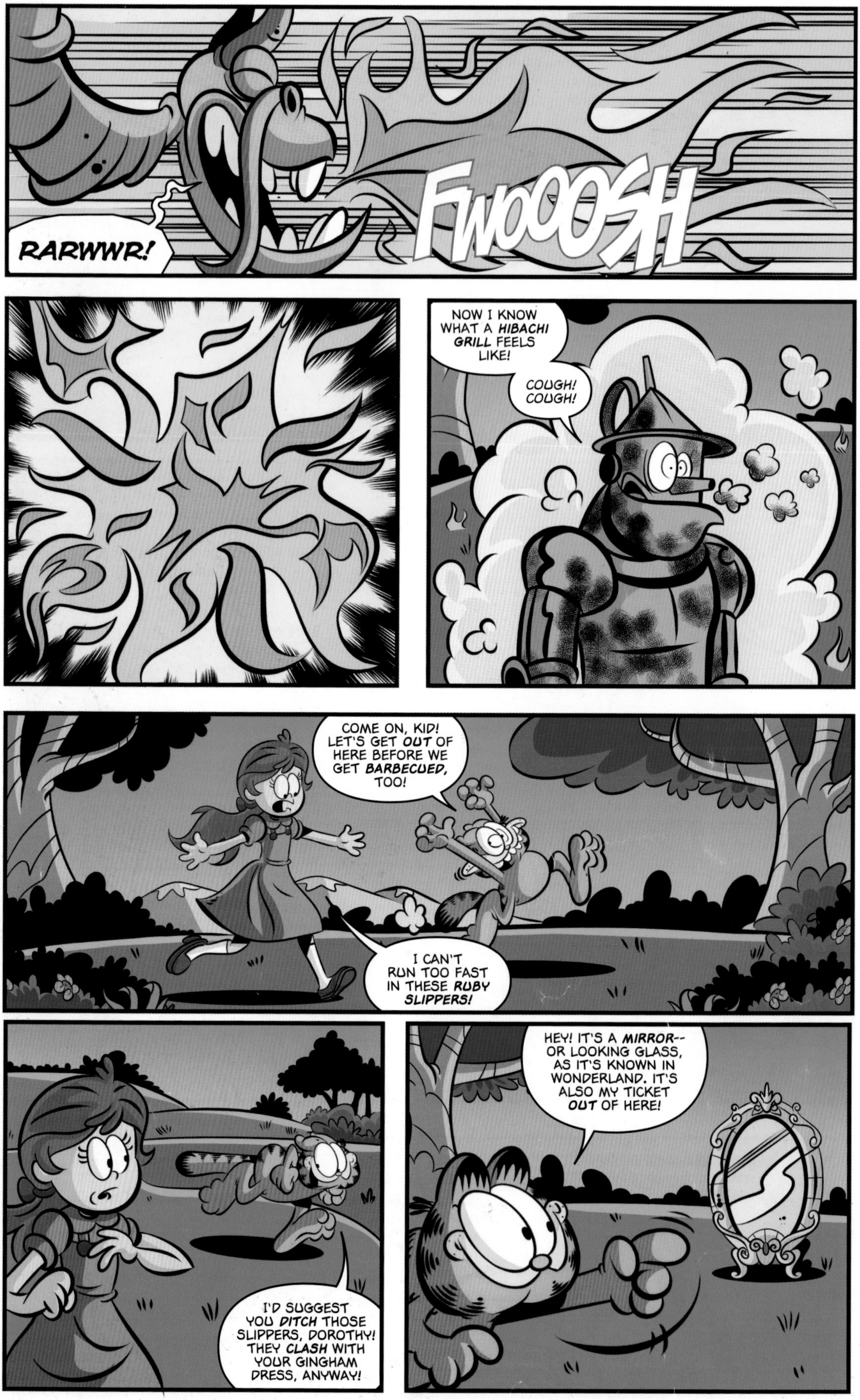
RARWWR!
FWOOOSH
NOW I KNOW WHAT A HIBACHI GRILL FEELS LIKE!
COUGH! COUGH!
COME ON, KID! LET'S GET OUT OF HERE BEFORE WE GET BARBECUED, TOO!
I CAN'T RUN TOO FAST IN THESE RUBY SLIPPERS!
I'D SUGGEST YOU DITCH THOSE SLIPPERS, DOROTHY! THEY CLASH WITH YOUR GINGHAM DRESS, ANYWAY!
HEY! IT'S A MIRROR-- OR LOOKING GLASS, AS IT'S KNOWN IN WONDERLAND. IT'S ALSO MY TICKET OUT OF HERE!

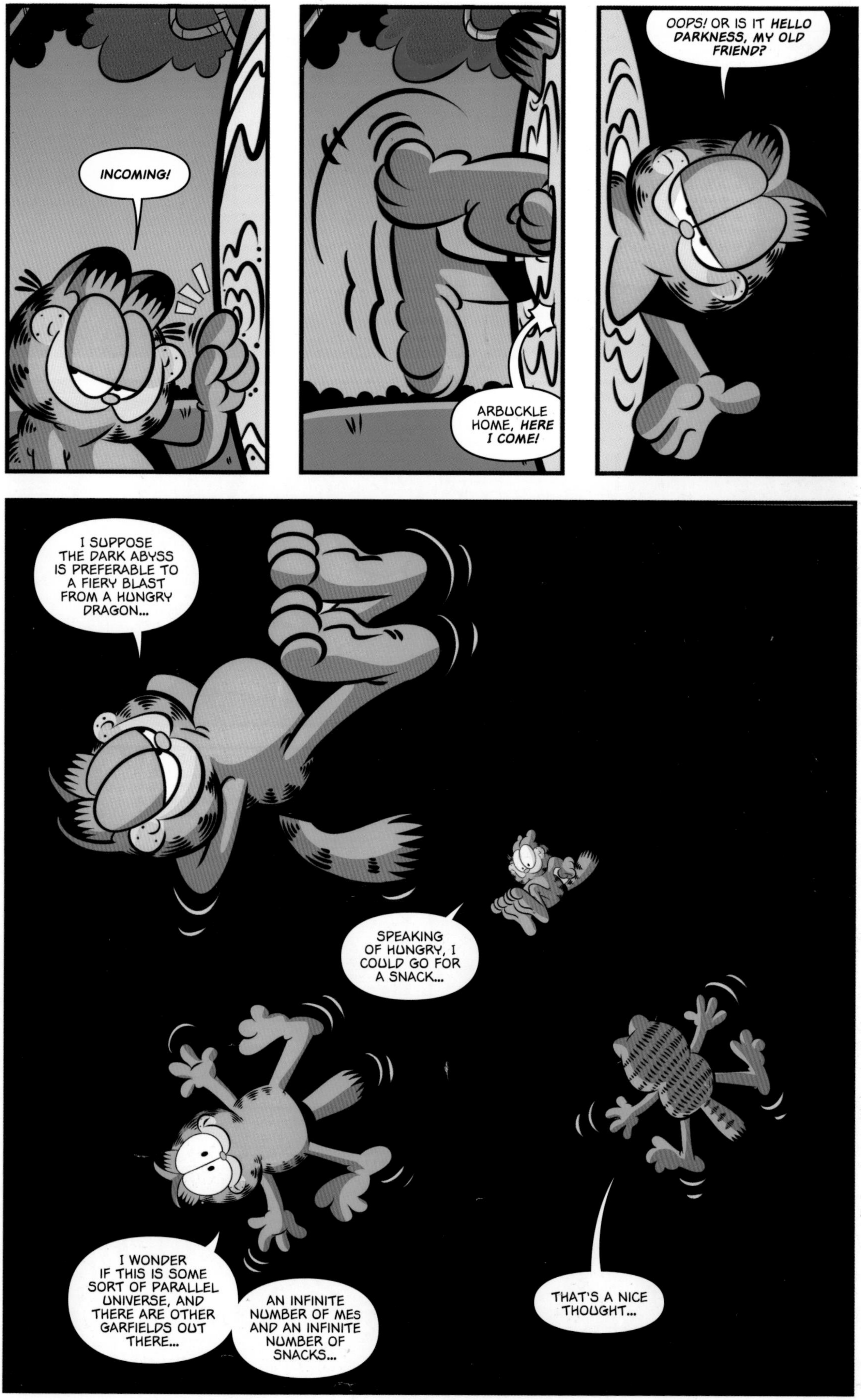
INCOMING!
ARBUCKLE HOME, HERE I COME!
OOPS! OR IS IT HELLO DARKNESS, MY OLD FRIEND?
I SUPPOSE THE DARK ABYSS IS PREFERABLE TO A FIERY BLAST FROM A HUNGRY DRAGON...
SPEAKING OF HUNGRY, I COULD GO FOR A SNACK...
I WONDER IF THIS IS SOME SORT OF PARALLEL UNIVERSE, AND THERE ARE OTHER GARFIELDS OUT THERE...
AN INFINITE NUMBER OF MES AND AN INFINITE NUMBER OF SNACKS...
THAT'S A NICE THOUGHT...

...THE RABBIT-HOLE WENT STRAIGHT ON LIKE A TUNNEL FOR SOME WAY, AND THEN DIPPED SUDDENLY DOWN...

...SO SUDDENLY THAT ALICE HAD NOT A MOMENT TO THINK ABOUT STOPPING HERSELF BEFORE SHE FOUND HERSELF FALLING DOWN A VERY DEEP WELL.

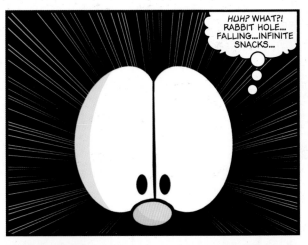

HUH? WHAT?! RABBIT HOLE... FALLING...INFINITE SNACKS...

GARFIELD, YOU'RE AWAKE? I JUST STARTED READING TO YOU A MINUTE AGO.

FORGET THAT BOOK! IT GIVES ME BAD DREAMS!

READ THIS INSTEAD.

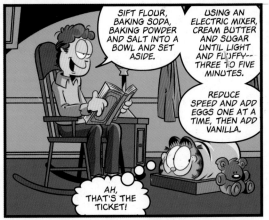

SIFT FLOUR, BAKING SODA, BAKING POWDER AND SALT INTO A BOWL AND SET ASIDE.

USING AN ELECTRIC MIXER, CREAM BUTTER AND SUGAR UNTIL LIGHT AND FLUFFY-- THREE TO FIVE MINUTES.

REDUCE SPEED AND ADD EGGS ONE AT A TIME, THEN ADD VANILLA.

AH, THAT'S THE TICKET!

MIX ALL INGREDIENTS UNTIL JUST COMBINED.

FOLD IN CHOCOLATE CHIPS. REFRIGERATE DOUGH FOR TWENTY-FOUR TO THIRTY-SIX HOURS...

SWEET DREAMS, GARFIELD!

THE END

Jon Arbuckle's Very Important Summer Vacation

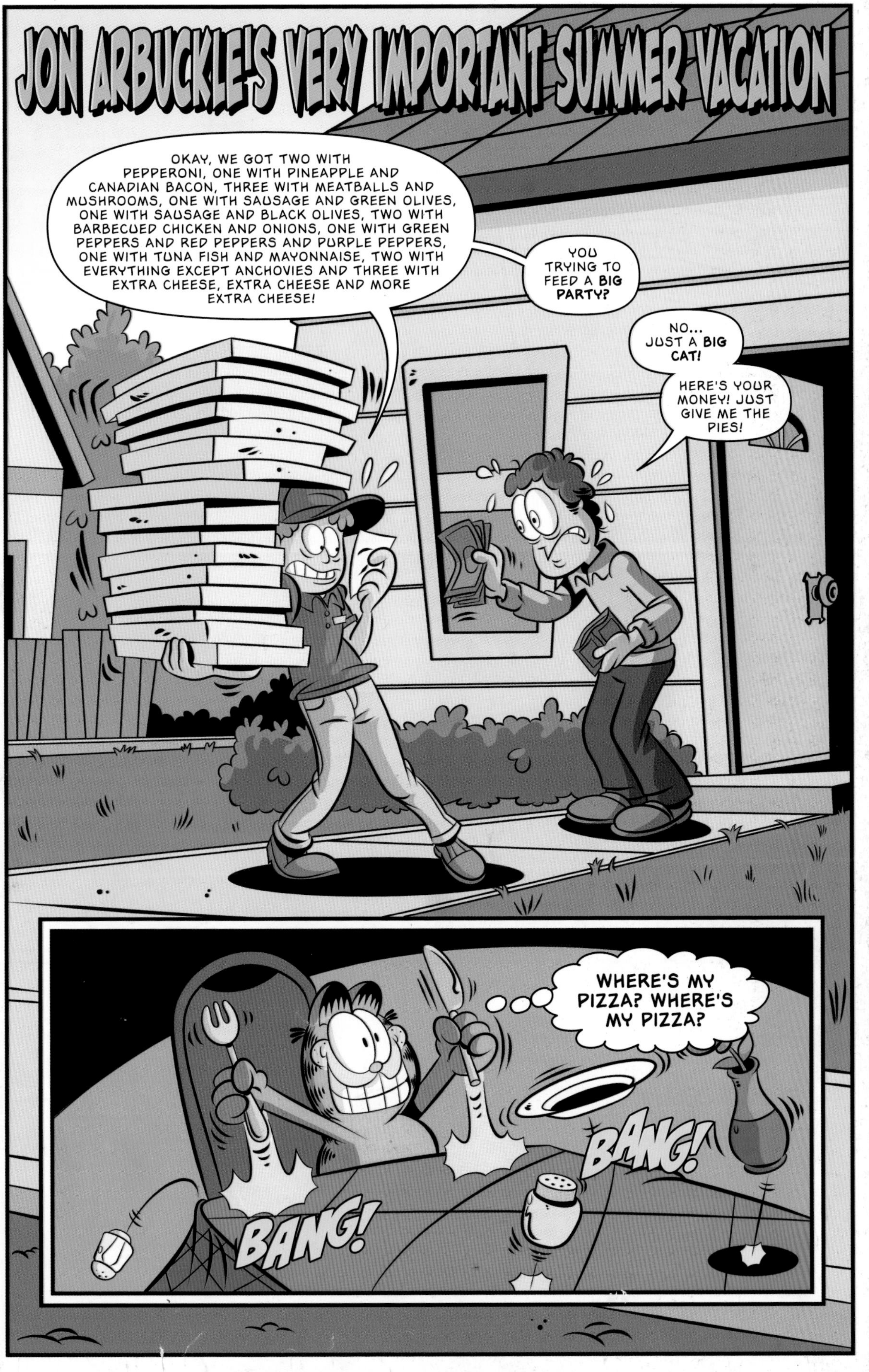
JON ARBUCKLE'S VERY IMPORTANT SUMMER VACATION
OKAY, WE GOT TWO WITH PEPPERONI, ONE WITH PINEAPPLE AND CANADIAN BACON, THREE WITH MEATBALLS AND MUSHROOMS, ONE WITH SAUSAGE AND GREEN OLIVES, ONE WITH SAUSAGE AND BLACK OLIVES, TWO WITH BARBECUED CHICKEN AND ONIONS, ONE WITH GREEN PEPPERS AND RED PEPPERS AND PURPLE PEPPERS, ONE WITH TUNA FISH AND MAYONNAISE, TWO WITH EVERYTHING EXCEPT ANCHOVIES AND THREE WITH EXTRA CHEESE, EXTRA CHEESE AND MORE EXTRA CHEESE!
YOU TRYING TO FEED A BIG PARTY?
NO... JUST A BIG CAT!
HERE'S YOUR MONEY! JUST GIVE ME THE PIES!
WHERE'S MY PIZZA? WHERE'S MY PIZZA?
BANG!
BANG!

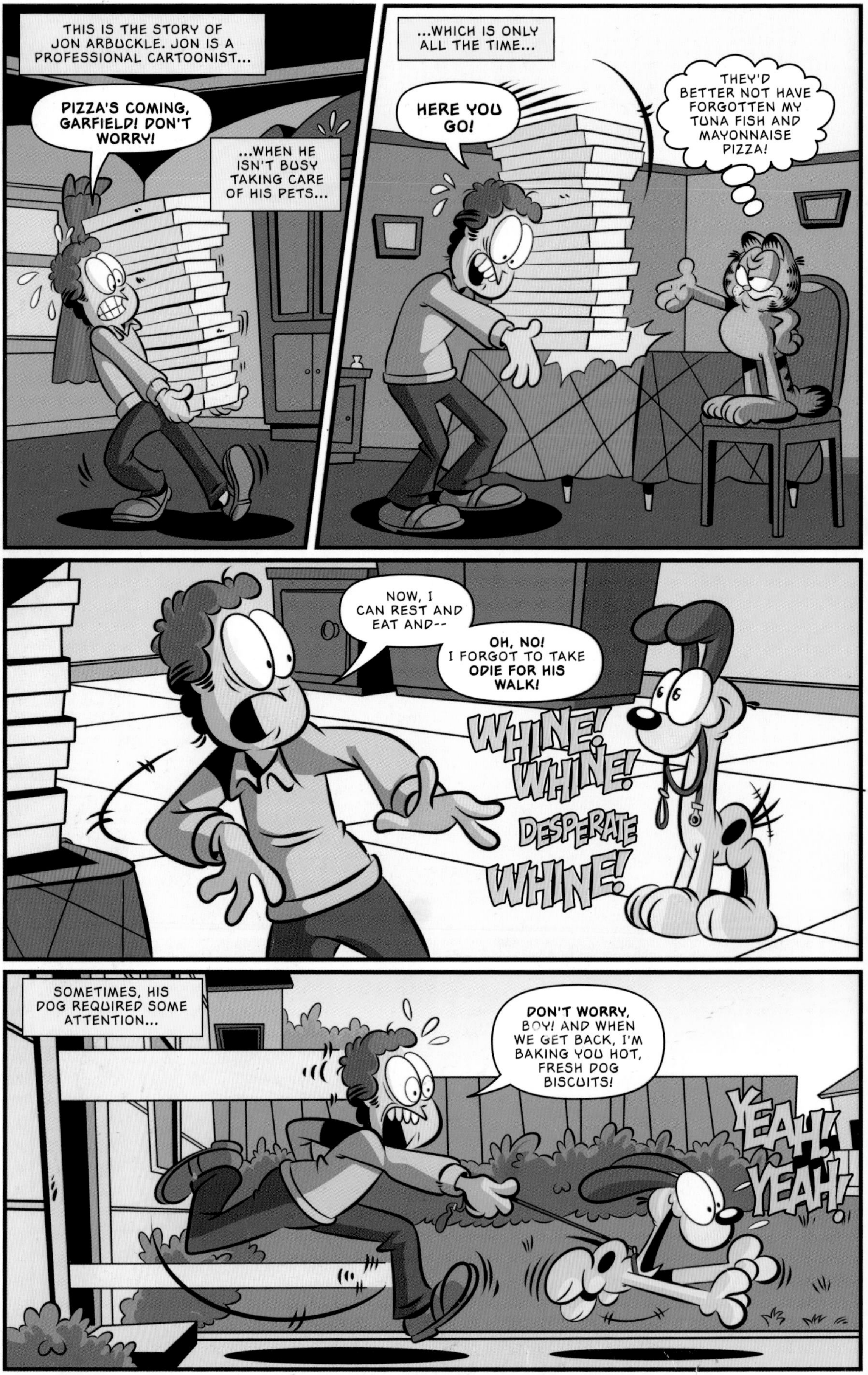

THIS IS THE STORY OF JON ARBUCKLE. JON IS A PROFESSIONAL CARTOONIST...
PIZZA'S COMING, GARFIELD! DON'T WORRY!
...WHEN HE ISN'T BUSY TAKING CARE OF HIS PETS...
...WHICH IS ONLY ALL THE TIME...
HERE YOU GO!
THEY'D BETTER NOT HAVE FORGOTTEN MY TUNA FISH AND MAYONNAISE PIZZA!
NOW, I CAN REST AND EAT AND--
OH, NO! I FORGOT TO TAKE ODIE FOR HIS WALK!
WHINE! WHINE!
DESPERATE WHINE!
SOMETIMES, HIS DOG REQUIRED SOME ATTENTION...
DON'T WORRY, BOY! AND WHEN WE GET BACK, I'M BAKING YOU HOT, FRESH DOG BISCUITS!
YEAH! YEAH!

BUT MOST OF THE TIME, IT'S HIS CAT...

WOULDN'T YOU KNOW IT? THEY FORGOT THE MAYONNAISE!

FOR JON ARBUCKLE, CAT CARE IS A 24/7 JOB...

JUST WAIT HERE A FEW MINUTES, ODIE! I'VE GOT TO PICK UP WHAT I NEED FOR **GARFIELD'S BREAKFAST** TOMORROW MORNING!

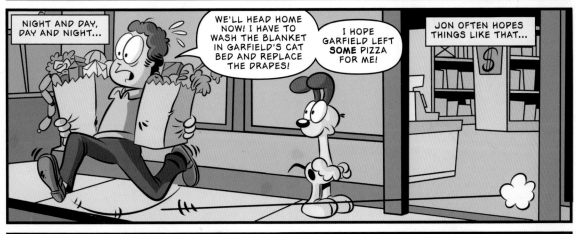

NIGHT AND DAY, DAY AND NIGHT...

WE'LL HEAD HOME NOW! I HAVE TO WASH THE BLANKET IN GARFIELD'S CAT BED AND REPLACE THE DRAPES!

I HOPE GARFIELD LEFT **SOME** PIZZA FOR ME!

JON OFTEN HOPES THINGS LIKE THAT...

...AND HIS HOPES NEVER SEEM TO COME THROUGH...

YOU ATE ALL **SIXTEEN PIZZAS** AND EVEN PART OF **THREE BOXES!** WHAT DO YOU HAVE TO SAY FOR YOURSELF?

BURP!!!

IT NEVER SEEMS TO CHANGE...

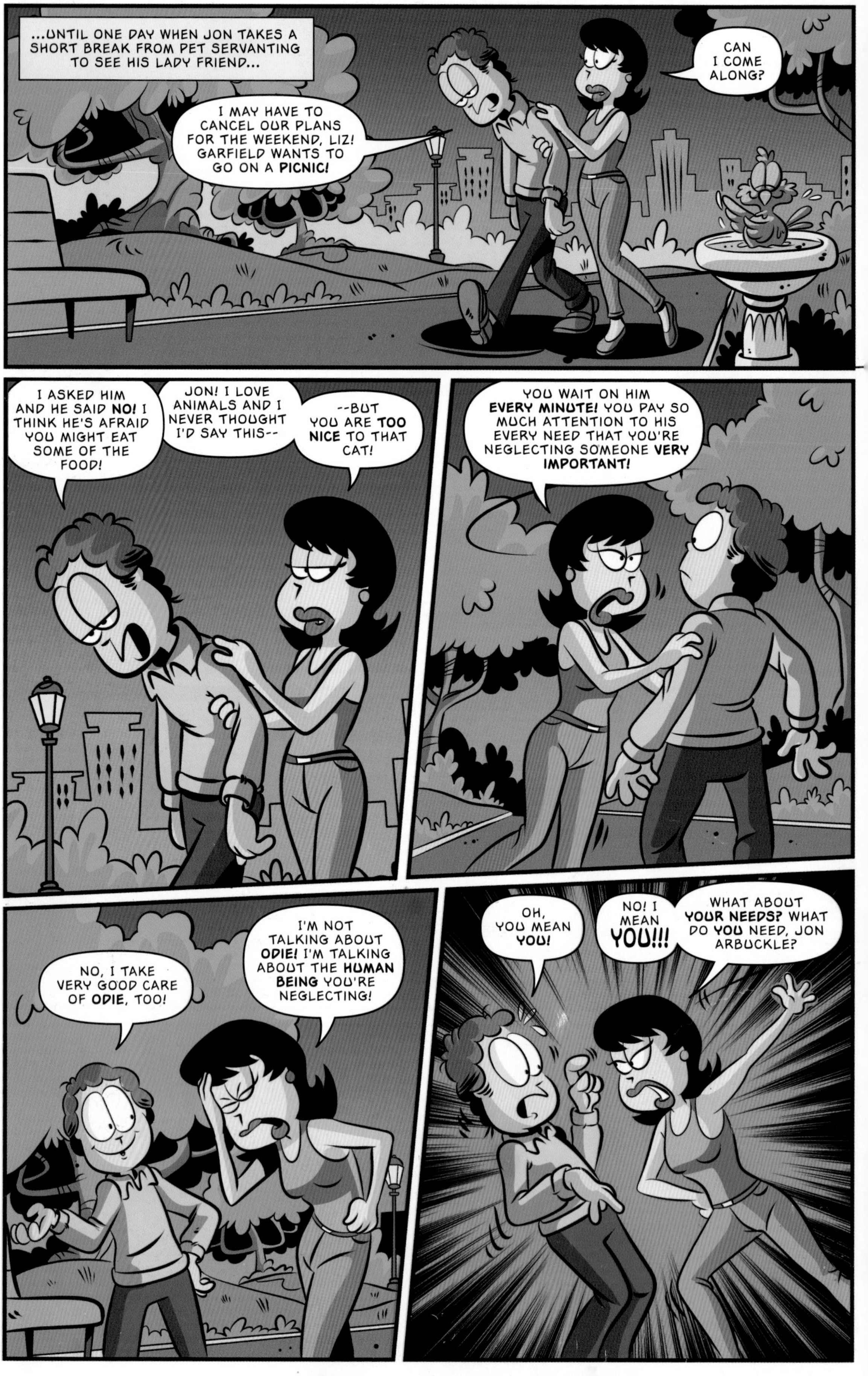
...UNTIL ONE DAY WHEN JON TAKES A SHORT BREAK FROM PET SERVANTING TO SEE HIS LADY FRIEND...
I MAY HAVE TO CANCEL OUR PLANS FOR THE WEEKEND, LIZ! GARFIELD WANTS TO GO ON A PICNIC!
CAN I COME ALONG?
I ASKED HIM AND HE SAID NO! I THINK HE'S AFRAID YOU MIGHT EAT SOME OF THE FOOD!
JON! I LOVE ANIMALS AND I NEVER THOUGHT I'D SAY THIS--
--BUT YOU ARE TOO NICE TO THAT CAT!
YOU WAIT ON HIM EVERY MINUTE! YOU PAY SO MUCH ATTENTION TO HIS EVERY NEED THAT YOU'RE NEGLECTING SOMEONE VERY IMPORTANT!
NO, I TAKE VERY GOOD CARE OF ODIE, TOO!
I'M NOT TALKING ABOUT ODIE! I'M TALKING ABOUT THE HUMAN BEING YOU'RE NEGLECTING!
OH, YOU MEAN YOU!
NO! I MEAN YOU!!!
WHAT ABOUT YOUR NEEDS? WHAT DO YOU NEED, JON ARBUCKLE?

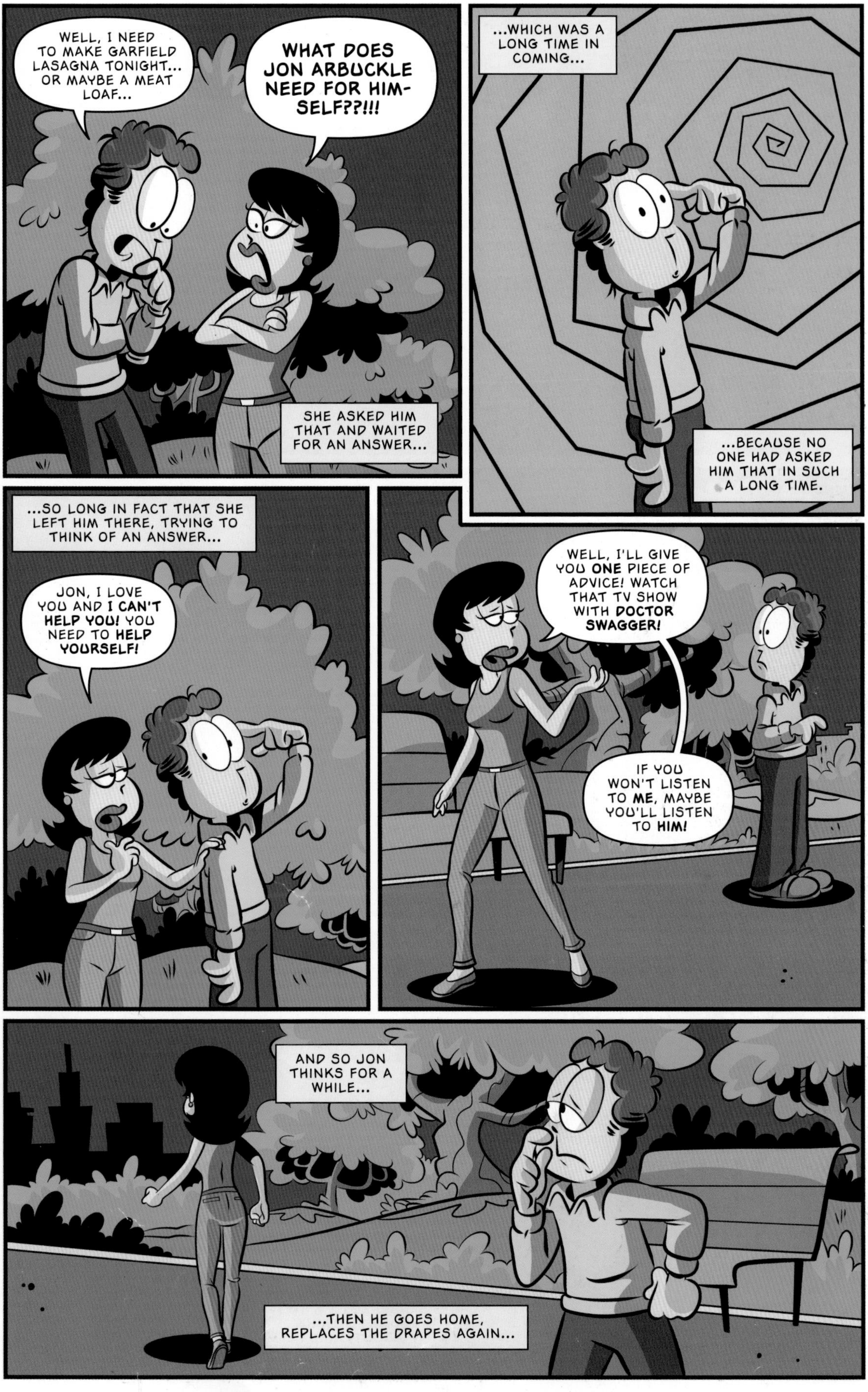

WELL, I NEED TO MAKE GARFIELD LASAGNA TONIGHT... OR MAYBE A MEAT LOAF...
WHAT DOES JON ARBUCKLE NEED FOR HIM-SELF??!!!
SHE ASKED HIM THAT AND WAITED FOR AN ANSWER...
...WHICH WAS A LONG TIME IN COMING...
...BECAUSE NO ONE HAD ASKED HIM THAT IN SUCH A LONG TIME.
...SO LONG IN FACT THAT SHE LEFT HIM THERE, TRYING TO THINK OF AN ANSWER...
JON, I LOVE YOU AND I CAN'T HELP YOU! YOU NEED TO HELP YOURSELF!
WELL, I'LL GIVE YOU ONE PIECE OF ADVICE! WATCH THAT TV SHOW WITH DOCTOR SWAGGER!
IF YOU WON'T LISTEN TO ME, MAYBE YOU'LL LISTEN TO HIM!
AND SO JON THINKS FOR A WHILE...
...THEN HE GOES HOME, REPLACES THE DRAPES AGAIN...

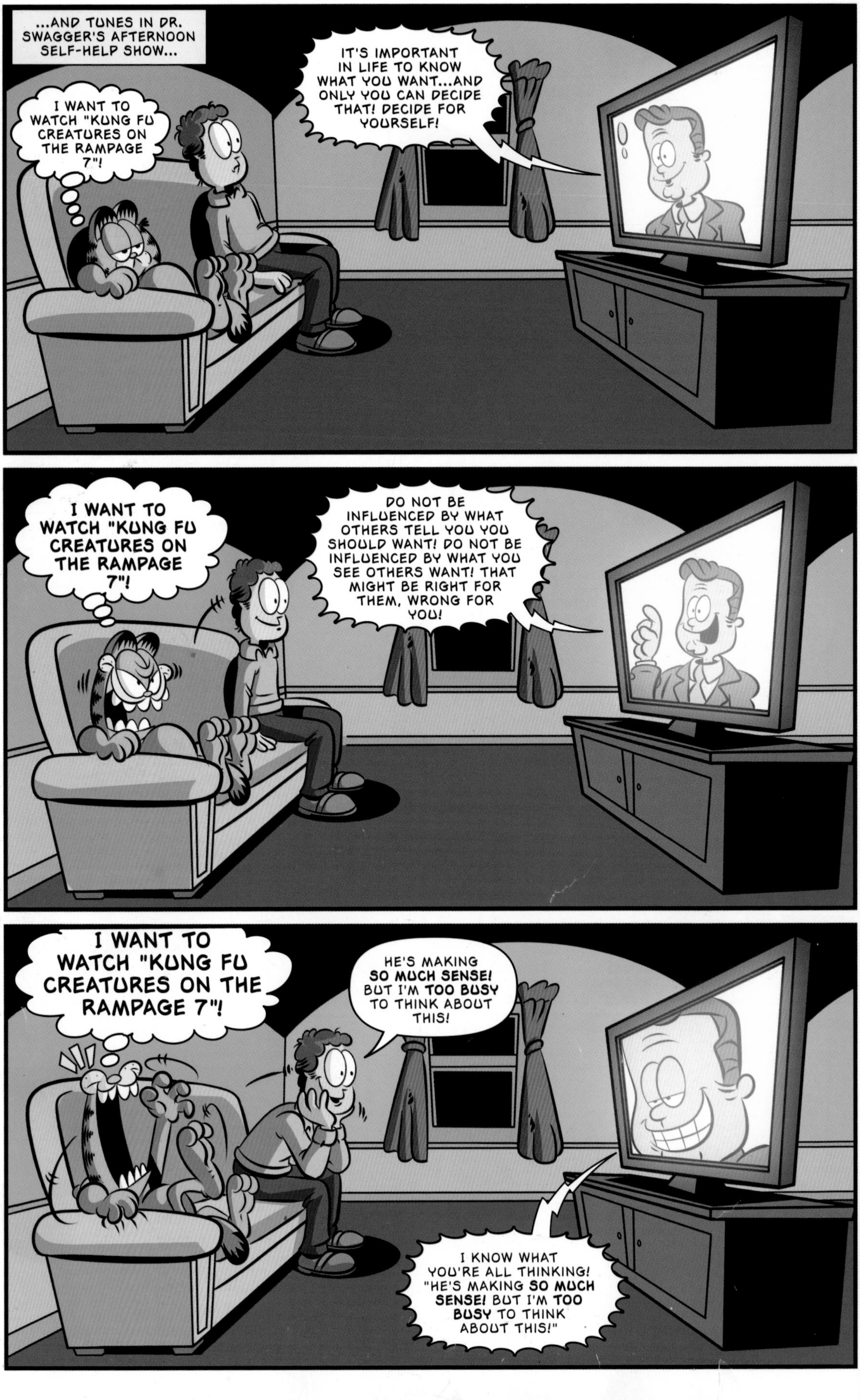
...AND TUNES IN DR. SWAGGER'S AFTERNOON SELF-HELP SHOW...
I WANT TO WATCH "KUNG FU CREATURES ON THE RAMPAGE 7"!
IT'S IMPORTANT IN LIFE TO KNOW WHAT YOU WANT...AND ONLY YOU CAN DECIDE THAT! DECIDE FOR YOURSELF!
I WANT TO WATCH "KUNG FU CREATURES ON THE RAMPAGE 7"!
DO NOT BE INFLUENCED BY WHAT OTHERS TELL YOU YOU SHOULD WANT! DO NOT BE INFLUENCED BY WHAT YOU SEE OTHERS WANT! THAT MIGHT BE RIGHT FOR THEM, WRONG FOR YOU!
I WANT TO WATCH "KUNG FU CREATURES ON THE RAMPAGE 7"!
HE'S MAKING **SO MUCH SENSE!** BUT I'M **TOO BUSY** TO THINK ABOUT THIS!
I KNOW WHAT YOU'RE ALL THINKING! "HE'S MAKING **SO MUCH SENSE!** BUT I'M **TOO BUSY** TO THINK ABOUT THIS!"

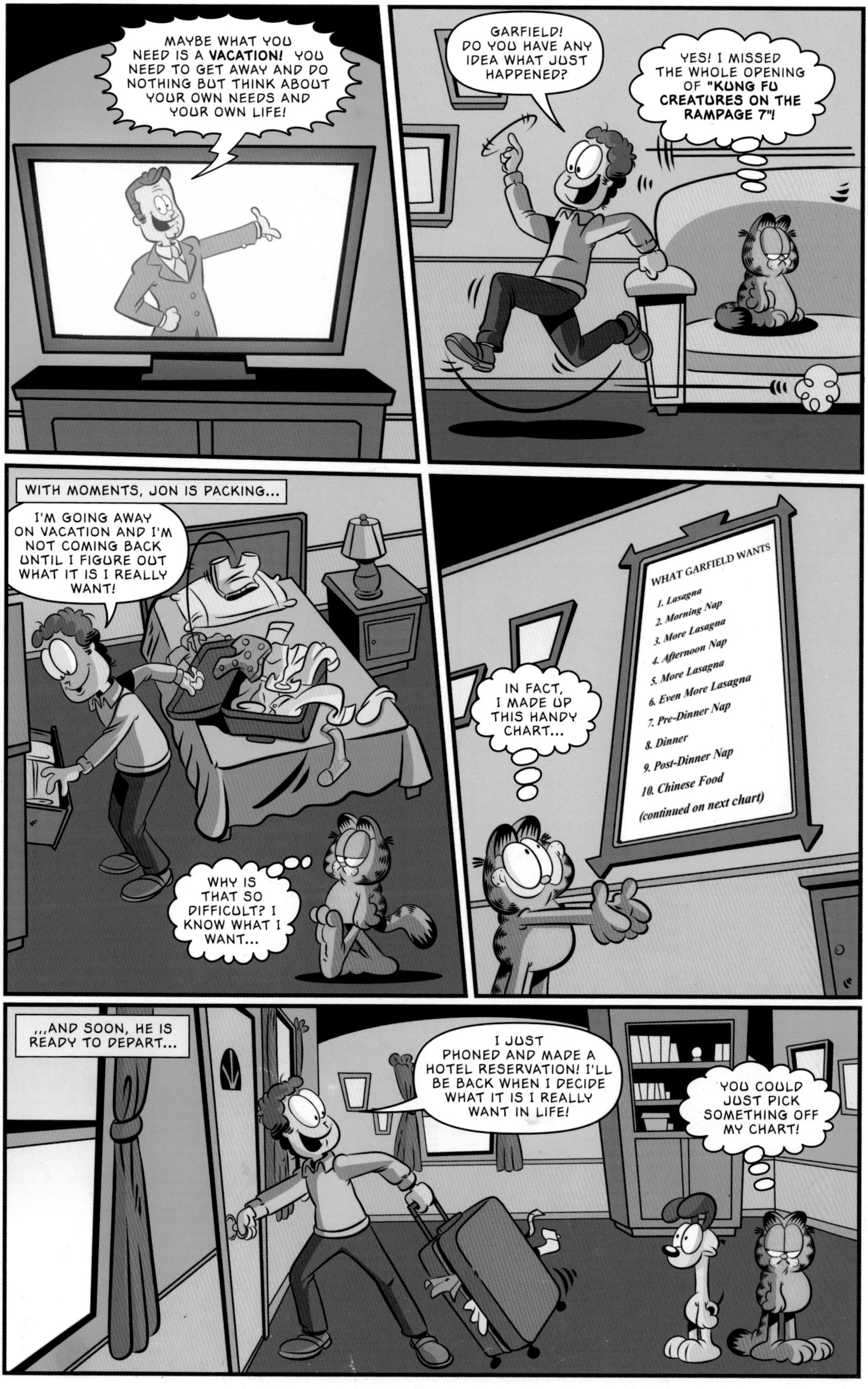
MAYBE WHAT YOU NEED IS A **VACATION!** YOU NEED TO GET AWAY AND DO NOTHING BUT THINK ABOUT YOUR OWN NEEDS AND YOUR OWN LIFE!
GARFIELD! DO YOU HAVE ANY IDEA WHAT JUST HAPPENED?
YES! I MISSED THE WHOLE OPENING OF **"KUNG FU CREATURES ON THE RAMPAGE 7"**!
WITH MOMENTS, JON IS PACKING...
I'M GOING AWAY ON VACATION AND I'M NOT COMING BACK UNTIL I FIGURE OUT WHAT IT IS I REALLY WANT!
WHY IS THAT SO DIFFICULT? I KNOW WHAT I WANT...
IN FACT, I MADE UP THIS HANDY CHART...
WHAT GARFIELD WANTS
1. Lasagna
2. Morning Nap
3. More Lasagna
4. Afternoon Nap
5. More Lasagna
6. Even More Lasagna
7. Pre-Dinner Nap
8. Dinner
9. Post-Dinner Nap
10. Chinese Food
(continued on next chart)
...AND SOON, HE IS READY TO DEPART...
I JUST PHONED AND MADE A HOTEL RESERVATION! I'LL BE BACK WHEN I DECIDE WHAT IT IS I REALLY WANT IN LIFE!
YOU COULD JUST PICK SOMETHING OFF MY CHART!

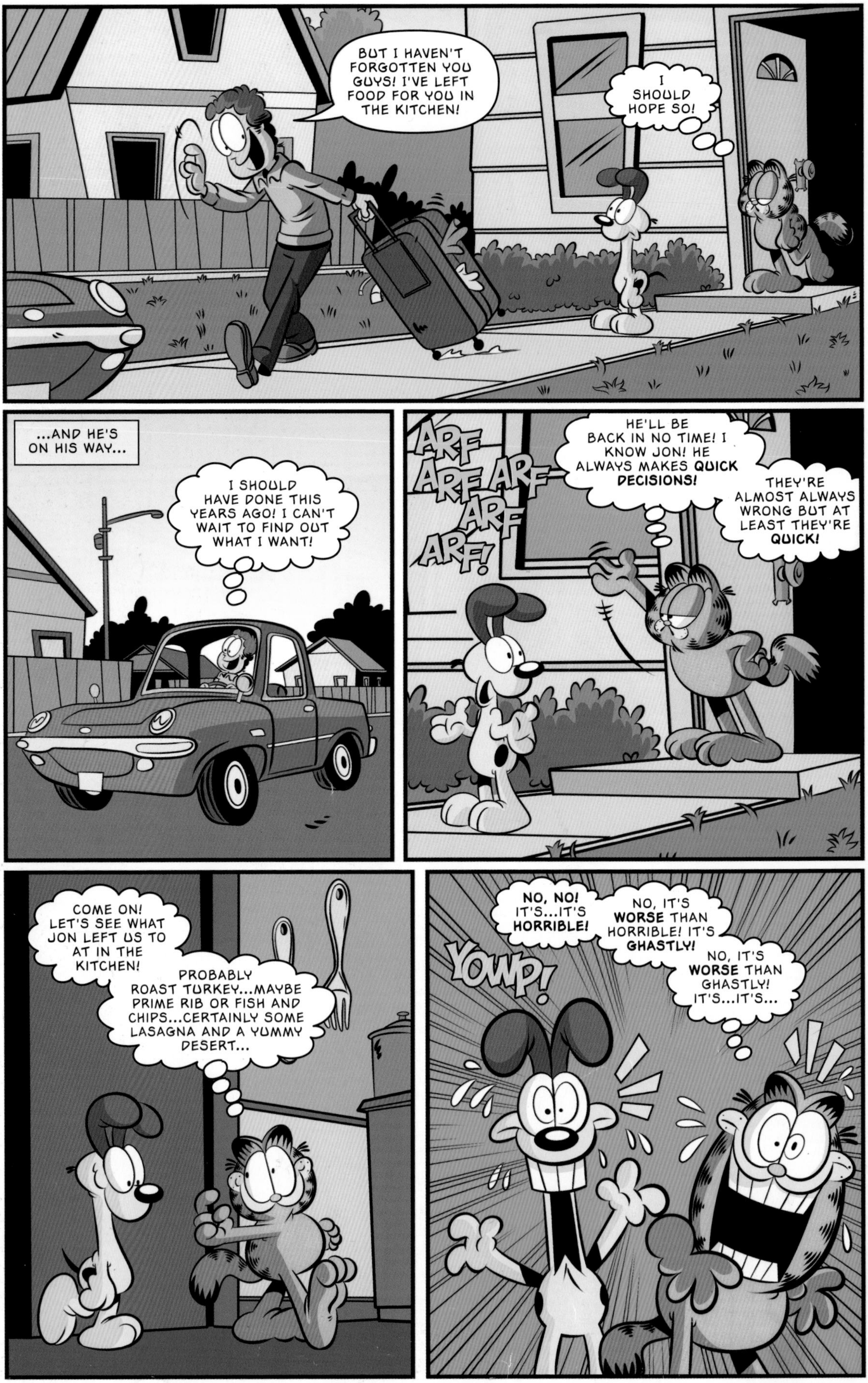
BUT I HAVEN'T FORGOTTEN YOU GUYS! I'VE LEFT FOOD FOR YOU IN THE KITCHEN!
I SHOULD HOPE SO!
...AND HE'S ON HIS WAY...
I SHOULD HAVE DONE THIS YEARS AGO! I CAN'T WAIT TO FIND OUT WHAT I WANT!
ARF ARF ARF ARF ARF!
HE'LL BE BACK IN NO TIME! I KNOW JON! HE ALWAYS MAKES **QUICK DECISIONS!**
THEY'RE ALMOST ALWAYS WRONG BUT AT LEAST THEY'RE **QUICK!**
COME ON! LET'S SEE WHAT JON LEFT US TO AT IN THE KITCHEN!
PROBABLY ROAST TURKEY...MAYBE PRIME RIB OR FISH AND CHIPS...CERTAINLY SOME LASAGNA AND A YUMMY DESERT...
YOWP!
NO, NO! IT'S...IT'S **HORRIBLE!**
NO, IT'S **WORSE** THAN HORRIBLE! IT'S **GHASTLY!**
NO, IT'S **WORSE** THAN GHASTLY! IT'S...IT'S...

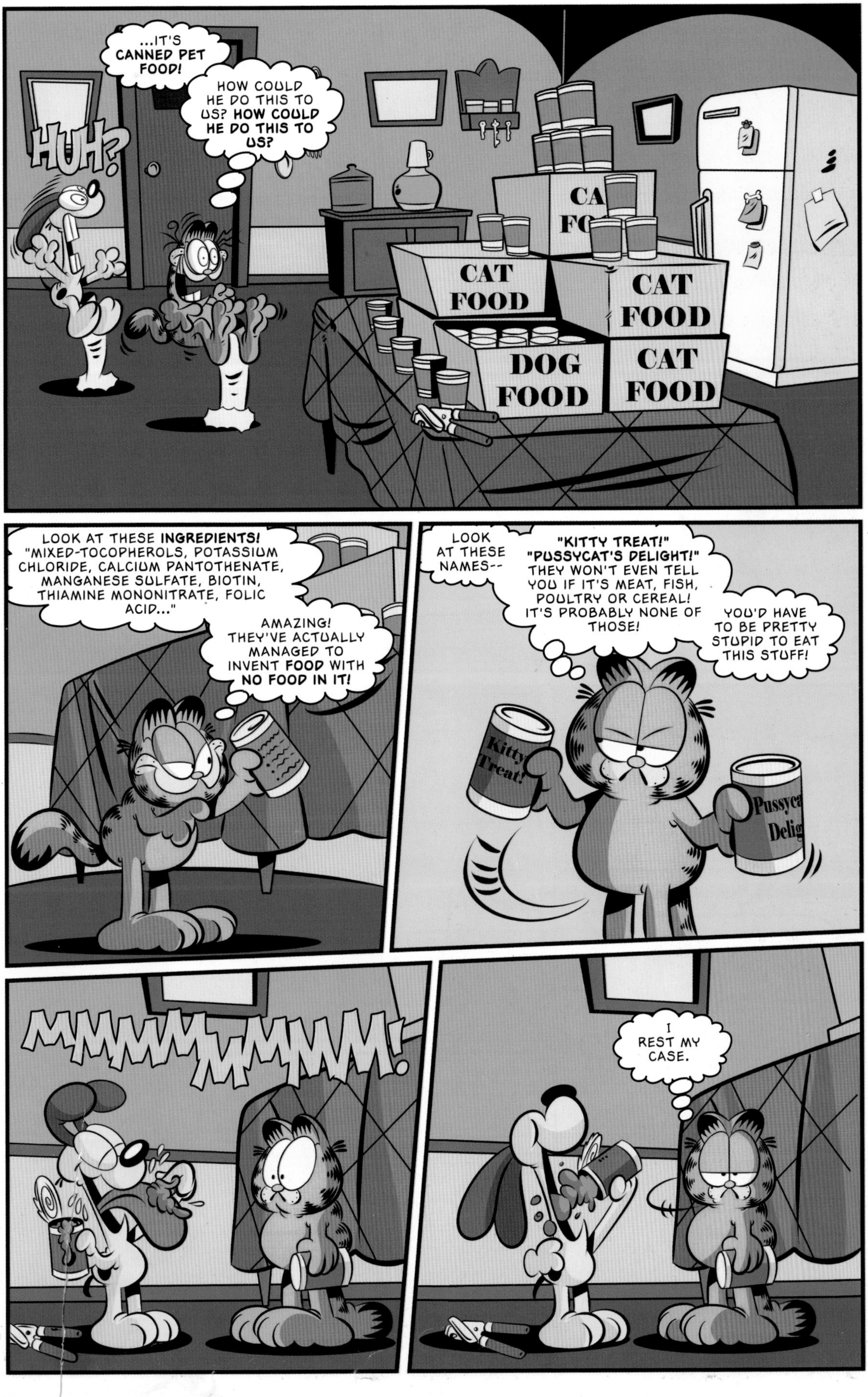
...IT'S CANNED PET FOOD!
HUH?
HOW COULD HE DO THIS TO US? HOW COULD HE DO THIS TO US?
CAT FOOD
CAT FOOD
CAT FOOD
DOG FOOD
LOOK AT THESE INGREDIENTS! "MIXED-TOCOPHEROLS, POTASSIUM CHLORIDE, CALCIUM PANTOTHENATE, MANGANESE SULFATE, BIOTIN, THIAMINE MONONITRATE, FOLIC ACID..."
AMAZING! THEY'VE ACTUALLY MANAGED TO INVENT FOOD WITH NO FOOD IN IT!
LOOK AT THESE NAMES--
"KITTY TREAT!" "PUSSYCAT'S DELIGHT!" THEY WON'T EVEN TELL YOU IF IT'S MEAT, FISH, POULTRY OR CEREAL! IT'S PROBABLY NONE OF THOSE!
YOU'D HAVE TO BE PRETTY STUPID TO EAT THIS STUFF!
Kitty Treat!
MMMMMMMMM!
I REST MY CASE.

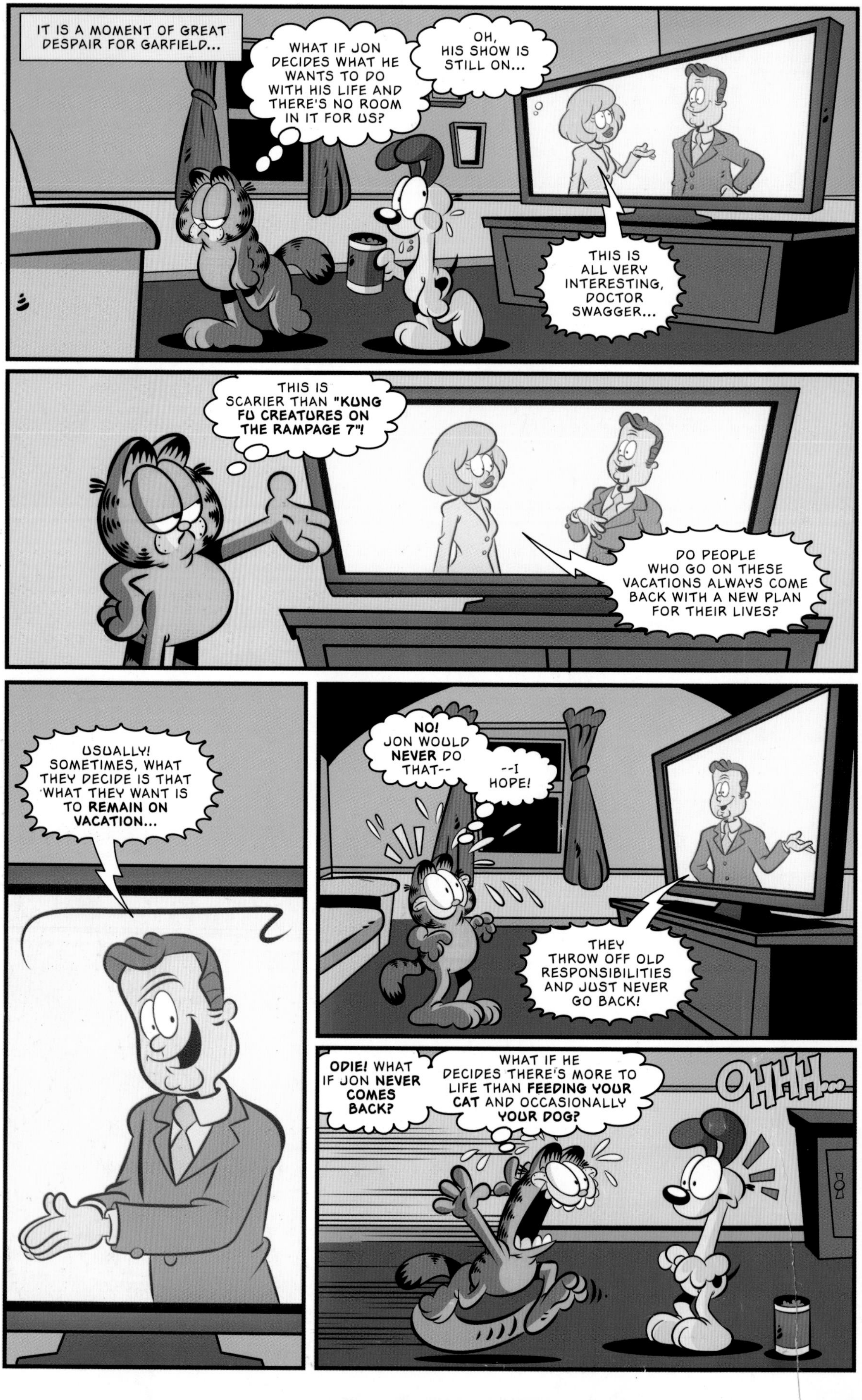
IT IS A MOMENT OF GREAT DESPAIR FOR GARFIELD...
WHAT IF JON DECIDES WHAT HE WANTS TO DO WITH HIS LIFE AND THERE'S NO ROOM IN IT FOR US?
OH, HIS SHOW IS STILL ON...
THIS IS ALL VERY INTERESTING, DOCTOR SWAGGER...
THIS IS SCARIER THAN "KUNG FU CREATURES ON THE RAMPAGE 7"!
DO PEOPLE WHO GO ON THESE VACATIONS ALWAYS COME BACK WITH A NEW PLAN FOR THEIR LIVES?
USUALLY! SOMETIMES, WHAT THEY DECIDE IS THAT WHAT THEY WANT IS TO REMAIN ON VACATION...
NO! JON WOULD NEVER DO THAT--
--I HOPE!
THEY THROW OFF OLD RESPONSIBILITIES AND JUST NEVER GO BACK!
ODIE! WHAT IF JON NEVER COMES BACK?
WHAT IF HE DECIDES THERE'S MORE TO LIFE THAN FEEDING YOUR CAT AND OCCASIONALLY YOUR DOG?
OHHH...

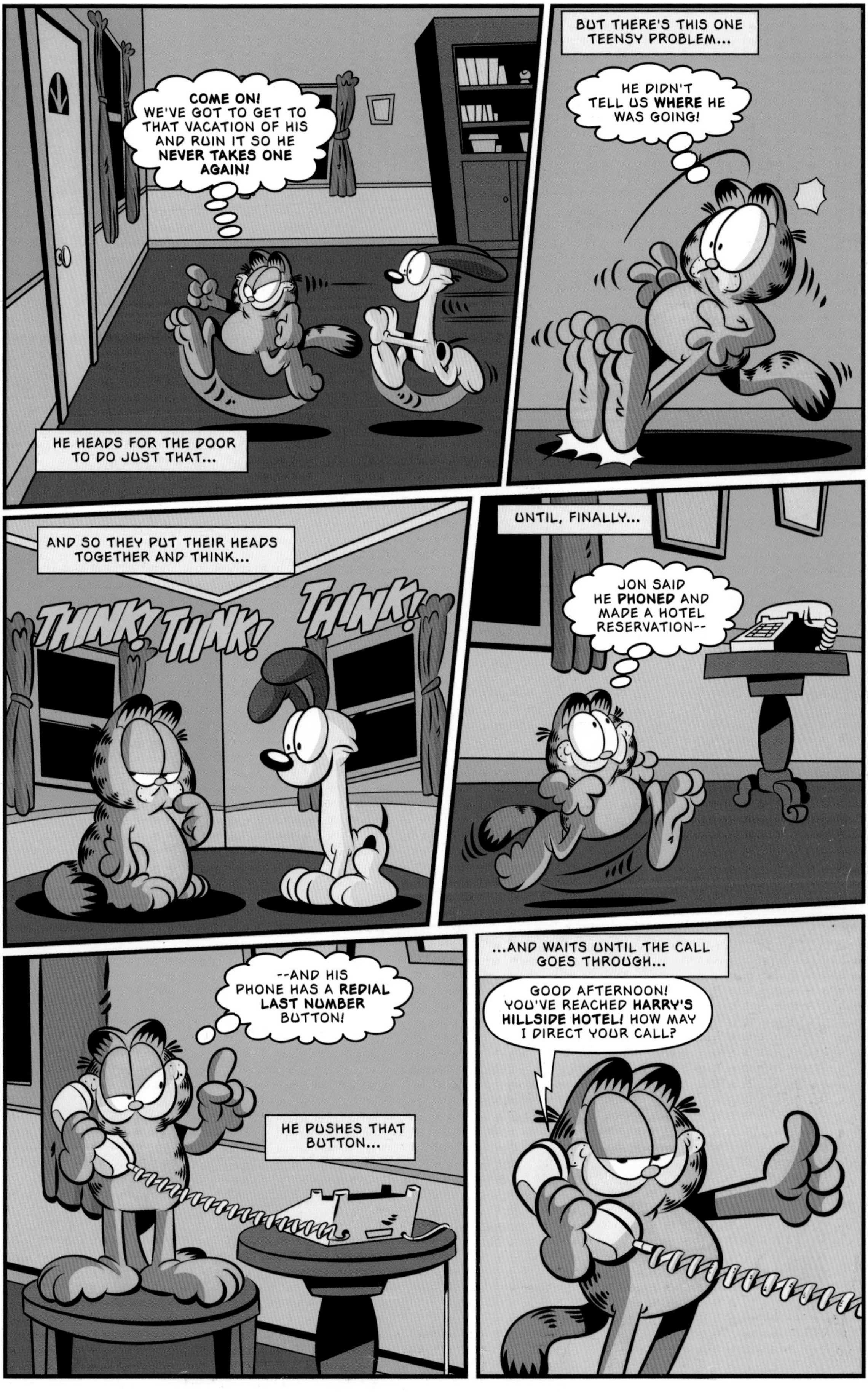
COME ON! WE'VE GOT TO GET TO THAT VACATION OF HIS AND RUIN IT SO HE NEVER TAKES ONE AGAIN!
HE HEADS FOR THE DOOR TO DO JUST THAT...
BUT THERE'S THIS ONE TEENSY PROBLEM...
HE DIDN'T TELL US WHERE HE WAS GOING!
AND SO THEY PUT THEIR HEADS TOGETHER AND THINK...
THINK! THINK! THINK!
UNTIL, FINALLY...
JON SAID HE PHONED AND MADE A HOTEL RESERVATION--
--AND HIS PHONE HAS A REDIAL LAST NUMBER BUTTON!
HE PUSHES THAT BUTTON...
...AND WAITS UNTIL THE CALL GOES THROUGH...
GOOD AFTERNOON! YOU'VE REACHED HARRY'S HILLSIDE HOTEL! HOW MAY I DIRECT YOUR CALL?

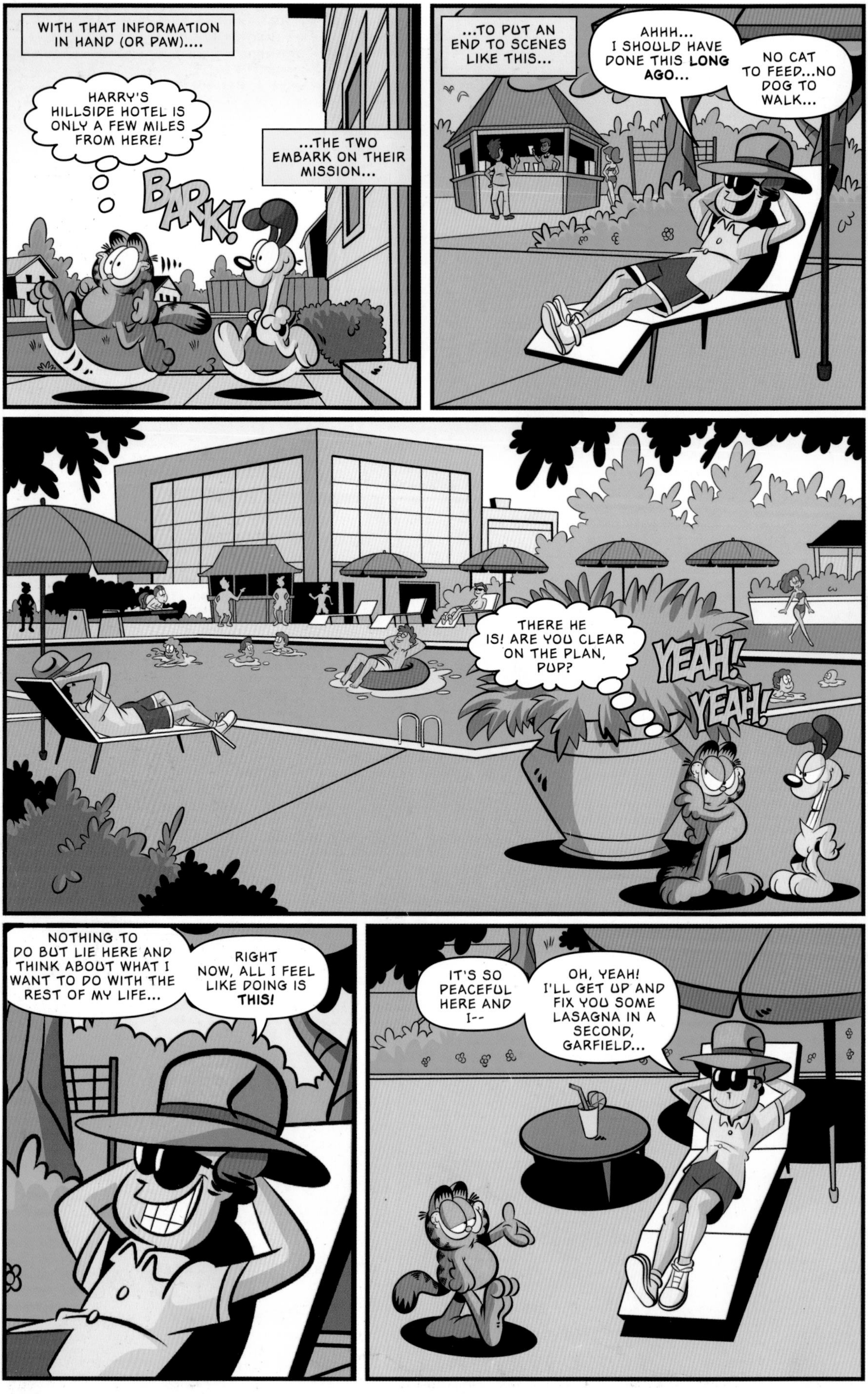
WITH THAT INFORMATION IN HAND (OR PAW)....
HARRY'S HILLSIDE HOTEL IS ONLY A FEW MILES FROM HERE!
...THE TWO EMBARK ON THEIR MISSION...
BARK!
...TO PUT AN END TO SCENES LIKE THIS...
AHHH... I SHOULD HAVE DONE THIS LONG AGO...
NO CAT TO FEED...NO DOG TO WALK...
THERE HE IS! ARE YOU CLEAR ON THE PLAN, PUP?
YEAH! YEAH!
NOTHING TO DO BUT LIE HERE AND THINK ABOUT WHAT I WANT TO DO WITH THE REST OF MY LIFE...
RIGHT NOW, ALL I FEEL LIKE DOING IS THIS!
IT'S SO PEACEFUL HERE AND I--
OH, YEAH! I'LL GET UP AND FIX YOU SOME LASAGNA IN A SECOND, GARFIELD...

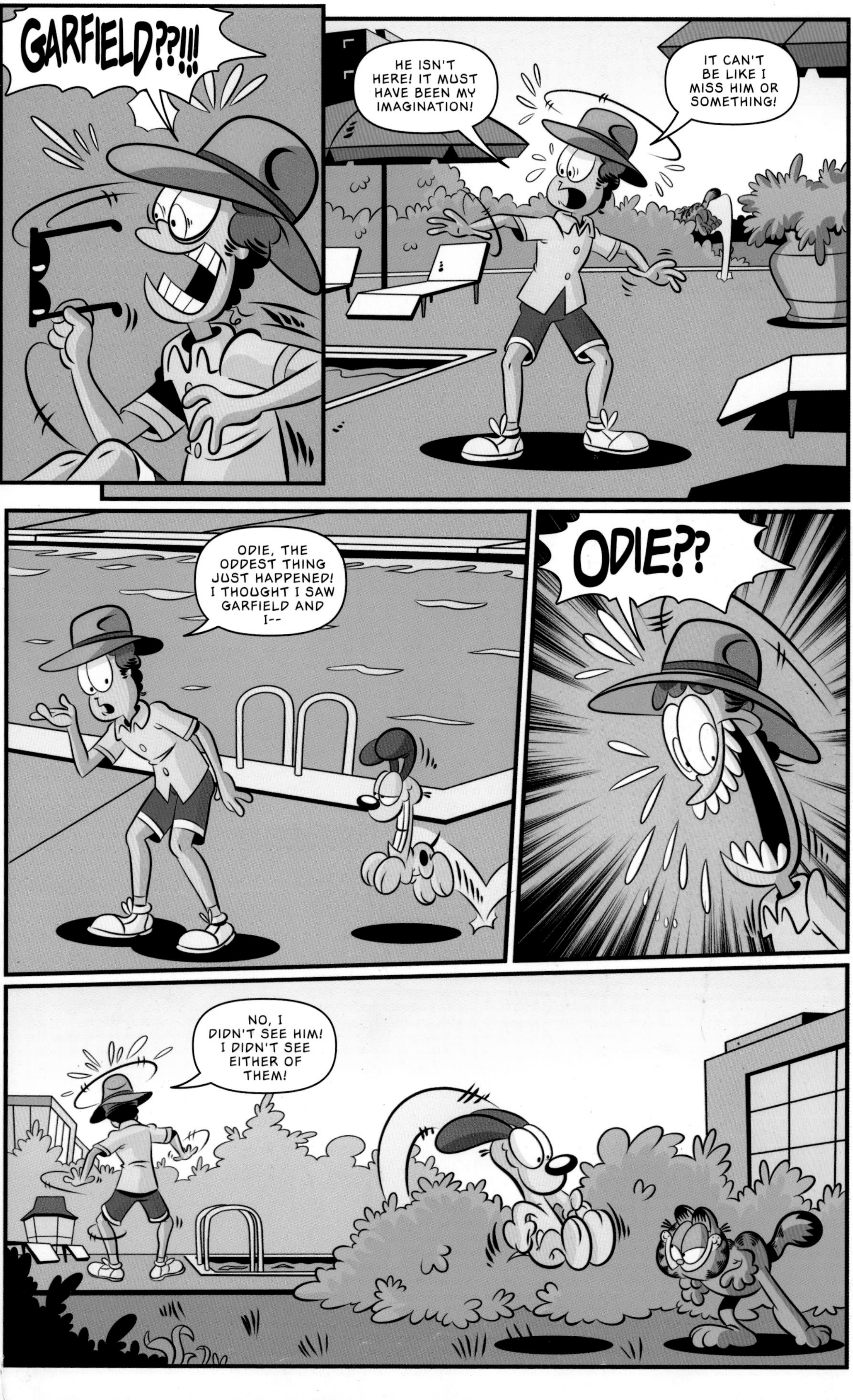
GARFIELD??!!!
HE ISN'T HERE! IT MUST HAVE BEEN MY IMAGINATION!
IT CAN'T BE LIKE I MISS HIM OR SOMETHING!
ODIE, THE ODDEST THING JUST HAPPENED! I THOUGHT I SAW GARFIELD AND I--
ODIE??
NO, I DIDN'T SEE HIM! I DIDN'T SEE EITHER OF THEM!

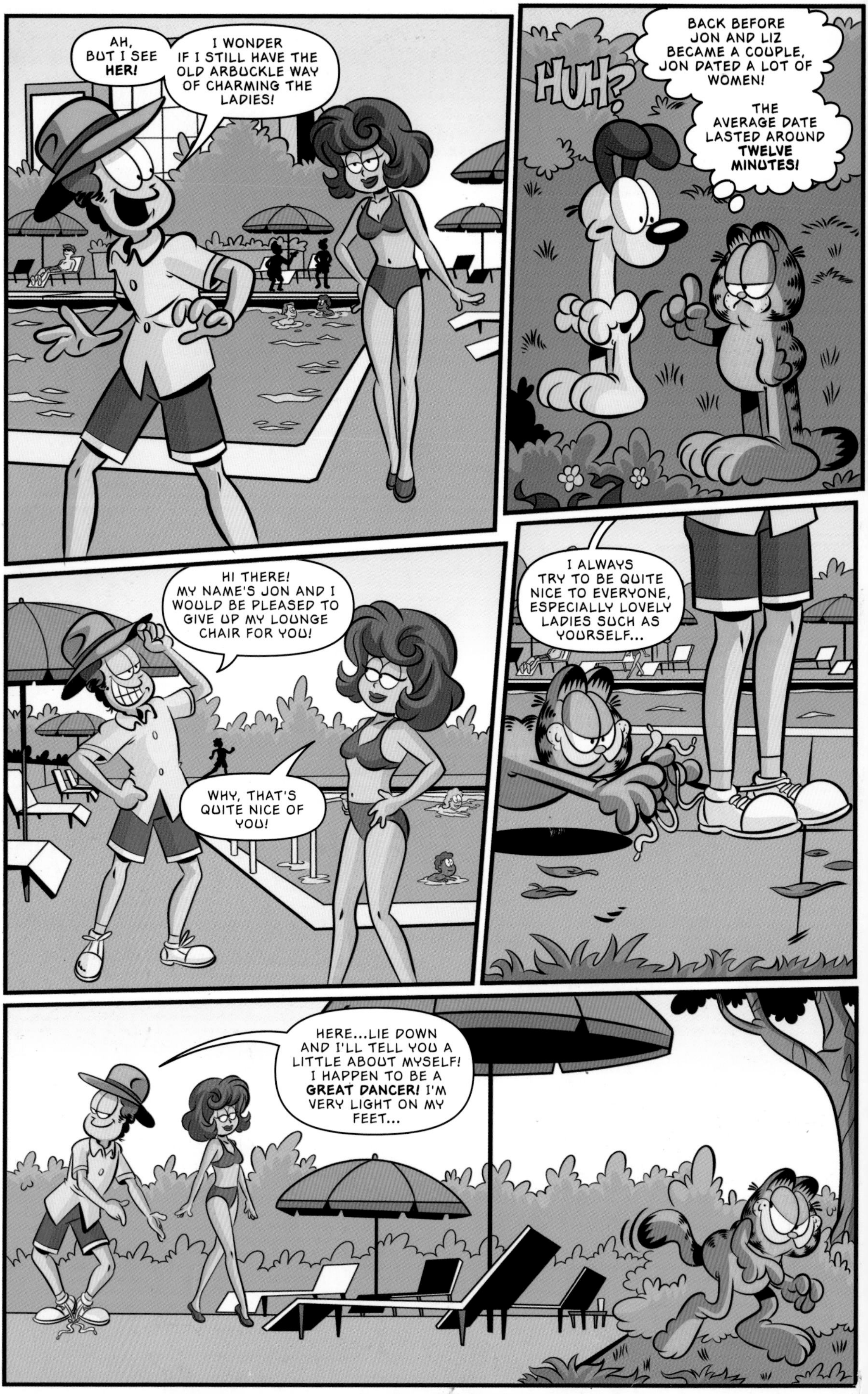
AH, BUT I SEE HER!
I WONDER IF I STILL HAVE THE OLD ARBUCKLE WAY OF CHARMING THE LADIES!
HUH?
BACK BEFORE JON AND LIZ BECAME A COUPLE, JON DATED A LOT OF WOMEN!
THE AVERAGE DATE LASTED AROUND TWELVE MINUTES!
HI THERE! MY NAME'S JON AND I WOULD BE PLEASED TO GIVE UP MY LOUNGE CHAIR FOR YOU!
WHY, THAT'S QUITE NICE OF YOU!
I ALWAYS TRY TO BE QUITE NICE TO EVERYONE, ESPECIALLY LOVELY LADIES SUCH AS YOURSELF...
HERE...LIE DOWN AND I'LL TELL YOU A LITTLE ABOUT MYSELF! I HAPPEN TO BE A GREAT DANCER! I'M VERY LIGHT ON MY FEET...

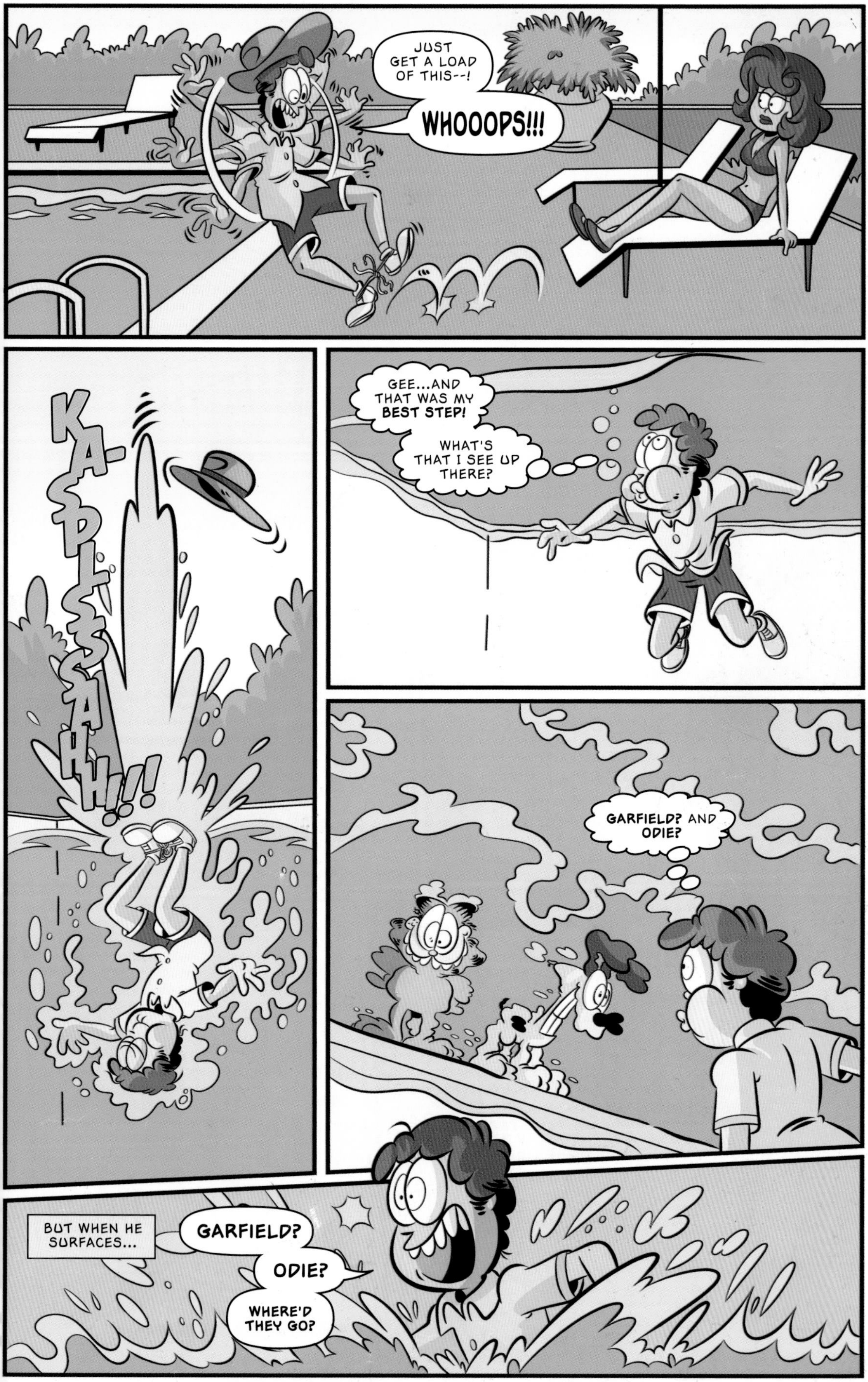
JUST GET A LOAD OF THIS--!
WHOOOPS!!!
KA-SPLISSAHH!!!
GEE...AND THAT WAS MY BEST STEP!
WHAT'S THAT I SEE UP THERE?
GARFIELD? AND ODIE?
BUT WHEN HE SURFACES...
GARFIELD?
ODIE?
WHERE'D THEY GO?

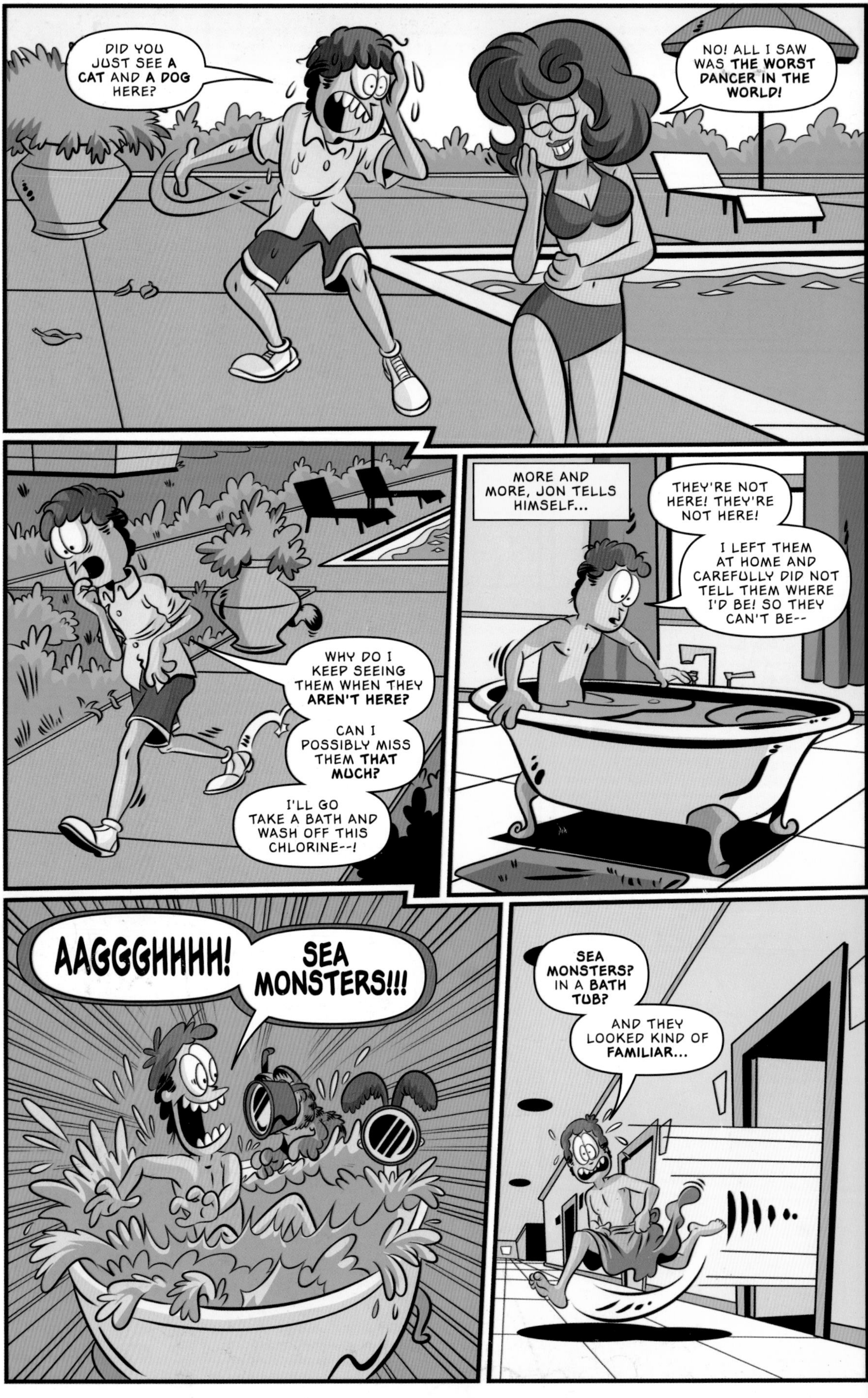
DID YOU JUST SEE A CAT AND A DOG HERE?
NO! ALL I SAW WAS THE WORST DANCER IN THE WORLD!
WHY DO I KEEP SEEING THEM WHEN THEY AREN'T HERE?
CAN I POSSIBLY MISS THEM THAT MUCH?
I'LL GO TAKE A BATH AND WASH OFF THIS CHLORINE--!
MORE AND MORE, JON TELLS HIMSELF...
THEY'RE NOT HERE! THEY'RE NOT HERE!
I LEFT THEM AT HOME AND CAREFULLY DID NOT TELL THEM WHERE I'D BE! SO THEY CAN'T BE--
AAGGGHHHH!
SEA MONSTERS!!!
SEA MONSTERS? IN A BATH TUB?
AND THEY LOOKED KIND OF FAMILIAR...

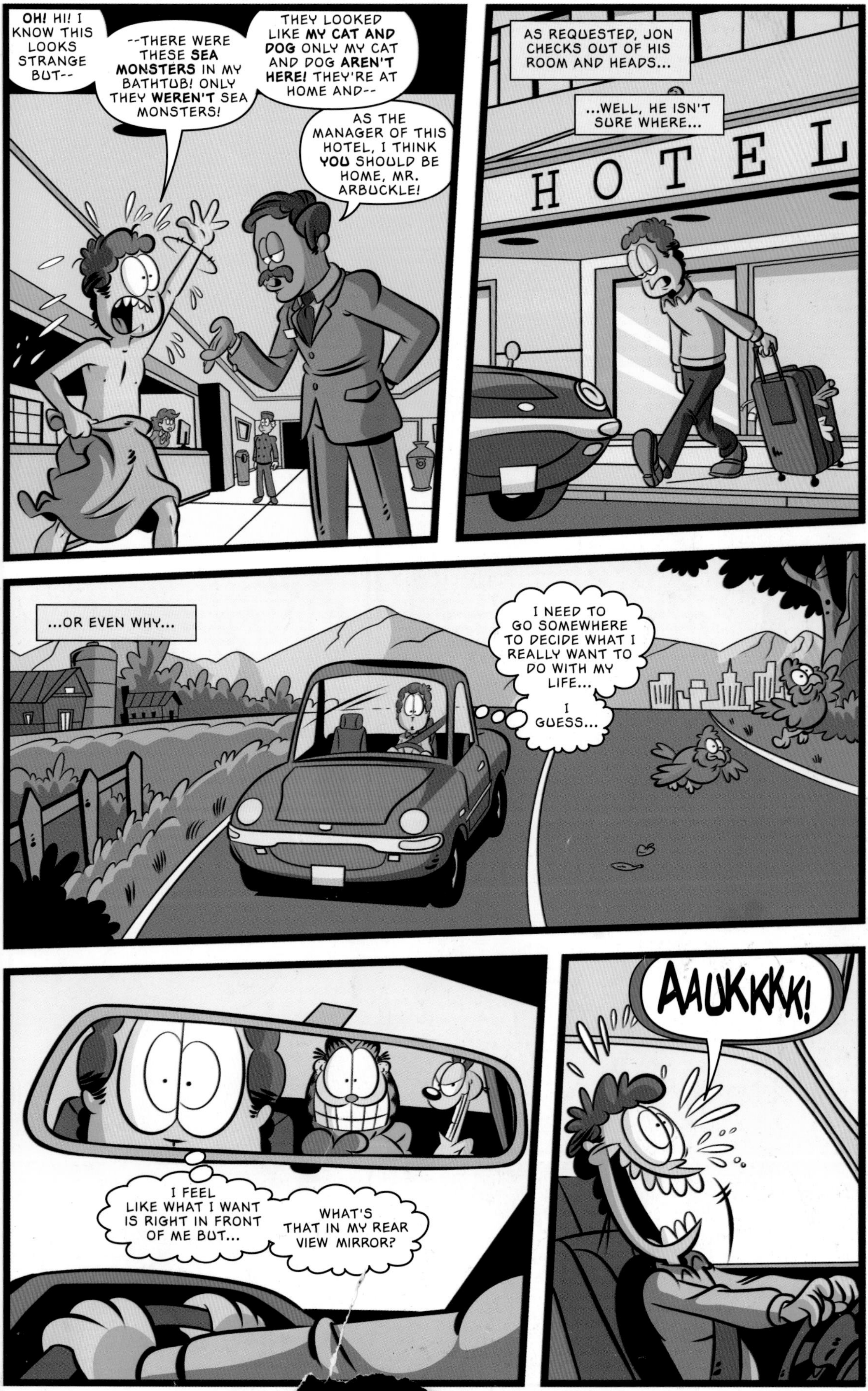
OH! HI! I KNOW THIS LOOKS STRANGE BUT--
--THERE WERE THESE SEA MONSTERS IN MY BATHTUB! ONLY THEY WEREN'T SEA MONSTERS!
THEY LOOKED LIKE MY CAT AND DOG ONLY MY CAT AND DOG AREN'T HERE! THEY'RE AT HOME AND--
AS THE MANAGER OF THIS HOTEL, I THINK YOU SHOULD BE HOME, MR. ARBUCKLE!
AS REQUESTED, JON CHECKS OUT OF HIS ROOM AND HEADS...
...WELL, HE ISN'T SURE WHERE...
HOTEL
...OR EVEN WHY...
I NEED TO GO SOMEWHERE TO DECIDE WHAT I REALLY WANT TO DO WITH MY LIFE...
I GUESS...
I FEEL LIKE WHAT I WANT IS RIGHT IN FRONT OF ME BUT...
WHAT'S THAT IN MY REAR VIEW MIRROR?
AAUKKKK!

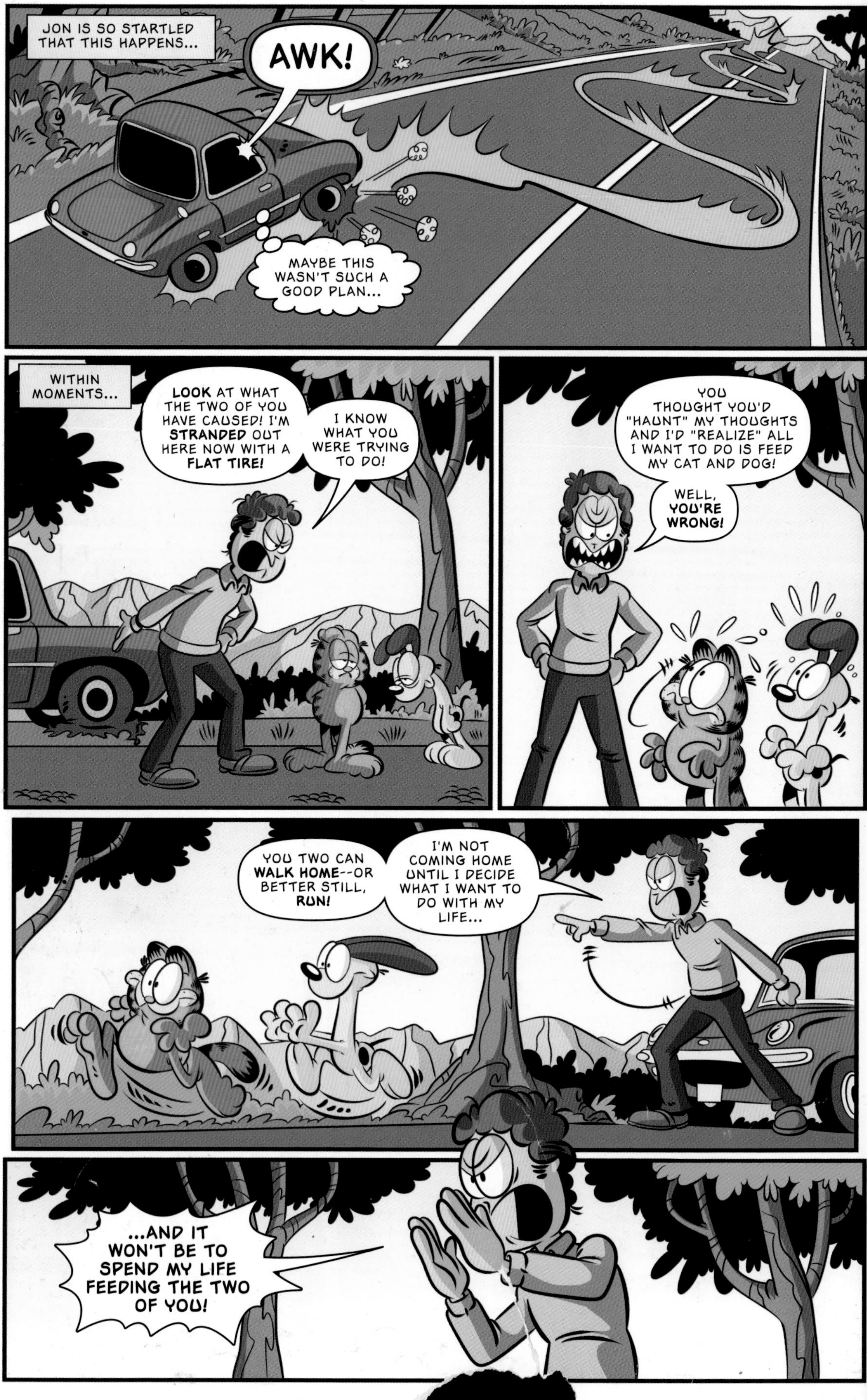
JON IS SO STARTLED THAT THIS HAPPENS...
AWK!
MAYBE THIS WASN'T SUCH A GOOD PLAN...
WITHIN MOMENTS...
LOOK AT WHAT THE TWO OF YOU HAVE CAUSED! I'M STRANDED OUT HERE NOW WITH A FLAT TIRE!
I KNOW WHAT YOU WERE TRYING TO DO!
YOU THOUGHT YOU'D "HAUNT" MY THOUGHTS AND I'D "REALIZE" ALL I WANT TO DO IS FEED MY CAT AND DOG!
WELL, YOU'RE WRONG!
YOU TWO CAN WALK HOME--OR BETTER STILL, RUN!
I'M NOT COMING HOME UNTIL I DECIDE WHAT I WANT TO DO WITH MY LIFE...
...AND IT WON'T BE TO SPEND MY LIFE FEEDING THE TWO OF YOU!

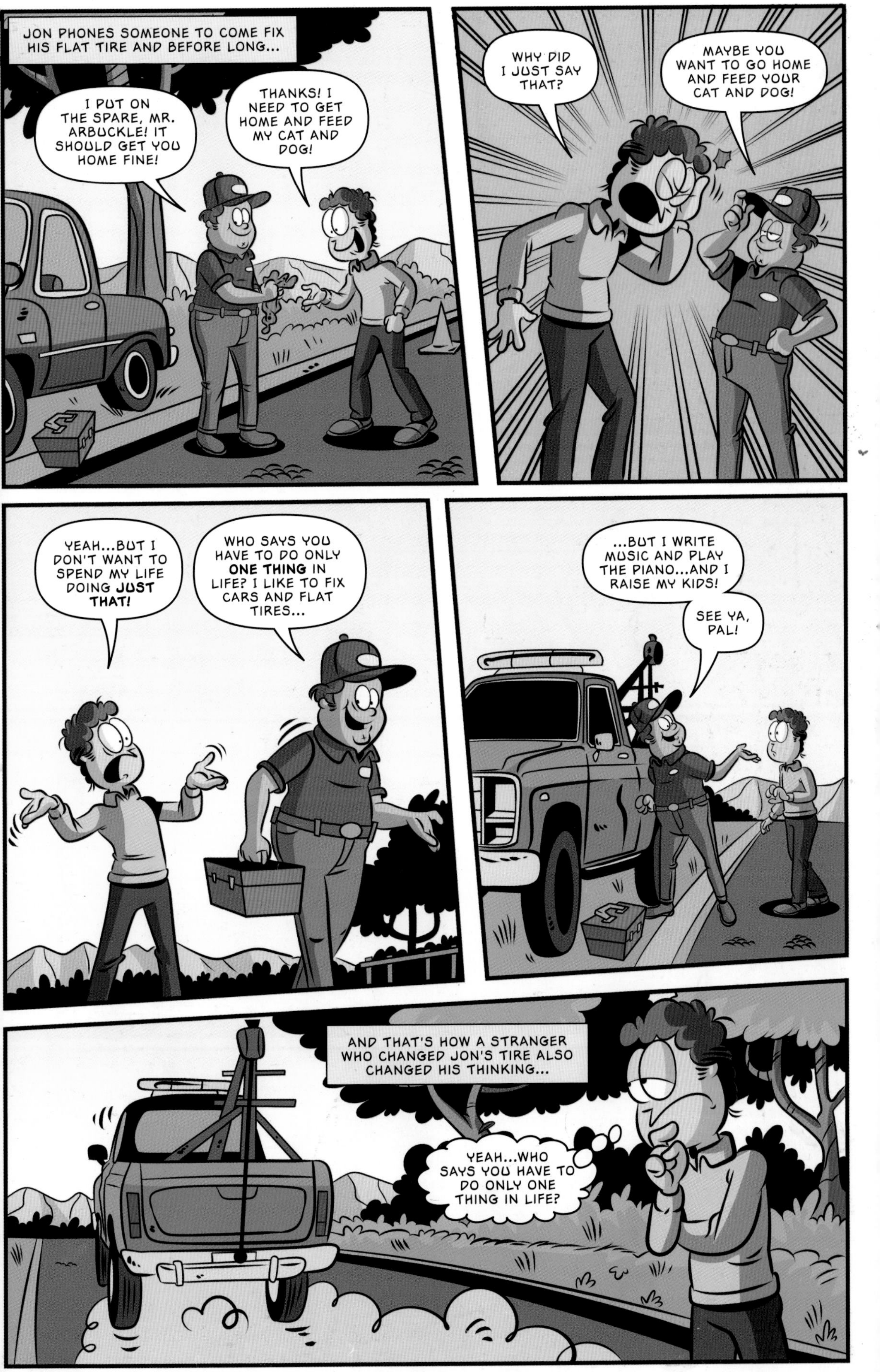
JON PHONES SOMEONE TO COME FIX HIS FLAT TIRE AND BEFORE LONG...
I PUT ON THE SPARE, MR. ARBUCKLE! IT SHOULD GET YOU HOME FINE!
THANKS! I NEED TO GET HOME AND FEED MY CAT AND DOG!
WHY DID I JUST SAY THAT?
MAYBE YOU WANT TO GO HOME AND FEED YOUR CAT AND DOG!
YEAH...BUT I DON'T WANT TO SPEND MY LIFE DOING **JUST THAT!**
WHO SAYS YOU HAVE TO DO ONLY **ONE THING** IN LIFE? I LIKE TO FIX CARS AND FLAT TIRES...
...BUT I WRITE MUSIC AND PLAY THE PIANO...AND I RAISE MY KIDS!
SEE YA, PAL!
AND THAT'S HOW A STRANGER WHO CHANGED JON'S TIRE ALSO CHANGED HIS THINKING...
YEAH...WHO SAYS YOU HAVE TO DO ONLY ONE THING IN LIFE?

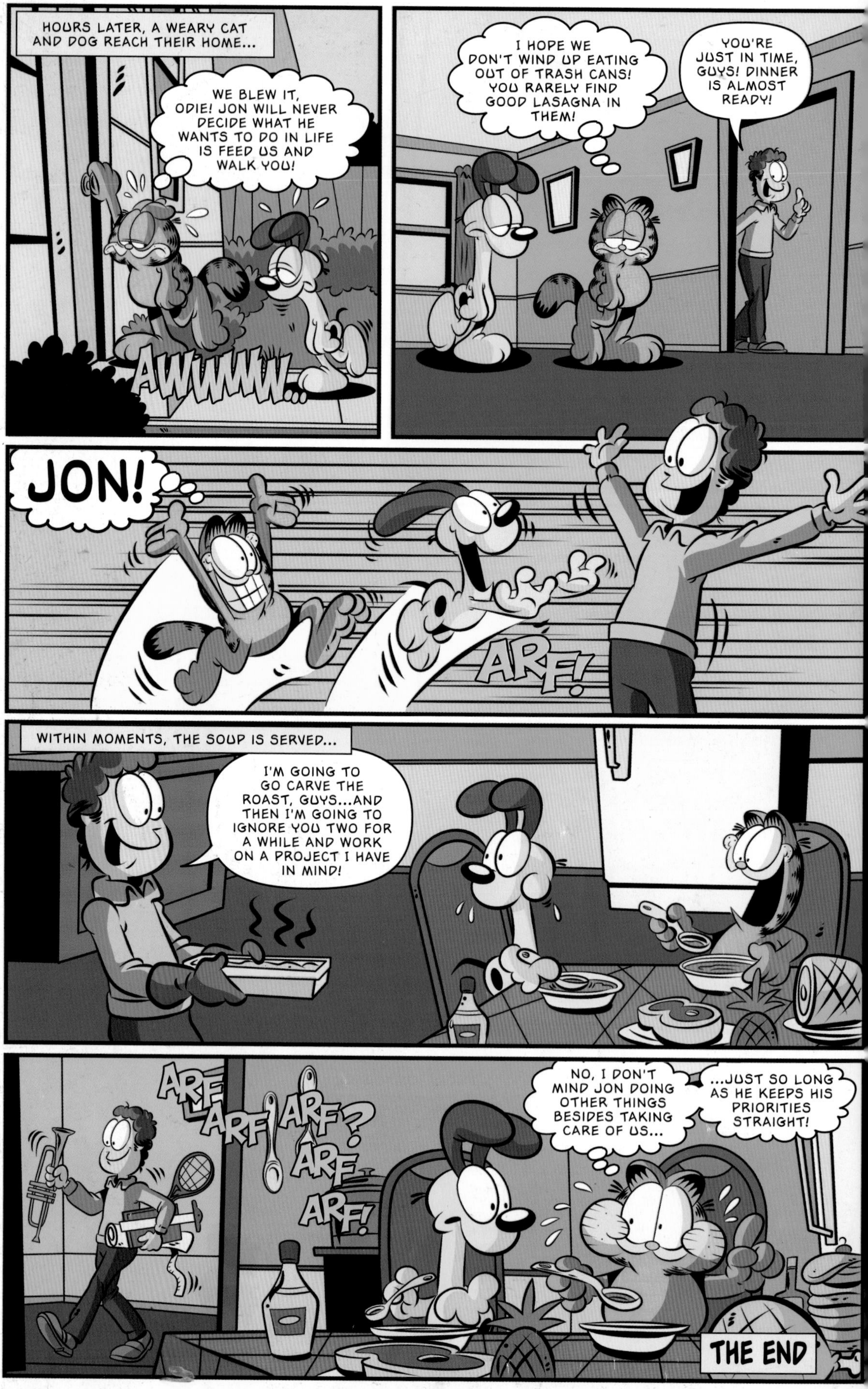
HOURS LATER, A WEARY CAT AND DOG REACH THEIR HOME...
WE BLEW IT, ODIE! JON WILL NEVER DECIDE WHAT HE WANTS TO DO IN LIFE IS FEED US AND WALK YOU!
AWWWW...
I HOPE WE DON'T WIND UP EATING OUT OF TRASH CANS! YOU RARELY FIND GOOD LASAGNA IN THEM!
YOU'RE JUST IN TIME, GUYS! DINNER IS ALMOST READY!
JON!
ARF!
WITHIN MOMENTS, THE SOUP IS SERVED...
I'M GOING TO GO CARVE THE ROAST, GUYS...AND THEN I'M GOING TO IGNORE YOU TWO FOR A WHILE AND WORK ON A PROJECT I HAVE IN MIND!
ARF
ARF
ARF?
ARF
ARF!
NO, I DON'T MIND JON DOING OTHER THINGS BESIDES TAKING CARE OF US...
...JUST SO LONG AS HE KEEPS HIS PRIORITIES STRAIGHT!
THE END

Spring
Breakup

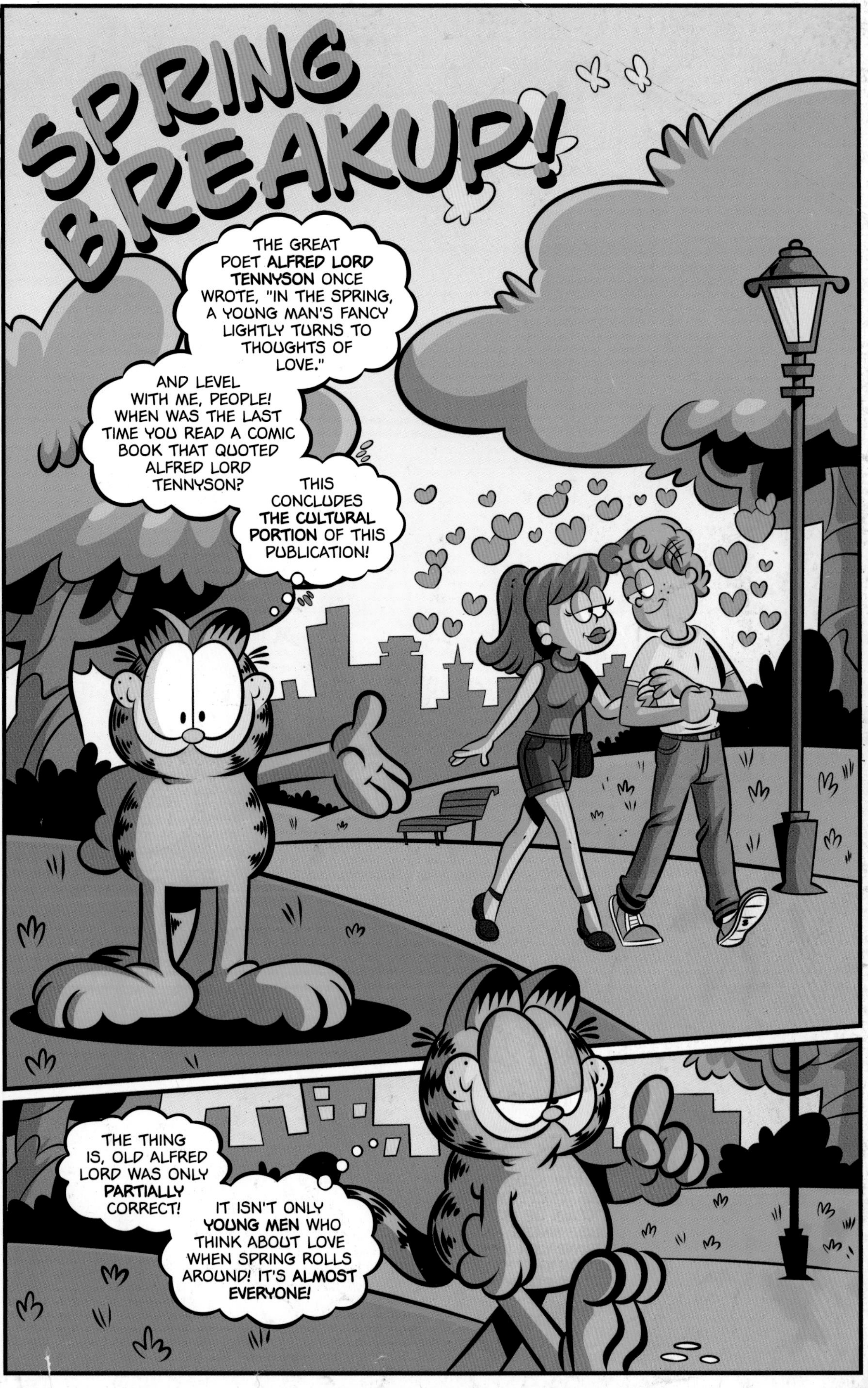
SPRING BREAKUP!
THE GREAT POET ALFRED LORD TENNYSON ONCE WROTE, "IN THE SPRING, A YOUNG MAN'S FANCY LIGHTLY TURNS TO THOUGHTS OF LOVE."
AND LEVEL WITH ME, PEOPLE! WHEN WAS THE LAST TIME YOU READ A COMIC BOOK THAT QUOTED ALFRED LORD TENNYSON?
THIS CONCLUDES THE CULTURAL PORTION OF THIS PUBLICATION!
THE THING IS, OLD ALFRED LORD WAS ONLY PARTIALLY CORRECT!
IT ISN'T ONLY YOUNG MEN WHO THINK ABOUT LOVE WHEN SPRING ROLLS AROUND! IT'S ALMOST EVERYONE!

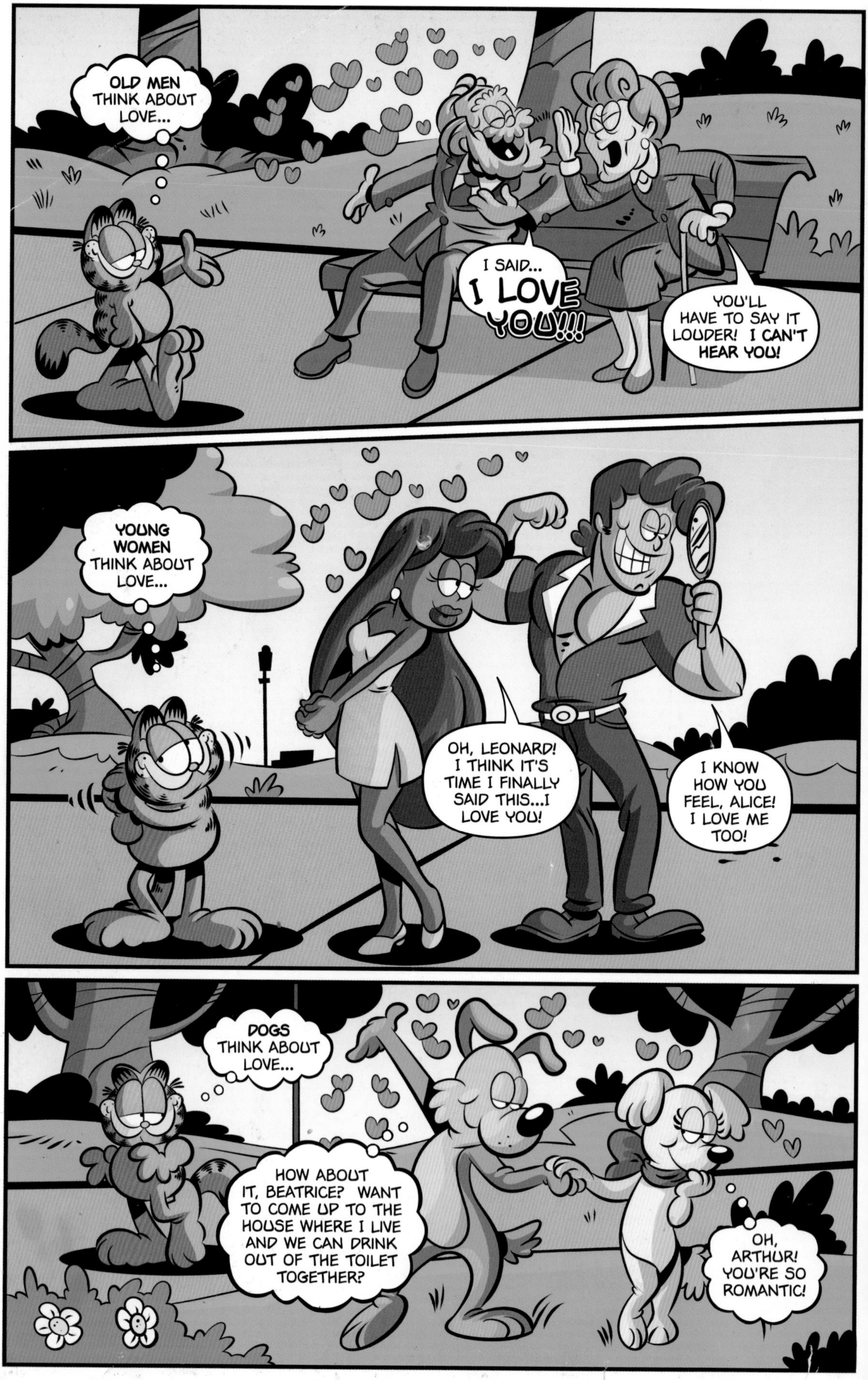

OLD MEN THINK ABOUT LOVE...
I SAID... I LOVE YOU!!!
YOU'LL HAVE TO SAY IT LOUDER! I CAN'T HEAR YOU!
YOUNG WOMEN THINK ABOUT LOVE...
OH, LEONARD! I THINK IT'S TIME I FINALLY SAID THIS...I LOVE YOU!
I KNOW HOW YOU FEEL, ALICE! I LOVE ME TOO!
DOGS THINK ABOUT LOVE...
HOW ABOUT IT, BEATRICE? WANT TO COME UP TO THE HOUSE WHERE I LIVE AND WE CAN DRINK OUT OF THE TOILET TOGETHER?
OH, ARTHUR! YOU'RE SO ROMANTIC!

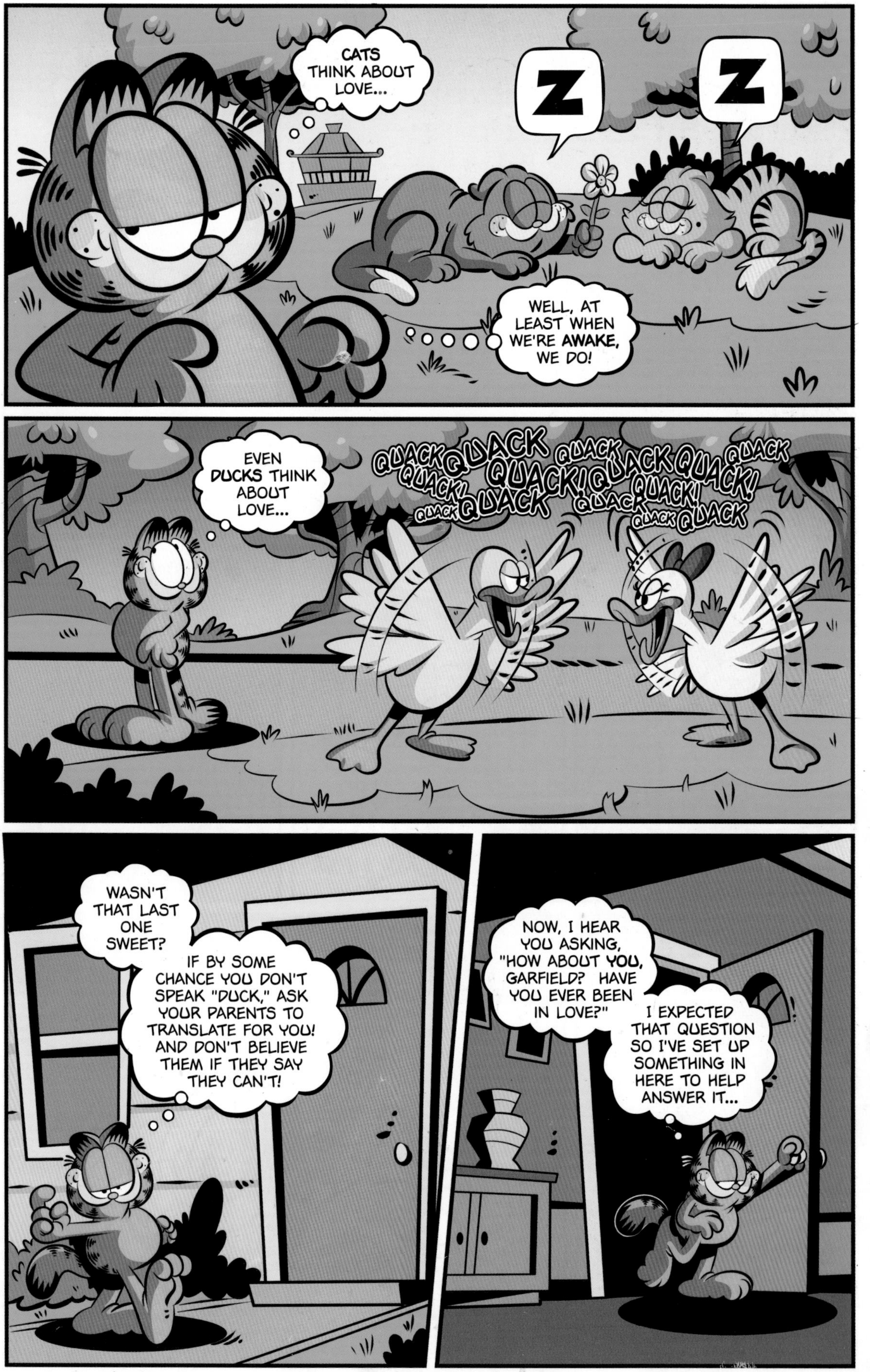
CATS THINK ABOUT LOVE...
Z
Z
WELL, AT LEAST WHEN WE'RE AWAKE, WE DO!
EVEN DUCKS THINK ABOUT LOVE...
QUACK QUACK QUACK QUACK QUACK QUACK QUACK! QUACK! QUACK QUACK QUACK! QUACK QUACK QUACK! QUACK QUACK
WASN'T THAT LAST ONE SWEET?
IF BY SOME CHANCE YOU DON'T SPEAK "DUCK," ASK YOUR PARENTS TO TRANSLATE FOR YOU! AND DON'T BELIEVE THEM IF THEY SAY THEY CAN'T!
NOW, I HEAR YOU ASKING, "HOW ABOUT YOU, GARFIELD? HAVE YOU EVER BEEN IN LOVE?"
I EXPECTED THAT QUESTION SO I'VE SET UP SOMETHING IN HERE TO HELP ANSWER IT...

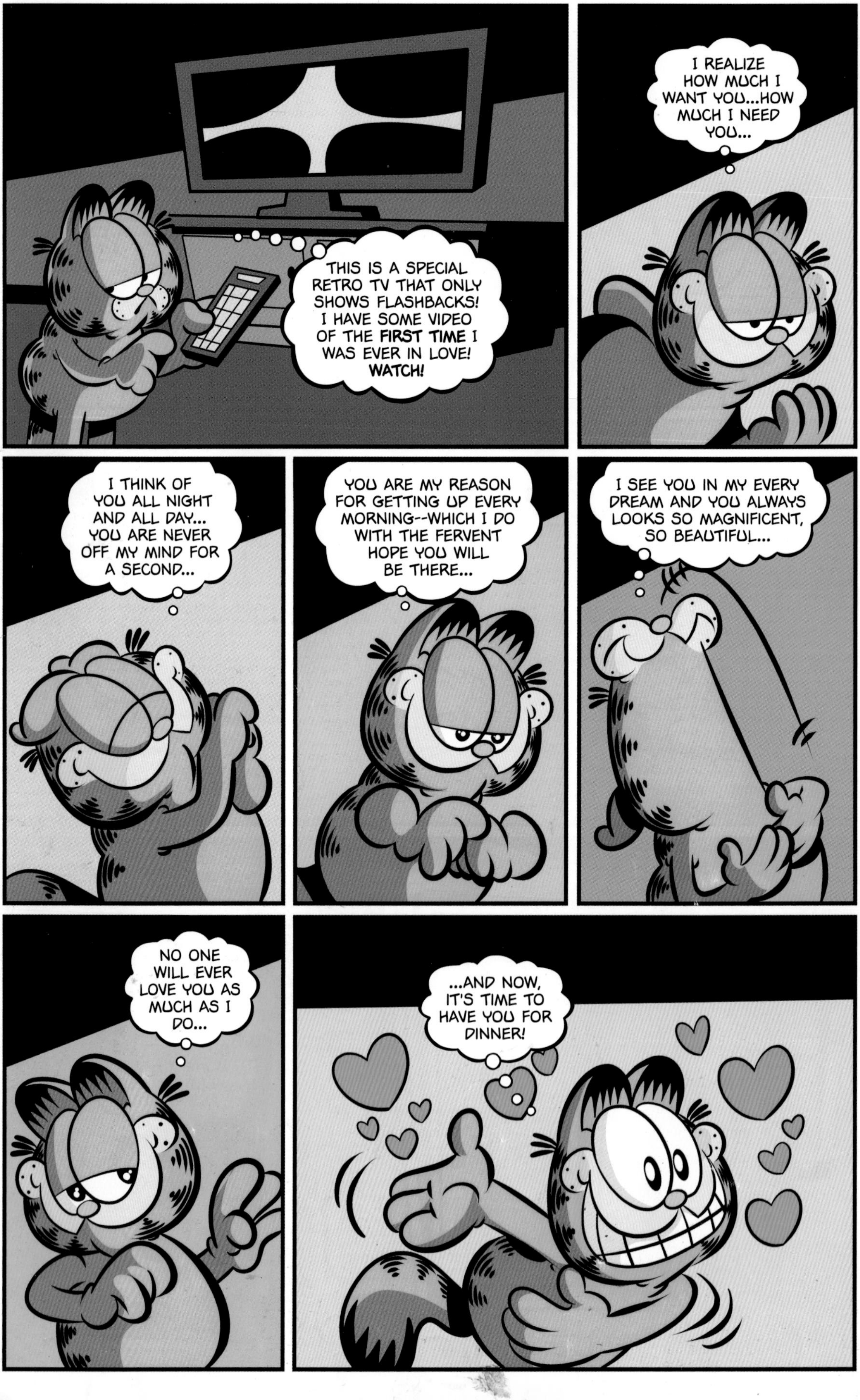
THIS IS A SPECIAL RETRO TV THAT ONLY SHOWS FLASHBACKS! I HAVE SOME VIDEO OF THE FIRST TIME I WAS EVER IN LOVE! WATCH!
I REALIZE HOW MUCH I WANT YOU...HOW MUCH I NEED YOU...
I THINK OF YOU ALL NIGHT AND ALL DAY... YOU ARE NEVER OFF MY MIND FOR A SECOND...
YOU ARE MY REASON FOR GETTING UP EVERY MORNING--WHICH I DO WITH THE FERVENT HOPE YOU WILL BE THERE...
I SEE YOU IN MY EVERY DREAM AND YOU ALWAYS LOOKS SO MAGNIFICENT, SO BEAUTIFUL...
NO ONE WILL EVER LOVE YOU AS MUCH AS I DO...
...AND NOW, IT'S TIME TO HAVE YOU FOR DINNER!

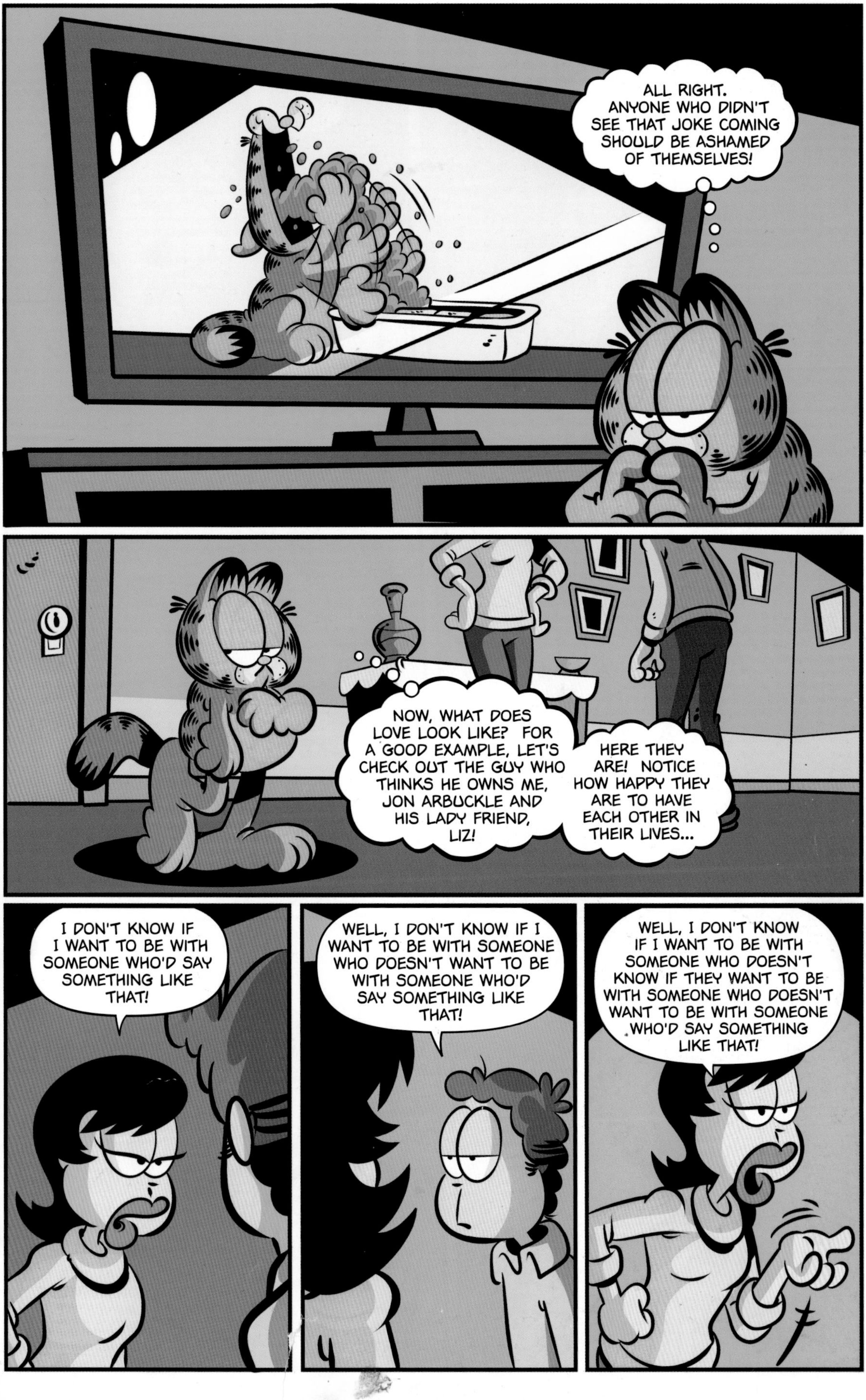
ALL RIGHT. ANYONE WHO DIDN'T SEE THAT JOKE COMING SHOULD BE ASHAMED OF THEMSELVES!
NOW, WHAT DOES LOVE LOOK LIKE? FOR A GOOD EXAMPLE, LET'S CHECK OUT THE GUY WHO THINKS HE OWNS ME, JON ARBUCKLE AND HIS LADY FRIEND, LIZ!
HERE THEY ARE! NOTICE HOW HAPPY THEY ARE TO HAVE EACH OTHER IN THEIR LIVES...
I DON'T KNOW IF I WANT TO BE WITH SOMEONE WHO'D SAY SOMETHING LIKE THAT!
WELL, I DON'T KNOW IF I WANT TO BE WITH SOMEONE WHO DOESN'T WANT TO BE WITH SOMEONE WHO'D SAY SOMETHING LIKE THAT!
WELL, I DON'T KNOW IF I WANT TO BE WITH SOMEONE WHO DOESN'T KNOW IF THEY WANT TO BE WITH SOMEONE WHO DOESN'T WANT TO BE WITH SOMEONE WHO'D SAY SOMETHING LIKE THAT!

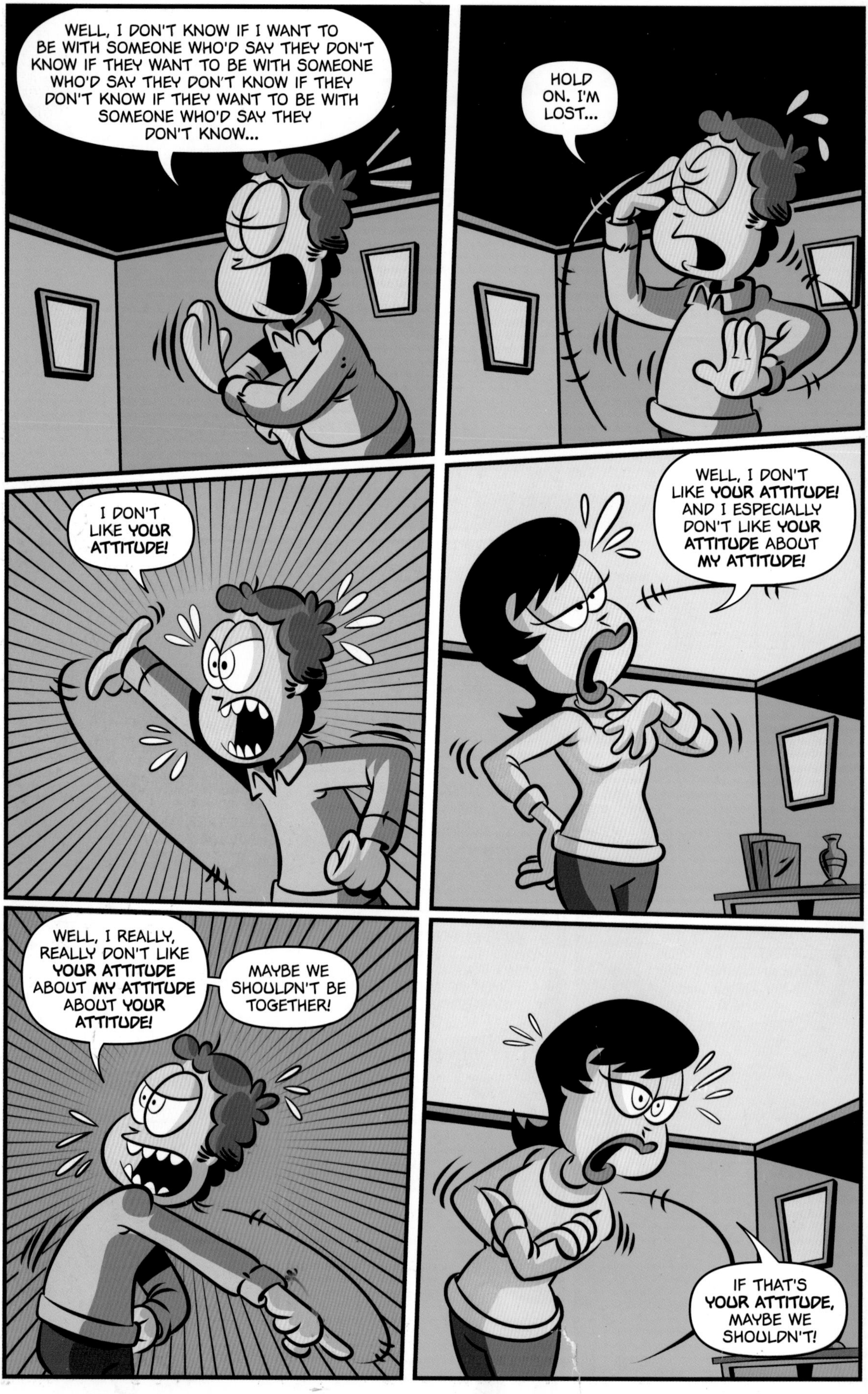
WELL, I DON'T KNOW IF I WANT TO BE WITH SOMEONE WHO'D SAY THEY DON'T KNOW IF THEY WANT TO BE WITH SOMEONE WHO'D SAY THEY DON'T KNOW IF THEY DON'T KNOW IF THEY WANT TO BE WITH SOMEONE WHO'D SAY THEY DON'T KNOW...
HOLD ON. I'M LOST...
I DON'T LIKE YOUR ATTITUDE!
WELL, I DON'T LIKE YOUR ATTITUDE! AND I ESPECIALLY DON'T LIKE YOUR ATTITUDE ABOUT MY ATTITUDE!
WELL, I REALLY, REALLY DON'T LIKE YOUR ATTITUDE ABOUT MY ATTITUDE ABOUT YOUR ATTITUDE!
MAYBE WE SHOULDN'T BE TOGETHER!
IF THAT'S YOUR ATTITUDE, MAYBE WE SHOULDN'T!

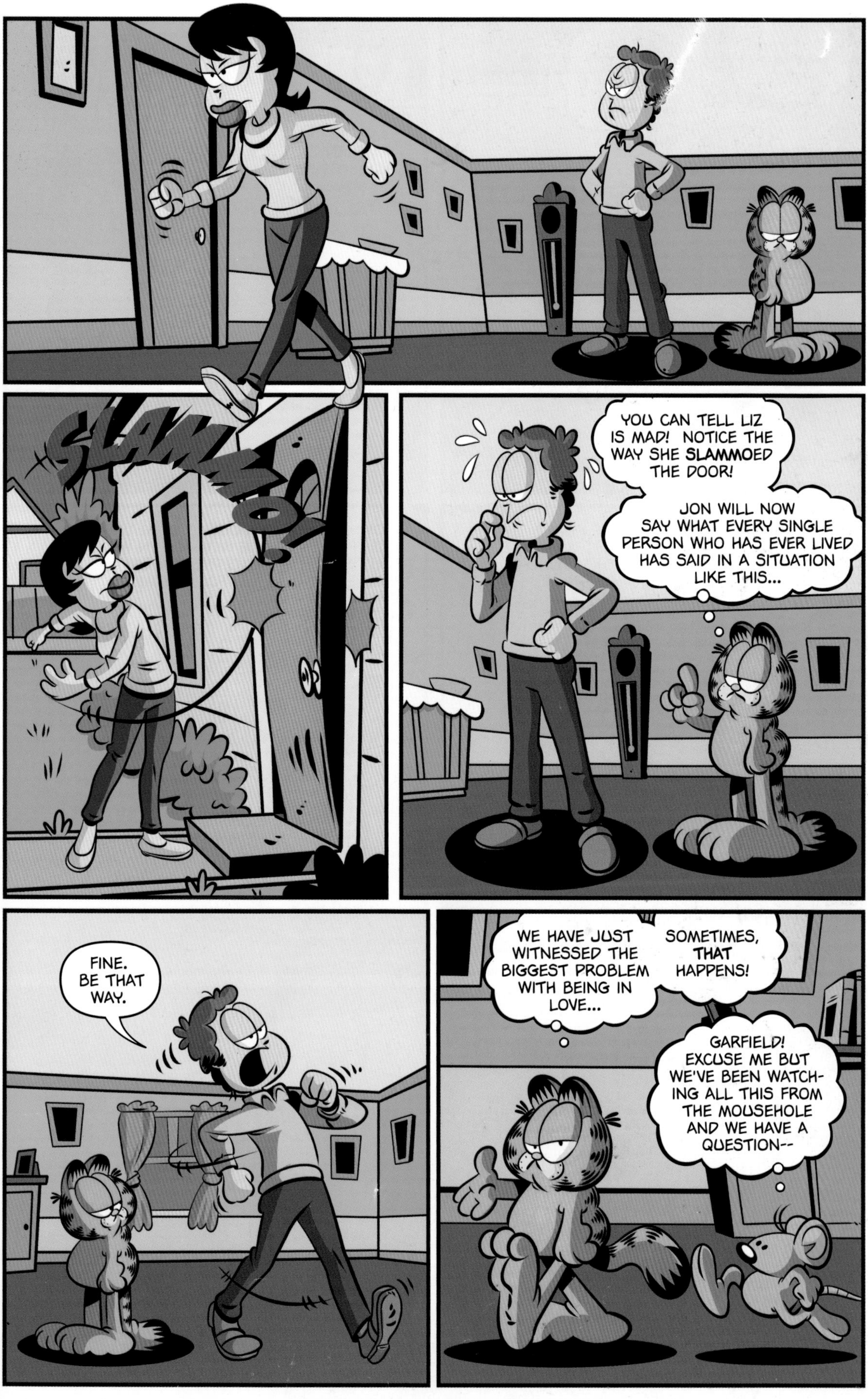
SLAMMO!
YOU CAN TELL LIZ IS MAD! NOTICE THE WAY SHE SLAMMOED THE DOOR!
JON WILL NOW SAY WHAT EVERY SINGLE PERSON WHO HAS EVER LIVED HAS SAID IN A SITUATION LIKE THIS...
FINE. BE THAT WAY.
WE HAVE JUST WITNESSED THE BIGGEST PROBLEM WITH BEING IN LOVE...
SOMETIMES, THAT HAPPENS!
GARFIELD! EXCUSE ME BUT WE'VE BEEN WATCHING ALL THIS FROM THE MOUSEHOLE AND WE HAVE A QUESTION--

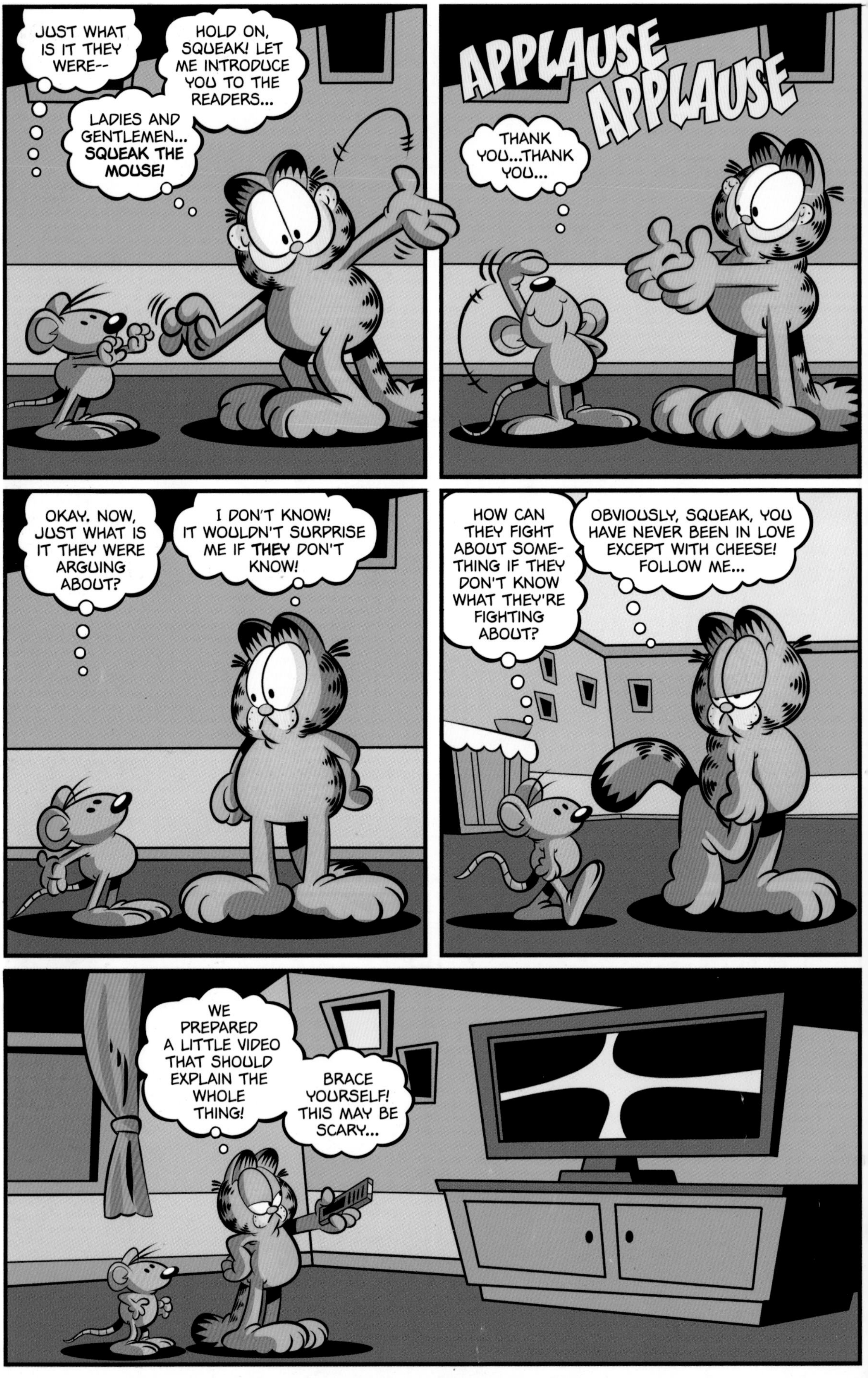
JUST WHAT IS IT THEY WERE--
HOLD ON, SQUEAK! LET ME INTRODUCE YOU TO THE READERS...
LADIES AND GENTLEMEN... SQUEAK THE MOUSE!
APPLAUSE APPLAUSE
THANK YOU...THANK YOU...
OKAY. NOW, JUST WHAT IS IT THEY WERE ARGUING ABOUT?
I DON'T KNOW! IT WOULDN'T SURPRISE ME IF THEY DON'T KNOW!
HOW CAN THEY FIGHT ABOUT SOMETHING IF THEY DON'T KNOW WHAT THEY'RE FIGHTING ABOUT?
OBVIOUSLY, SQUEAK, YOU HAVE NEVER BEEN IN LOVE EXCEPT WITH CHEESE! FOLLOW ME...
WE PREPARED A LITTLE VIDEO THAT SHOULD EXPLAIN THE WHOLE THING!
BRACE YOURSELF! THIS MAY BE SCARY...

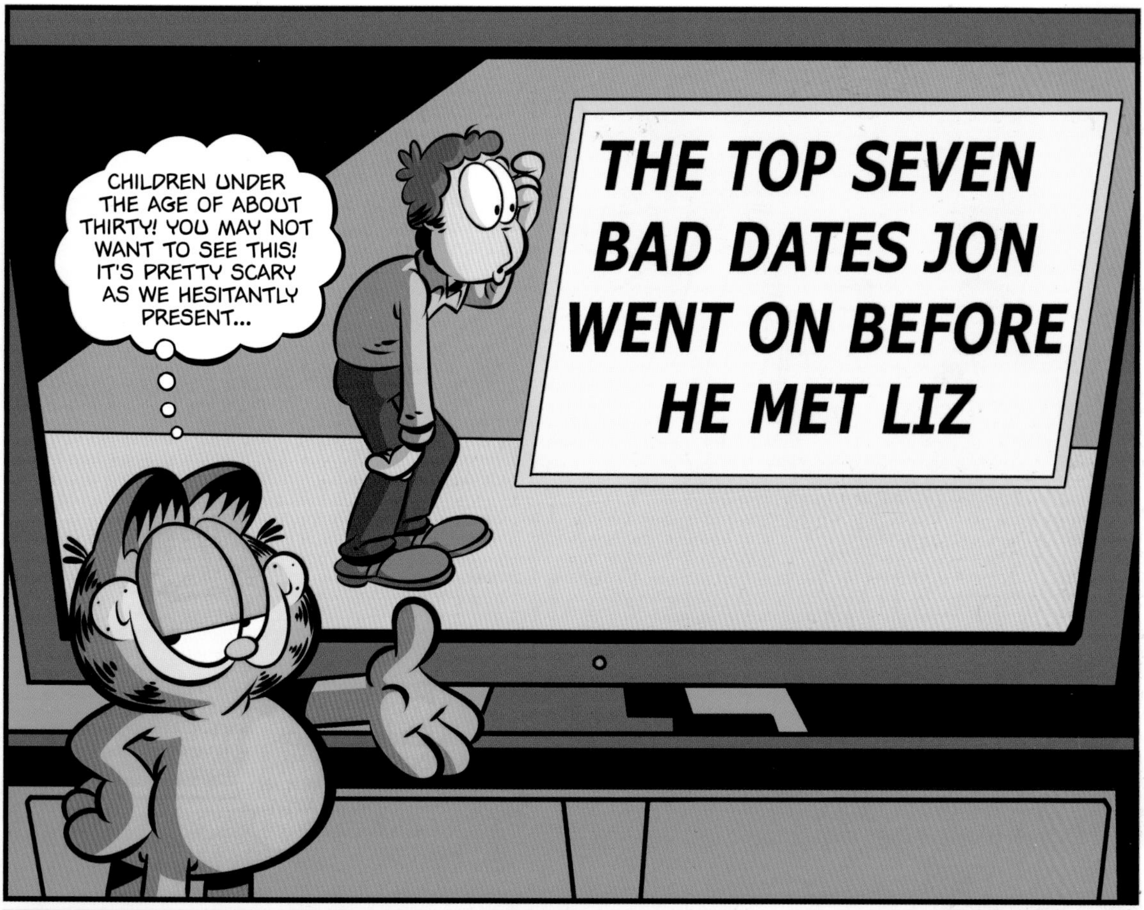
CHILDREN UNDER THE AGE OF ABOUT THIRTY! YOU MAY NOT WANT TO SEE THIS! IT'S PRETTY SCARY AS WE HESITANTLY PRESENT...
THE TOP SEVEN BAD DATES JON WENT ON BEFORE HE MET LIZ

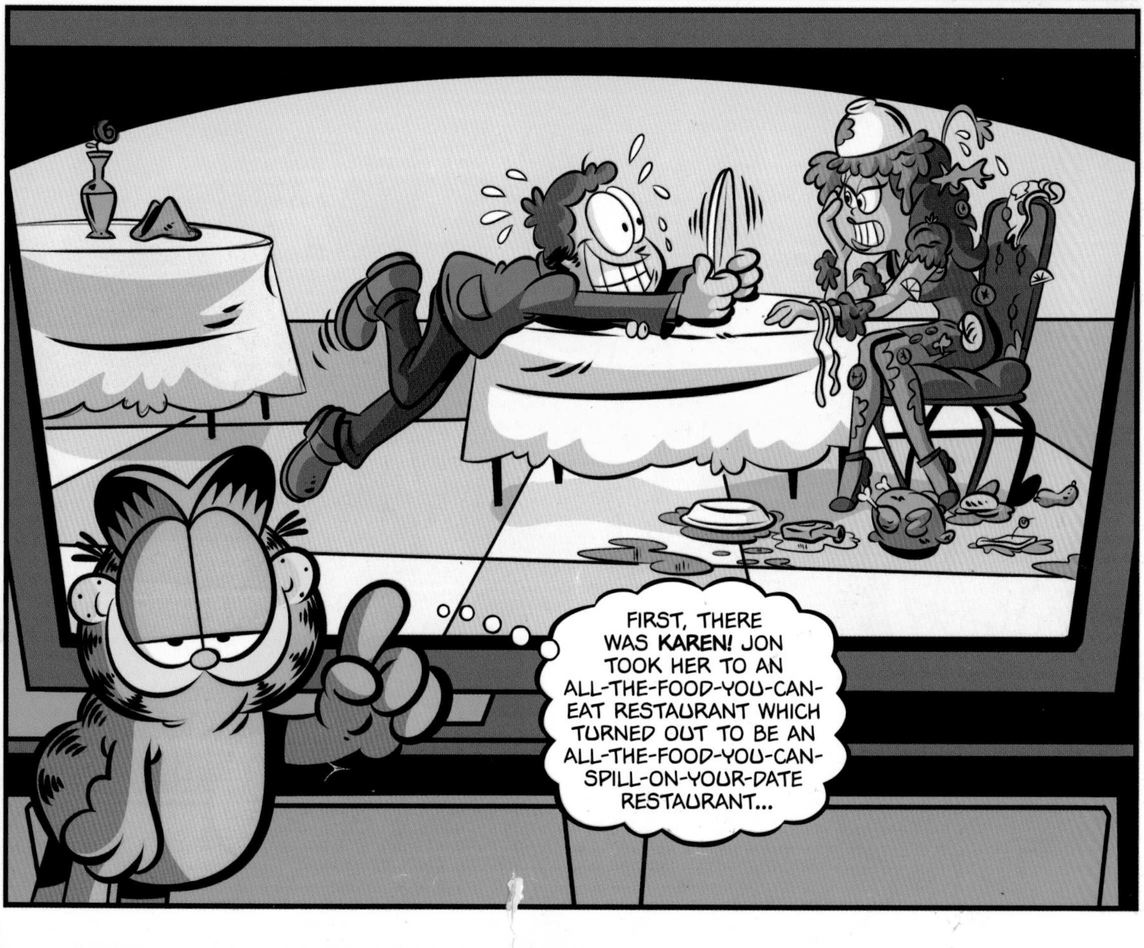
FIRST, THERE WAS KAREN! JON TOOK HER TO AN ALL-THE-FOOD-YOU-CAN-EAT RESTAURANT WHICH TURNED OUT TO BE AN ALL-THE-FOOD-YOU-CAN-SPILL-ON-YOUR-DATE RESTAURANT...

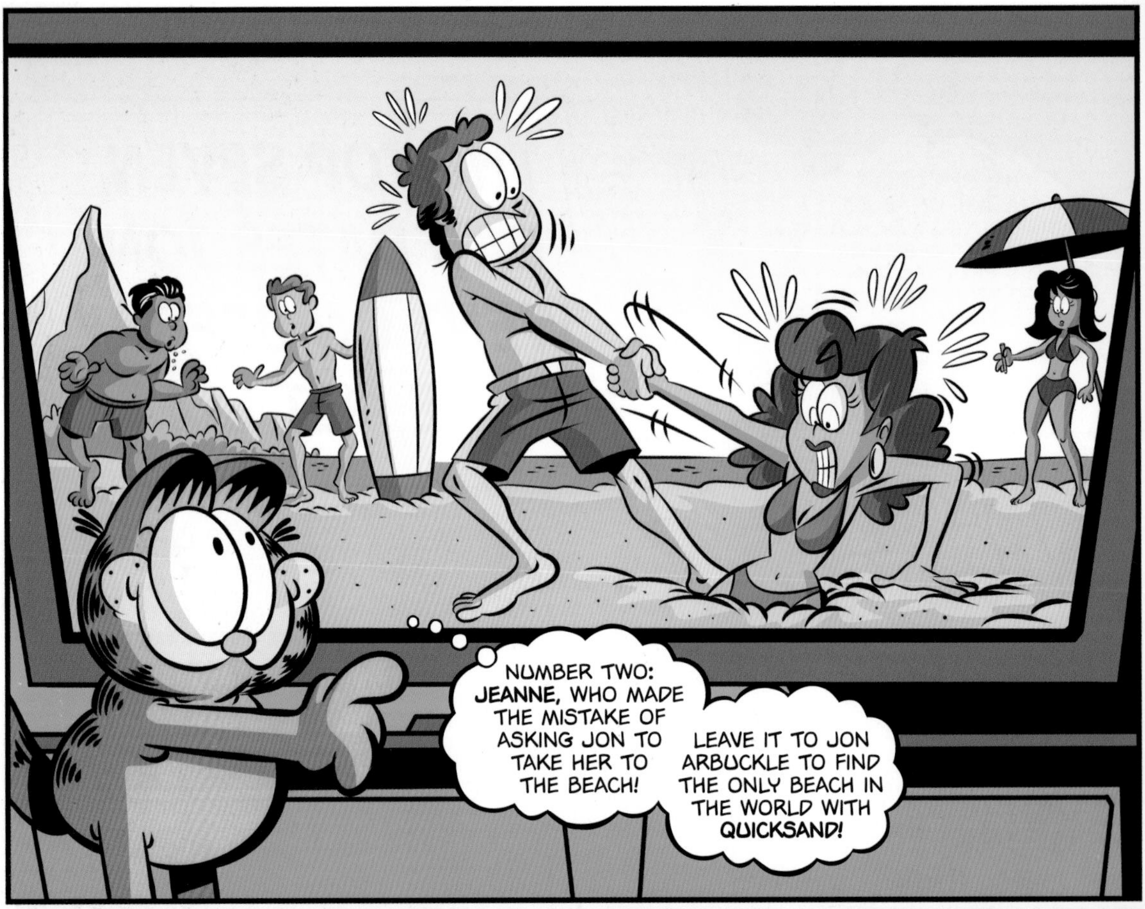
NUMBER TWO: **JEANNE**, WHO MADE THE MISTAKE OF ASKING JON TO TAKE HER TO THE BEACH!
LEAVE IT TO JON ARBUCKLE TO FIND THE ONLY BEACH IN THE WORLD WITH **QUICKSAND!**

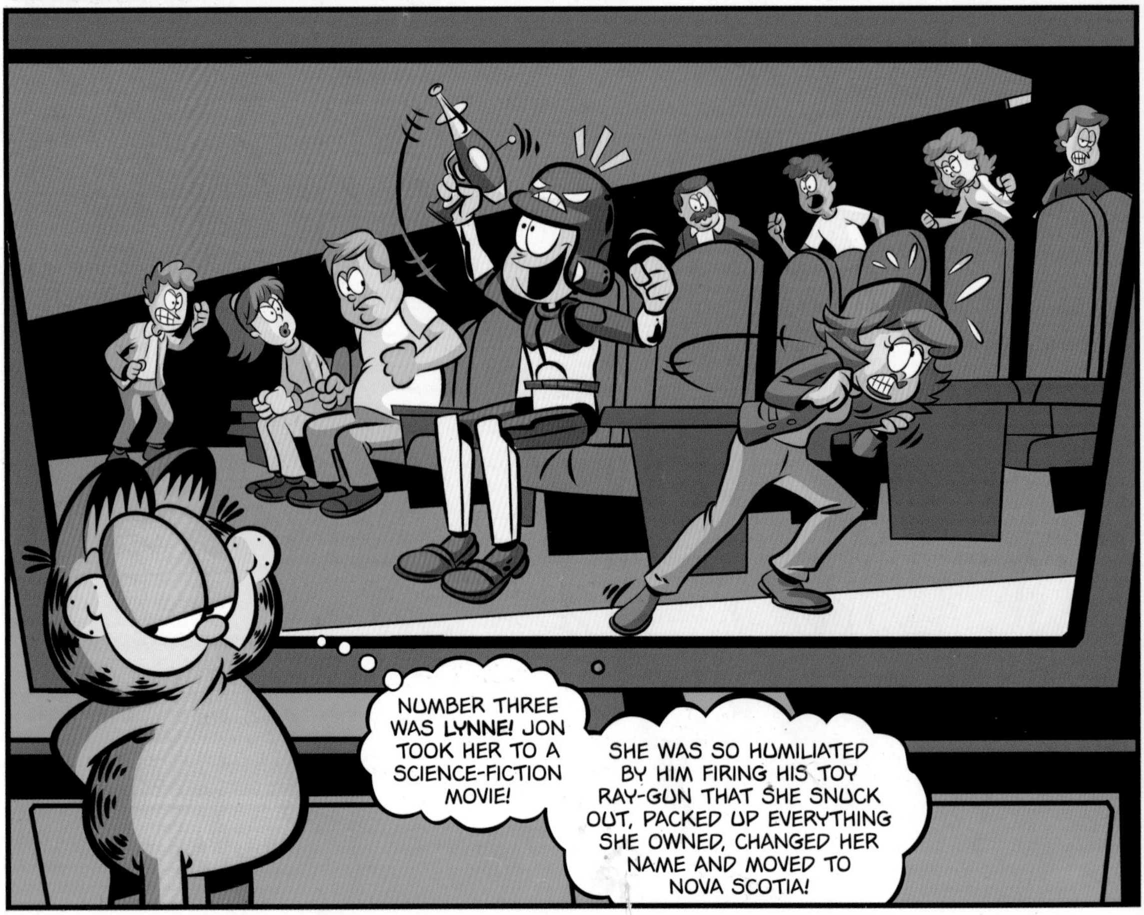
NUMBER THREE WAS **LYNNE!** JON TOOK HER TO A SCIENCE-FICTION MOVIE!
SHE WAS SO HUMILIATED BY HIM FIRING HIS TOY RAY-GUN THAT SHE SNUCK OUT, PACKED UP EVERYTHING SHE OWNED, CHANGED HER NAME AND MOVED TO NOVA SCOTIA!

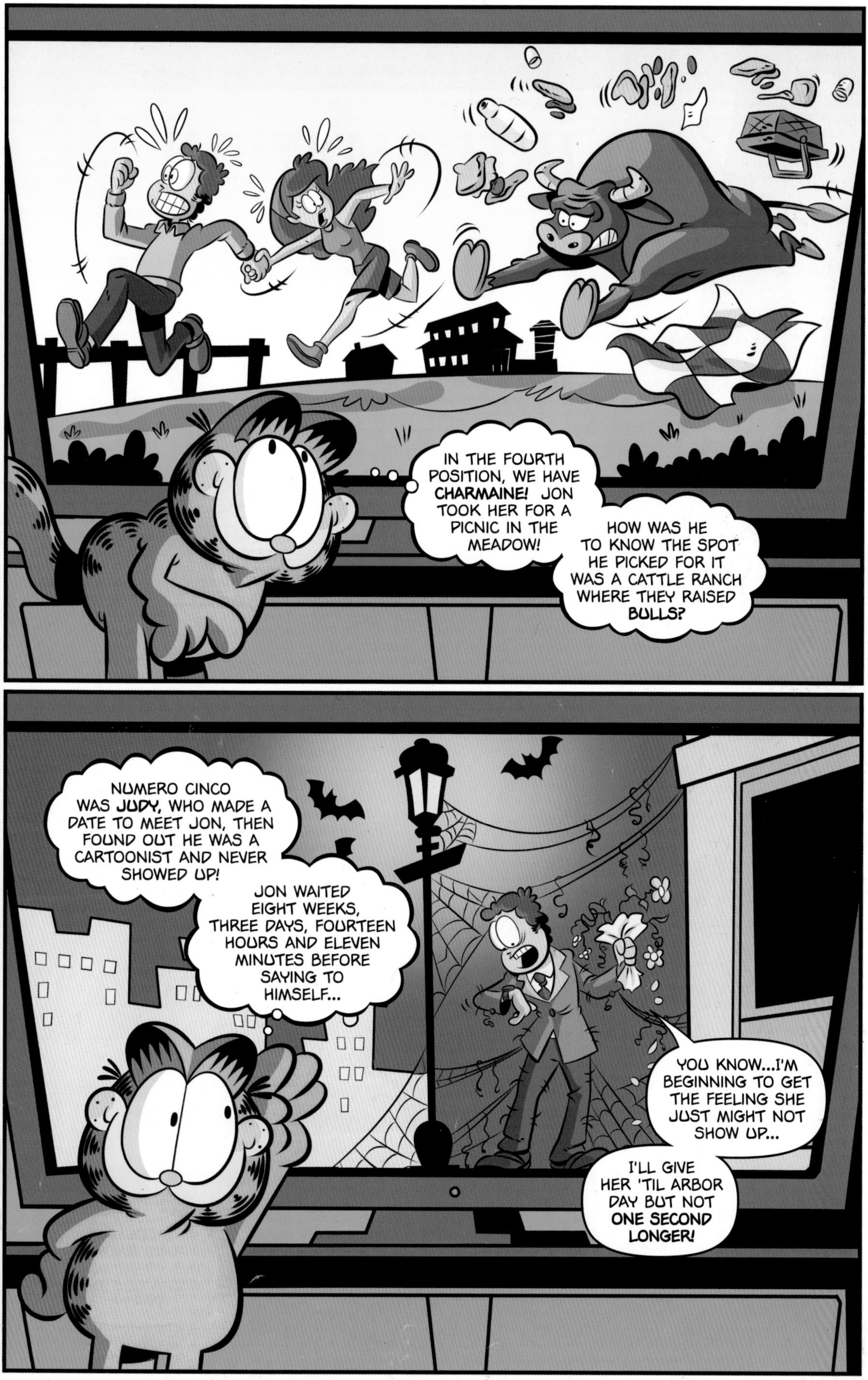
IN THE FOURTH POSITION, WE HAVE CHARMAINE! JON TOOK HER FOR A PICNIC IN THE MEADOW!
HOW WAS HE TO KNOW THE SPOT HE PICKED FOR IT WAS A CATTLE RANCH WHERE THEY RAISED BULLS?
NUMERO CINCO WAS JUDY, WHO MADE A DATE TO MEET JON, THEN FOUND OUT HE WAS A CARTOONIST AND NEVER SHOWED UP!
JON WAITED EIGHT WEEKS, THREE DAYS, FOURTEEN HOURS AND ELEVEN MINUTES BEFORE SAYING TO HIMSELF...
YOU KNOW...I'M BEGINNING TO GET THE FEELING SHE JUST MIGHT NOT SHOW UP...
I'LL GIVE HER 'TIL ARBOR DAY BUT NOT ONE SECOND LONGER!

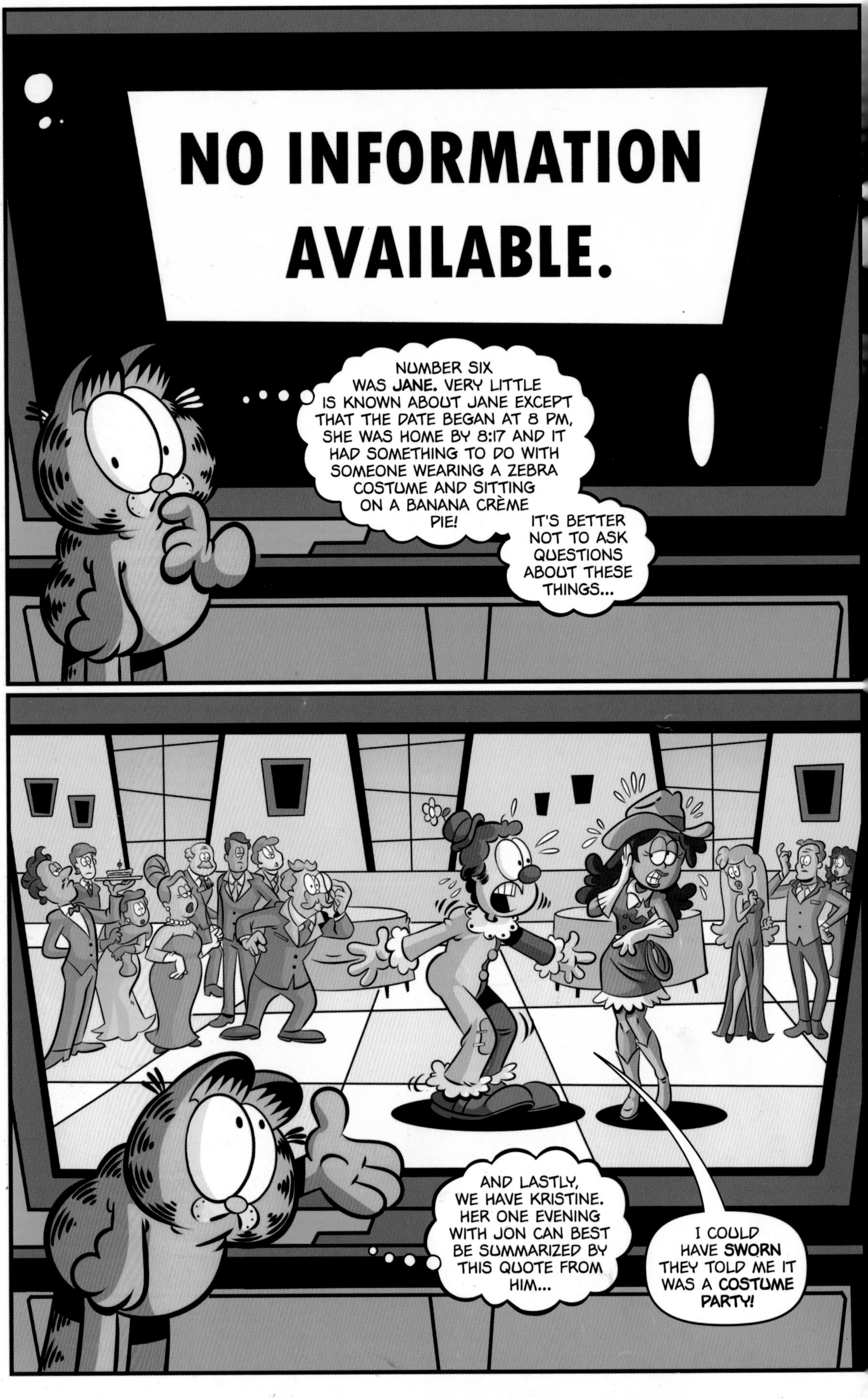
NO INFORMATION AVAILABLE.
NUMBER SIX WAS JANE. VERY LITTLE IS KNOWN ABOUT JANE EXCEPT THAT THE DATE BEGAN AT 8 PM, SHE WAS HOME BY 8:17 AND IT HAD SOMETHING TO DO WITH SOMEONE WEARING A ZEBRA COSTUME AND SITTING ON A BANANA CRÈME PIE!
IT'S BETTER NOT TO ASK QUESTIONS ABOUT THESE THINGS...
AND LASTLY, WE HAVE KRISTINE. HER ONE EVENING WITH JON CAN BEST BE SUMMARIZED BY THIS QUOTE FROM HIM...
I COULD HAVE SWORN THEY TOLD ME IT WAS A COSTUME PARTY!

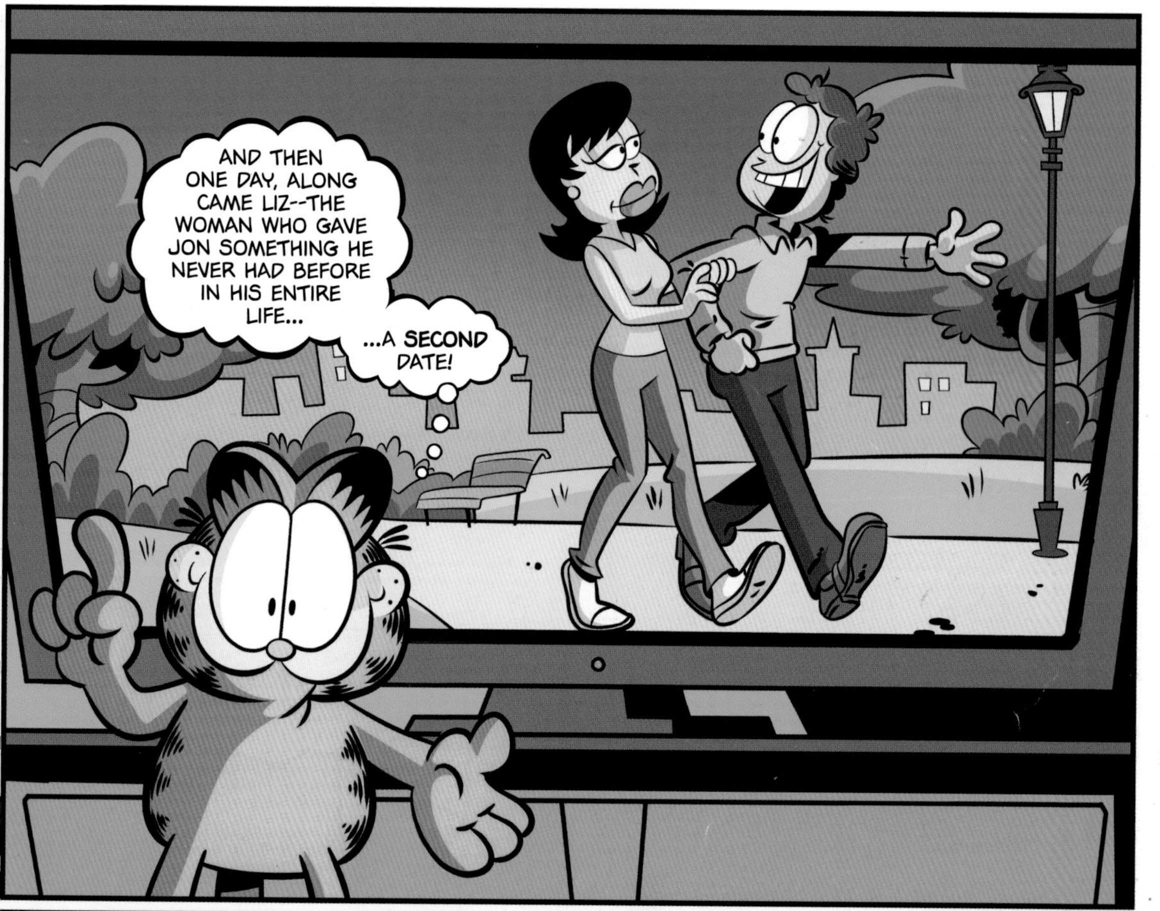
AND THEN ONE DAY, ALONG CAME LIZ--THE WOMAN WHO GAVE JON SOMETHING HE NEVER HAD BEFORE IN HIS ENTIRE LIFE...
...A **SECOND** DATE!
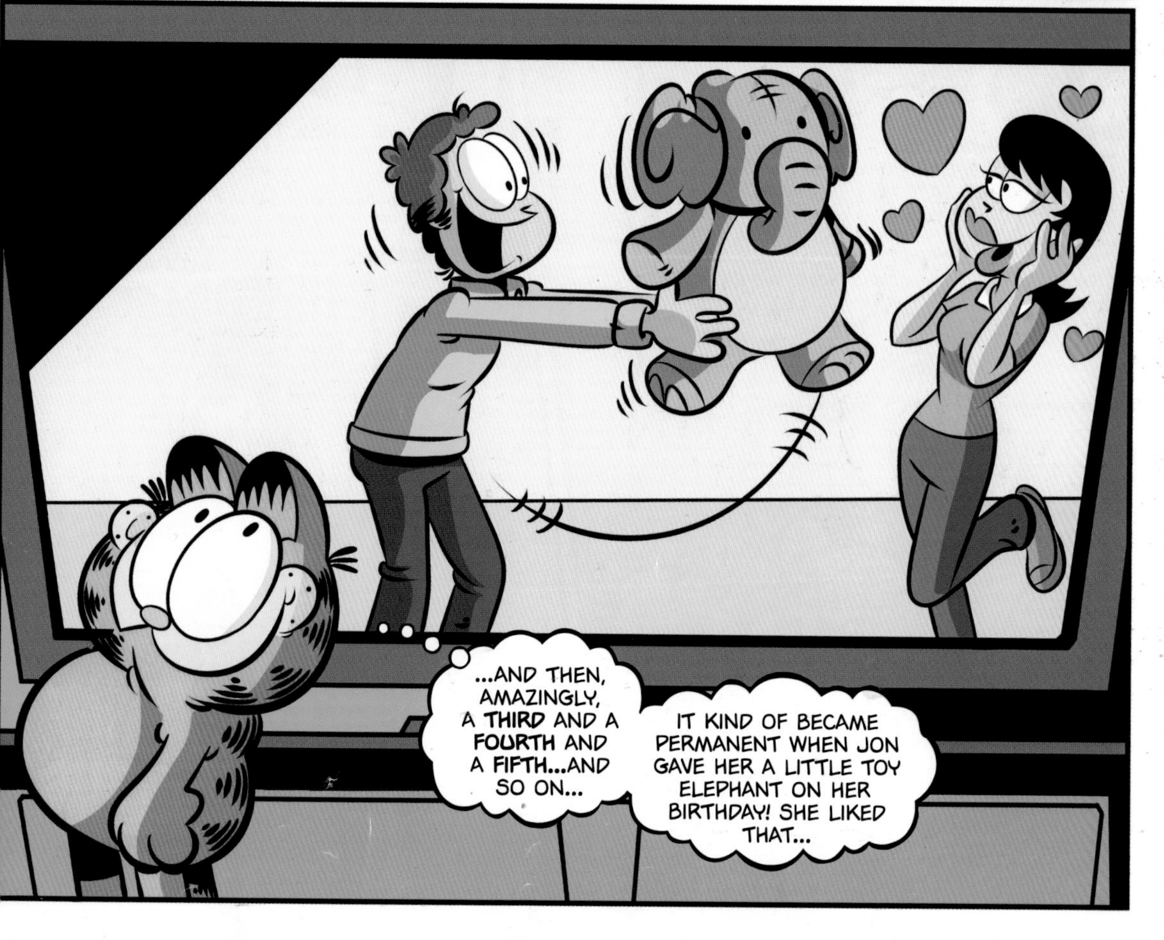
...AND THEN, AMAZINGLY, A **THIRD** AND A **FOURTH** AND A **FIFTH**...AND SO ON...
IT KIND OF BECAME PERMANENT WHEN JON GAVE HER A LITTLE TOY ELEPHANT ON HER BIRTHDAY! SHE LIKED THAT...

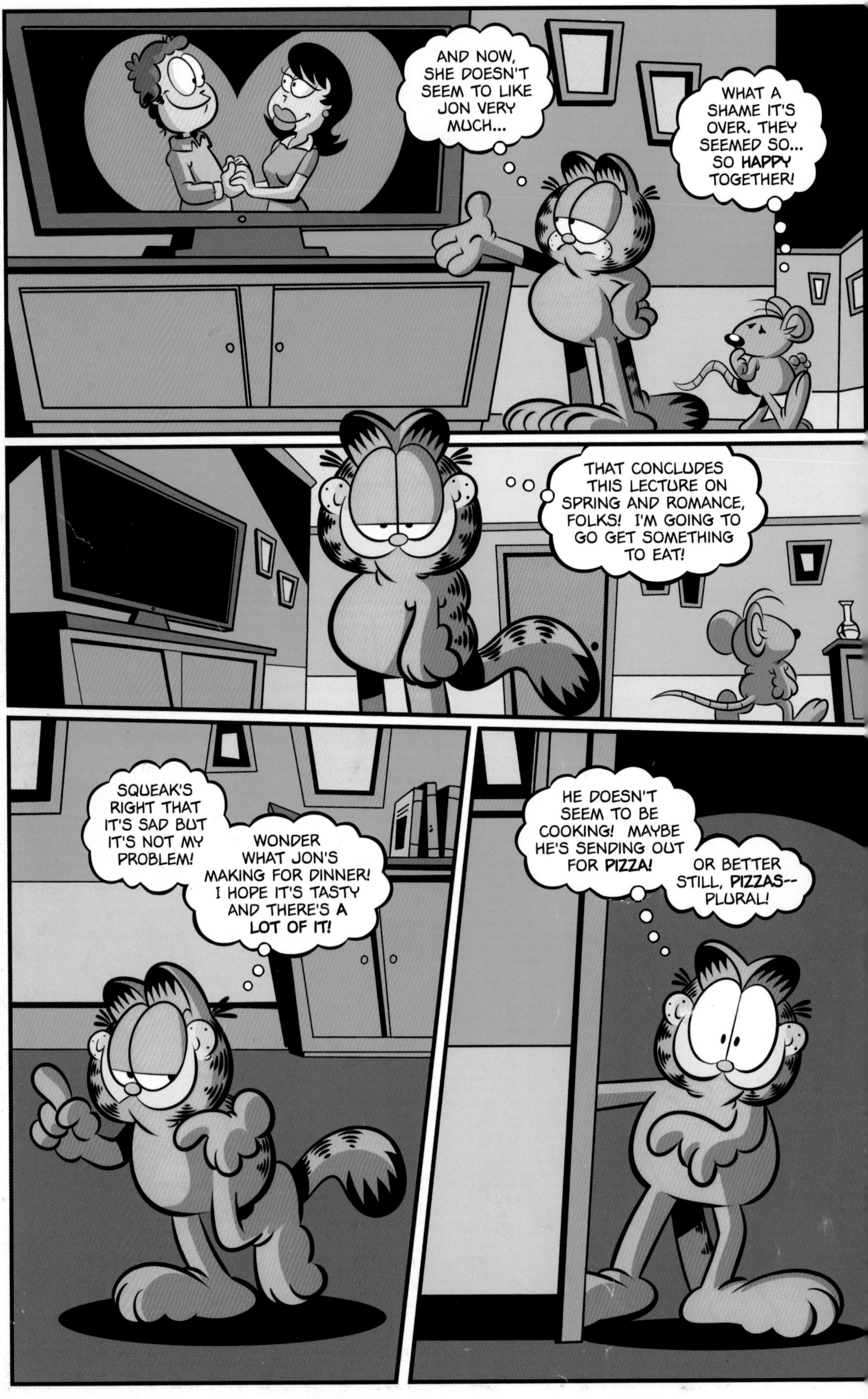

AND NOW, SHE DOESN'T SEEM TO LIKE JON VERY MUCH...
WHAT A SHAME IT'S OVER. THEY SEEMED SO... SO HAPPY TOGETHER!
THAT CONCLUDES THIS LECTURE ON SPRING AND ROMANCE, FOLKS! I'M GOING TO GO GET SOMETHING TO EAT!
SQUEAK'S RIGHT THAT IT'S SAD BUT IT'S NOT MY PROBLEM!
WONDER WHAT JON'S MAKING FOR DINNER! I HOPE IT'S TASTY AND THERE'S A LOT OF IT!
HE DOESN'T SEEM TO BE COOKING! MAYBE HE'S SENDING OUT FOR PIZZA!
OR BETTER STILL, PIZZAS--PLURAL!

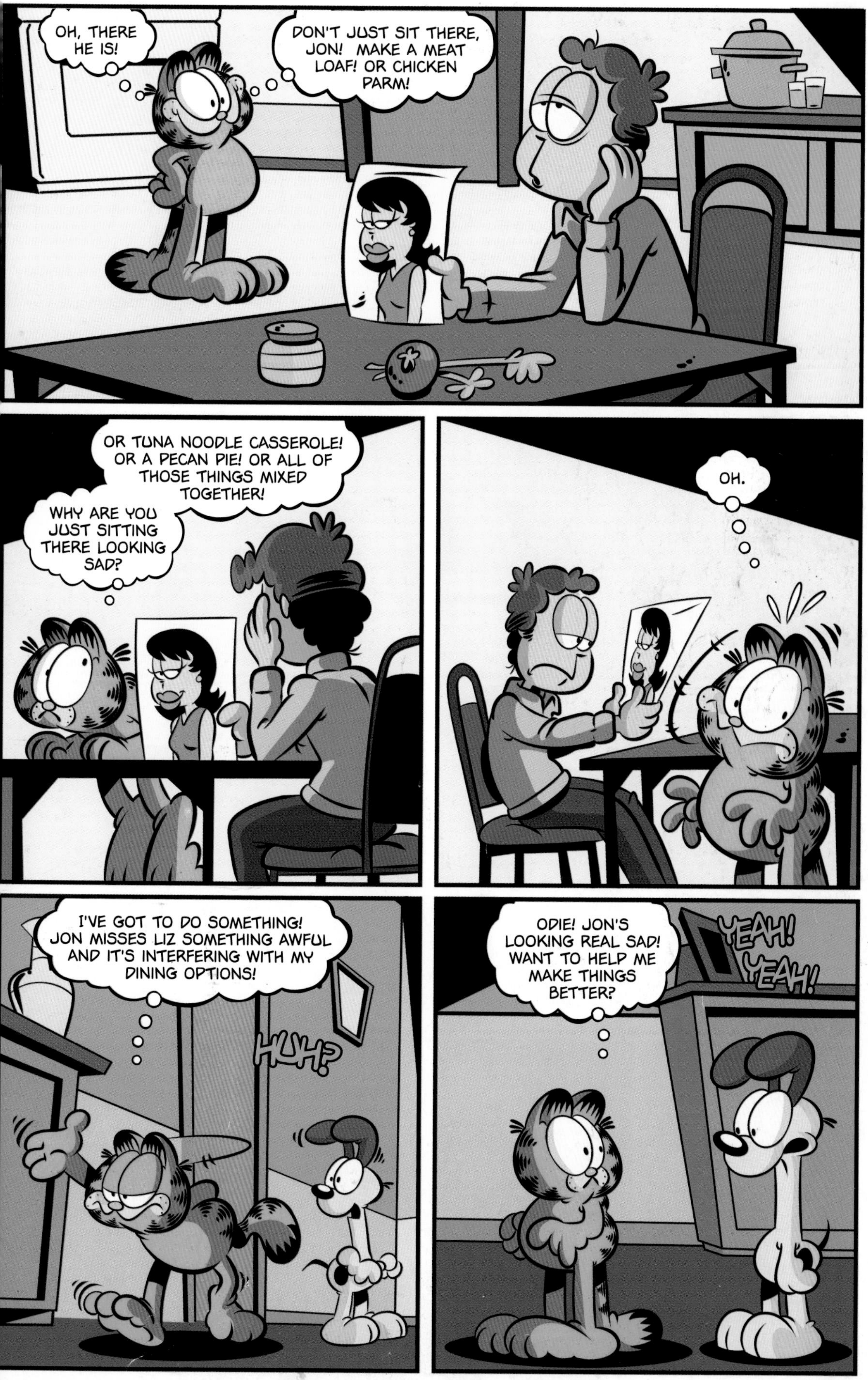
OH, THERE HE IS!
DON'T JUST SIT THERE, JON! MAKE A MEAT LOAF! OR CHICKEN PARM!
OR TUNA NOODLE CASSEROLE! OR A PECAN PIE! OR ALL OF THOSE THINGS MIXED TOGETHER!
WHY ARE YOU JUST SITTING THERE LOOKING SAD?
OH.
I'VE GOT TO DO SOMETHING! JON MISSES LIZ SOMETHING AWFUL AND IT'S INTERFERING WITH MY DINING OPTIONS!
HUH?
ODIE! JON'S LOOKING REAL SAD! WANT TO HELP ME MAKE THINGS BETTER?
YEAH! YEAH!

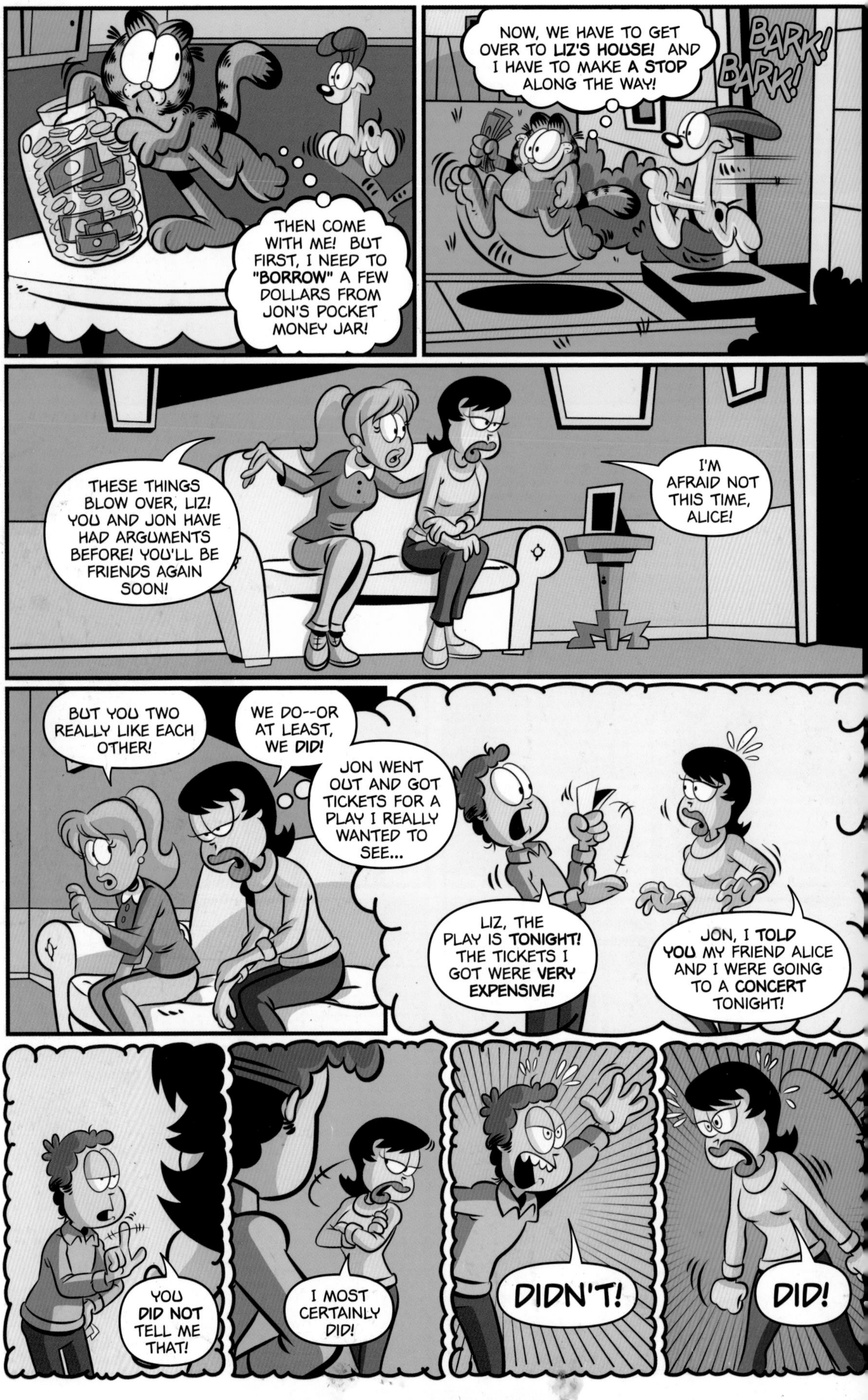
THEN COME WITH ME! BUT FIRST, I NEED TO "BORROW" A FEW DOLLARS FROM JON'S POCKET MONEY JAR!
NOW, WE HAVE TO GET OVER TO LIZ'S HOUSE! AND I HAVE TO MAKE A STOP ALONG THE WAY!
BARK! BARK!
THESE THINGS BLOW OVER, LIZ! YOU AND JON HAVE HAD ARGUMENTS BEFORE! YOU'LL BE FRIENDS AGAIN SOON!
I'M AFRAID NOT THIS TIME, ALICE!
BUT YOU TWO REALLY LIKE EACH OTHER!
WE DO--OR AT LEAST, WE DID!
JON WENT OUT AND GOT TICKETS FOR A PLAY I REALLY WANTED TO SEE...
LIZ, THE PLAY IS TONIGHT! THE TICKETS I GOT WERE VERY EXPENSIVE!
JON, I TOLD YOU MY FRIEND ALICE AND I WERE GOING TO A CONCERT TONIGHT!
YOU DID NOT TELL ME THAT!
I MOST CERTAINLY DID!
DIDN'T!
DID!

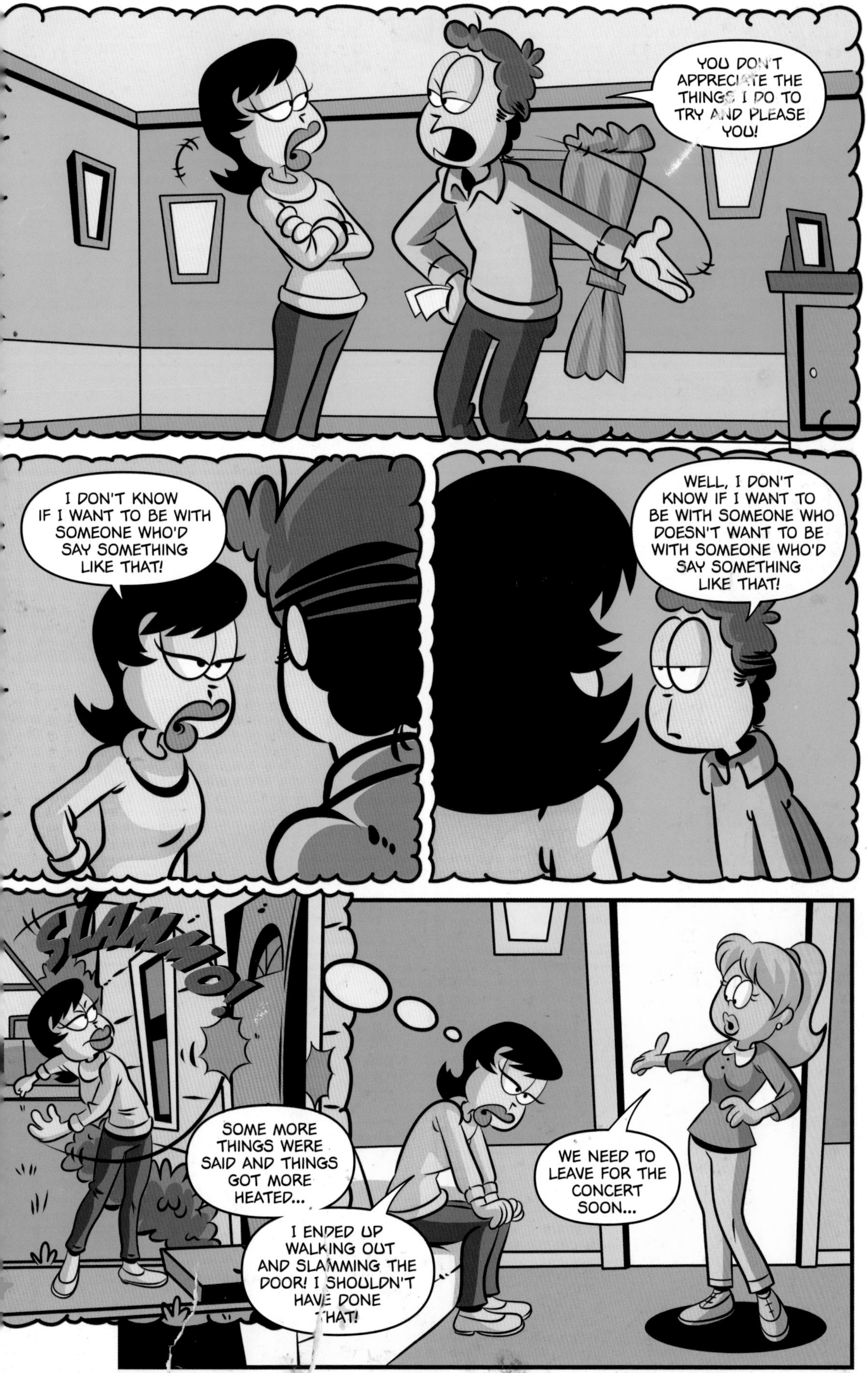
YOU DON'T APPRECIATE THE THINGS I DO TO TRY AND PLEASE YOU!
I DON'T KNOW IF I WANT TO BE WITH SOMEONE WHO'D SAY SOMETHING LIKE THAT!
WELL, I DON'T KNOW IF I WANT TO BE WITH SOMEONE WHO DOESN'T WANT TO BE WITH SOMEONE WHO'D SAY SOMETHING LIKE THAT!
SLAMMO!
SOME MORE THINGS WERE SAID AND THINGS GOT MORE HEATED...
I ENDED UP WALKING OUT AND SLAMMING THE DOOR! I SHOULDN'T HAVE DONE THAT!
WE NEED TO LEAVE FOR THE CONCERT SOON...

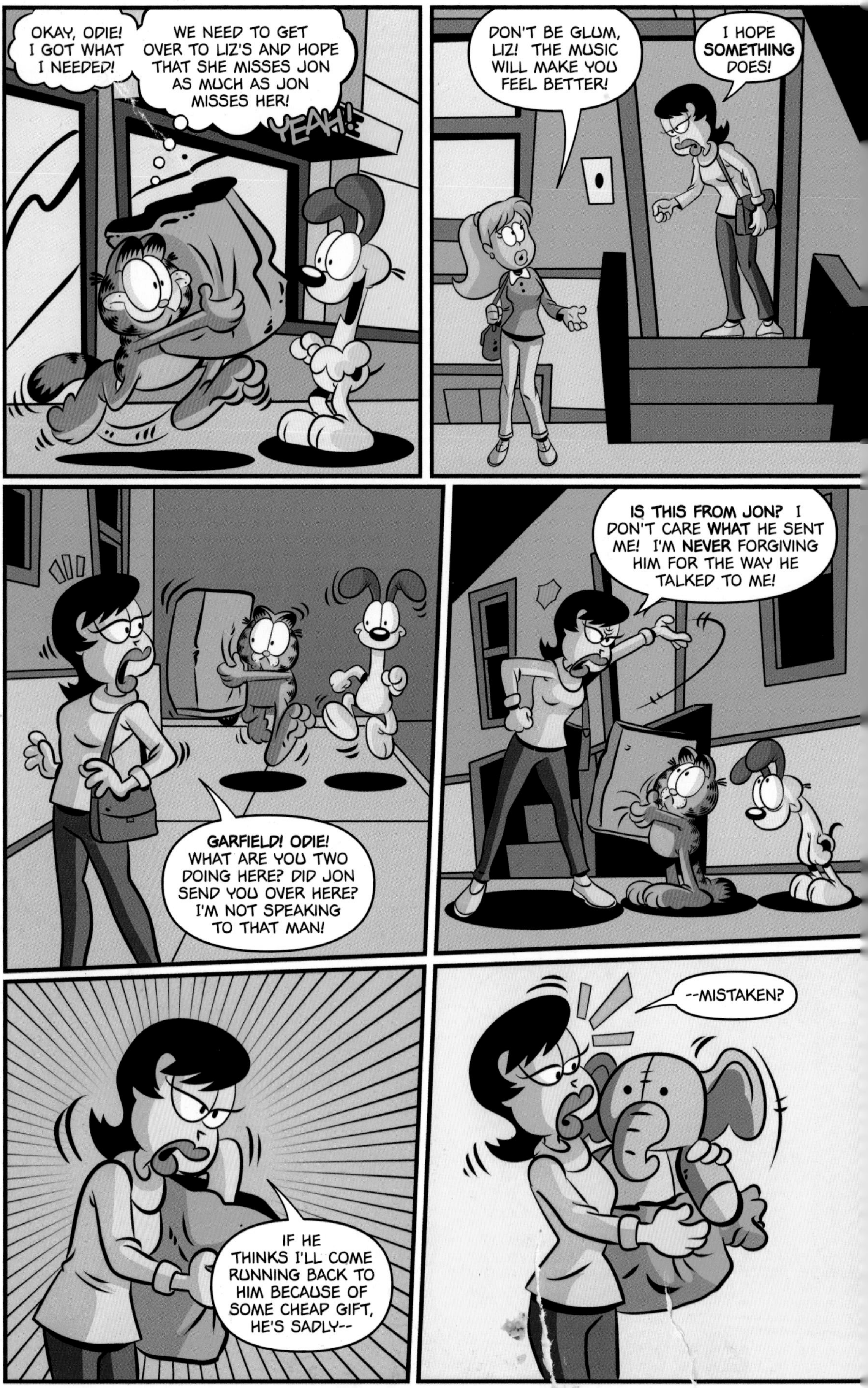

OKAY, ODIE! I GOT WHAT I NEEDED!
WE NEED TO GET OVER TO LIZ'S AND HOPE THAT SHE MISSES JON AS MUCH AS JON MISSES HER!
YEAH!
DON'T BE GLUM, LIZ! THE MUSIC WILL MAKE YOU FEEL BETTER!
I HOPE SOMETHING DOES!
GARFIELD! ODIE! WHAT ARE YOU TWO DOING HERE? DID JON SEND YOU OVER HERE? I'M NOT SPEAKING TO THAT MAN!
IS THIS FROM JON? I DON'T CARE WHAT HE SENT ME! I'M NEVER FORGIVING HIM FOR THE WAY HE TALKED TO ME!
IF HE THINKS I'LL COME RUNNING BACK TO HIM BECAUSE OF SOME CHEAP GIFT, HE'S SADLY--
--MISTAKEN?

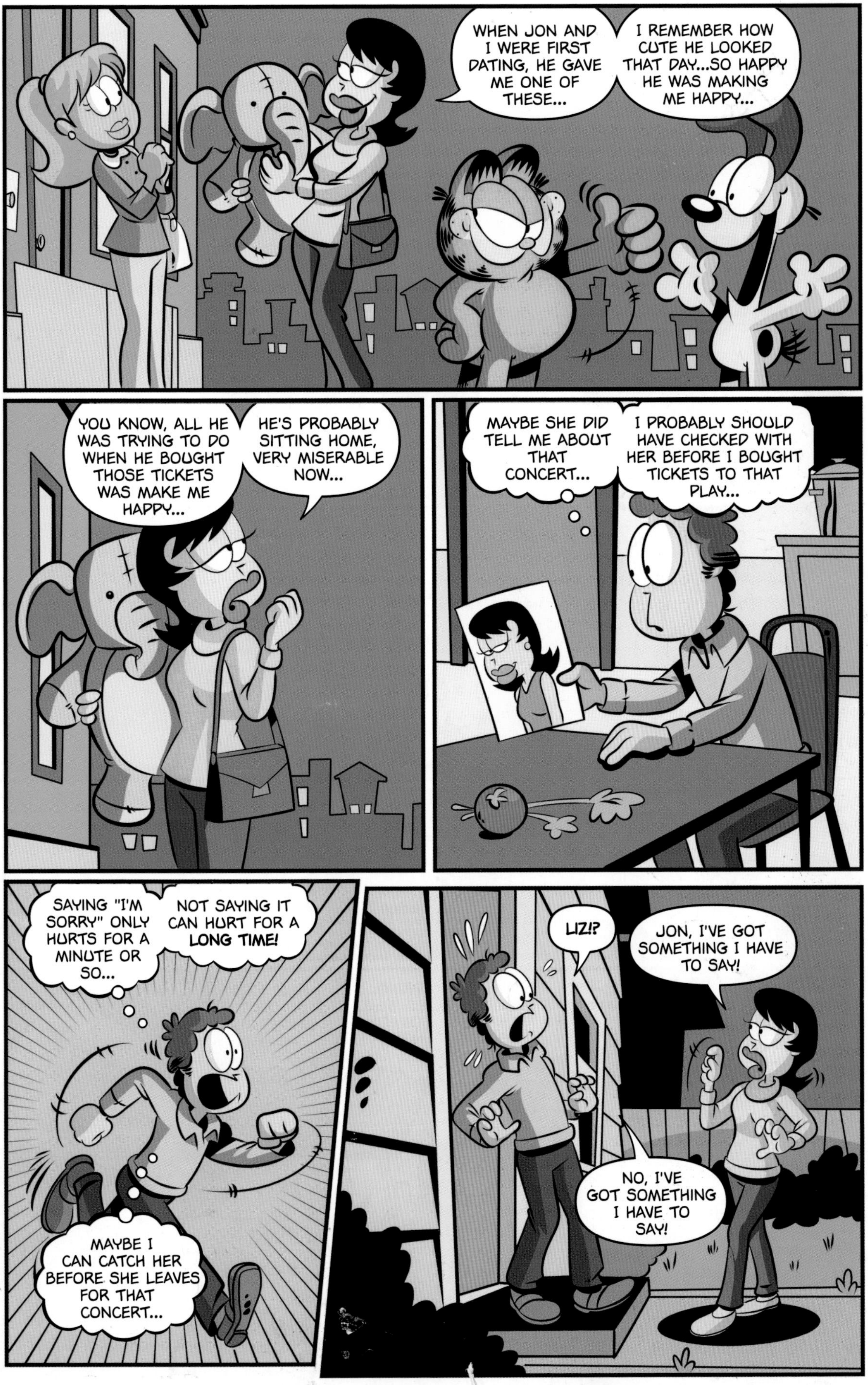
WHEN JON AND I WERE FIRST DATING, HE GAVE ME ONE OF THESE...
I REMEMBER HOW CUTE HE LOOKED THAT DAY...SO HAPPY HE WAS MAKING ME HAPPY...
YOU KNOW, ALL HE WAS TRYING TO DO WHEN HE BOUGHT THOSE TICKETS WAS MAKE ME HAPPY...
HE'S PROBABLY SITTING HOME, VERY MISERABLE NOW...
MAYBE SHE DID TELL ME ABOUT THAT CONCERT...
I PROBABLY SHOULD HAVE CHECKED WITH HER BEFORE I BOUGHT TICKETS TO THAT PLAY...
SAYING "I'M SORRY" ONLY HURTS FOR A MINUTE OR SO...
NOT SAYING IT CAN HURT FOR A **LONG TIME!**
MAYBE I CAN CATCH HER BEFORE SHE LEAVES FOR THAT CONCERT...
LIZ!?
JON, I'VE GOT SOMETHING I HAVE TO SAY!
NO, I'VE GOT SOMETHING I HAVE TO SAY!

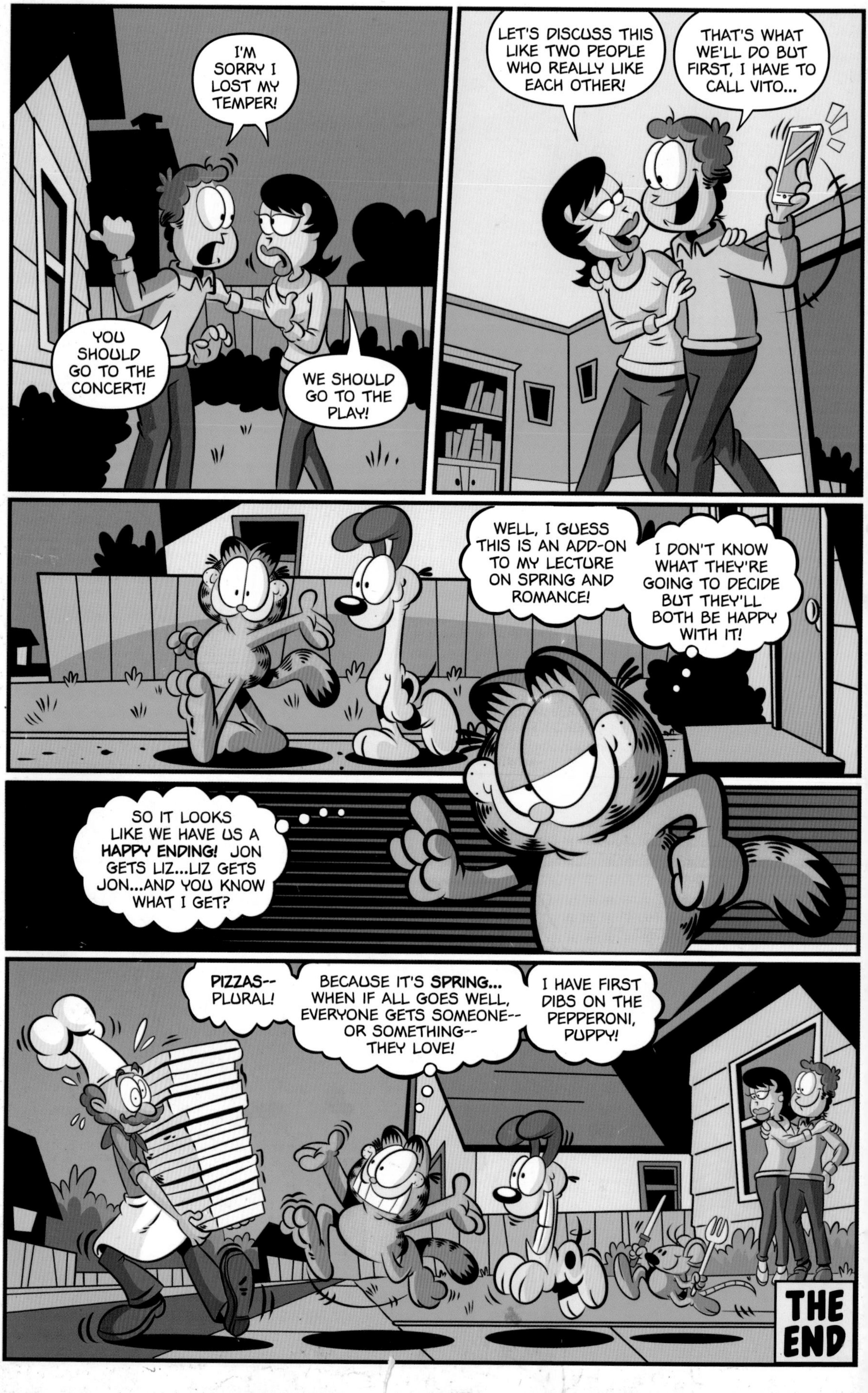
I'M SORRY I LOST MY TEMPER!
YOU SHOULD GO TO THE CONCERT!
WE SHOULD GO TO THE PLAY!
LET'S DISCUSS THIS LIKE TWO PEOPLE WHO REALLY LIKE EACH OTHER!
THAT'S WHAT WE'LL DO BUT FIRST, I HAVE TO CALL VITO...
WELL, I GUESS THIS IS AN ADD-ON TO MY LECTURE ON SPRING AND ROMANCE!
I DON'T KNOW WHAT THEY'RE GOING TO DECIDE BUT THEY'LL BOTH BE HAPPY WITH IT!
SO IT LOOKS LIKE WE HAVE US A **HAPPY ENDING!** JON GETS LIZ...LIZ GETS JON...AND YOU KNOW WHAT I GET?
PIZZAS--PLURAL!
BECAUSE IT'S **SPRING...** WHEN IF ALL GOES WELL, EVERYONE GETS SOMEONE--OR SOMETHING--THEY LOVE!
I HAVE FIRST DIBS ON THE PEPPERONI, PUPPY!
THE END

Garfield Sunday Classics

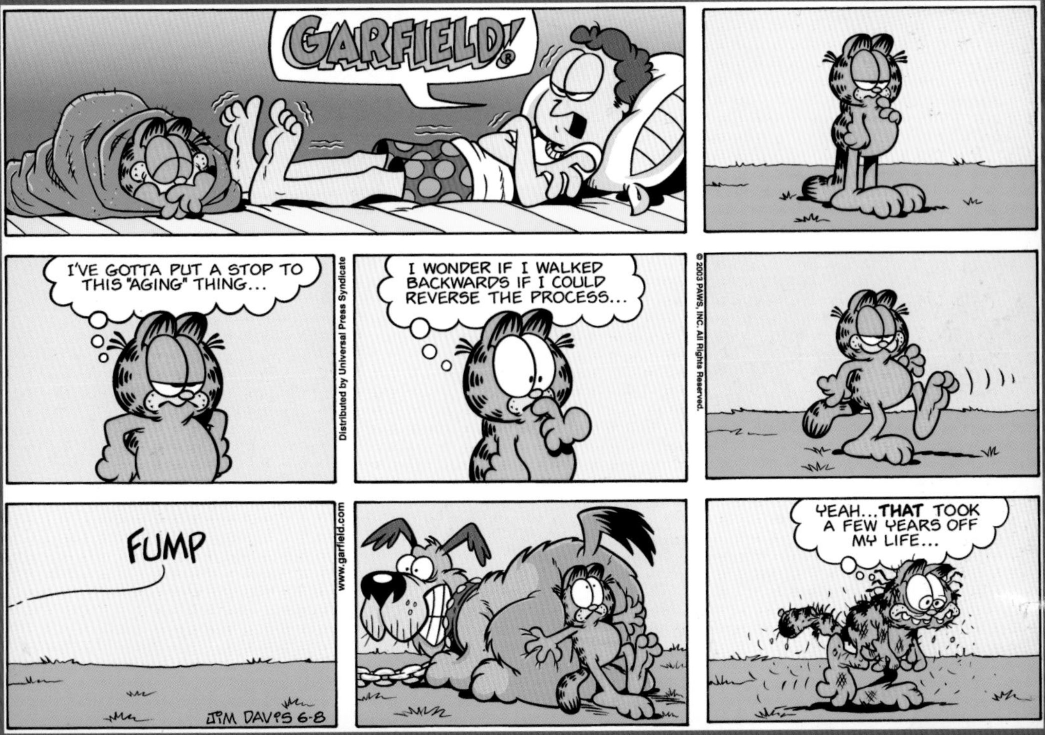
GARFIELD!
I'VE GOTTA PUT A STOP TO THIS "AGING" THING...
Distributed by Universal Press Syndicate
I WONDER IF I WALKED BACKWARDS IF I COULD REVERSE THE PROCESS...
© 2003 PAWS, INC. All Rights Reserved.
FUMP
JIM DAVIS 6-8
www.garfield.com
YEAH...THAT TOOK A FEW YEARS OFF MY LIFE...

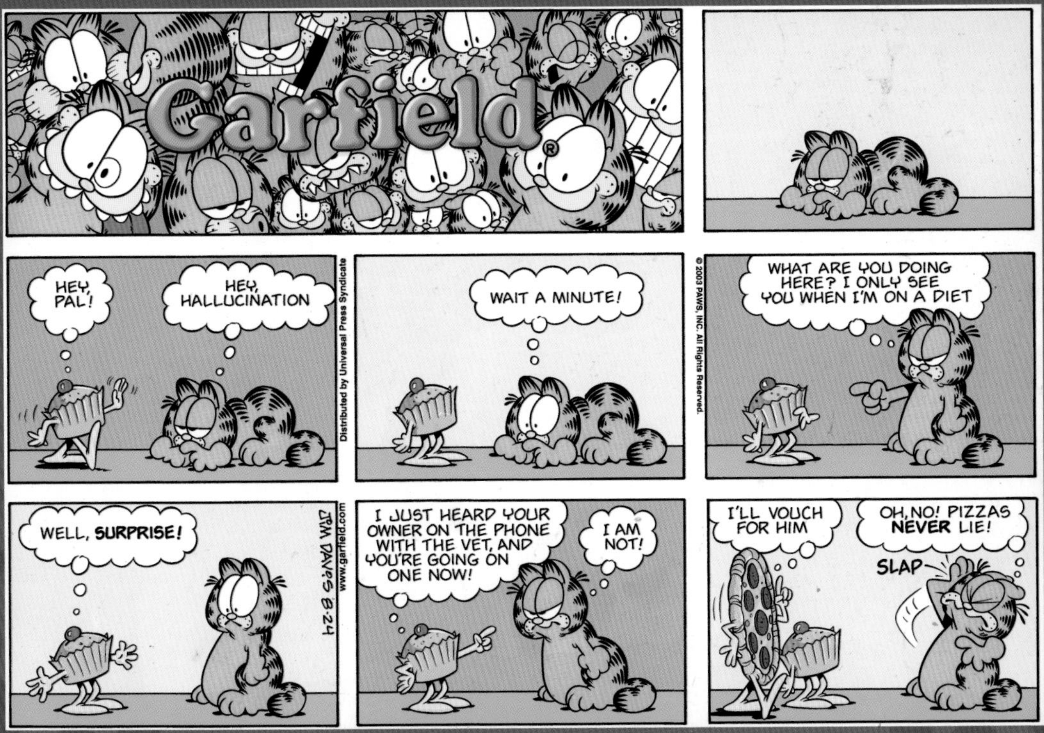
Garfield
www.garfield.com
HEY, PAL!
HEY, HALLUCINATION
Distributed by Universal Press Syndicate
WAIT A MINUTE!
© 2003 PAWS, INC. All Rights Reserved.
WHAT ARE YOU DOING HERE? I ONLY SEE YOU WHEN I'M ON A DIET
WELL, SURPRISE!
JIM DAVIS 8-24
www.garfield.com
I JUST HEARD YOUR OWNER ON THE PHONE WITH THE VET, AND YOU'RE GOING ON ONE NOW!
I AM NOT!
I'LL VOUCH FOR HIM
OH, NO! PIZZAS NEVER LIE!
SLAP

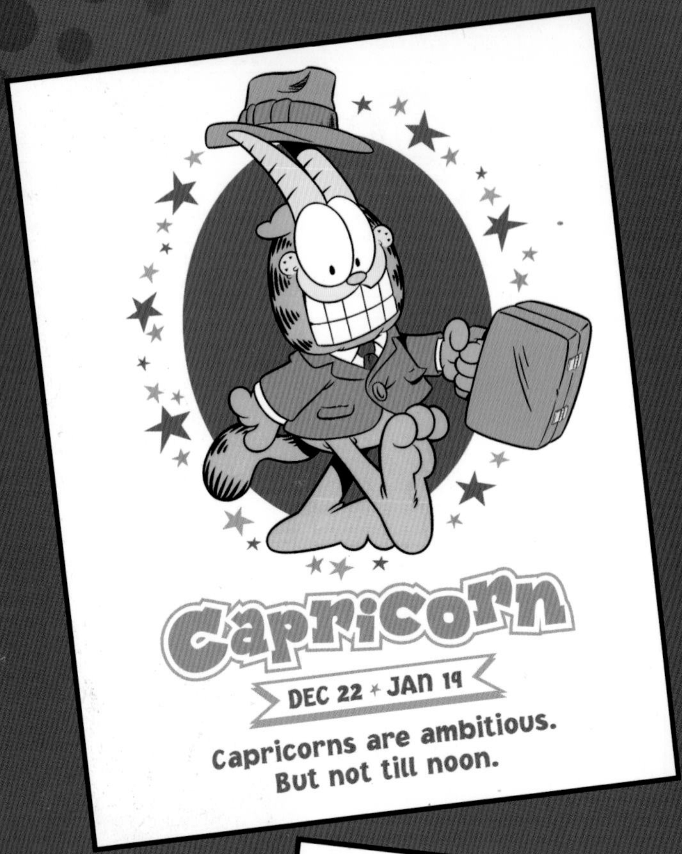
Capricorn
DEC 22 ★ JAN 19
Capricorns are ambitious.
But not till noon.

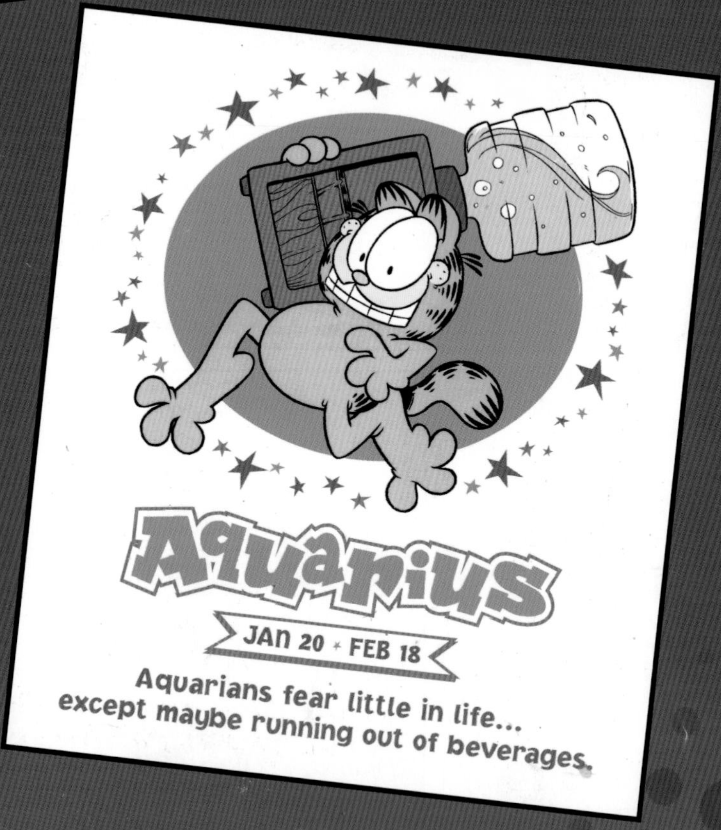
Aquarius
JAN 20 ★ FEB 18
Aquarians fear little in life...
except maybe running out of beverages.

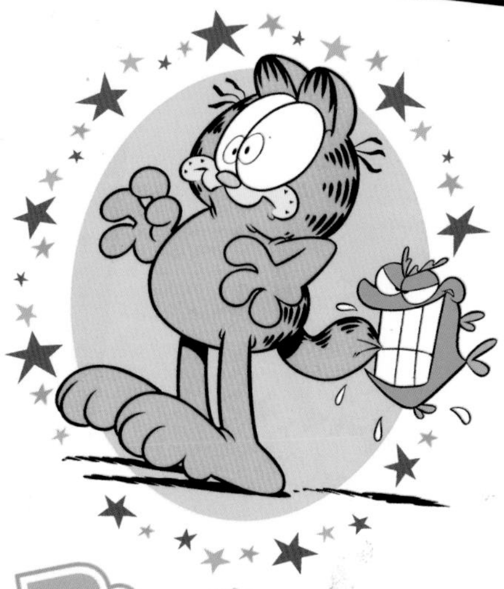

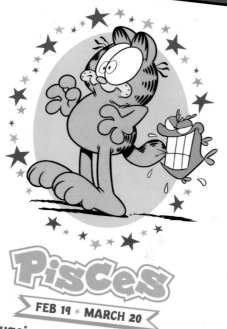

Pisces

FEB 19 ★ MARCH 20

Easygoing, Pisces will join a gym when they put in a dessert bar.

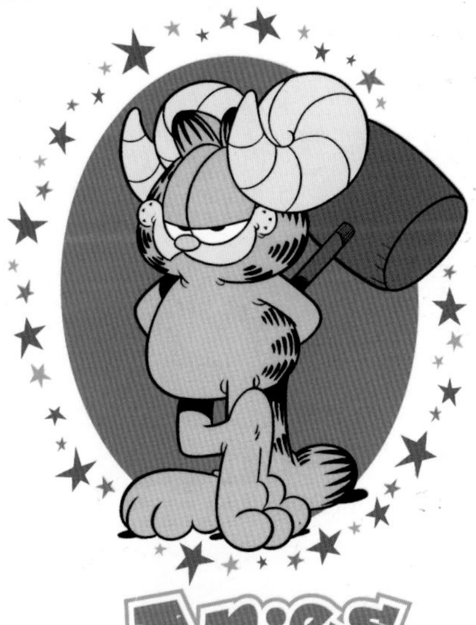

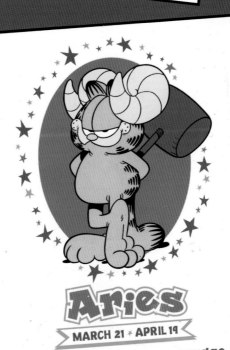

Aries

MARCH 21 ★ APRIL 19

An Aries never holds a grudge. They get even right away.

Taurus

APRIL 20 * MAY 20

Straightforward, Taurus always gives two choices: take it or leave it.

Gemini

MAY 21 * JUNE 20

Geminis believe in half the work and twice the fun!

Cancer

JUNE 21 * JULY 22

Cancers prefer the domestic joys...
family, security, and
a well-stocked refrigerator.

Leo

JULY 23 * AUG 22

Leos are brave and loyal, kind and caring.
Their generosity is exceeded only by the
size of their credit-card bills.

Virgo

AUG 23 ✦ SEPT 22

Industrious and meticulous,
Virgos always do a good job...
and look good doing it.

Libra

SEPT 23 ✦ OCT 22

Fiercely independent,
Libras hate rules...
especially limits on dessert.

Scorpio

OCT 23 ✦ NOV 21

Scorpios can resist temptation, but they'd rather not.

Sagittarius

NOV 22 ✦ DEC 21

Expressive and sincere (whether they mean it or not), Sagittarians have a voracious appetite for life.

Ask a Dog

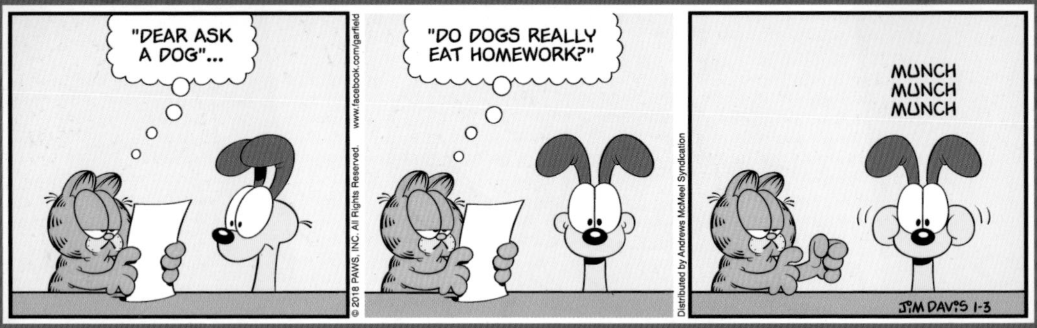
"DEAR ASK A DOG"...
"DO DOGS REALLY EAT HOMEWORK?"
MUNCH MUNCH MUNCH
© 2018 PAWS, INC. All Rights Reserved. www.facebook.com/garfield
Distributed by Andrews McMeel Syndication
JIM DAVIS 1-3

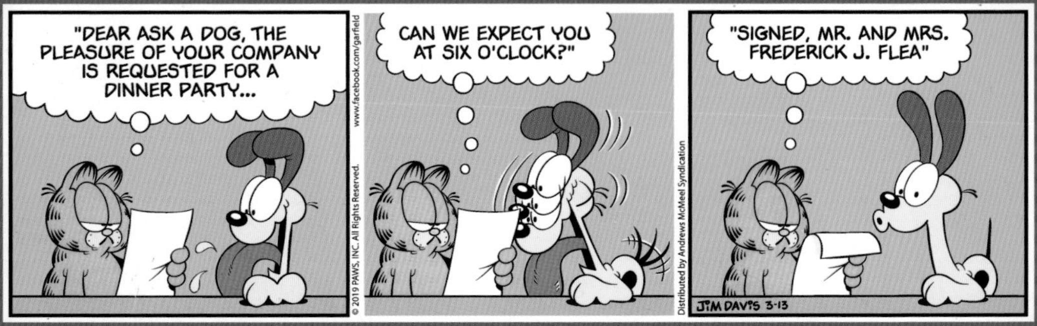
"DEAR ASK A DOG, THE PLEASURE OF YOUR COMPANY IS REQUESTED FOR A DINNER PARTY...
CAN WE EXPECT YOU AT SIX O'CLOCK?"
"SIGNED, MR. AND MRS. FREDERICK J. FLEA"
© 2019 PAWS, INC. All Rights Reserved. www.facebook.com/garfield
Distributed by Andrews McMeel Syndication
JIM DAVIS 3-13

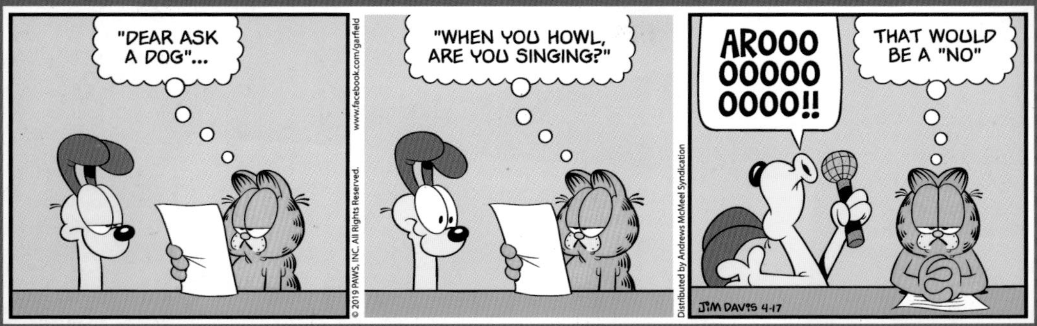
"DEAR ASK A DOG"...
"WHEN YOU HOWL, ARE YOU SINGING?"
AROOO OOOOO OOOO!!
THAT WOULD BE A "NO"
© 2019 PAWS, INC. All Rights Reserved. www.facebook.com/garfield
Distributed by Andrews McMeel Syndication
JIM DAVIS 4-17

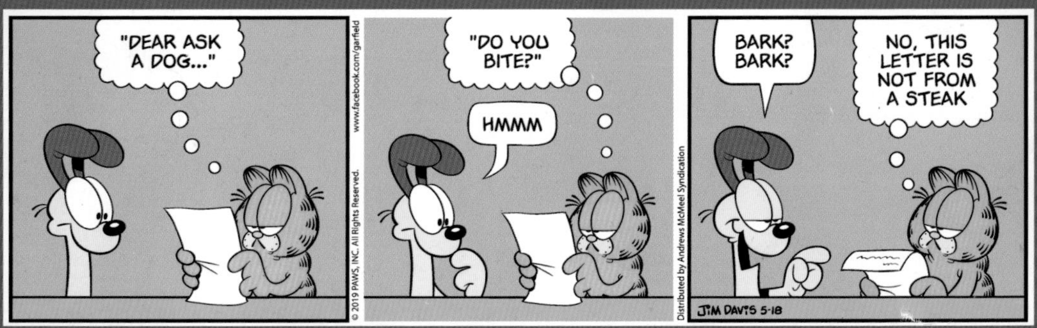
"DEAR ASK A DOG..."
"DO YOU BITE?"
HMMM
BARK? BARK?
NO, THIS LETTER IS NOT FROM A STEAK
© 2019 PAWS, INC. All Rights Reserved. www.facebook.com/garfield
Distributed by Andrews McMeel Syndication
JIM DAVIS 5-18

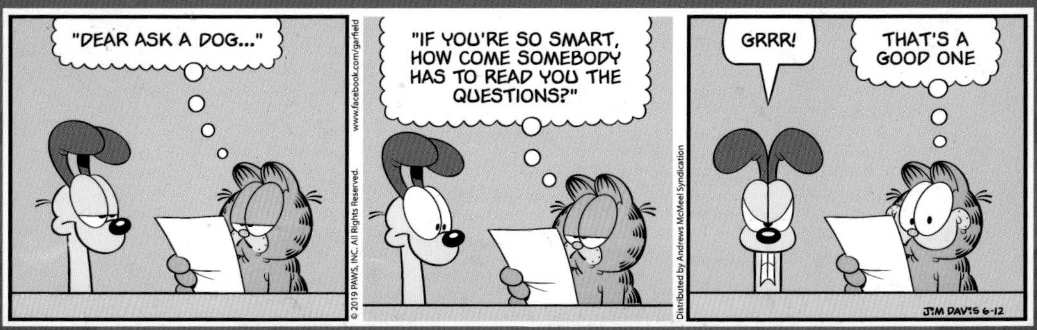
"DEAR ASK A DOG..."
"IF YOU'RE SO SMART, HOW COME SOMEBODY HAS TO READ YOU THE QUESTIONS?"
GRRR!
THAT'S A GOOD ONE
© 2019 PAWS, INC. All Rights Reserved. www.facebook.com/garfield
Distributed by Andrews McMeel Syndication
JIM DAVIS 6-12

Phone Fun

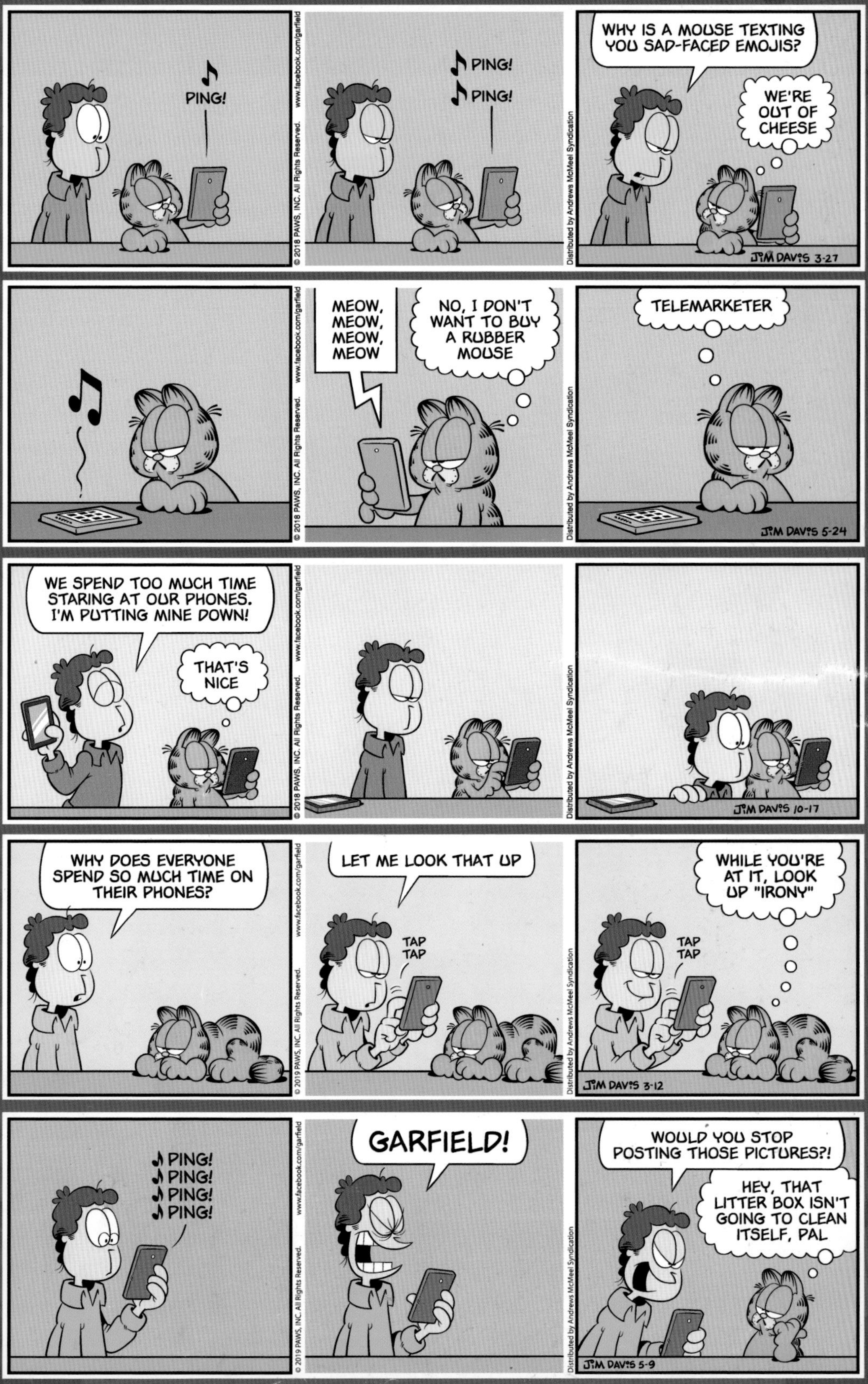
PING!
PING!
PING!
WHY IS A MOUSE TEXTING YOU SAD-FACED EMOJIS?
WE'RE OUT OF CHEESE
JIM DAVIS 3-27
© 2018 PAWS, INC. All Rights Reserved. www.facebook.com/garfield
Distributed by Andrews McMeel Syndication
MEOW, MEOW, MEOW, MEOW
NO, I DON'T WANT TO BUY A RUBBER MOUSE
TELEMARKETER
JIM DAVIS 5-24
© 2018 PAWS, INC. All Rights Reserved. www.facebook.com/garfield
Distributed by Andrews McMeel Syndication
WE SPEND TOO MUCH TIME STARING AT OUR PHONES. I'M PUTTING MINE DOWN!
THAT'S NICE
JIM DAVIS 10-17
© 2018 PAWS, INC. All Rights Reserved. www.facebook.com/garfield
Distributed by Andrews McMeel Syndication
WHY DOES EVERYONE SPEND SO MUCH TIME ON THEIR PHONES?
LET ME LOOK THAT UP
TAP TAP
TAP TAP
WHILE YOU'RE AT IT, LOOK UP "IRONY"
JIM DAVIS 3-12
© 2019 PAWS, INC. All Rights Reserved. www.facebook.com/garfield
Distributed by Andrews McMeel Syndication
PING! PING! PING! PING!
GARFIELD!
WOULD YOU STOP POSTING THOSE PICTURES?!
HEY, THAT LITTER BOX ISN'T GOING TO CLEAN ITSELF, PAL
JIM DAVIS 5-9
© 2019 PAWS, INC. All Rights Reserved. www.facebook.com/garfield
Distributed by Andrews McMeel Syndication

Life's a Beach!

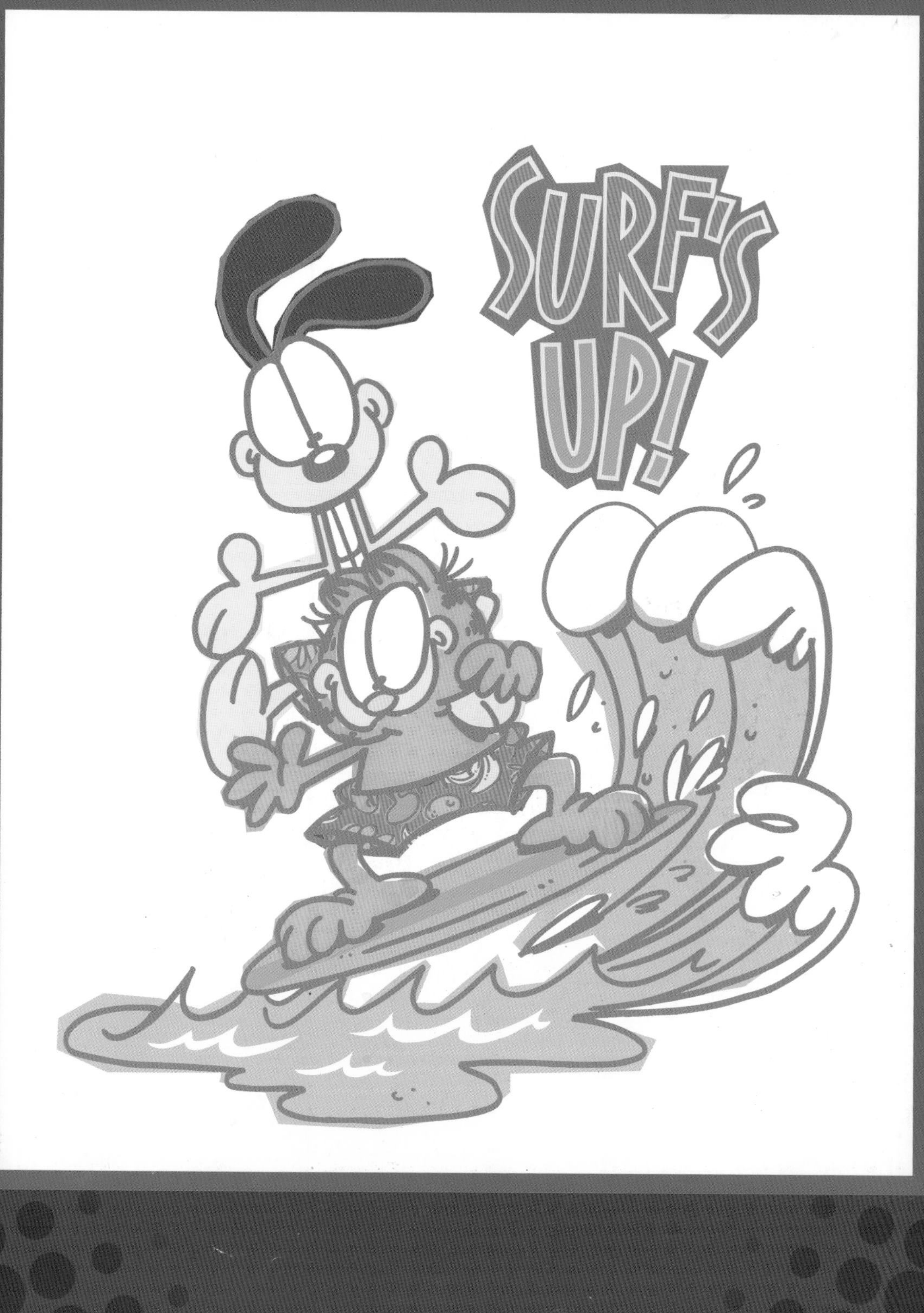
SURF'S UP!

Accordion Jon

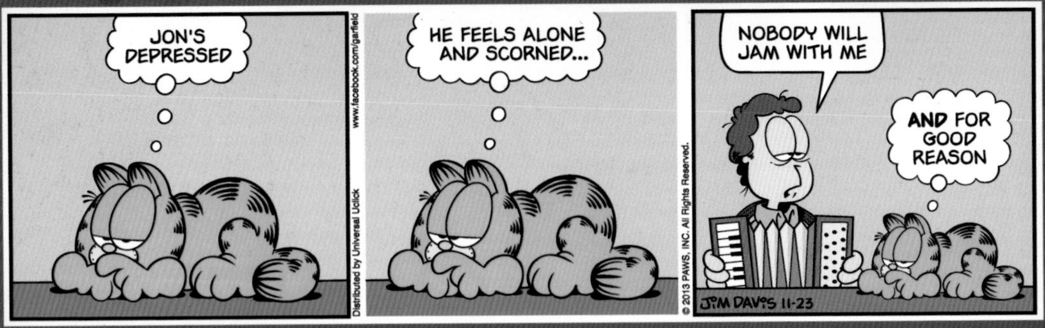

JON'S DEPRESSED
HE FEELS ALONE AND SCORNED...
NOBODY WILL JAM WITH ME
AND FOR GOOD REASON
JIM DAVIS 11-23
Distributed by Universal Uclick www.facebook.com/garfield
© 2013 PAWS, INC. All Rights Reserved.

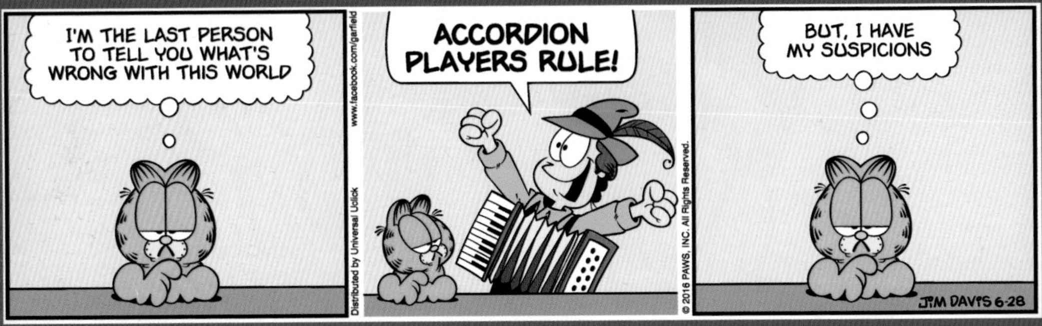

I'M THE LAST PERSON TO TELL YOU WHAT'S WRONG WITH THIS WORLD
ACCORDION PLAYERS RULE!
BUT, I HAVE MY SUSPICIONS
JIM DAVIS 6-28
Distributed by Universal Uclick www.facebook.com/garfield
© 2016 PAWS, INC. All Rights Reserved.

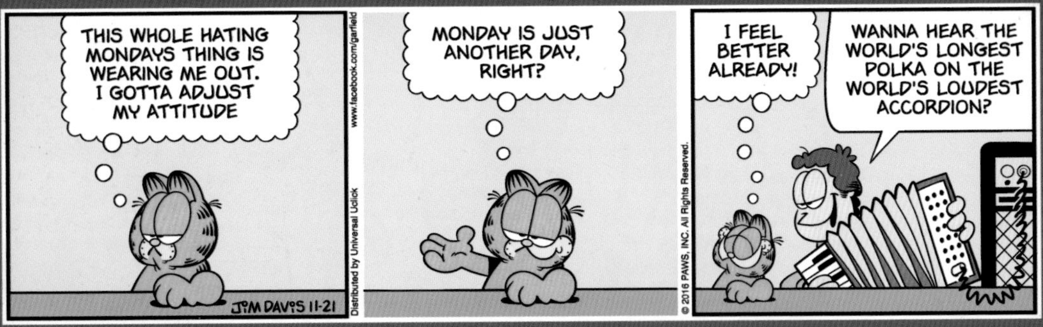

THIS WHOLE HATING MONDAYS THING IS WEARING ME OUT. I GOTTA ADJUST MY ATTITUDE
MONDAY IS JUST ANOTHER DAY, RIGHT?
I FEEL BETTER ALREADY!
WANNA HEAR THE WORLD'S LONGEST POLKA ON THE WORLD'S LOUDEST ACCORDION?
JIM DAVIS 11-21
Distributed by Universal Uclick www.facebook.com/garfield
© 2016 PAWS, INC. All Rights Reserved.

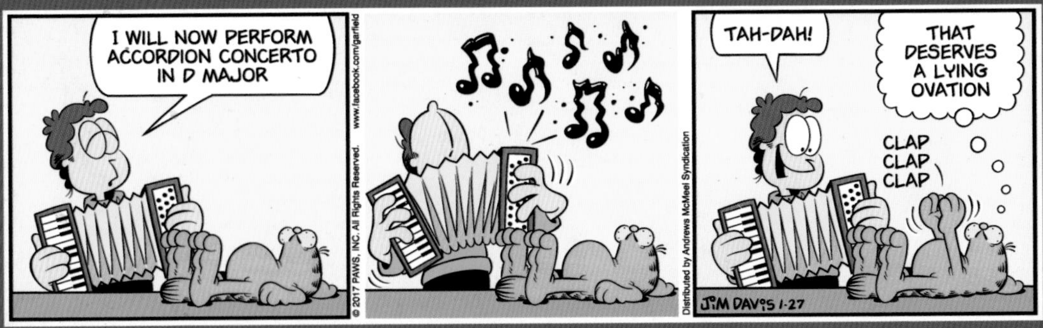

I WILL NOW PERFORM ACCORDION CONCERTO IN D MAJOR
TAH-DAH!
THAT DESERVES A LYING OVATION
CLAP CLAP CLAP
JIM DAVIS 1-27
© 2017 PAWS, INC. All Rights Reserved. www.facebook.com/garfield
Distributed by Andrews McMeel Syndication

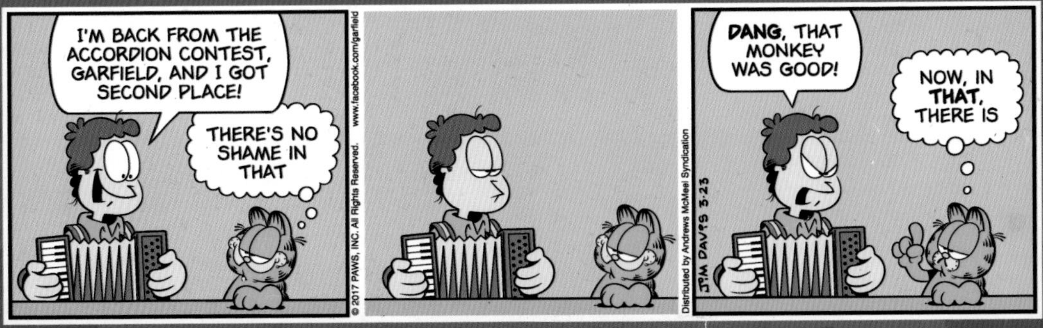

I'M BACK FROM THE ACCORDION CONTEST, GARFIELD, AND I GOT SECOND PLACE!
THERE'S NO SHAME IN THAT
DANG, THAT MONKEY WAS GOOD!
NOW, IN THAT, THERE IS
JIM DAVIS 3-23
© 2017 PAWS, INC. All Rights Reserved. www.facebook.com/garfield
Distributed by Andrews McMeel Syndication

Liz Biz

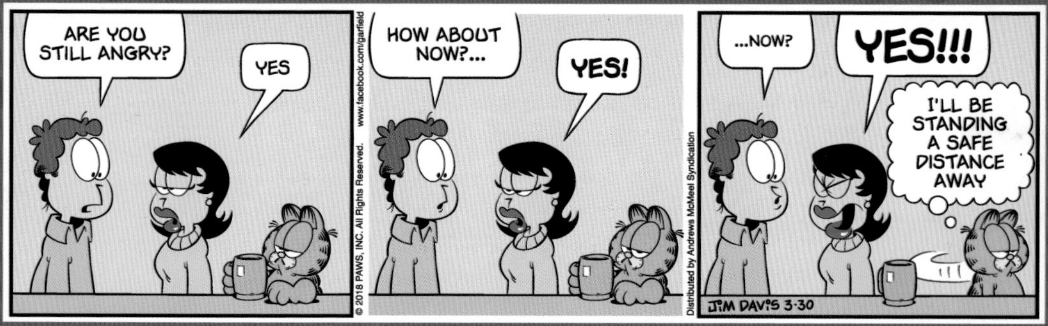

ARE YOU STILL ANGRY?
YES
HOW ABOUT NOW?...
YES!
...NOW?
YES!!!
I'LL BE STANDING A SAFE DISTANCE AWAY
© 2018 PAWS, INC. All Rights Reserved. www.facebook.com/garfield
Distributed by Andrews McMeel Syndication
JIM DAVIS 3-30

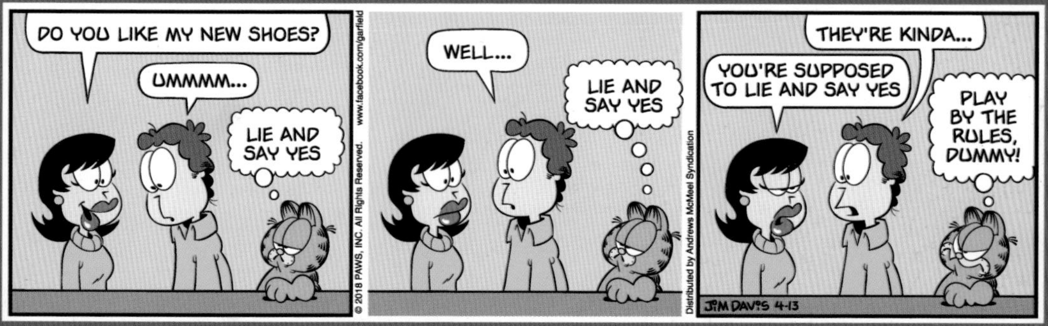

DO YOU LIKE MY NEW SHOES?
UMMMM...
LIE AND SAY YES
WELL...
LIE AND SAY YES
THEY'RE KINDA...
YOU'RE SUPPOSED TO LIE AND SAY YES
PLAY BY THE RULES, DUMMY!
© 2018 PAWS, INC. All Rights Reserved. www.facebook.com/garfield
Distributed by Andrews McMeel Syndication
JIM DAVIS 4-13

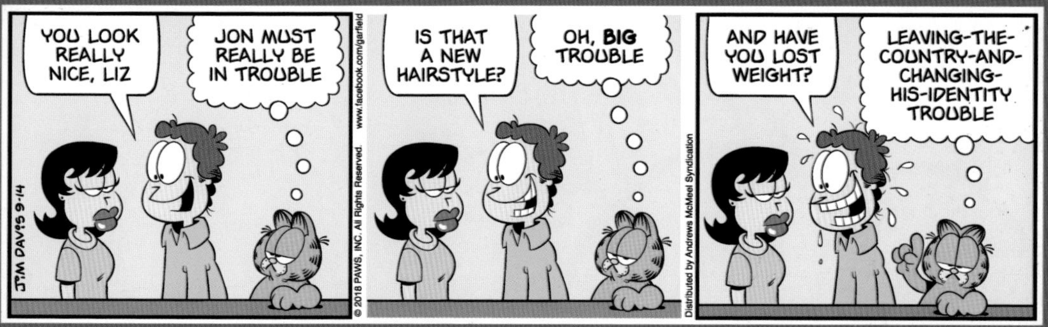

YOU LOOK REALLY NICE, LIZ
JON MUST REALLY BE IN TROUBLE
JIM DAVIS 9-14
IS THAT A NEW HAIRSTYLE?
OH, **BIG** TROUBLE
AND HAVE YOU LOST WEIGHT?
LEAVING-THE-COUNTRY-AND-CHANGING-HIS-IDENTITY TROUBLE
© 2018 PAWS, INC. All Rights Reserved. www.facebook.com/garfield
Distributed by Andrews McMeel Syndication

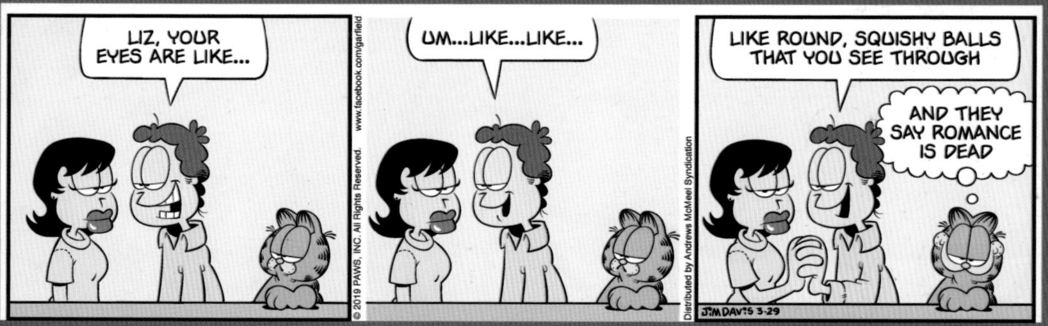

LIZ, YOUR EYES ARE LIKE...
UM...LIKE...LIKE...
LIKE ROUND, SQUISHY BALLS THAT YOU SEE THROUGH
AND THEY SAY ROMANCE IS DEAD
© 2019 PAWS, INC. All Rights Reserved. www.facebook.com/garfield
Distributed by Andrews McMeel Syndication
JIM DAVIS 3-29

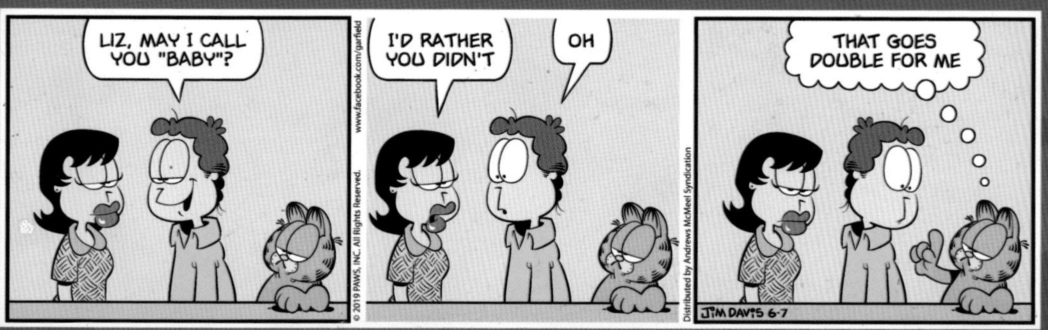

LIZ, MAY I CALL YOU "BABY"?
I'D RATHER YOU DIDN'T
OH
THAT GOES DOUBLE FOR ME
© 2019 PAWS, INC. All Rights Reserved. www.facebook.com/garfield
Distributed by Andrews McMeel Syndication
JIM DAVIS 6-7

If life is a test, I want a CHEAT SHEET

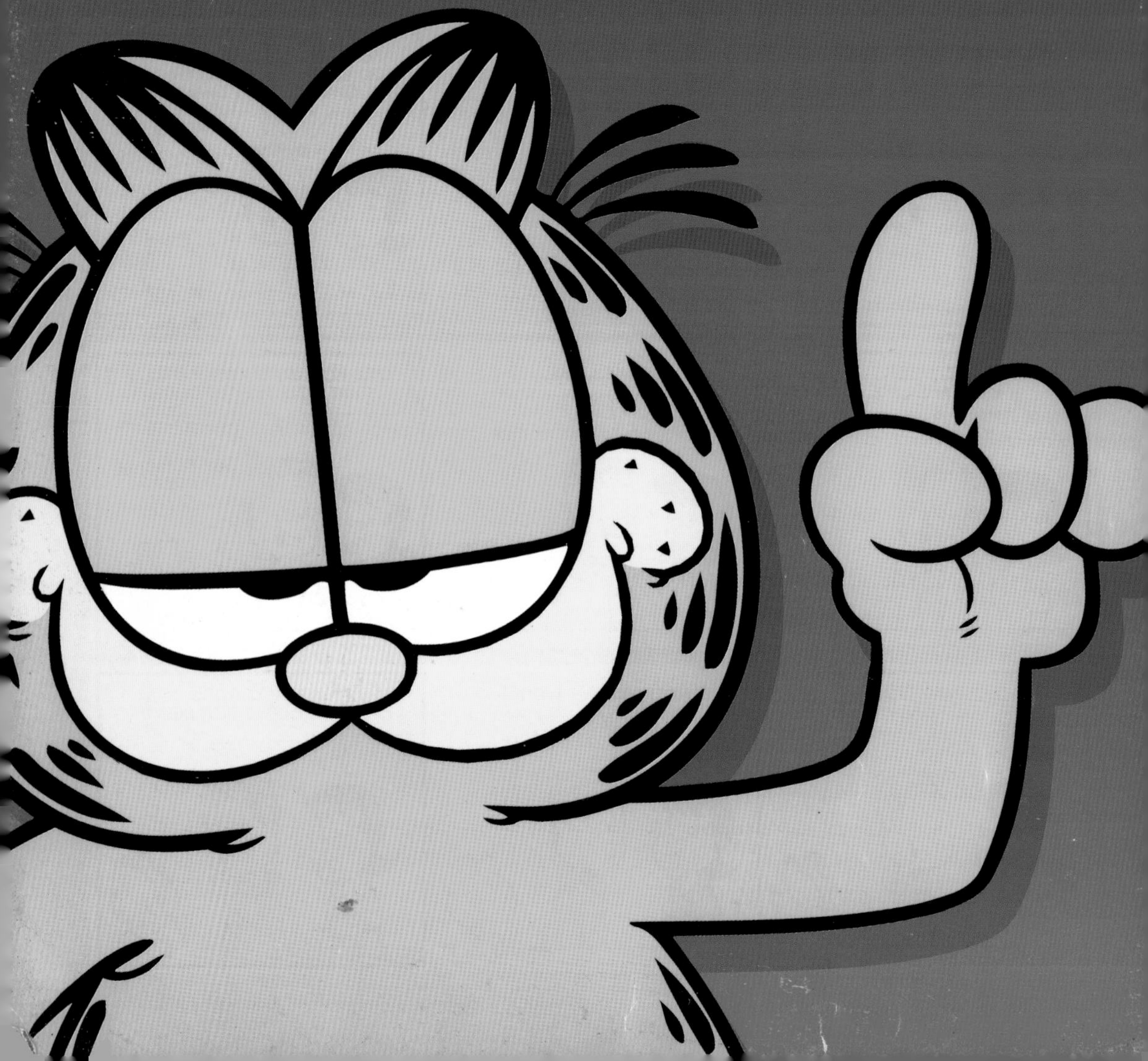

Dog Talk

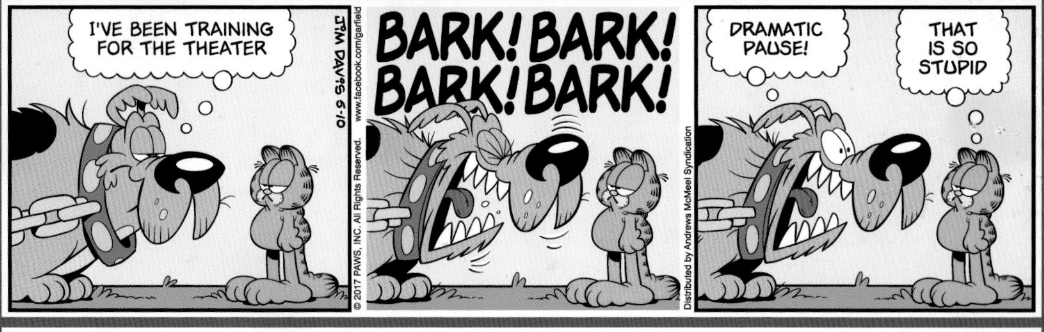

I'VE BEEN TRAINING FOR THE THEATER
JIM DAVIS 6-10
BARK! BARK! BARK! BARK!
DRAMATIC PAUSE!
THAT IS SO STUPID
© 2017 PAWS, INC. All Rights Reserved. www.facebook.com/garfield
Distributed by Andrews McMeel Syndication

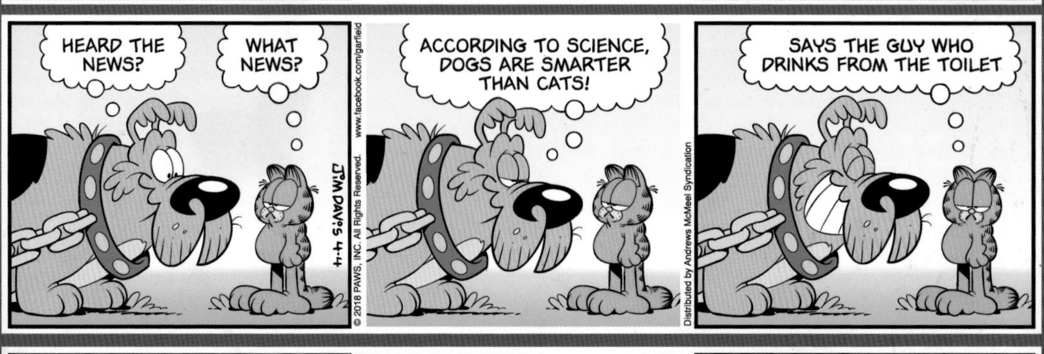

HEARD THE NEWS?
WHAT NEWS?
JIM DAVIS 4-4
ACCORDING TO SCIENCE, DOGS ARE SMARTER THAN CATS!
SAYS THE GUY WHO DRINKS FROM THE TOILET
© 2018 PAWS, INC. All Rights Reserved. www.facebook.com/garfield
Distributed by Andrews McMeel Syndication

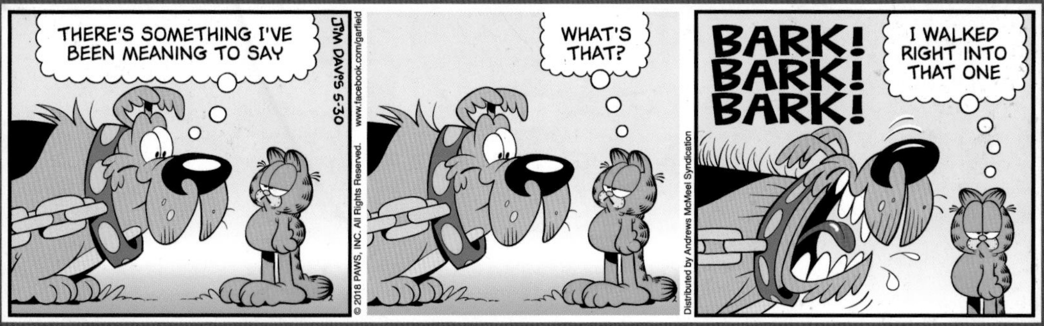

THERE'S SOMETHING I'VE BEEN MEANING TO SAY
JIM DAVIS 5-30
WHAT'S THAT?
BARK! BARK! BARK!
I WALKED RIGHT INTO THAT ONE
© 2018 PAWS, INC. All Rights Reserved. www.facebook.com/garfield
Distributed by Andrews McMeel Syndication

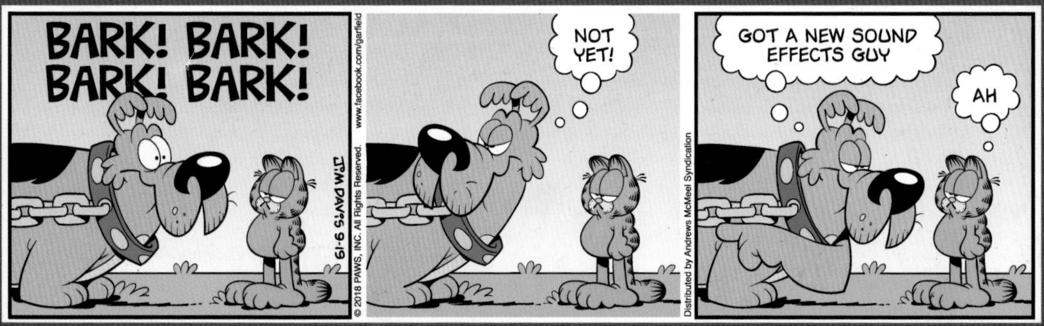

BARK! BARK! BARK! BARK!
JIM DAVIS 9-19
NOT YET!
GOT A NEW SOUND EFFECTS GUY
AH
© 2018 PAWS, INC. All Rights Reserved. www.facebook.com/garfield
Distributed by Andrews McMeel Syndication

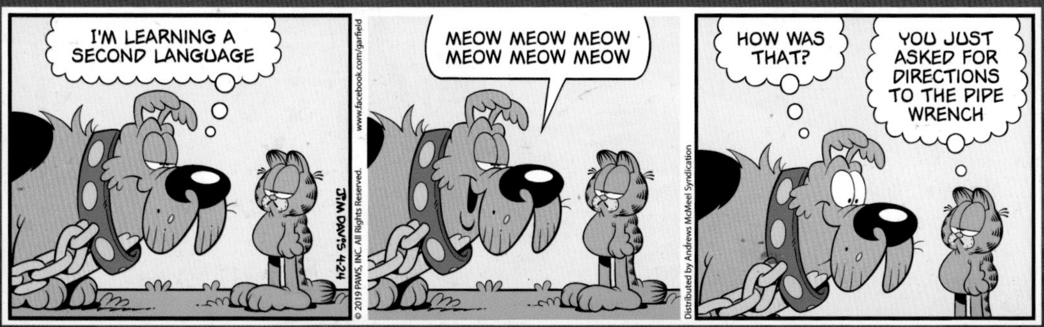

I'M LEARNING A SECOND LANGUAGE
MEOW MEOW MEOW MEOW MEOW MEOW
JIM DAVIS 4-24
HOW WAS THAT?
YOU JUST ASKED FOR DIRECTIONS TO THE PIPE WRENCH
© 2019 PAWS, INC. All Rights Reserved. www.facebook.com/garfield
Distributed by Andrews McMeel Syndication

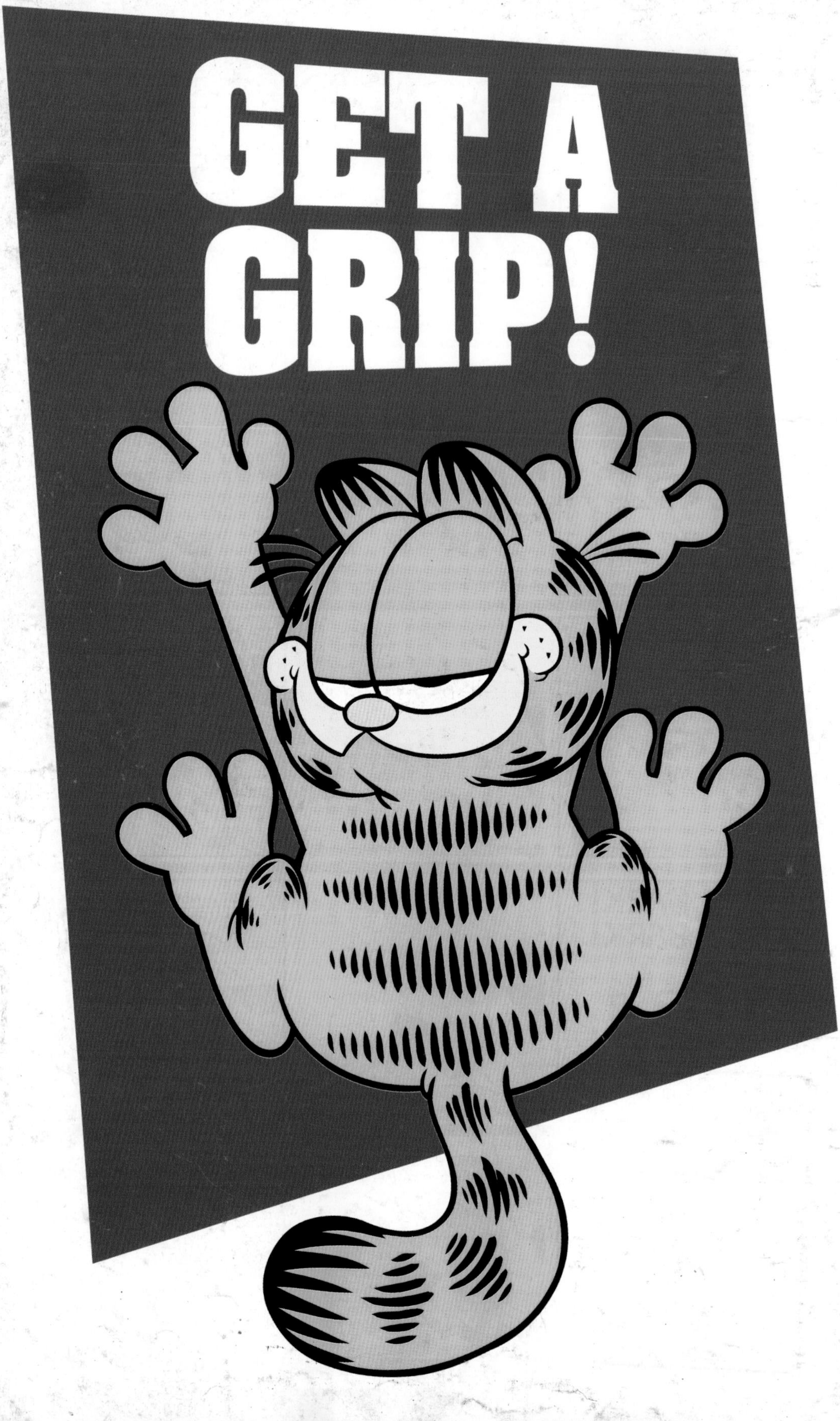
GET A
GRIP!

Garfield Sunday Classics

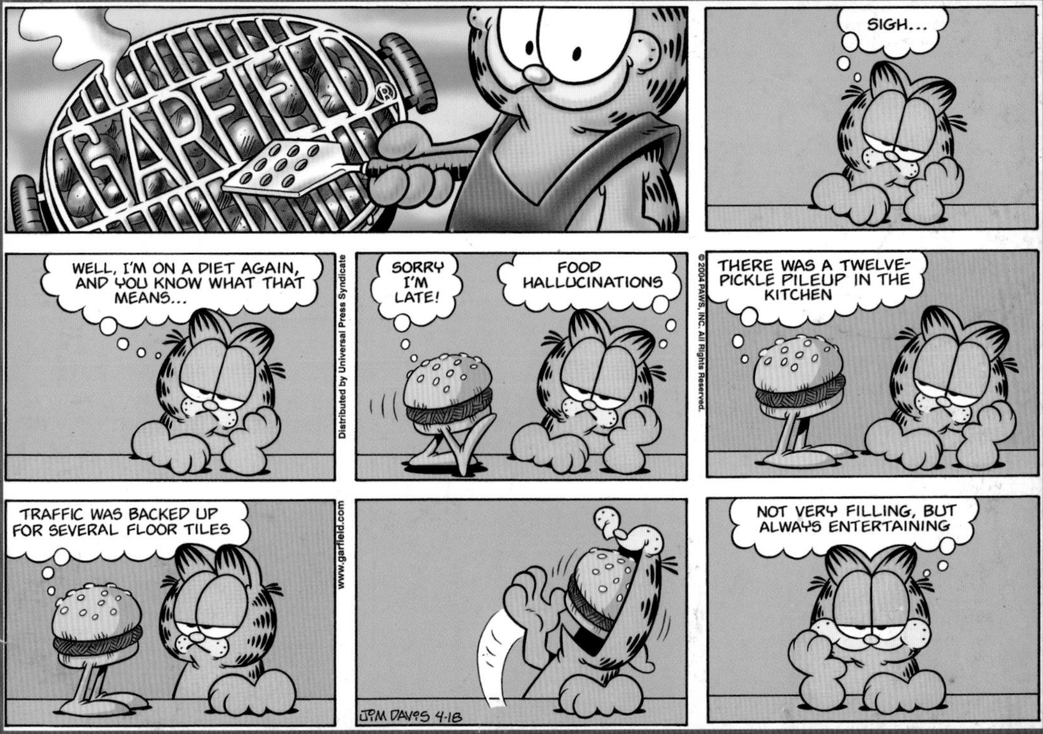
GARFIELD
SIGH...
WELL, I'M ON A DIET AGAIN, AND YOU KNOW WHAT THAT MEANS...
Distributed by Universal Press Syndicate
SORRY I'M LATE!
FOOD HALLUCINATIONS
© 2004 PAWS, INC. All Rights Reserved.
THERE WAS A TWELVE-PICKLE PILEUP IN THE KITCHEN
TRAFFIC WAS BACKED UP FOR SEVERAL FLOOR TILES
www.garfield.com
JIM DAVIS 4-18
NOT VERY FILLING, BUT ALWAYS ENTERTAINING

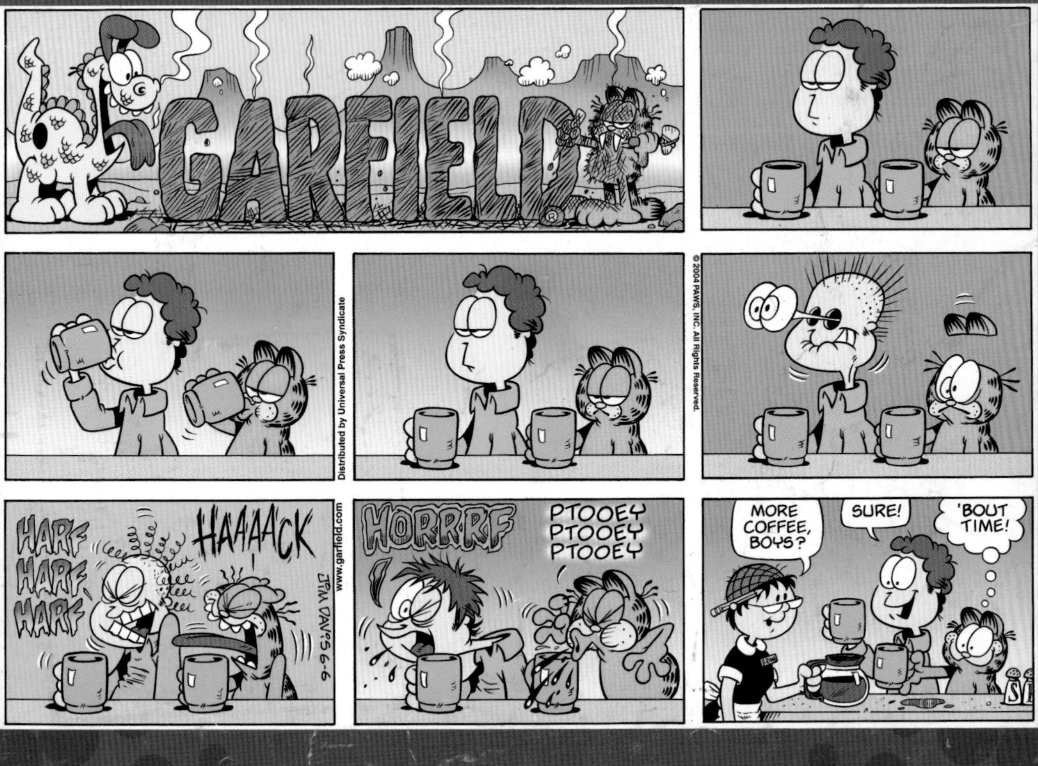
GARFIELD
Distributed by Universal Press Syndicate
© 2004 PAWS, INC. All Rights Reserved.
HARF HARF HARF
HAAAACK
www.garfield.com
JIM DAVIS 6-6
HORRRF
PTOOEY PTOOEY PTOOEY
MORE COFFEE, BOYS?
SURE!
'BOUT TIME!

DISCOVER
EXPLOSIVE NEW WORLDS

ADVENTURE TIME

Sam Sykes · Selina Espiritu · Sarah Stern
BRAVE CHEF BRIANNA

KELLY THOMPSON BRIANNE DROUHARD M. VICTORIA ROBADO
MEGA PRINCESS

THE NOT-SO SECRET SOCIETY
DALEY · CRAFTS · CLARK · BRUNI

OVER THE GARDEN WALL

STEVEN UNIVERSE
VOLUME ONE

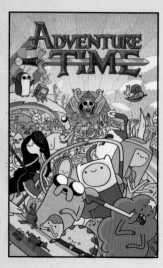

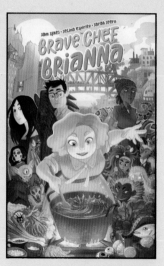

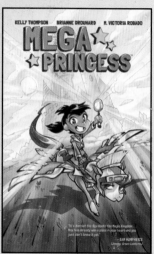

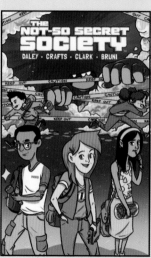

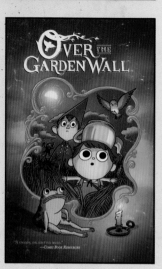

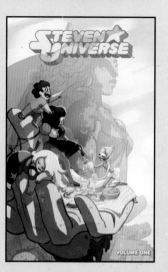

Adventure Time
Pendleton Ward and Others
Volume 1
ISBN: 978-1-60886-280-1 | $14.99 US
Volume 2
ISBN: 978-1-60886-323-5 | $14.99 US
Adventure Time: Islands
ISBN: 978-1-60886-972-5 | $9.99 US

The Amazing World of Gumball
Ben Bocquelet and Others
Volume 1
ISBN: 978-1-60886-488-1 | $14.99 US
Volume 2
ISBN: 978-1-60886-793-6 | $14.99 US

Brave Chef Brianna
Sam Sykes, Selina Espiritu
ISBN: 978-1-68415-050-2 | $14.99 US

Mega Princess
Kelly Thompson, Brianne Drouhard
ISBN: 978-1-68415-007-6 | $14.99 US

The Not-So Secret Society
Matthew Daley, Arlene Daley, Wook Jin Clark
ISBN: 978-1-60886-997-8 | $9.99 US

Over the Garden Wall
Patrick McHale, Jim Campbell and Others
Volume 1
ISBN: 978-1-60886-940-4 | $14.99 US
Volume 2
ISBN: 978-1-68415-006-9 | $14.99 US

Steven Universe
Rebecca Sugar and Others
Volume 1
ISBN: 978-1-60886-706-6 | $14.99 US
Volume 2
ISBN: 978-1-60886-796-7 | $14.99 US

Steven Universe & The Crystal Gems
ISBN: 978-1-60886-921-3 | $14.99 US

Steven Universe: Too Cool for School
ISBN: 978-1-60886-771-4 | $14.99 US

kaboom!™

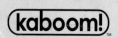

AVAILABLE AT YOUR LOCAL COMICS SHOP AND BOOKSTORE
To find a comics shop in your area, visit www.comicshoplocator.com
WWW.**BOOM-STUDIOS**.COM